CW01597536

Val Morgan

The Remarkable Tale of the Bull and the Sheep

Limited Special Edition. No. 8 of 10 Paperbacks

Val Morgan is a writer and retired academic. She lives near Colchester.

For Ros

Val Morgan

The Remarkable Tale of the Bull and the Sheep

Austin Macauley Publishers™
London • Cambridge • New York • Sharjah

A CIP catalogue record for this title is available from the British Library.

ISBN 9781788234009 (Paperback)
ISBN 9781788234016 (Hardback)
ISBN 9781528953375 (ePub e-book)

www.austinmacauley.com

First Published (2019)
Austin Macauley Publishers Ltd
25 Canada Square
Canary Wharf
London
E14 5LQ

"The plough in England is drawn by two oxen outstanding among the rest: the King and the Archbishop of Canterbury. These two, drawing the plough, rule the land, one by human justice and sovereignty, the other by divine doctrine and authority. My lords, you are trying to harness together at the plough under one yoke an untamed bull and an old and feeble sheep. What will come of it?"

—Archbishop Anselm, 1093

Chapter One

The King at Kingsholm

No-one could ignore the atmosphere. In the palace, hangers-on and place-seekers drifted about in aimless groups. Courtiers and ministers gathered to exchange mistrustful whispers. Servants tip-toed about, mute and fearful. What was going to happen if the king died? Even in the best-governed kingdom with a legitimate heir to succeed, the imminent death of the sovereign was a perilous moment. But this sovereign had no heir and no-one could say that England in 1093 was well-governed. In fact many called the king's illness an affliction of God, a punishment for the ills of his reign and his battles with the church. He was being called to account. He should have been a better king.

King William Rufus, son of the Conqueror, a man of biting humour and furious energy, had spent the six years of his reign in rancorous relations with the church. His propensity to joke about sacred things, to mock pompous prelates and exploit ecclesiastical treasuries had led to bitter wrangles with the clergy. Now, laid low on a bed of sickness, he was surrounded by priests to whom he was giving unaccustomed ear. His old subversive appetite for levity had left him. There were no more *bons mots* or cruel jokes for his attendants, no disarming bluff *raillerie* for his ministers or companions. The old provocation about how he was thinking of converting to Judaism, so often trotted out to ruffle clerics in the act of reprimanding him, had died on his lips. Those lips, now dry and cracked, had begun to pray: "Christ Jesus, have pity on the dying…" Dared they believe what seemed to be apparent, that the reign of William Rufus was about to end?

The king had fallen ill at the beginning of March while he was at Alveston, north of Bristol, a royal manor that had once belonged to King Harold. It was whispered among superstitious folk that it was no coincidence that the king was stricken in this place. In revenge for the terrible slaughter at Hastings and the subsequent massacres of the people, King Harold's tormented spirit had risen from his blood-soaked ancestral lands to strike down the son of his old enemy. Yet, though struck, William was not stopped at Alveston. He had insisted on going on to Gloucester, from where he intended to plan how he would prevent the incursions of the malcontent Malcolm, King of Scotland. But the twenty-five mile ride to his palace at Kingsholm drained him utterly. A burning fever had ensued and, on Wednesday 2nd March, he took to his bed feeling so wretched that he sent messengers up to St Peter's Abbey in Gloucester asking Abbot Serlo to speed to his side with all the medical and spiritual aid that such a renowned place of learning might afford.

Far away from the court, at the obscure East Anglian Priory of St Sepulchre's, Aefled heard the news when she rode over to the priory from her home nearby at Castle St Mary's in answer to a summons.

'Come quickly,' the Prioress had written, 'there are people I want you to meet.'

Lady Agnes had been prioress at St Sepulchre's for the last thirteen years and was godmother to all Aefled's children. Two of those children, Robert and William, twelve and ten years old, had left to travel north with their father, Robert, who intended to place the boys in the service of his overlord, Count Alan Rufus of Richmond. Immediately on her arrival, Aefled was told of the perilous state of the king.

'He has certainly fasted this Lent,' said Agnes, 'I dare say it's the first time he has ever done so. They say he cannot eat, cannot keep anything down. He rails against everyone, not even sparing God.'

She paused a moment before asking abruptly: 'Have you heard from your husband?'

'Not for many weeks.'

'Is he with the king?'

'I don't know. It's more likely that Robert will stay with Count Alan Rufus until the outcome is clear. If the king dies, there will be war.'

'Count Alan is a powerful man. He has ambitions.'

'What do you mean?'

'I sometimes wonder if you are wise to choose Count Alan's household for the training of your sons.'

Every conversation with Lady Agnes left Aefled feeling inadequate, embarrassed at her own unworldliness. It seemed a strange irony that a cloistered woman, living in a remote provincial convent, should enjoy more knowledge of current affairs than herself, whose own husband was moving among the highest nobles of the land. But then Agnes was not someone who conformed to expectations, being youthful, handsome and without a religious vocation. Where her information came from was a mystery, but she appeared confident of her sources which had often proved reliable. This made her, as well as a charming and amusing friend, a necessary person to know.

'Count Alan has ambitions,' she went on, 'but where they might lead him, no one can tell. We must wait. We must hope for a happy outcome, whatever that might be.'

Hoping and praying for their own versions of a 'happy outcome' was the preoccupation of the ruling class, at that moment assembled in great numbers at Kingsholm. Throughout the palace, courtiers were doing deals or jostling for position as everybody tried to keep one step ahead of developments. They had, at the very least, to prepare for the death of a king. William Rufus was generally reckoned an eccentric king, a flawed king, certainly an unpopular one. Never destined for a throne, it had come to him as the result of family feuding and sheer luck. But, once in his grasp, he had known how to occupy it.

The third son of the Conqueror, born into the middle ranks of the aristocracy and still a landless knight bachelor when his father had died in 1087, William was an unlikely successor to the kingdom his father had conquered. But neither his eldest brother, Robert, nor his second brother, Richard, nor his youngest brother, Henry, had been favoured by fortune or the regard of their father. Richard had been killed in a hunting accident many years ago; Henry had been set to study and at one time seemed likely to be destined for the church, while Robert, being short and inclined to overweight, had suffered from his father's mockery for years. "Short legs", "Fat legs", "Gambaron", these contemptuous names had perpetually dogged him through his youth, finally settling down into the insulting nickname "Curthose" by which he was widely known. Contempt and mockery, compounded with unfair treatment and preference for his brothers, eventually drove him to rebellion. Although later reconciled, father and eldest son were never again on mutually trustful terms. So William had inherited the throne of England while Robert Curthose got only the duchy of Normandy, for which he had to do fealty to the French king. And the two realms which the Conqueror had unified, were split apart.

Among the Norman aristocracy, there was much discontent about this division. It seemed to them preferable that England and Normandy should continue to be governed as a single administration, as it had been in the Conqueror's time. Noblemen and castellans enjoying vast estates in both realms did not want to be beholden to two overlords, or to have their loyalties split by owing allegiance to two contending rulers. So when William had taken up arms against his brother, he found many supporters who wanted to see the two realms under a single ruler. Thus his early years on the throne had been marked by aggressive policies against Robert Curthose as he sought to bring Normandy within his control. With the exception of a few periods of truce, they were to go on battling all their lives. Now it seemed, one of those lives might be on the point of ending.

In the face of that possibility, three broad camps were emerging: men who were committed to William and stood to lose if he died, men who were already looking to align themselves with whichever of the two brothers seemed likely to come out on top, and men of the church. At serious sick beds, the latter were always dominant, especially where great sinners were concerned. And William was a great sinner. Clerics called to attend at his bedside were likely to be nursing grudges about the high handed way William had treated the church in the past, imposing requisitions, keeping bishoprics vacant in order to siphon off revenues, or selling clerical offices and benefices thereby raking in tidy sums for his own coffers. These practices infuriated churchmen who felt constantly embattled by a king who refused to acknowledge the rights of the church, fill vacancies or even recognise a pope.

In England, thanks to William's obstructive practices, neither of the two papal claimants then in contention had been recognised. Was it to be Pope Urban or Pope Clement? Although it amused William to keep everyone guessing, non-recognition was a deliberate policy designed to keep papal authority at a minimum and prevent interference from the *curia* in any of the disputes between church and king. This left the higher clergy free to pursue their own interests without having to undertake long consultations with the Holy See and it left William in control of the English church. Such was the divisive and unreformed state of affairs which had persisted for many years and which William wished to prolong since it was incontrovertibly to his advantage.

But now he lay prostrate, in naked need of God's favour and the prayers of churchmen. He wished to be spared, he enjoyed the feasts of life too much, the hunts, the battles, the roaring days among his field companions, the nights of drink and dissolution. He must reject all that, said the priests. God forgave sinners, they assured him, but only if penitence was ardent and sincere. Days passed while the heart of the kingdom beat feebly at Gloucester. Noblemen and courtiers gathered around the bed of a king who began to believe that he was being punished by God for his past profligacies and high handed treatment of the clergy. Entertaining visions of Hell and fiery punishments as he burned with fever, William was struggling to think of his soul while his bowels and guts spurted forth corruption.

Prayers were said for the king at St Sepulchre's, as they were at religious houses up and down the country. As was usual on her visits, Aefled attended the offices. On the evening of her arrival, she went to compline where the prayer: 'Oh Lord, grant us a quiet night and a perfect end,' seemed most suited to the king's situation. Afterwards, she stayed overnight in Agnes's quarters, not the cell of a nun but a comfortable, heated room. It was late when she went to bed, but even so, she lay awake thinking of her daughter, Eleanor, now eight years old, regretting that she had been unable to bring her on this visit. Eleanor was very fond of her godmother and loved to ride her palfrey. The child found Lady Agnes the most exciting person she knew and had been greatly disappointed when Aefled had refused to take her.

'But, mama,' she said, 'why can't I come?'

'Not this time, my sweet, I have some important matters to discuss.'

Aefled did not want to tell Eleanor that she was not going to see her godmother because her godmother had, for some unknown reason, asked that she should not be present at the meeting arranged for the following day. Before she fell asleep, Aefled's mind returned again to the unusual secrecy surrounding tomorrow's meeting. Who were these people she was to meet and why was Agnes being so artful and wary?

****

Gloucester was packed. Never had so many prelates and churchmen been gathered together around the king. The town filled up with ministers and clergy, officials, small post holders of the king's suite and all those who could not be lodged at a castle already filled to bursting with courtiers and their followers. The feeding of such numbers began to put a strain on the surrounding food stores. Barns were forcibly opened and the contents seized. Local manor farms lost livestock. In whatever way the situation was to be resolved, the people of Gloucester wished it would be soon. Saint Peter's Abbey resounded with chants and prayers, incense swirled in clouds, monks sang the *Kyrie eleison*. Meanwhile, physicians plied their craft around the sallow royal body, effecting no cure, while bishops and priests came and went with equal redundancy. The king's personal physician, Baldwin, Abbot of St Edmundsbury, had been summoned but was still on his way across country and not expected for several days. A Mass was said in the sick room, monks intoned incessantly in an antechamber. Hopes were raised when, late on Friday, Abbot Baldwin finally appeared, looking in need of his own cures. Then, on Sunday, 6th March, a great stir was caused by the arrival of Anselm, the sixty-year-old Abbot of Bec, one of the most renowned monks in Christendom. Had he been summoned? If not, why was he here? Whispers went round among the courtiers. What was Anselm up to? Had a genuine concern for the king compelled him to bring the consolation of prayers? Or was there an ulterior motive, the search for a post, perhaps? Was Anselm at last signalling his readiness to end the great scandal of William's reign?

For the past four years, since the death of the previous Archbishop of Canterbury, Lanfranc, there had been a great gap in the organisation of the church in England. Many times, William had signalled his intention to offer the post to Anselm, who had many times signalled his intention to refuse, a reaction that William was counting on since it was entirely in his interests to keep the huge wealth of the archbishopric flowing into his coffers. The longer the see was vacant, the more money was diverted to the royal treasury. And so a game was begun, William continually hinting that the post would go to Anselm who continually stressed his unfittedness. In this way, the status quo was maintained, along with the flow of wealth into the king's exchequer.

Many of those at Gloucester were aware of the reputation of the man who rode through the bailey gate that Sunday. He had been born in Aosta, then in Burgundian territory and had spent many years at the Abbey of Bec in Normandy during the time when Lanfranc was abbot there. When Lanfranc went to take up the post of Archbishop of Canterbury, Anselm succeeded him as abbot. In this role, he had become distinguished in ecclesiastical circles, famous for his *privata conversatio,* little pep talks to the monks full of instructive matter but without the dreariness of sermons.

As they watched him dismount, they saw a man of average height and build, a little bowed but with a fine broad head from which his grey hair grew in drifts around his tonsure, a strong Roman nose, straight lips—not incapable of smiling, dark eyes with an intelligent gaze that seemed to look inward. Anselm liked to claim that it was only with the strongest urging that he had been prevailed upon to accept the post of Abbot of Bec. Despite great shows of reluctance and continual disavowals, he had finally taken on the abbacy in 1079 and, once installed, had shown a moderate talent for organisation and leadership. But there, he said, his ambitions ended. 'I am a meditative man,' he protested, 'ill-suited to worldly affairs. I desire a simple life in which I might continue to write and teach.' And he promised the monks of Bec to remain with them and not to seek higher office. Certainly, he did not appear to seek it, but how much did he hope it would be pressed on him?

Last Christmas Anselm had composed a special prayer asking God to move the king's mind to appoint an Archbishop of Canterbury and so end the scandal of the vacancy. This prayer, promulgated around the churches of England, was well-known among the bishops gathered at Gloucester that day. They began to suspect that, having brought such scrutiny to the vacancy, Anselm was now presenting himself as the one to fill it.

Followed by his secretary, Baldwin, and a little monk from Bec called Eustace, Anselm crossed the bailey and entered the lower hall where Abbot Serlo of Gloucester received him in a chamber full of the king's ministers and councillors. Unusually for such a large gathering of powerful men, they made little noise, keeping their voices low and stepping quietly, like monks in a chapter house before the work of the day begins. Anselm had already met a few of them but most were unknown, including the one who came over to hand him a goblet and inquire pleasingly after his health. Anselm replied that his health was good but that he was most distressed to learn of the king's illness.

'Indeed, it is most distressing. In a few moments, I will escort you to his sickroom but first I wish to alert you to something.'

Anselm exchanged a glance with Baldwin. Although not naturally suspicious, they were unsettled by the concentration of power represented by the magnates and barons in the room. These men, who commanded wealth, armies and vast feudatories, would be required, if the king should die, to carry on the government until a new king could be eased or battled into place. Anselm looked at the man in front of him: tall, bold faced, smiling, giving nothing away. He must be one of them. Why did he not give his name?

'Abbot Anselm, forgive me, my name is Ranulf Flambard.' Anselm nodded. The name, which he would come to loathe, along with the man who now uttered it with such gracious goodwill, would never be forgotten.

'As you know, the king is gravely ill. He speaks with difficulty and does not always know what he is saying. Fever burns words out of him that sometimes shock. Even in his days of health, his sense of humour has sometimes offended. But I want to assure you that he only insults men he admires and he insults most those he admires most. Praise from the king does not come tricked out in golden phrases.'

Anselm looked questioningly at Baldwin, not knowing what to make of this speech, but before he could reply, Ranulf Flambard had taken him by the arm and was steering him from the room.

'Let me take you to the king,' he said.

The king lay in a grand bed in a decorated chamber, hung about with fleabane and horsemint and strewn with fresh reeds. Ember pans burning curative herbs doused the air with pungent fumes which struggled to disguise the nauseous stench. At his bedside was Abbot Baldwin of St Edmundsbury, the royal physician. Experienced though he was, having ministered both to the Conqueror and his predecessor, King Edward, no skill of his had power over this disease and he was entirely at a loss. Spiritual appeals now seemed the only remedy. Throwing off any pretence to Galenic science, he was praying over the tormented royal body. The king had cast aside his covers; his arms, encased in linen sleeves, lay limply at his sides so that he looked like a corpse already in his shroud. Sweat poured from him as he burned and shivered. Plastered hair framed a drawn, pinched face, occasionally distorted in pain. As Abbot Anselm's procession entered, the king's physician drew back. Everyone in the room, except perhaps William, noticed that the Abbot of St Edmundsbury, one of the great representatives of the English Church, was giving place to the Abbot of Bec. Anselm, dressed in the black Benedictine robes of his order, moved sedately towards the bed.

'Holy Face of Lucca!' William's voice was cracked like his lips and his favourite oath lacked the energy that usually gave it a provocative edge. An unseemly oath at the best of times, in the mouth of a dying man it became almost shocking.

Out of his dry body from which all fluids had been expelled during a morning of vomiting, his words came sere and brittle. 'Have you come to chide me?'

'My lord king,' said Anselm, with the greatest dignity, 'I bring you the consolation of Christ's mercy. I have come to pray for you.'

'There are enough of them doing that. They never leave off. Bring me something I can use. Like a cure.' William stared at the prelate for some time with fierce, glittering yellow eyes, before giving in and complying with his illness. 'Welcome, Abbot Anselm, I am right glad of you.'

'May Christ's blessing be upon you.'

'If it was, I wouldn't be lying here.' William paused for breath; every word seemed an effort. 'Did I send for you?'

'You did, my lord. I happened to be close by. Earl Hugh of Chester is desirous of founding a monastery. He sought my advice and I have been to visit him.'

'How convenient.'

'My lord king, do you consider yourself in a state to make confession?'

William lay considering for a moment, closing his eyes as if in sleep. He had often been asked that question and had often thrown back an insolent answer to some elderly priest already half inclined to view the mere fact of his youth and vitality as a form of insolence. On one occasion, he had replied to that same question: 'Don't ask me now. Come back when I'm dying.'

After a while, he confirmed that he was ready. 'Clear everybody out,' he said with something of his old vigour. 'Everybody, do you hear? My confession is for you alone.' The king raised a hand and pointed at Baldwin and Eustace. 'They must go, too. Everybody. Get out.'

Once confession was made, absolution followed and, seizing the moment, Anselm extracted from the king a promise to amend his life. Then the chamber began to fill again. If Anselm had had his way, no further business would have been conducted that day. If the king was to die in the night, he would be pure of stain with no sin on him. If he was to live, tomorrow was soon enough to conduct further business.

But others thought otherwise.

While Anselm withdrew a little way, half a dozen of the most prominent barons and a number of clergy assembled around the royal sick bed and began speaking in low, urgent voices. After a time, the king raised himself on one elbow and said simply, 'Anselm.'

Anselm heard the king say his name in little more than a whisper but it seemed to ignite the room. What happened next passed in a barely comprehended whirl. In after years, Anselm would never quite be able to recall the scene of embarrassment and confusion. At one moment, he was hearing the king's confession and giving absolution. The next, he was surrounded by barons and prelates breaking into uproar, pressing around him with urgent clamouring. He was plunged into a scene from one of his nightmares, when black robed demons roil around him and he is calling out for some impossible aid. Someone presses into his hand a pastoral staff, but he fails to clutch it. He pushes it away but they force open his fingers and thrust it again into his grip. He hears himself objecting, refusing, pushing away the thing once more, all the while wanting to seize it, make it his. It is as if he is being forced against his will, not simply to take the proffered symbol of office, but to confront something in his own soul. He desires the thing he must not want. Although a battle is going on around him, it is in himself that the conflict is greatest.

Again, they clamour about him. Voices are raised in unseemly fulminations above the king's bed. Someone shouts, brings them to their senses and urges him out into an antechamber, pulling at his robes. He is being conducted into the next room where they continue to press about him, once again forcing his hand in the most literal sense, opening his fist around the pastoral staff then clenching it around the shaft, impelling him to their will, overcoming his objections, sensing they have cornered him. Again, he rejects it, but he wants it. Undoubtedly he wants it. Somewhere in his nature, ambition has been revealed, a tiny figure prancing naked. He is suddenly confronting in himself a quality he despises. Then, abruptly, the uproar turns to acclamation. He has the staff in his hand. He is holding it and they are rushing to congratulate him. When he wakes from the nightmare, it is to find that he has been elected Archbishop of Canterbury.

Wide awake, he is borne into the church where he hears every note of the *Te Deum Laudamus* ringing out in celebration of an election to which he is not sure he has consented. What has happened seems no more than a disorderly series of unreal scenes. But could he really have been taken by surprise? He had long been aware of the rumours and expectations; he knew his reputation for scholarship and sanctity; he knew he could do much for the church if elected. If he was lacking in administrative skills, a few well-chosen appointments and a staff of episcopal clerks would steer him around the pitfalls. Surely he might have suspected that his summons to Gloucester was not only for the purpose of administering absolution to the dying king. Had that king, sick though he was, outwitted him by forcing on him this most onerous burden?

At the end of the momentous day, exhausted and bewildered, Anselm found himself escorted to his lodgings by some of the king's magnates, burly men, under orders to ensure that he did not try to slip away before the king had a chance to announce his appointment. When Baldwin re-joined his master that evening, he tried to pluck up the courage to ask him about what had happened. But Anselm's face was showing the fixed, impenetrable expression which signalled: 'Ask me nothing.'

The following day, Monday, 7th March, the king was found to be still living. He spent the morning without vomiting but was only able to keep down pure spring water. A feverish headache had left him feeling mulish and defiant. But ill though he was, William was still only fitfully contrite.

'I suppose you have come to have your will of me,' he said to Anselm.

'My lord king, yesterday you promised that I should have an amendment. Do you feel capable of such an undertaking?'

'Did I make a promise? I must have been raving. What do you want of me, Anselm? A promise to be good?'

'Articles of amendment, reformation of your life, a statement of good intentions. That you will fill vacancies, enact good laws, release prisoners, amend your life. We will have them written down and placed upon the altar. They will be sacred pledges.'

'You are gloating. You stand before a lion and gloat.' William embarked on a coughing fit which came from lying too long in bed. Phlegm wheezed up from his lungs. Someone came to prop him on bolsters and he expelled a huge gobbet into a well-placed copper dish, before settling back to pursue his line of thought. 'That's what I am, a sick lion. You know what the bestiaries say about a sick lion, don't you? "A sick lion will seek out an ape and devour it in order to be cured." Are you my ape?'

As Ranulf Flambard had warned, the king loved to provoke with ill-timed jests, like a naughty child. Indeed, there was in him something of the boy who had been dragged around the great cities of England and Normandy, desperate to catch the attention of a remote and preoccupied father, often resorting to pranks and japes in order to secure it. In those days, Anselm had enjoyed the high regard of William's parents, the Conqueror and Queen Matilda, who had at one time considered him for the role of tutor to the boy when William, a mere third son, seemed likely to be destined for the church. But on the death of his brother, Richard, William's scholastic education had ended. Now a second son, he became a youth of some importance and was dubbed a knight at seventeen. From then on, his father had ensured his presence at important occasions, allowing him to participate in the witnessing of documents or attending great ecclesiastical ceremonies, such as the dedication of Uncle Odo's new cathedral at Bayeux.

Anselm's response to William's sardonic humour was to remain calm and maintain at all times the dignity of the church.

'My lord king,' he said in a low voice, 'shall we consider the ways in which you might, in this extremity, seek the mercy of the Lord?'

William held forth his hand and spoke in a changed tone. 'Give me counsel, Anselm, I have no wish to die.'

Anselm took his hand and held it as a father might hold the hand of his son, in comfort or compassion or to steer him on a better path. It was a touch William had never known and it ran through his enfeebled spirit like a regret.

'God's will be done. If you are to live, live in justice and right; if to die, die in penitence. Shall we think about the amendments?'

Weak with inanition and ground down by days of vomiting, fearful of God's wrath against his sinful life, William conceded. 'Call in the bishops,' he said.

When the pledges were written out and witnessed, they were placed on the altar in the church. The king bound himself to fill vacancies, donate lands to various monasteries and introduce "good laws", that is to say, curtail the royal prerogative. He filled one of the lapsed vacancies by appointing Robert Bloet as Bishop of Lincoln. There now followed a stage of parrying, a back and forth between the two, as William promised to reform and Anselm maintained a show of reluctance about the archbishopric. A heightened mood, brought on by the king's weakness, made them behave in a restrained, subdued way in contrast to the shameful scrimmage around the king's bed the previous day.

'My lord king,' said Anselm, 'there are certain obstacles that may take any decision about Canterbury out of my hands. Firstly, I have recognised a pope whom you do not recognise and given obedience to Urban II. I cannot retract that obedience. Secondly, your brother, Robert, Duke of Normandy may refuse consent. Then the community at Bec may raise objections. Then again, the Archbishop of Rouen may protest my unworthiness.'

'None of that matters,' said William, fully aware that Anselm was stalling. 'They will accept what is done. The point is, do you? Go and think about it. Think deeply, Anselm.'

The king lay back, too exhausted to engage in battle. 'Send my physician,' he said.

****

As well as thinking deeply about what had happened, Anselm discussed what had happened with his friend and secretary, Baldwin, who knew him as well as anyone could know such a contradictory character.

'Did you notice?' said Anselm. 'I felt it most strongly. There was every emotion around that bed except pity.'

'A dying king excites more fear than pity.'

'But the man, a man in the last extremity of man's condition. Hoping for salvation as we all must. The *man* is to be pitied.'

'Master,' said Baldwin. 'You are now in a position to do the church much good.'

Anselm looked past him. His mind was far from Canterbury.

'If he lives, this king will be my adversary. I feel it. For his parents' sake, I would not think ill of him, but many men speak against him. They call him licentious, given up to pleasures and corruption. Others say that is not true; that monks write false, cruel things about him because he does not make concessions to the church. But even his worst detractors often use a particular phrase about him. They talk of his *magnanimity.* What do they mean by that, Baldwin?'

'Master,' said Baldwin, wishing to turn his thoughts away from the king and towards Canterbury, 'do you wish me to write to the chapter house, to inform them of your election? Surely fortune has smiled on them as well as on you.'

Anselm's face hardened. 'If the world smiles on you with favours, do not smile in return. It does not smile that you may smile, but that it may mock.'

Baldwin had heard this sentiment before, it was Anselm's way of denying good fortune the power to deprive him of insecurity.

'But *magnanimity*? What is it to have a great soul? Why do they use that term of a man of such little charity, such little spirituality? Is it what they see as energy and dash, the colossal appetite for life? Can one be a great-souled sinner?'

Baldwin did not understand Anselm's preoccupation.

'Master, will you accept the appointment? Have you accepted it?'

'It is in God's hands, Baldwin. If the king dies, everything will depend on his successor. I will make no move, say no word, until God shows the way.'

Meanwhile, up and down the castle, in chambers, anterooms and lodgings, the barons and prelates who had done so much to bring about the election drew together in little groups, holding impromptu counsels to discuss what had been done. In the great council chamber, a larger group had gathered, grand men who lugged half the countryside of England in their titles: Lichfield, Durham, Rochester, Lincoln, Winchester. The Abbot of St Edmundsbury alone measured whole swathes of Norfolk, Suffolk and Essex in his entitlement. These men had personal names and patrimonies, but they were walking shires, counties and vast feudatories. Men of this stamp were by nature politicians and they formed the semblance of a government. Under the king, they administered as diplomats, negotiators, ambassadors. Then there were chamberlains, treasurers and clerks like Gerard Chancellor and William Warelwast, the king's most subtle fixers. Some were men of probity, some scoundrels, most simply trying to make their way. The greatest of these self-makers, Ranulf Flambard, belonged to another group, men of obscure origins, servants, clerks and menials, the sort who knew their way around the legalistic jargon of royal writs, inventories and accounts. Without birth or family, such men were generally despised by the nobility who resented their natural aptitude and regarded them as interlopers. One of King William's underrated strengths was his ability to recognise talent and employ it to the best advantage, whatever its origin. This had enabled Ranulf Flambard to work his way up to become the king's most trusted minister. But when the king's illness deprived Flambard of active protection, he found himself excluded from the secret councils of the nobility.

In the great chamber at Kingsholm, they sat, or stood, or lounged or strode about, mulling over the events of the last few days. Among them, the royal chancellors: Maurice of London and Osmund of Sarum, one time tutor to the king's brother, Henry; the royal chaplain, Robert of Lichfield; Robert Bloet, a handsome, agreeable courtier who had just become Bishop of Lincoln and William St Calais, the one-time rebel, now a staunch king's man. It said much for the king's capacity to value men of merit that he had not only forgiven St Calais but rewarded him and advanced his career.

'We wanted an archbishop in place in case the king should die,' he said to no one in particular. 'But what if he lives? What is the king to gain from this appointment?'

'The king thinks he might be able to control him in the way his father did Lanfranc. But Lanfranc was subtle, able to parry and hop and had the king's interests at heart.' Robert Bloet was well pleased with the events of the last few days which had seen him appointed to a bishopric without having to pay the lump sum the king usually demanded for the award of a benefice. This custom of cash for appointments, known as simony, was increasingly under attack from the church hierarchy and many reforming clergy were outspokenly against it.

'Is Anselm a reformer?' asked Maurice, one of the king's chancellors. 'When there is contention between king and pope, where will his loyalty lie?'

'Which pope?' said Bloet. 'Anselm has recognised Urban, as he made plain to us at the time of his election. But the king has failed to recognise a pope for the last several years. It is more fun, he says, to keep everyone guessing. But in truth, he must recognise Urban II, as his brother of Normandy has done.'

'But until he does so, Anselm will be treading a difficult path.'

'Anselm pretends that he is unfitted for administration. But last year when he came to England to negotiate a reduction of taxes on the monastery at Bec, he got his way.'

'Anselm has no sense of occasion, he fails to adapt to the moment. His response to challenges is to do nothing for a long time before doing something completely inappropriate.'

Robert Bloet laughed. 'Anselm was right in what he said this morning.'

Everyone knew what he meant. That morning Anselm had addressed the barons in a speech designed to impress on them the folly of what they had done. It was a warning as well as a rebuke and he finished with an unforgettable image. 'The plough in England,' he had said, 'is drawn by two oxen outstanding among the rest: the King and the Archbishop of Canterbury. These two, drawing the plough, rule the land, one by human justice and sovereignty, the other by divine doctrine and authority. My lords, you are trying to harness together at the plough under one yoke an untamed bull and an old and feeble sheep. What will come of it?'

'What will come of it, indeed?' said Bloet. 'We have yoked the most secular man in England to the most pious. A perfectly ill-matched pair.'

'Shouldn't we have had this conversation before?' said William St Calais. 'If no one here supports him, why did we agree to force the king's hand?'

But William St Calais knew that they had agreed to force the appointment of Anselm because they believed the king would die. In that event, having an archbishop in place would reduce the power of a successor king, making him more dependent on themselves for a swift transfer of power which would be acceptable to Scotland. As Bishop of Durham, St Calais was a major player in the politics of the north, especially at a time when Malcolm of Scotland and the great Northumbrian magnate Count Alan Rufus were showing signs of discontent. It was in response to these restless stirrings that, before the king's illness, St Calais had been summoned to Gloucester to confer with the king about what was to be done in the borderlands.

But when the king had fallen ill, all negotiations had been halted.

****

Negotiations of some sort, however, were going on at St Sepulchre's. Waking to the bell calling the sisters to morning prayers, Aefled dressed and went looking for Agnes. She found her in deep whispers with another lady whom she had not seen the previous day.

'Aefled, my dear. Come and join us. Meet the lady Christina.'

Aefled gave a warm salutation to Christina who responded with strict politeness but little warmth. She was tall and gaunt with high cheekbones, large eyes, a deeply lined forehead and a sour mouth. She wore a nun's habit and hid her hair under a veil. She looked about forty years old but might have looked younger if she had smiled.

Lady Agnes eyed them both as if making a calculation before speaking. 'Lady Christina has travelled from Wilton Abbey. She is an old friend of mine. We used to know each other years ago when we were both at Romsey Abbey and then, later, at Wilton. We like to meet to remember those days when we can. Unhappily, that is not often.' Almost every conversation with Agnes revealed another aspect of her life, some reminiscence or unexpected reference pointing towards a mysterious past, strewn like nuggets through the most trivial utterances, seemingly without design on her part. So, evidently, Agnes had been at two of the most illustrious conventual houses in the country, but why had someone so notably unspiritual pursued a life of devotion?

Desperate to find something to say, Aefled seized on the weather. 'It has been fine for travelling this last week. How are you accompanied?'

'I have an escort,' said Christina, 'in keeping with my rank.'

The rank of a nun? What did that mean? Aefled looked at Agnes for an explanation. Why was she being introduced to this sour lady?

Before Agnes could answer, one of the nuns came into the room, leading a small girl by the hand. Christina rose and embraced her. 'Edith, my dear, come and eat.'

The child was about thirteen years old, small grown, with a round face, a neat mouth, a somewhat pointed nose which gave her a *jolie laide* look in profile and watchful blue eyes. She was dressed in the dark habit of a Benedictine nun and wore a covering on her head, a dark cap with flappets which draped her neck. She held herself stiffly and looked unhappy. Aefled thought how different this muted child was from her own lively daughter.

'Edith is Christina's niece,' explained Agnes embracing her, 'and my own dear godchild.'

Evidently, whatever it was that Agnes wanted to explain could not be done in the presence of this child so an hour was spent in conjecturing on the king's illness, the whereabouts of Aefled's husband and the prospects for peace if the king should die.

At length, Edith and her aunt went out to walk in the cloister and finally, Aefled got her explanation.

'You have no idea who Christina is, do you?' said Agnes as Aefled looked at her expectantly.

'Let me amaze you then. She is the sister of the Queen of Scotland. And little Edith there, her niece, is the daughter of Malcolm, the Scottish king who is currently not on the best terms with our poor sick King William.'

Lady Agnes enjoyed Aefled's surprise. 'Yes, it is quite astonishing, isn't it? You are thinking at this minute: What is such a person doing at this little out-of-the way convent? Well, at the moment, she is hiding. Call it a retreat.' Agnes laughed. 'She is in retreat from a nunnery'

'But I don't understand. Why?'

'Aefled, can you imagine what that little slip of a girl is worth in marriage? Can you imagine what might be done to secure her? Christina is at her wits' end. Men with various pretexts keep turning up at Wilton to view her, to make inquiries on their own behalf or someone else's. It is even said someone came from William himself before he fell ill, although I don't believe it.'

'Why don't her parents remove her from Wilton?'

'Queen Margaret has a special fondness for the place. Besides, she wants the best education for her daughter. Perhaps you don't know but Wilton has a famous reputation for piety and learning. Edith can read and write, she can compose in various styles, she knows several languages and has been educated in the accomplishments of *courtoisie* and wifely conduct.'

'In other words, she is a great prize.'

'Yes. And so the question is: who will have her?'

'Whoever her father chooses, I suppose. That's the way of things.'

'And who do you think King Malcolm seems to be on the verge of choosing?'

'Oh, Agnes, I have no idea about such things.'

'Count Alan Rufus! The very man you have chosen to educate your sons.'

'But won't everything depend on the king's health? If he dies, the whole politics of the north will change as his successor makes his own terms with the northern baronage.'

'Yes, of course. But if he does not? Oh, you cannot begin to imagine all the turns of fortune that may depend on this child's small body. Edith is sweet, but she has no vocation for the religious life. I think she wants to marry to get away from her suffocating aunt. As you've seen, she dresses her like a nun and makes her wear a little black hood which gives the impression she is veiled. Christina is a good woman, she is genuinely concerned for her niece, but she's frightened and that makes her defensive.'

'What is she afraid of?'

'She is afraid of men, men's bodies, sweat, seed and procreation. She is in revolt from them and tries to take Edith with her. But I think the girl is suited to a life in the world. I think she will blossom. She in in love with the idea of love, but what she really wants is power.'

‘Marriages of such status cannot take place without the king’s consent,’ said Aefled. ‘If she is to marry a king’s liegeman, like Count Alan Rufus, he will have to obtain the king’s consent.’

‘Indeed. And the king is in no condition to give it. So we will have to wait. And in the meantime, Christina is here, spending a little time with an old friend and her niece’s godmother in peace and quiet while we await the outcome. Then they will go back to Wilton.’

‘But why did you want me to meet them? I cannot do them any good. I have no counsel for them. I have no court contacts.’

‘No, but it may do you good, Aefled, to know a little more about the great world where your sons will have a place.’

So, for the next few days, Aefled spent time with Christina and her niece. Edith gave the impression that she knew nothing of the adult world or any plans for her future. It became clear that Christina wanted to keep her for the church and was bitterly opposed to marriage. Such was Christina’s determination that Aefled began to wonder whether she would even dare to defy prospective suitors, turning them away, refusing access to the girl.

Towards evening on Friday, 11th of March, during Lent, Edith was sitting in the Priory house with a book of devotion in her hand, a psalter, richly illuminated. She was not reading, but tracing the swirls of red and gold with her fingertip, chasing their coils around the capital ‘I’ the first letter of *Intende voci orationis… Attend to the voice of my prayer*. By chance, Aefled came upon her and stood observing for a moment her unselfconscious absorption in the game. Over the last few days, she had become much drawn to Edith, seeing in her prospects the very same that confronted her own daughter. Marriage or the nunnery. Innocent, unworldly, subdued, Edith did not seem ready for either one of these. But, once out of her aunt’s company she opened up, began to unbend, smiled a little and even laughed. An unpractised laugh with shrill notes, hiding doubtful amusement.

‘Do you like the colours?’ asked Aefled, watching her finger trace the lines.

‘Yes, I love the colours, they change in different lights, they flow and stream over the parchment, they have deep shadows and bright tints. I feel they are drawing me, not just to the words, but to adventures, dreams, to their own world.’

‘Is that what you want, Edith, to go into the world?’

‘I don’t know. I think so. But Aunt Christina says the world is not bright like these colours, but full of darkness and shadows.’

'The world has both shade and brightness. You can see both, even in a cloister garden. Do you like it at Wilton?'

'Sometimes. I like to be with my sister. She's smaller than me. She's called Mary.'

'Ah, I see.'

Edith put aside the book at which she had been staring intently all this time and turned her eyes full on Aefled. It was an intelligent, open stare, not the demure, fluttering, shamefast look of a girl of subdued spirit.

'You don't wear a habit,' she said, 'are you worldly?'

Aefled smiled. 'Indeed, I am not fitted for the religious life. I am married. I have three children, my youngest child is a daughter called Eleanor.'

Edith seemed pleased by this. 'How old is she?'

'She will be eight at the end of this month.'

'Younger than Mary.' Edith fell silent.

'Where is your aunt?' Aefled looked around noticing that they were quite alone.

'She has gone to vespers.'

The conversation seemed to have stalled and Aefled tried to think of something that might interest the girl, induce her to open up and speak of her life at Wilton, or tell something about her aunt or her illustrious royal parents. She looked very ordinary sitting there in her sombre habit, a nun's caul on her hair. But Aefled sensed a submerged menace in that ordinariness. She seemed like a still place from which immensities might rush, a small dry fissure that might suddenly vent a summer flood.

'Lady Aefled, what will happen if the king dies? Will my father try to set up new baronies in the north and throw his fortunes in with Robert of Normandy and Edgar Aetheling?'

'Bless you, child, I have no idea of these matters! I cannot say.' Again, Aefled felt an embarrassing ignorance of worldly affairs. In spite of her wide education and her acquaintance with classical philosophers, she was unaware of the world beyond her own locality, the world of privilege, politics, power; just those things that were going to matter to her sons. Where were they now, her sons? She had the terrible fear that before she saw them again they would be utterly changed, grown faint in her memory as she in theirs. They were far away in a world with which she had nothing to do, of courtiers, ministers, high churchmen. *On the other hand,* thought Aefled, *here I am sitting in the company of the daughter of the king of Scotland. How surprised Robert will be!*

Edith looked disappointed at Aefled's response. Being privy to some of the discussions at Wilton and of a naturally attuned and curious disposition, she had picked up more than her aunt intended and was always on the lookout for new opinions and information.

'Do you know who Edgar Aetheling is?'

When Aefled shook her head, Edith went on: 'He is my uncle. He is my mother Margaret's brother. He is my father's friend and my godfather. My father says Edgar has just as much right to the throne of England as William. More, because his right goes back to the old days, the old dynasty, before the Normans came. My father says they are upstarts. He says William is breaking the promises he made the year before last. He says he cannot bear to have to do homage to William. He says he will not bear it much longer.'

'My dear child, your father says a great deal. Have you heard him say these things or is this just what others have told you?'

'I listen when Aunt Christina talks to the abbess when they think I'm not there. I remember it all.'

'Do you know what plans he has for you?'

Edith looked up, alert, coy, arch. She closed the book.

'Lady Aefled, can I come to meet your daughter one day? Can I come to visit you? I would like to see where you live.'

'Of course, we would be very happy to welcome you. But such a visit would very much depend on your aunt.'

When, not long after, that same aunt appeared, accompanied by Lady Agnes, the conversation ended. But Aefled was intrigued by the child. She found her small person enchantingly odd, her circumstances obscure and piquant with mysteries and her aunt peculiarly closed, haughty, fearful. Why were they really here? If there was to be trouble between England and Scotland, what role was Edith destined to play in it?

****

Chapter Two
A Cup of Anjou

By the second week of March, there was still no improvement in the king's condition. He lay prostrate, barely eating, hardly speaking. He might spend a whole day only half aware of those around him, the barons and bishops, clerks and menials who questioned him, prayed over him, tended him or just wished him either to stand up or die so that the interminable wait would be over.

One of those who came frequently to the king's bedside was Ranulf Flambard. If he found it surrounded by grandees and higher nobility, he would wait, hanging back, caught awkwardly between knowing his place and being confident of favour. Ranulf was the exact contemporary of William, born in the same year of 1060, which made them both thirty-three. Ranulf's father, Thurstin, had been a poor village priest in the diocese of Bayeux where he had known Bishop Odo. Through Odo's patronage, Ranulf had acquired a Latin education and had entered the old king's household as a clerk and chaplain. By hard work, energy, clever networking and an intuition for what the king wanted, he had progressed steadily in favour and advancement. When William Rufus succeeded in 1087, Ranulf had been on hand and had come to notice as a man who could fix things by exploiting the royal rights and maximising revenue. He was generally reckoned to be physically good looking, tall, strong-jawed, energetic and able to mix with all types and degrees of men. Never wholly accepted into the highest circles, he had friends and supporters in every rank and the gift of not making serious enemies. He liked to dress brightly in the latest fashions, a factor which pleased the king, himself inclined to flamboyant tastes. This quality had earned him the title Flambard, from *flambeau* or torch, one in the vanguard of fashion who burns brightly with wit, imaginative schemes and ideas for every occasion. But the occasion of the king's illness left him short of ideas. The longer it went on, the more unlikely seemed a recovery, the more Ranulf Flambard found himself on precarious ground.

Towards evening on Friday, March 11th, he brought the king a goblet of Anjou wine and offered it to him.

The king opened one eye and stared at it. 'Face of Lucca. What's that? Take it away. Their cures have done for me, Flambard. I don't need more.'

'My lord, I swear this will do you good.'

'What is it?' The king raised himself on one elbow.

'It's a message from Anjou, reminding you of the vineyards there. Or you might think of the Vexin and the lands you have taken back from the French King and your brother of Normandy. So much done, my lord king, and so much yet to do.'

No one had spoken to William like this for days. It was as if a sudden freshening breeze had blown through the stale room. He drank several sips from the goblet then sank back, closing his eyes. When he opened them again, Ranulf was still there with the goblet in his hand. William was about to sign to him to give him more when his physician, Abbot Baldwin, approached the bed.

'What's that?' he asked sharply. 'Did the king send for that? What are you giving him? I have in hand the most careful supervision of his food and drink.'

Hearing this, the king lifted a weak arm and pulled at Baldwin's robe.

'Abbot,' he whispered, 'I pray you, all is well.'

When the abbot had gone, the king drank again.

He lay back as if exhausted by the mere act of drinking, his eyes roving between Ranulf's face and the goblet in his hand.

'That was bold, Flambard,' he said in a faint whisper. 'If I die now, you are dead too.'

The boldness of this act went whispering around the palace and Ranulf spent an anxious night wondering if he was to go down in the chronicles as the man who had killed the king. But it was typical of him and men of his sort to force their fortunes at necessary points: chancers playing for high stakes, never forgetting the drag of their humble origins, the low birth and lack of blood links. Yet, in spite of indications to the contrary, which would become a law to historians, Ranulf Flambard believed he was living in progressive times. Times when a nobody son of a minor cleric could ascend to the ranks of national fixers with a finger in every plot and a plant in every faction. Personal good looks, a ready laugh, a quick mind and a strong stomach for dark and ugly deeds could propel the right man upward in a steady progression. As long as every upward step was measured with care, the ramifications of every action carefully judged and secret ambitions hidden under bowings and scrapings, steady progress could be made. If you slipped, you could expect help only from those you had helped in the past. That was why, though you went along taking fortune's pawns, you always made sure to guard against the moves of bishops and knights. This analogy, occurring to Ranulf when he had drunk copiously of the Anjou, suffered from one great impairment. It would not work because there was no queen.

William Rufus really ought to have married. It was high time that a man of thirty-three in possession of a throne should get himself a wife and breed an heir. Ranulf Flambard was not the only one to see that there was a perfect candidate close to home, the elder daughter of the King of Scotland, Edith, who was even now being educated at an English nunnery. Not the best kind of preparation for life with William, one might say, but hadn't she been destined for one of the Conqueror's sons since birth? Her mother, Queen Margaret, granddaughter of Edmund Ironside, placed Edith in a direct line of heritage from the pre-Conquest kings. Marriage with William would please the English, and more importantly, the Scots, so that the union might bring peace to the northern borders for years. Moreover, it would avoid the necessity of entering into negotiations with foreign princes who would make greedy demands, exact payments and tie William up in inconvenient treaties. Many advisers had counselled this course of action which was sure to win the king popular favour and forestall any plottings by his younger brother, Henry. Once William had heirs, Henry's prospects of inheriting would be considerably reduced.

So why had the king avoided marriage so long? It was not as if, like himself, the king had a complaisant mistress. His own Aelfgifu, a woman of wealthy Anglo-Danish stock, tucked away in Huntingdon, had already given him several children whose care he financed from his growing resources. But the king showed little interest in women, other than the merest groping encounter when drunk. He had certainly never entered into serious negotiations with noble families on that point. Some said he preferred the company of his favourites, like Robert FitzHaimo or Walter Tirel, his mates from the 'grease time' when they went out hunting stags. He himself protested that, between attending to affairs, travelling endlessly around his kingdom or crossing to and from Normandy, battling his brother, skirmishing with the church, issuing writs and charters, wrangling with Malcolm, there was no time left for protracted marriage negotiations. *None of that seemed to matter much now,* thought Ranulf, as he sat at his writing table that night in the cramped lodging he shared with his servant. He helped himself to some more of the Anjou. In spite of his bold act, the king's life seemed about to end. So he had better think hard about the wording of the letter he was drafting to the king's brother, Henry, who might not, if things worked out in a certain way, look too harshly on the matter of the wine.

After an hour, he threw down his pen.

'I can't do it, Firmin,' he said to his servant, a lad he had brought from Huntingdon to look after his bodily comforts; a bold young fellow of about ten or eleven, who could keep his ears and eyes open, especially amongst the stablemen who were often the first to talk to messengers and note their comings and goings. Firmin was slight but well grown, with a great mop of brown hair, energetic and enterprising like his master. Ranulf had scraped him out of orphaned poverty, put him to learn the basics of Latin and given him the semblance of a life of adventure. All this he repaid with devotion.

'What can't you do, master?'

'I can't write this letter. I can't write to Henry. It seems disloyal while the king lives. I can't do it.' He got up and strode about. 'Dear God, this interminable waiting! Is there any news?'

'Everyone is talking about you. It's reached the kitchens.'

'What about Anselm? What's he up to?'

'Anselm has taken lodgings at St Oswald's. He has exchanged letters with Canterbury.'

'Well, well, he's been quick with the news, hasn't he? I dare say he would like to hurry down to Canterbury and get himself consecrated. But he's stuck like the rest of us until this dreadful wait is over. Let's hope his prayers find favour with heaven. It's about time one of these holy men was listened to.'

Anselm had withdrawn to the Priory of St Oswald which lay between St Peter's Abbey and Kingsholm Palace, an island of ancient Benedictine calm going back to the days of its founder Aethelflaed, daughter of Alfred the Great. There, in the company of Baldwin, Eustace and his entourage, he was seeking spiritual guidance in a place where the relics of the old English saint were kept in the crypt. A sudden interest in English saints might be connected to the idea that he was now the primate of the English church. But it was an idea he fought against. His soul was still reeling from the events of the 6th of March. That was why the palace of Kingsholm with its masses of people and worldly preoccupations had forced him to flee to a spiritual sanctuary where he might contemplate the magnitude of what had happened. How was he to interpret it? Was it an indication of God's will? A knavish trick by courtiers who were terrified that the king would die before an archbishop was in place? The crowning of a life's work of discipline, study and intellectual application? Or the most terrible blow of a malign fortune? Still, it was a long road between being proclaimed and being fully installed as archbishop. All along that road were little lay-bys where he could choose to sit for long periods and do nothing. Acceptance of high office was a particular problem for him. As a monk, he had renounced all exercise of self-will. Yet, once self-will was taken out of the picture, he was staring at conflicting indications which made no sense. If he asked himself, 'what do I want?' he got no answer. So he asked Baldwin.

The reply came pat. 'Master, you want whatever is right for the church in England.'

'But my loyalty is with Bec. It lies with Normandy, with the ducal power of Robert. It lies in Rome with the Pope Urban II. If I am archbishop of the premier see in England, I will be like the child in the parable of Solomon, split down the middle.'

'Master, don't you think we should wait for God's hand in this? The king could die tomorrow and everything will change.'

'No, some things do not change with the vanities of the world. Kings come and go, but principles, a sense of rightness in a man's soul, these are lasting. In the matter of worldly promotion, I have been consulted on many occasions. Do you know what I always said? I said, follow these principles: first, make sure you do not *want* to be promoted, for that is ambition; second, do all you can to avoid it, thus you test the strength of your renunciation; third, the best advisers available must have urged you to accept, thus you receive counsel from those more wise than you. That's what I always replied when monks, on the verge of being offered promotion, sought my opinion. The question is: can I benefit from my own advice?'

'Master, we should go to the shrine of St Oswald and ask for guidance. But first, the Prior has asked that you join the monks for their meal so that they might benefit from your discourse. He would regard that as the greatest courtesy.'

'Indeed, Baldwin, one of my chief consolations is to bury myself in a cloister with monks of the rule. I would rather be the lowliest creature in a monastic community than have the pastoral care of the whole of Britain.'

Such declarations were like the writhings of a chained man. For all his devotion to his master, Baldwin sometimes tired of them. The chains were on. He should accept them.

'Master,' he said. 'You must give yourself permission to accept this election.'

'Ah, Baldwin,' said Anselm, rising stiffly to go to the meal. 'Permission is something which deceives many. In monastic rule, obedience and disobedience are contraries; permission lies between these extremes. Permission is given by a superior, it cannot be given to oneself, for it will only follow self-will.'

This is the key, thought Baldwin. He wants permission. The permission of a superior. Permission of a father. As far as Baldwin could glean from the few references to his early life, Anselm had never got on with his father. Instead, he had transferred all his sense of filial duty to the church, where, in the person of Lanfranc, he had found his surrogate father at the age of twenty-six. When Lanfranc moved from Bec to Canterbury, Anselm had taken his place and for many years struggled to find his way as the leader of a great monastic foundation. Without a superior to make decisions for him, he became a prey to self-doubt. So he took as father, the father of the church itself, the pope. At Bec, in Normandy, that was fairly straightforward. He could abide by the decretals of Urban II who had been recognised by Robert, Duke of Normandy. But in England, being a true son of the Holy Father was of no benefit whatever because England did not recognise a pope. Once, when he had remonstrated with William about this issue, the king had rounded on him. 'By the Holy Face of Lucca! No one shall force my hand in the matter of the pope.'

That was the sort of scene Anselm recoiled from, and yet, somehow, provoked. Another man of Anselm's age might have played father to William's wilful youth and assuaged the anger with fair and soothing words. But Anselm could not play the role of father, since he himself was in search of one. Over the course of the next few months, Baldwin would rehearse at great length these and suchlike arguments with himself as Anselm delayed, made excuses, wavered, sought advice and generally whirled about in a frenzy of soul searching and an anguish of paternal absence. Sometimes Baldwin was moved to pity. Sometimes he would have liked to grab the cantankerous old man by his robes and given him a good shaking. But he recognised that Anselm, through sharpness of mind and genuine spiritual insecurity, had probably understood better than anyone the immensity of what had been granted to him.

Anselm was assuming the mantle of a saint. To become the Archbishop of Canterbury, he must take on the persona of the saint to whom his church was dedicated. He must not just represent but in some sense embody St Augustine, the founder of the English Church. He must become the mystical embodiment of a founding moment, a perpetual origin which had happened five hundred years ago but was still mysteriously and continuously present in the Old English Church. He must become the inheritor and guardian of a tradition that was in fact quite alien to him: the stewardship of obscure saints, a different calendar of saints' days, an array of impenetrable traditions, a vast inheritance of pre-Conquest documents going back hundreds of years, in a language he couldn't even read. Although Lanfranc had attempted to sweep away some of the English rituals and put in place a body of continental observances, Canterbury remained distinct in its origins and practices. It observed purely English feasts and was firmly attached to its saints. All this contributed to Anselm's uneasiness. He was neither English, nor a saint, nor familiar with the English church. He wondered what the Canterbury monks would make of him. But these practical doubts were nothing compared to the spiritual torments which, during the coming months of delay and uncertainty, would impale him on a cross of indecision.

As the days of March dragged on, the king's illness took its excruciating course. Courtiers became restless at being held so long away from their estates while all government business was suspended. No charters were witnessed, no writs or statutes given, no official letters went out via envoys, no messengers were sent to foreign courts, no orders came from the king and only good news was carried to him. Even the pleasant distraction of hunting was suspended out of respect for the king whose great passion it was. Out of boredom, men began to get careless, dropped their guard, began to say things they ought not to say. Firmin was quick to pick this up.

'William St Calais is talking of going north,' he said to his master one morning.

'Good lad, that's the sort of gossip I like. Anything else?'

'Not really, something about enlisting the aid of St Cuthbert.'

'Ah yes, the Bishop of Durham is a particular devotee of that saint. The cult of St Cuthbert is greatly respected in the north. Even the king makes a show of devotion to the saint as a way of asserting dominion over the north.'

'So does St Calais think St Cuthbert will intervene to save the king?'

'He either does, or pretends to. But it's nonsense. How long will it take him to get to Durham? Ten days? What's the point? The king will either be dead or recovered before he gets there.'

'Perhaps it's an excuse for something else.'

'Now that's what I like, Firmin. You're thinking. What else?'

'Well, if the king dies, St Calais will be in place to defend his position.'

'Good, good lad. Now run along to the stables and put your ear about.'

So, what was St Calais up to? Presumably he was concerned for the security of the north and with good reason. It would be the first place to blow apart when the king died. Durham and the whole of Northumberland would be destabilised, including the vast territories of Count Alan Rufus. *Another Rufus, God save us*, thought Ranulf. Why, a man has only to have one reddish whisker and people call him Rufus. Count Alan held the honour of Richmond, one of the largest estates in the realm, with territories extending over eight counties, including the important communication routes through the Pennines. Then there was Robert of Mowbray who held the great castle at Bamborough and lordships in the eastern marches. Above all, there was King Malcolm of Scotland, aggrieved by the terms of the Peace of Abernethy and still smarting from the capture of Carlisle two years before. Even though his own saintly wife, Margaret, and her brother, Edgar Aetheling, made no secret of their Anglo-Norman leanings and constantly lectured him on the benefits of good relations with his southern neighbour, Malcolm prowled about the border, looking for opportunities to exert his influence, fomenting discontent wherever he could. Perhaps St Calais was right, maybe he should go north and keep a lid on things. After all, before the king fell ill, there were talks in hand for a conference with Malcolm later in the year. Perhaps reassurances should be sent, affirming the king's intention to receive Malcolm and negotiate a new settlement of their differences as soon as he had recovered. Perhaps St Calais should be advised to move everything forward as if the king was not going to die. So why not, while he was at it, make overtures for Edith's hand?

****

On the last day of her visit, towards evening, Aefled was walking with Edith in the cloister garden. During the few days she had spent with Edith, she had been enchanted by her strange, contradictory personality. By turns warm and peremptory, she could baffle and delight at the same time. She was an array of accomplishments that hung about her like finery on a statue. But though she might have her marble moods, or give the impression of a cold exterior, Edith was capable of changing in a moment into the malleable softness of childish warmth and charm. Her fluency, intelligence, a sharpness of mind far beyond her years, caused Aefled to wonder what sort of place Wilton might be. Was Edith an example of what was produced there? What sort of education could have formed the mind of this girl? A mind that seemed so much the cultivation of its own nature, germinating thoughts in its own private soils. Undoubtedly Edith was sharp-witted, shrewd and sly. Although at times, she seemed genuinely pious, joining the nuns for the offices of the day, reading holy works and speaking knowledgeably about saints' lives and the value of the spiritual life, she was also capable of presenting an entirely contradictory personality, when she wished. That was it, thought Aefled—when she wished. This girl could do anything if she wished and, if she didn't wish, nothing would coerce her. Humility was a badge she put on and took off just as it suited her to play to her aunt's moods. The things she was supposed to learn in the convent, self-denying, quiet, patient virtue, were like little honed skills that might be employed from time to time and then put down. Sometimes Aefled caught the glimpse of an unguarded expression in those watchful blue eyes, calculating, cold, as if to say, how may I use this person's interest, how may I benefit from this acquaintance? Aefled even got the impression that Edith was trying to play off the new acquaintance with herself against Christina and Lady Agnes, to make them jealous, working on the suspected weaknesses of women twice her age. Even her juvenile prattle, as they loitered in the cloister garden that evening, had in it the unmistakeable notes of manipulative duplicity. Aefled was intrigued. Her time with Edith was as if she had taken up a volume filled with a wondrous tale and did not want to put it down until she got to the end.

Edith was pursuing a tale of her own, one she had read in the 'Life of Mary of Egypt.'

'There was an old monk called Zozimus,' she explained. 'He chases a naked figure fleeing across a desert. Have you heard it?'

'No, I have never read it or heard it told.'

'The naked figure is St Mary of Egypt. They end up at a dried out creek and Mary calls out for a blanket to cover her body. "Why do you have such a need to see me, Zozimus," she asks, "me a sinful woman?" And the monk prostrates himself, recognising her holy beauty. Don't you think that is marvellous? Of course, the nuns say that Zozimus is us, pursuing the way to a holy encounter, true communion with those blessed by God. We all desire to see the naked truth of holiness. But I don't think that's the most interesting thing about the story. I think the old man is in search of something else.'

From little more than a tone as she said this and an arch look in the eye, Aefled had the impression that the sexual symbolism of the story with its pattern of desire and shame was not altogether unknown to her.

'What do you think he's in search of?'

'The sort of thing Lady Agnes knew years before she entered the convent. An old nobleman wanted to marry her and threatened to distrain her father when she said no. He chased her across deserts of shame to see her naked, like Zozimus. But he was not in search of holiness.'

'Did Lady Agnes tell you this?'

'No. My aunt told me. Something similar happened to my aunt. It was a man who drove her to the convent.' Edith laughed. 'Can I tell you something strange?' she said.

Aefled nodded eagerly. What was this little rosebud mouth going to come out with next?

'If you would learn about the ways of men, go to Wilton. The convent is full of women escaping from angry fathers, irate lovers, thwarted suitors, cheated husbands. Women in flight from all manner of amorous adventures. You can learn a great deal about the world by just sitting quietly and listening at Wilton.'

'Well, I suppose it is not good to be ignorant of these things. I have always believed that ignorance fosters fear and that knowledge, every kind of knowledge, is to be desired.'

'That's what I admire in you, Lady Aefled. You see, unlike my aunt and godmother, you are a married woman and have children. You have knowledge of the flesh and you are not afraid.'

Just then, Christina, looking pale and peremptory, arm in arm with Agnes, came to seek them in the cloister garth. It was almost time for vespers and the nuns were preparing for the service in the abbey church.

'Your aunt has received a letter,' said Agnes. 'The news is not good.'

'Is it the king?' asked Edith.

'No. News from Wilton,' said Christina. 'We must return immediately. We will set out as soon as it is light tomorrow. Lady Agnes will arrange for some of the brothers of St John's to escort us. When you say your prayers tonight, pray that your father finds good counsel.'

That night Aefled lay wondering what news had been contained in Christina's letter. What was the meaning of those enigmatic words about Edith's father and 'wise counsel'? She thought it must have something to do with the king's illness, but Christina seemed to have quashed that possibility. In the morning, when the escort arrived from the Abbey, Christina and Edith, with a little party of lay servants, were already dressed for travelling, their horses tacked and their luggage stowed in the panniers of baggage donkeys. Edith embraced Aefled and seemed to cling to her, reluctant to part. 'I wish I could stay,' she whispered, 'I like to talk to you. Please say that we will meet again.' Edith seemed again the small, vulnerable, innocent child, shrunk into herself that she had been at the very beginning of their acquaintance. Aefled wondered if she had been foolish to impute to this little girl qualities that were merely the product of her own imagining. Surely she was only what she seemed, a small figure at the mercy of the immense forces of Scottish and English power.

'We will meet again,' Aefled replied, genuinely hoping it would be so.

****

The chain of circumstances that had brought an urgent letter to Christina at St Sepulchre's had its origin in developments at the Scottish court. When Malcolm heard of the king's illness, he had called a council to discuss how to react in the case of death or recovery. The hurriedly convened council performed wonders of non-committal or conflicting advice as each noble and prelate looked to his own advantage. In the end, Malcolm dismissed them and, with biblical aptitude, took counsel with himself. His greatest difficulty was ignorance. Policy decisions were hampered by the slow progress of news. It would take a week to ten days for a messenger on good horses to cover the route from Gloucester to whichever stronghold Malcolm's court happened to be occupying.

Longer by ship if winds were contrary. If he was in the field, it might take another few days to find him. So Malcolm was staring at the possibility that, if William died, a new king might be proclaimed and crowned before news of the death had even reached him.

He had to look at options in advance and decide where he stood. First, there was the question of a likely successor, that is to say which of the two brothers, Robert, Duke of Normandy or Henry, Count of Cotentin, was most likely to make the first move to snatch the crown. Henry was a blank space, reputed to be studious, with plenty of cash, having received five thousand pounds of silver as legacy from his father, but not a hide of land. Though he had acquired lands in subsequent years, they were scattered in Normandy and he lacked a cohesive body of loyal nobles to support his cause. Robert was a known quantity, a small man with a great chip on his shoulder, capable of sporadic energy, though feckless and unreliable. But Robert had a good relationship with Edgar Aetheling and was not wholly ill-disposed to Malcolm. Robert might have made a good match for Edith had it not been for the awkward fact that he was her godfather and therefore ineligible. From whatever angle he viewed his prospects, Malcolm saw that his little daughter was his most important stake in the bid for alliances. For years he had believed William would marry her. There was never any formal agreement but rather an unwritten, informal assumption that went back to the Conqueror's time. Edith was fast approaching marriageable age and it was high time some deal was done. Now the king was ill and might have forever lost his chance to leave an heir. What a fool, thought Malcolm, to turn away the chance to ally himself to the Old English line. He should have had her years ago, by formal betrothal and solemn undertakings.

In the spring of 1093, Malcolm was once again looking back on a year filled with disputes and wrangling. William had refused to honour previous agreements, such as reducing the aggressive garrison at Carlisle and returning territory seized in Cumbria. These lands had been transferred in lordships to William's henchmen and it seemed unlikely that they would ever be recovered. Therefore, he must take steps to strengthen his position in the face of damaging alliances between the new lords planted by William and the established forces of Robert of Mowbray. He needed a northern ally, someone endowed with firmly held territories who could muster an army of knights, someone loyal to northern interests. Someone old enough to lead in the field and young enough to be in need of a wife.

When he looked around for a likely candidate, he found no one better qualified for the role than Count Alan Rufus of Richmond. In Malcolm's view, he was a typical man of the warrior class, not given to contemplation, a man who valued actions more than anything else. More importantly, he was immensely wealthy, enjoying the income from vast estates which he administered from his great castle stronghold of Richmond. He controlled important roads and communication routes from the south and could put into the field a large body of knights at short notice. *Perhaps,* thought Malcolm, *it is time to make some friendly overtures to Count Alan Rufus.* If the king dies, we can take steps to secure a good negotiating position with his successor. Faced with an alliance of two such powerful leaders in the north, an incoming king would at the very least have to negotiate. If the king recovers, Malcolm told himself, I will go south to confront him. I shall force him to an interview and he will either grant my request or provoke me to war against him.

The result of all Malcolm's considerations was that he was still in a waiting time, unable to take immediate action until he knew what God had in store for the reprobate king. For the moment, instead of marching south, he would edge south, drifting towards Durham for example. What could be the harm in offering prayers at the place where the sacred bones of St Cuthbert were deposited? In a few weeks, it would be Easter, the season of resurrection and renewal. By then, he would most likely be in possession of definite information which would help him formulate definite plans. In the meantime, he called for his clerk and commanded him to write three letters. One was to his sister-in-law, Christina; the letter that had called her back to Wilton. The other was to Count Alan Rufus suggesting a meeting in which he would hear a proposal that might be of great interest. The third was a matter of great delicacy, a letter to William himself, with prayers for his recovery and a request for a meeting to discuss a settlement of all differences. Feeling that he had taken steps to deal with every possible outcome, Malcolm reconvened his council and informed them of what had been done.

****

When Christina and Edith had left St Sepulchre's to return to Wilton Abbey, Aefled spent the morning with Agnes before she herself would be leaving to travel the short distance home to Castle St Mary's, a matter of half a day's ride. By now, she was anxious to be home although there was no real need. Robert's men, Arnoud, the constable, and Hugh, the steward, were more than capable of protecting his interests. Nor need she be anxious about her daughter since her friends, Maria and Gyft, were completely devoted to Eleanor. So Aefled delayed her return in order to have a few hours of private conversation with Agnes. The visit had been a delight to her. She had been intrigued and enchanted by Edith, impressed by the imperious royalty of Christina, calmed by the slow pace of life among the nuns and warmed by Agnes's friendship. But with her curiosity piqued by Edith's remarks, she wished to learn more of Agnes's past.

'What do you want to know?' Agnes seemed at ease with the question.

'Everything. How you came to be at Romsey and then Wilton? When and how you met Christina? When did Edith join her aunt? These will do for a start.'

'It's quite simple. As you know, there are no nunneries in Scotland, so when royal and noble girls require an education they are sent south. Christina came to Romsey about fifteen years ago where she discovered a vocation for the spiritual life and took the veil. When Edith was about six years old, she was sent to Romsey to join her aunt. That was when I first knew them.'

'But you said you were Edith's godmother. How can that be when you met her when she was six?'

'Oh, that's a little charade on our part. Edith once said she wished I was her godmother and I said I would be to her everything a godmother should be. But her real godmother is her aunt.'

'Why did you go to Wilton?'

'I was asked to go and take up a role as companion to the abbess who had become frail and unable to perform all her duties. She was a relative of mine. So I went to Wilton and soon afterwards Christina and Edith got permission to follow me. Wilton was a different sort of community with strong links to the old English aristocracy, pre-Conquest ladies seeking sanctuary. Aefled, you can't imagine the tales I heard there, the dreadful oppressions, deceptions, cruelties and betrayals, stories of broken hearts and real physical danger. The worst ones were those of the English women whose menfolk had been slaughtered in the Conquest and its terrible aftermath. Those days may be long gone but the damage goes on. No one thinks of it much now, but, believe me, there are many fugitives at Wilton who remember those times with grieving and bitterness.'

Agnes was telling a tale of terror and danger about Wilton, whereas Edith had told it as an excited awakening of sexuality.

Aefled wondered if Wilton would ever come into clear focus. Perhaps it was a place where you only found what was already in you.

As though to cool her mind, Agnes removed her headdress and ran her fingers through her long hair with slow, meditative movements. This luxuriance of hair and the way Agnes played with it, convinced Aefled that the nun's life was no calling for her, that she would never have her head shaved or take binding vows.

'Let me give you an example,' she said, as though coming to a decision. 'Have you ever heard of a woman called Gunhild?'

'No.'

'No, hardly anybody has. Yet, everyone has heard of her father. She is the last child of King Harold and Edith the Fair. That makes her a living link to the English line. She is a friend of Christina. A remarkable person, still in her prime, about your age, Aefled. Like many living at Wilton, she is in sanctuary and has never taken the veil. She is a distant relative of little Edith. Like Edith, she is of the English royal house, as is, of course, Margaret, Queen of Scotland.'

'The mother of our little Edith?'

'Yes, you see now why she bears that name? It's a family link that goes back into the mists of time. I say that advisedly. It goes back into the mists of King Edward's time, to be precise. Do you know the story? When Edward was on his deathbed, he had a dream about a blasted tree split asunder. The tree was England, the split was the sundering of the English line by Norman invasion. But the dream foretold a time when the two parts of the tree would be brought together and Normans and English would fuse in one strong vigorous growth, bearing greenery and fruit.'

'And Edith is the means to that union?'

'Indeed, a prize of great worth. Should the king die, there will be an almighty upheaval, as you know. Sides will be taken, alliances formed as the great magnates back their chosen candidates. Edith will suddenly become a figure of immense importance. You see now why Christina is anxious?'

It took Aefled a little while to absorb this information. Once more Agnes had astonished her with unexpected revelations; once more she had sidetracked the conversation by avoiding the subject of her own past.

'Tell me about yourself,' urged Aefled.

Agnes stopped playing with her hair and raised uncompromising eyes to her friend.

‘What is there to tell?’ Agnes went on. ‘I spent several years at both Romsey and Wilton and later I came here to St Sepulchre’s where I was made Prioress by special charter. There is really nothing more, Aefled. What adventures can one have in a nunnery?’

‘But, Agnes, as you have often said, you are not devout and have no bent for the religious life. So why were you at Romsey in the first place?’

‘Ah, I daresay Edith has been telling some wonderful tales of lost love and heartbreak. Her imagination is, shall we say, vivid and creative. Pay no mind to her stories.’

‘Can you tell me what was in Christina’s letter?’

‘A summons to return to Wilton without delay.’

‘Tell me one thing more,’ said Aefled, trying not to show her disappointment and wondering why Agnes had to be so frustratingly secretive. ‘As you know, my husband Robert and my sons are at this moment seeking the patronage of Count Alan Rufus. Do you think that the death of the king might endanger them in some way?’

‘Aefled,’ said Agnes with great seriousness. ‘If the king dies, no one will escape some sort of danger.’

****

Chapter Three

Easter Rising

King William was confined to his sick chamber throughout the period of Lent, from early March to mid-April. Never before had he fasted so long or so completely. Nor had he spent so much time thinking about sin and salvation. When the penitential psalms were read to him, he listened and promised again to abide by the sacred pledges that now lay on the altar of the abbey church of St Peter's. He would reform, he said, dismiss his favourites, enact good laws and deal justly with everybody. During one of the worst crises, he sent for Anselm and entreated him not to let him perish in body and soul. He begged him to accept the archbishopric and enter upon the office with full grace so that he would not have a great sin against the church on his conscience at his death. Cynics sneered, but there was no doubt that William was so dangerously ill and the fear of death so genuine that he was at last in naked confrontation with his soul.

It was into this situation that, early in April, the envoys from Malcolm entered, causing a quarrel among the courtiers who were adamant that no business could be conducted. Getting wind of this, Ranulf Flambard sent for them and, when he learned that nothing had been done for their immediate comfort, invited them to supper and gave instructions for the stabling of their horses and their own lodging. Having won them over, he lost no time in bringing himself up to date with Malcolm's plans. The senior envoy was a lord of Moray, called Dunmore. And it was to this bearded ox of a man that Ranulf addressed himself.

'As the King's Chief Minister,' he said, 'all the king's correspondence has to come through me. You must understand he is gravely ill.'

'I know that. That's why these letters bring prayers along with a proposal of reconcilement.'

'What kind of reconcilement?'

'A fair settlement of the terms of 1091. Renewing the Treaty of Abernethy. Reducing the garrison at Carlisle, restoring lands. A firm peace must be rooted in these things. Malcolm wants friendly relations with William. But William must keep his word.'

'Of course, as we all must,' said Ranulf. 'For the moment, let us set aside Malcolm's rampage into England when William was in Normandy two years past. Let us ignore the fact that Malcolm has reneged on oaths made to the king after Edgar Aetheling brokered a peace.'

Flambard was more than ready to counter every complaint of Dunmore's with an equally valid one of his own. But the whole thing would be likely to last indefinitely.

'Let's not trawl over the past or we shall be swopping tit for tat all night. Show me the letter. If I consider the proposals valid, I will bring them to the king's ear.'

So Ranulf spent an evening discussing affairs of state with Dunmore. *Not bad,* he thought, *for the son of a semi-literate Norman priest.* And if he wasn't quite the king's chief minister, he soon would be. Unless, of course, the king died. Then he would have to climb his way up all over again. In which case, the forging of good relations with a Lord of Moray and the King of Scotland would certainly not hamper the process.

At the appointed time next day, Ranulf turned up to brief the king. One look at the royal face would instruct him on what was safe to report and what must be held back. His washers and dressers had been busy, he looked clean and his hair had been combed. A thin beard was growing back, without the reddish tinge. But his flesh was sallow, clammy, his eyeballs yellow, his cheeks hollow and the orbits of his eyes stained with black and purple blotches.

'My lord king,' he whispered, 'please God you are better today.'

'Face of Lucca, Flambard. Do I look better?' The voice was weak but surely there was a spark in it, the spark Flambard so often ignited in the king. Ranulf decided not to admit the recent news from Wales to the king's sickbed. Rhys ap Tewdwr, a client king of the Norman court who had maintained stability in south Wales, was dead, killed in a random skirmish. This was a great blow requiring a vigorous response, something the king was in no position to give. The Scottish news, however, concerning peaceful diplomacy and the restoration of good relations was altogether more fitted for the king's ear. When Ranulf had briefly explained that Malcolm wanted a meeting, William seemed willing to agree. 'Let him come. Invite him. I will deal fairly with him. If God spares me.'

The simple impulse of these few words may possibly have been lost in translation as they were modified for the official reply later despatched to Malcolm. If, in the course of the drafting, Flambard appeared to offer rather more than was intended, it might be no more than the overwarm glow of his desire for ready solutions. These were based on a principle of balance: on the one side avoidance of war, always costly and with uncertain outcomes; on the other side a due regard for the king's honour. Not that the royal word must, at all times, be kept but rather that an action must entail a perceived quotient of justifiability in the long term. What did it matter if the king had not kept his word in regard to the terms made with Malcolm last year and the year before, when he could potentially do so this year or next? In undertaking a reply on the king's behalf, Flambard relied heavily on the future tense and laced that future with the indistinct and misty prospect of an offer for Edith's hand. Phrases such as 'joining our two great realms' and the 'royal lines of England and Scotland in a new commingling' and similar vague verbiage found its way effortlessly into the document. Ranulf did not consider himself in the business of false promises, but if the king was to die, proffered hopes could only enhance his posthumous reputation. If he was to live, William's hand would have been gently guided in the right direction.

Satisfied that the mission had been successful, Dunmore and the envoys left the court the following day to return north. In his turn, Flambard was satisfied that he had handled the marriage business with subtlety. He had thought to employ William St Calais in these initial overtures, but St Calais had made no move northward and was still hanging around, stuck in a swamp of uncertainty, as they all were. Meanwhile, far away in the north, powerful forces were stirring.

****

The keep of Richmond castle rose like a great incisor, biting into the territory of North Yorkshire. Count Alan Rufus, latest of the line of Breton Counts of Penthièvre, one of the wealthiest men in England, held a stronghold to match his status. Great stone walls, strengthened with turreted bastions, curved away from the keep along two sides of the triangular hilltop fortress. On the third side, a sheer drop fell steeply down to the River Swale. From these heights a complete survey of the surrounding country could be taken, the road winding up the valley, the Swale looping through pastures and *bosquets*, the dales and hills rolling away to distant crests. Up against the south-west corner of the castle site, as far from the town's rowdy pullulations as possible, close to the sheer drop down to the water, stood Count Alan Rufus's great hall.

In contrast to the militaristic keep, the great hall was a place where the habitual fierce hardihood of a warrior overlord could be seen giving way to embryonic luxury. A two-storey well-heated, well-decorated set of rooms, which a Roman Praetor on leave from the Wall might not have scorned, formed the focal point of domestic living for the count's private household. It was accessed via an undercroft where all the menial services were housed, but once up the wide flight of steps and through a magnificent doorway with columns and a moulded inner arch, brightly painted with scenes of the Penthièvre ancestors, an impressive effect of wealth, power and opulence met the eye. A rectangular hall with flued fireplaces and wide recessed windows was the setting for formal occasions, feasts and ritual entertainments. Beyond this large hall, and divided by a stone wall at one end, was a smaller, intimate chamber or solar, where Count Alan would receive his closest friends, or those he wanted to impress.

It was to this place and this man that Aefled's husband, Robert, had brought his sons for the enlargement of their education. The man he knew, having fought under his command in the vassal army raised after the revolt of 1071. But in those days they had been continually in the field. Robert had never entered Richmond, never seen the magnificent stronghold of his suzerain. On his arrival, Count Alan received him warmly, as if remembering an old comrade in arms.

'They are eager boys,' said Robert when he had explained his purpose. 'They can read and write a little, say their catechism. The eldest, Robert, is in his thirteenth year, William in his eleventh.'

Count Alan looked them over, smiling as he saw them stare back boldly. 'Well grown for their years. What do you want me to do for them?'

Robert spread his arms wide, indicating the magnificence of his surroundings. 'This is a new world to them, my lord. I want them to learn how to conduct themselves in it.'

'If they stay with me, Sieur Robert, they will begin, like all the squires, in the lower hall among the servants. They will wait on me and the lords and clerks of my household. They will train on foot and horseback. And for that, you will supply them with equipment, pay their keep and maintain their mounts. In return, I will make men of them.'

That was the deal and Robert thought it a good one.

'One thing more, if I find them lads of merit, I will allow them to accompany me when I travel. The terrain here, rugged high uplands, cut by valleys and precipices, with few good roads, is very different from your soft southern acres. My holdings in Nottinghamshire and Lincolnshire are flat, good for corn and turnips, but much of it is fenland, boggy fields, marsh and mire. Here you stand upright on solid ground and learn to lean into the wind.'

'That is what I would have them learn, my lord.'

'Good, then we are agreed. But while you are here, Sieur Robert, I might want to employ you on a mission of my own. Come to the solar this evening after supper and we will talk.'

After this conversation, Robert's first impulse was to write to Aefled. It was at least two months since he had seen her and in all that time he had not been able to send word of his whereabouts. Or perhaps he should wait until he had been received in private interview by Count Alan. She would be sure to want a detailed report on the count's private life. So he waited and that evening, leaving the boys to their own devices, went off to his meeting with Count Alan.

To arrive at Count Alan's solar was to have the ineradicable feeling that one had arrived *somewhere*. Tapestry wall coverings, plump cushions, silken hangings, silver goblets chased with arms and mottoes, delicate iron-wrought hand lamps, proclaimed not only wealth but taste. Curious, rare, fine things offered delight to every glance. This was the setting for a man who competed in fascination with the opulence of his surroundings. Large-boned and solid, he stood or sat foursquare like his keep. In spite of the tag of Rufus, or *le roux*, he was neither florid nor red-haired, nor given to flaming tempers. In a conversation with the steward, Robert learned that Rufus had the same colour hair as his brother who, bizarrely, was called Alan 'Niger' or *noir*.

'But black or red does not matter,' said the steward, 'they are not counters on a board.'

On the contrary, he explained, they maintained close relations, perhaps because the younger Alan behaved in all things as a liegeman of his brother. Besides, there were so many of them—seven legitimate brothers, several called Alan, and innumerable half-brothers—that it was often joked that the lord of Richmond could muster an army from his relatives alone. In fact, Count Alan Rufus was a grizzle-headed warrior of fifty-three with the energy and enthusiasm of a man half his age, limber as a well-oiled hinge, still able to spend all day in the hunting field, wield a two-handed sword or couch a lance.

While gratified by his *entrée* to Count Alan's intimate circle, Robert felt outclassed, unable to compete with the splendour of his host. A minor provincial lord of estates that might fit into one of Count Alan's parks, without connections at court, he had never felt so much a vassal. His manor of Castle St Mary's was not much bigger than Richmond town market and his new stone keep was built on a hill that could be lost in a fold of Swale valley. But in one respect he felt superior to his lord since he had two fine sons, heirs of his line. Alan Rufus had no heir save his brother. However, in the north that was not necessarily a disadvantage. Here an ancient code of property transference called *tanistry* was still in existence. Based on a Celtic tradition, it involved the selection of an heir by the senior members of a clan. This was often practised in Scotland and the border country where there was every likelihood that a minor would be struck down by his own relatives before he could enter on his inheritance. So his brother, Alan Niger, was heir designate to the entirety of the Northumbrian and Cumbrian possessions. One day this situation would involve both brothers in the unfolding of a strange tale of passion and tragedy, so unlikely and bizarre that, had it not been for the subsequent interventions of Anselm, it might never have come to light. Unknown to Robert, the beginnings of that tale lay in the interview he was about to have with his magnificent overlord.

Minstrels were playing in a corner of the solar, wine flowed. Late evening light poured into the room through large windows. The sun had an hour or two to drop before setting. Robert felt light-headed. His belly was full from the impressive array of dishes served in the great hall. Feigning to be at ease with himself and the world, he lounged on an upholstered bench, waiting for Count Alan's attention, wondering what kind of mission was going to be proposed. He waited a long time.

Count Alan's attention was a prize for which men and women competed, and the ladies were the winners. Well-dressed Breton dames presented their daughters and delayed him in conversation. He spent long with them, appearing to enjoy their company, laughing and talking or encouraging them to skip around to the music or sing the traditional old songs from Brittany. If he was such a success with women, thought Robert, why had he never married? For a big man, he had an unusual delicacy, a gracious way of speaking. His accent was distinctive, Norman French laced with Breton and a sprinkling of Border gutterals. He has *finesse,* thought Robert, look how he calls me "Sieur". The more he observed and listened, the more he realised that Count Alan was one of those rare beings who win confidence by giving full attention when you speak. The way he held your gaze, the way his replies were fashioned for you alone, not stock courtiers' phrases or commonplaces, but something growing entirely out of the momentary meeting of your interest with his, these were winning, not to say gallant, qualities. A kind of discerning amiability enveloped this hard man without the least trace of counterfeit. But his reputation of old, when Robert had fought for him in the campaigns after 1071, was of a different order. No one could be harder, more implacable, more resolute than Count Alan Rufus in those days. And yet something about him fascinated men and women alike, drew them to his magnificent presence on threads of gossamer. In his own house, thought Robert, he is more kingly than the king himself.

At last, it was Robert's turn to receive the undiluted attention of his host. They sat alone at one end of the solar, now darkening in the twilight.

'What is the news from Gloucester? How is the king?'

'He survives, my lord, but merely. I have heard nothing certain for many days.'

'You know, of course, that if the king dies, the repercussions here are likely to be grave. The barons will be ready to make war over the succession. Conflict in the border country will attract the interest of King Malcolm.'

Although Robert had little understanding of the power politics of the north, he listened intently without feeling it necessary to answer.

'I have had word from King Malcolm of Scotland,' the Count went on. 'He has suggested that we meet. He wants to discuss a matter of some importance, though he gives no hint of what it might be. In view of the king's illness, I am not sure whether to be alarmed or flattered by these royal attentions.'

Again, Robert did not see what sort of answer was required.

'You are a man of few words,' said the Count approvingly. 'I like that. You are discreet and I know you to be a loyal fealty man, as I am. You are from the south, therefore not embroiled in the alliances and clannish rivalries of these parts. So let me ask you, will you conduct some business for me?'

'Willingly, my lord.'

'It will require no great hardship.'

Count Alan signalled to an attendant to bring a flagon of wine and attend to their empty goblets.

'I want you to establish communications with King Malcolm. Take an escort of my vavasours. Clean men, fighting men, straight, honourable men is what I want. Do you take my meaning?'

'I do, my lord.'

Simple men, thought Robert, ignorant, close-mouthed, obedient men, is what he wants. Men like me. But how well he phrases it.

'Good, I see we understand each other.'

Between this conversation and Robert's departure, there was a long delay as arrangements were adjusted in the light of Malcolm's continual restless movements around his kingdom. During this time Robert was able at last to despatch a letter to Aefled, though it was far from certain that she would receive it. As always in this remote country, difficulties of communication, poor roads and, latterly, dreadful weather, rendered all plans uncertain. Robert was still at Richmond trying to finalise the details of his mission when news came from the south and the outcome of King William's long agony was known.

****

On Holy Thursday, the 14th day of April, the king's illness reached its frightful crisis in a seizure so violent that he had to be held down. Afterwards, he fell into a dull, shivering torpor and was silent. For two days, he was barely conscious.

Anselm stayed on at the Priory of St Oswald's, offering up prayers. William St Calais, Bloet, Meulan and other members of the council, no longer came to speak to the king. Even Ranulf Flambard had lost all hope. By turns, they stood in vigil, waiting, punctuating the days and nights with horrible suspension.

By the end of the second day, Holy Saturday, all hope had departed. William was going to his tomb as surely as Christ when he was taken down from the cross. Words that William had scorned all his life now seemed to mock his semi-conscious form with fitting reproofs: 'Grant O Lord that as we are baptised into the death of our Blessed Saviour, so by continual mortifying of our corruption we may be buried with him and pass to our joyful resurrection.'

Then, early on Easter Sunday, the 17th day of April, the morning of the Resurrection when Christ rose and walked in the garden, the king rallied. Fully conscious, he opened his eyes and asked what day it was. Ranulf Flambard, whose lonely vigil had lasted most of the night in hopes of catching the last words of the king, could barely master his relief. All the complicated plans he had been weaving fell away in an instant. Here was the simplest, most perfect, most symbolic solution to all his problems. The king would rise again. Then he thought about the possibility of a "false crisis", when sufferers appear to rally just before death. In a torment of hope and doubt, Ranulf hastily sent for Anselm and the chief courtiers to witness the ultimate outcome of the king's long ordeal.

'My lord king,' he whispered to the ravaged carcass, burnt up by weeks of fever, 'it is Easter morning, Holy Sunday. Please God you are saved.'

William touched his hand and gave him the shadow of a smile. 'God has spared me, Flambard. God in his mercy has spared me.' The last residue of fluid in his body squeezed out from the corners of his eyes.

'Believe me, I wept too, when I saw that he was indeed again among the living. The stone was rolled away. A miracle, although I could not say that any radiant figures appeared to announce it,' Ranulf told Firmin at the end of that memorable day. 'The best thing was, he kept down what he ate and took a little more of my Anjou. Perhaps that really was the beginning of the cure. He was clear of his fever and appeared out of all danger by evening.'

Firmin, along with all the servants of the various households and most of the people of Gloucester, spent the day in Easter celebrations such as had never been seen before. Bells rang out all over the town, messengers were despatched to all the great centres of the realm, to Winchester, Windsor, Rochester, Lincoln, York, Durham. The whole court was suddenly reanimated in the dissemination of joyful news. The message of Easter with all its hopes of renewal and the overcoming of death was enfolded in news of the resurrection of the king and went posting around the kingdom. Universal relief broke out among the townsfolk who hoped that their town might benefit from the king's gratitude because there, in their midst, he had been raised from the dead.

Ranulf thought that something should be done for them and gave orders for the palace cellars to be opened. Great iron-hooped casks were rolled into the marketplace where tables were furnished with food for a populace who had suffered long under the great burden of superfluous numbers. Fires were lit and, in the mad rampages of unbridled song and dance, people partook of celebratory bounty. If they thought this generosity came from the king, all to the good. As far as Flambard was concerned, this could be a turning point in William's reign. For once, the monks would be silenced in writing their scandalous reports of his reputation. Flambard positively flamed with a desire to serve. Now William's reign would take a path towards good laws, peace and wise administration, and he would be the man to lead it there. All those pledges on the altar of Gloucester Cathedral would be put into effect. Anselm would glide happily into his archbishopric, Malcolm would gladly give a pledge of peace and William would marry Edith to the sound of rejoicing every bit as gladsome as that taking place in Gloucester this day. So ran Ranulf's thoughts, heading blindly towards a quagmire of bitter disappointments.

The following week was spent in convalescence as the king recovered his vigour. He ate and drank with returning appetite, spent an entire day taking a bath, received individual ministers, dictated some private letters and ventured out once or twice on horseback, confining himself to the grounds of Kingsholm. He summoned and graciously thanked those who had attended him in his illness and those, like Ranulf Flambard, who had kept their fingers on the pulse of affairs.

'Believe me, Flambard,' he said, 'I am aware of you.'

It sounded like a threat but Ranulf knew better. This was the king in thanking mode.

William did not appear publicly until a triumphal celebratory mass in the abbey church at Gloucester on the following Sunday which marked the end of the Easter Octave. As might be expected, this was a magnificent occasion and, for once, involved an outflow of genuine warmth for the king. Ranulf worked hard in the background, organising a grand affair in which the court and the church united around a monarch who was, perhaps for the first and last time, indisputably popular. Tributes were paid, speeches were made, *laudes* were sung and the king paraded in his robes of state looking like a man who had been chastened but not subdued. Colour and firmness were coming back to his shaved cheeks. His freshly combed hair, though long, was not lank. Thinner, seemingly taller, he entered the abbey church to great acclamation. Ready to receive him and perform the mass, were William St Calais, Bishop of Durham, Robert Bloet, the recently appointed Bishop of Lincoln, the abbot and canons of Gloucester Abbey, Baldwin, Abbot of St

Edmundsbury, and a large number of bishops and priors from various parts of the kingdom, some who had attended him through his illness, some newly arrived for this splendid occasion. And there, in an honoured but not prominent position, was Anselm, former Abbot of Bec and now Archbishop of Canterbury.

But does he know he is? wondered Ranulf as he saw him wearing, not the alb and chasuble or richly embroidered cope that might be expected, but the ordinary tunic and scapular of a Benedictine monk. 'How like him to make his point by dressing down. This humility is simply a stylised form of vanity. What is he playing at?'

If William took it as a statement, he made no sign, but nodded graciously in his direction and proceeded with the ceremonial in which Anselm, pointedly, played no part. The spiritual intimacy of confession and absolution seemed, if it had happened at all, to have happened to other people.

From their first meeting, later that week in the great hall of Kingsholm, two things became clear. The first was that William was completely recovered from his illness and had regained his appetite for battle: the second that Anselm had not altered his attitude one bit. Mentally, he still considered himself Abbot of Bec and was on the look-out for obstacles to his acceptance of the archbishopric.

'The decision is not in my hands,' he pleaded lamely. 'Consent by Duke Robert of Normandy, by the Bishop of Rouen, by the monks of Bec, all these are necessary to my entering upon the office.'

'Face of Lucca!' replied William. 'Not one of these is a genuine obstacle. First, my brother's agreement arrived this very week. With it came the consent of Rouen. There only remains the matter of Bec. If you act with firmness, nominate your successor and tell them to get on without you, there will be no murmur from Bec, I assure you.'

It was this kind of trivial and inconclusive dispute that soured relations between them. The worst was, it was all so predictable.

'It's infuriating, Firmin,' said Ranulf that evening. 'In the persons of Anselm and William, the two great administrative arms of the state will do nothing but batter each other.'

'Master, it was well said that they are the bull and the sheep. They should never have been yoked.'

'And that was only the first exchange of blows. Later, they got on to the subject of money. "What will happen to the monies raised during the four-year vacancy?" says Anselm. As if William will return a penny! That's the trouble with these spiritual types.

Practical affairs require careful adjustment of ends and means. But Anselm lacks a pliable spirit. It's all torment and conscience with him.'

'Master,' said Firmin, in the casual tone he often used when about to drop a nugget of news. 'I've been speaking to Eustace. He told me that Baldwin is resolute that his master shall be archbishop and wants a meeting with you.'

'Does he, by God! Firmin, you might yet earn your keep. Get off, lad. Speak to that little Eustace again. Dig up facts about Baldwin and drop hints that I will be just as happy to speak to him.'

Baldwin of Tournai was a man born to business. He had pursued a distinguished career as a layman before becoming a monk of Bec seven years ago, attracted there, like many young men, by the growing reputation of Anselm. As a young man, he had been the chief agent of the Bishop of Tournai and had travelled around the courts of Europe with his master, whose titular he adopted. At Bec, Anselm had depended heavily on his expertise and Baldwin duly expected to be made head of his household when he became archbishop. These were the sort of facts Firmin supplied and Ranulf could use. A study of his character proved more difficult but, on the pretext of wanting to understand the nature of the Eucharist, Firmin cornered Eustace in the kitchens one day and began to probe.

'What do you want to know?' said Eustace, very willing at all times to enter into scholarly discussion, especially when a pan of roasted eels was offered with fresh bread.

'How does it happen,' said Firmin between mouthfuls, 'that the real body of Christ is present in the bread at communion? I mean, really present. Not just notionally present, or present in a rhetorical way. But really there, real, in front of you?'

'Ah,' said Eustace eagerly. 'Are you not aware of Lanfranc's definition? Lanfranc set it all out most brilliantly at the Council of 1059.'

'No, I've never heard of it. Tell me.'

'Well, he uses the logical arguments of Aristotle's doctrine of categories. In this doctrine, Aristotle holds that the visible world consists of a substratum of invisible primary substances of which the visible and tangible 'accidents' of colour, shape and so on, are the sensible evidence. Do you follow?'

Firmin nodded feebly.

'So, what happens in the Eucharist is that the invisible substance of Christ's body replaces the invisible primary substance of the bread while the 'accidents' of colour, appearance, shape and so on, remain unchanged.'

'So, basically, it looks like bread but isn't bread?'

'A little crude, but yes, I suppose so.'

'Then I don't see what my difficulty was!' Firmin pretended to be satisfied and turned his attention to the meal. 'You monks are amazingly clever,' he said, after a time. 'I admire your learning. I wish I had more Latin.'

'I would offer to teach you,' said Eustace, 'but we will be leaving soon.'

'Of course, I expect Anselm is eager to hurry down to Canterbury.'

'No, there are no plans to go there.'

Firmin seized on this piece of information as a clue to what Baldwin wanted to talk about. So Anselm was not going to Canterbury. He was trying to twist out of the election and Baldwin wanted him firmly kept in it.

'You are a clever man,' he coaxed. 'But it seems to me you are not given the respect you deserve. Baldwin, for instance, does he treat you well? '

'Well enough, but he is high-handed, domineering. I don't think he likes me.'

'I suppose he is a great scholar like you?'

Eustace laughed. 'Baldwin is no scholar, he's an organiser. He is in awe of Anselm's intellect. He believes him to be a person of intense spiritual powers. He even makes up stories to spread his fame.'

'Does he? By God! What sort of stories?'

Eustace leaned forward to whisper: 'Once, when we were all on board a boat at sea, rough weather made Anselm pray for a safe harbour and when we came safely to the port of Wissant Baldwin swore that there was a hole in the boat. Anselm's prayers had kept the boat afloat through the storm in spite of a great hole in the keel. That is what Baldwin swore.'

'And did you, or anyone else, see this hole?'

'No.' Eustace shook his head, while Firmin made mental notes about his appearance. An unremarkable person, small, thin and raw-boned, with pale freckled skin, a circle of sandy hair around his tonsure and a mole on his nose.

'I'll tell you something else. Baldwin believes Anselm to be a saint.'

From further discussions of this sort, Firmin was able to report that Baldwin was an image maker who knew how to spin out the threads of his master's reputation and was not above the invention of marvellous stories. No scholar himself, he was in awe of his master's intellect and never missed an opportunity to present him as a person of great holiness. Devoted, pragmatic, Baldwin could advise and guide the older man who trusted him implicitly and depended on him to take off his shoulders the responsibilities of practical daily life. Baldwin was eager to do so. Believing his master to be a saint, Baldwin was going to ensure he would be one.

With this report in mind, Ranulf met Baldwin about a week later in his cramped lodgings at Kingsholm, where space was still short. They were both adamant that Anselm must be steered towards acceptance of the archbishopric, though they took opposing attitudes to the tenderness of Anselm's conscience.

'You must understand that the motives of my master are complicated,' said Baldwin. 'He considers himself unfitted for the role, he is a spiritual man who wishes only to read, study and write great theological works. Basically, he fears the expense of time and energy on worldly things. He considers the office of archbishop a worldly office. Administration of lands, tenantries, running a household, receipts and disbursements. All that is of no interest to him.'

'So, what, primarily, is his position?'

'His official position is that he has not accepted the election and, before he can do so, he needs further assurances from the king.'

'About what, precisely?'

'That he must have all the Canterbury lands exactly as they were at Lanfranc's death and unencumbered by any claims upon them. That William must take him as his principal councillor. And that Anselm, as one who has recognised Pope Urban II, should continue in obedience to him and not another.'

'These do not sound like the tender qualms of conscience,' said Ranulf knowing full well that Baldwin, not Anselm, was the head and fount of these stipulations.

'My master would like to have the king's decision on these matters but does not press for a reply. He intends to travel around the Canterbury lands, testing opinion and listening to the wishes of the various communities. He proposes that he should meet with the king at Windsor in the summer.'

'So, what it comes to is that we still don't actually have an archbishop.'

‘If we understand that we are working together on this, we can have an archbishop in place by the end of the year.’

‘And what will it take to get us there?’

‘Patience, hard work. But I know Anselm better than he knows himself. He wants this office but he wants it without vanity, without the bite of conscience. He desires the thing he should not desire. That is how he thinks. So he will have to torment himself a little, for a few months or so. There will be arguments but I would wish you to understand that his fiercest arguments are with himself, not with the king.’

Ranulf found himself warming to this pragmatic, clear-headed monk. Indeed, faced with his astute, realistic appraisal of his master, it was difficult to believe that he could also be the purveyor of incredible tales. Ranulf was tempted to ask him about the hole in the boat but held back, not wishing to damage a newly established relationship. In all, he felt the meeting had been a great success. When Firmin returned after Baldwin’s departure, Ranulf spared a word of praise.

‘Well done, lad. Baldwin is a man I can work with. Now, I suppose, you want a reward?’

‘As it happens, master. I do.’

‘What do you want?’

Firmin’s reply was not what Ranulf expected.

‘Master, I want to perfect my Latin.’

‘What for? Are you proposing to become a monk?’

‘No, master. But if I was more learned I would be of much more use to you.’

‘I daresay you would, Firmin. In fact, that might not be a bad idea.’

****

Before the news of the king’s recovery had trickled to the obscurer parts of the realm, Aefled returned to Castle St Mary’s to pursue the domestic routine of the wife of a provincial castellan. When her daughter, Eleanor, asked questions about the visit, she said that she had met “some interesting ladies from another convent”, but made no mention of Wilton. As far as anybody was concerned, she had spent a few days in retreat at St Sepulchre’s, an item of news that would do no harm in fostering a reputation as a model Christian lady. She sent for Hugh, the steward, and Arnoud, the constable, who between them supervised the daily organisation of the household and security of the castle. They had nothing to report; everything was running smoothly, the village was quiet. As in towns and villages up and down the country, the people of Castle St Mary's were caught in the general hebetation of waiting, torpid with anxiety, expectant and fearful as they awaited news of the king. If the king died, there might be war. If there was war, there would inevitably come a war tax, sometimes as high as seventy pence per household.

During this waiting time, Aefled turned her attention to the running of what she thought of as her little 'school' to which her own sons, Robert and William had belonged before they had gone away to the household of Count Alan Rufus. This "school", in which English village boys and Norman sons of the household were raised together, learning to read and write, to say the catechism and acquire the basics of mutual understanding, was her own experiment in trying to foster Anglo-Norman relations. She had begun it when her sons were small and for some time it seemed quite successful. Even now, among the newest little members, there was a degree of mixing. But Aefled had learned that, at a certain age, around ten or twelve years old, something happened to the boys. They seemed, almost by instinct and in the face of a carefully nurtured ethos, to become aware of the differences of lineage which marked them out as members of superior or inferior groups. This was a great disappointment to Aefled and one she had written about many times to Isaac. Her old mentor, who had always been sceptical about her plans, was now living permanently in London. But from his letters, she deduced that he was not surprised by the ruin of what he termed her 'noble ideal.'

She had wanted to mould and shape men for the coming age, a new age of unity between two peoples. Or, as Agnes had put it, the binding of the great split trunk of the realm which had been sundered at Hastings. But unless the sealing of the trunk was to happen higher up the hierarchy, among the noble or royal houses, there was less chance of it happening further down. That was why the marriage prospects of Edith were of such national importance. If that odd little girl could be joined with William, or if William died, his successor, uniting the old English house with the new Norman monarchy, the trunk would be joined at the highest level. This way, a strong message of unity would be established for people at every level below. In order to be effective, the grandiose image of King Edward's dream required the imprint of the highest ranks. Without it, exclusion at the lowest levels would simply become entrenched.

This had always been Isaac's view but she had refused to see it. Strange that at each stage of her life she was finding it necessary to change her opinions. That ideal image of the unified trunk, giving forth green shoots, so happily organic and conformable to nature, was, she knew, unlikely in a world that dealt roughly with ideals. Practical, harsh, painful realities tended to get in the way.

She could see it happening in her own household where it was becoming apparent that the village boys, Edward and Alfred, were in the process of confronting such realities. Now that they were grown to the same age as her sons and it was obvious that they were not going to be sent away to learn the practice of knights in some noble household, as their playmates had been, they were feeling the affront of exclusion. As awareness of distinctions became apparent, that birth and lineage mattered more than talent and training, resentment grew. What could they expect from life except that they would be, like their fathers, the labourers and tenants of the Norman overlords who now held their land? They could read and write, but what good was that except to make them more discontented with their lot? One answer to their aspirations was to place them in a monastery to train as clerks so that they might advance in the church. One of the few openings for English boys to rise in the world was through the great international organisation of the church. But neither Edward nor Alfred showed any aptitude for such training and were beginning to run wild.

On Easter Sunday, a mass was said in the manor church of St Mary's and prayers were offered for the recovery of the king. Then, towards the end of April, the news came. Their prayers had been granted. The king had recovered. They heard that his miraculous restoration had begun on Easter Sunday when he rose unaccountably from what everyone had thought would be his deathbed. But now he was quite well again; so well, it was rumoured, that he had already fallen out with Anselm. The rejoicings at Castle St Mary's reflected the universal rejoicing up and down the country as people realised that, for a time at least, they were to be spared the horrors of war and the infliction of a war tax. This summer the Lammas harvest would be cut on time.

Aefled was still waiting for news of Robert's whereabouts by the beginning of June but no message came and she settled down to a routine of administration with the help of Hugh and Arnoud. Life went on in steady dullness. Aefled thought constantly of her trip to St Sepulchre's and the exciting glimpse she had had of a world beyond her own provincial sphere which now seemed remote and secluded. This was Aefled's state when, in early June, a message came from Robert. It was written in the hand of her eldest son, the distinctive cumbersome hand that she knew so well. It told briefly of their progress, gave an impression of the great fortress of Richmond, assured her of their health but made no mention of when she could expect to see them again. It brought an inadequate kind of reassurance, being already out of date before she could read it.

'They are well,' she told Maria, 'they are at Richmond.'

'Perhaps now you will not be so restless. What is it that disturbs you?'

Maria and Gyft had noticed her strange mood since her return from St Sepulchre's. Thinking it probably concerned some religious question, they did not press her and she, on her part, offered no information. They assumed that she had found the convent uncongenial, or fallen out with the lady Agnes over a spiritual matter. So they were surprised when, in the second week of June, Lady Agnes turned up suddenly in a distressed state asking to see Aefled urgently.

'It's Edith,' she said, when they were alone. 'Edith is ill and is asking for us. I want you to travel to Wilton with me. Now. Without delay. Christina writes that Edith needs us. She urges us to come as soon as we can.' Agnes read out Christina's letter while Aefled listened to a list of symptoms in mounting alarm. 'Come as quickly as you can,' it ended, 'for Edith's sake and mine. God bring you to us safely, dear friends in Christ. You are our only hope.'

Such an appeal could have only one reply.

In other circumstances, Aefled might have enjoyed travelling in June when the roads were dry and the weather mostly fine. She might even have considered taking Eleanor with her. But she could not take her daughter to a place where illness raged. Arrangements were hurriedly made. Escorted by Arnoud and a detachment of garrison soldiers, they travelled fast, stopping overnight at religious houses. When they reached Wilton Abbey late on the fourth day, they found Christina in an almost collapsed state, despairing of her niece's life.

'Praise God you have come,' she said. 'Praise God you have come.'

Preparing themselves for the very worst scene imaginable, a child's deathbed agony, Aefled and Agnes followed Christina to her chamber. It was not the cell of a nun but a plush, well decorated, airy room. They found Edith stretched in a comfortable bed draped with a brocade bedcover richly embroidered with the arms of

Scotland. It was a reminder that this was the bed of no ordinary child but one around which national destinies were to be played out. Edith lay still, eyes closed, breathing shallowly, looking rather more in a peaceful sleep than tormented by pain or fever.

'Edith, dear, the ladies Agnes and Aefled have come, just as you asked.' Christina's whisper caused the eyelids to flutter and the cold blue eyes to open in response, but she made no other movement.

'She has been like this for days. Hardly eats, speaks little.'

Aefled took her hand and touched her forehead. Both were cool.

'She seems clear of fever at least. How did this illness begin?'

'With her bleeding,' said Christina. 'She complained of pains when her bleeding began.'

'She is young to bleed,' said Agnes. 'We might not have expected it for years.'

'I was fifteen and thought it was early,' said Aefled. 'She is indeed young for the monthly burden.'

'She came to me in a terrible state, saying she was struck by the flux and would die. I explained what was happening but she did not seem to accept it. Poor Edith, it is the terrible mark of women's fate, the seal of sin, the curse of sex.'

If this is the sort of explanation Christina has been giving, thought Aefled, it is no wonder the child has taken to her bed in terror.

'Is this where you sleep, Christina?' asked Aefled seeing a second bed in the room.

'Yes, I stay with her night and day.'

Aefled and Agnes exchanged a glance of concern, suspecting that the cause of this malady lay in the tensions between aunt and niece. A heavy load of religious guilt on one side and a profound ignorance of the body's functioning on the other, had driven them into a destructive emotional conflict.

'Poor Edith,' said Aefled, leaning over the bed to take her hand, 'don't be afraid.' She bent low and whispered so that Christina would not hear. 'There is no harm in what is happening. It is not your fault. Nothing is your fault. There is no sin in womanhood, whatever the priests say.' She saw Edith's eyes open wide, cold and blue as ice and skies. A faint smile played over her little, pinched face. Christina and Agnes were talking on the other side of the room and did not see this response.

Aefled smiled back, seeing the likely scenario of events. Edith had been kept ignorant of any matters concerned with the body's preparation for sex and reproduction by her aunt who, having renounced them herself, was trying to force her niece into the same mould. Christina wanted to make her a nun. Her father wanted to make her a queen, or at least the wife of a high-ranking nobleman. Many men wanted her as a trophy. To Edith, this had all been a game in which her importance was gratifyingly magnified. She had strung her aunt along with her charms and pretences, believing she could always have her way. But with the onset of her menses, the game had suddenly become serious, threatening, frightening. It thrust her out of childhood into that murky, ill-understood world of adult relationships. Confronted with the real prospect of marriage, she had panicked and that state of panic had laid her low. But not so low that her clever little mind had ceased to work its precocious cunning in calling to her bedside women who would shield her from her aunt's oppressive virtue. This, as far as Aefled could see, was the true explanation of Edith's condition. But in refusing food she had weakened her body as though punishing it for escaping her command. Bleeding and the accompanying pain were like the afflictions of a disease that might be treated by fasting, a widely accepted practice in conventual houses where stick thin nuns boasted that they had escaped the curse.

Aefled saw what must be done.

'Edith,' she coaxed, taking hold of her hand and bending close to her ear. 'We have come to bring you back to health. Will you let us do that?'

Again, the wide-eyed smile, this time accompanied by a squeeze of Aefled's hand.

'The first thing you must do is take a little morsel to eat. If we bring you something nice from the kitchen, will you do that?'

'Yes,' said Edith.

From that first evening when Edith took some food, hopes of recovery rose. Christina took herself off to give thanks at the shrine of Saint Edith, the patron saint of the convent, for the restoration of her namesake. In her absence, Aefled and Agnes left Edith resting and wandered out into the cloister garden to discuss the situation and look at the June roses that grew there in great abundance. Some of the nuns were skilled plantswomen and collected the hips to make syrups and salves, and the petals to make scents. Not all the women in the convent were nuns and many wore fine clothes and maintained the customs of secular life. Aefled remembered Edith saying that if you wanted to learn about men, go to Wilton. But tonight there was a religious calm in the cloister. It was deserted and hushed in the twilight, a place holding its breath as if listening for the voice of God. The still air, heavy with the warmth of the day and the scent of flowers, scarcely stirred a leaf. Eventually, they walked in silence as if obeying the wishes of the air and the roses.

They were on the point of going inside when Agnes spotted someone approaching from the north side, through an arched doorway which led into the cloister. She stood for a moment as though making up her mind what to do, then said: 'Come Aefled, there's someone you should meet.'

Agnes approached the stranger, a tall graceful woman dressed in a nun's habit with a caul on her head but no veil.

'Agnes? Is that you?' she said. 'How delightful to see you again.'

They embraced like old friends while Aefled stood watching. 'How is the little one, how is Edith?' she asked in a low, soft voice. 'Christina told me she had sent for you, but I had no idea you were here. Is there any news?'

'Good news. Edith has taken food and is now resting while Christina has gone to compline. We are hopeful of a recovery, the danger has passed.'

'I wanted to do more to help but Christina wouldn't let anyone else near her. I'm so glad you've come.' She looked at Aefled. 'And not alone, I see.'

'Let me introduce you.'

The stranger greeted Aefled in a friendly manner, taking both her hands and holding them warmly. Her face, framed by the caul, was, as far as Aefled could make out in the gathering darkness, fair and handsome. Aefled guessed her age at a year or two off thirty. In the twilight, she made an impression of outlined grace, a gentleness of form and expression. The shadows of her face were arranged pleasantly around regular features; her large eyes were in deep shadow.

'Aefled,' said her companion, 'this is Gunhild, the daughter of King Harold.'

****

Chapter Four

In Search of a Bride

While King William spent the summer dashing about the southern counties exploiting the image of a sin-cleansed monarch embarking on a rejuvenated reign, William St Calais slipped away to his bishopric to attend to business of his own. Long before the king's illness, he had begun to strengthen the prestige and wealth of Durham against the prospect of a resurgent Canterbury. He had put in place a wide-ranging network of contacts, twinning his chapter with houses in Fécamp and Caen as well as his home monastery of St Calais in Maine. But the greatest of his projects was the building of a new cathedral church to replace the original foundation belonging to the old pre-Conquest monastery of St Cuthbert.

A great Romanesque edifice would rise from a rocky promontory towering over the river Wear. At its heart, would lie the shrine of St Cuthbert to be served by monks drawn from Benedictine houses in the area, replacing the secular married priests whose administration had grown lax and corrupt. Within a short time of his return, he had brought the project to such a state of readiness that the laying of the foundation stones was planned for early August. In preparation for this ceremony, he wrote to Count Alan and King Malcolm, inviting them to attend. Nothing could better ensure the peace of the north, he reasoned, than to involve two such powerful men of the region in the inauguration of a magnificent resting place for St Cuthbert's incorruptible remains.

Meanwhile, Robert was still ignorant of Count Alan's plans. After just a few weeks in his service he was convinced that, while he enjoyed the count's trust, he was not completely in his confidence. Few men were, and those few were close-mouthed types, of longstanding service, utterly devoted and often related through legitimate and illegitimate lines, forming a brotherhood of bonded kinship with fierce loyalties. But in his daily dealings, Robert found him a magnanimous and equable lord who called him

'Sieur Robert' and clapped him on the shoulder with real or pretended bonhomie.

'Some men will clap you on the shoulder and stab you a day later in the same casual style,' he said to his sons, Robert and William. 'But Count Alan is not one of them. You will do well here if you apply yourselves and learn.'

Although he was constantly looking for the opportunity to return home, leaving his sons in Count Alan's care, Robert found himself riding back and forth all summer on embassies to Malcolm. The last of these was to arrange a meeting at Durham in August when the foundation stones of the new cathedral were to be laid. But what this meeting was for Robert had no idea. Nor did he know that, along with his correspondence with Malcolm, Count Alan was also exchanging letters with the fully restored William.

On the morning of August 11th, 1093, the ceremony of laying the first stones of the new cathedral took place with as much pomp and splendour as a church founded on the renunciation of worldly things can provide. The workmen who had laboured during the previous weeks to dig the foundations were banished from the scene and in their place stood prelates draped in rich copes and chasubles, worked with threads that glittered in the sunlight. In front of huge crowds and assembled monks, St Cuthbert was invoked, *Te Deums* were sung, incense swung in great gold-leafed thuribles and bells pealed across the city. King Malcolm, sweltering in a hauberk and an ermine-edged cloak, knelt with Count Alan in the open air before an improvised altar and offered prayers for peace between England and Scotland, calling on St Cuthbert for benediction. Then they followed Bishop William St Calais and Prior Turgot around the stones as they splashed them with holy water. It was especially important that God would look favourably on this day. Many people had advised against the ceremony because of the inauspicious associations of August 11th. But William St Calais pressed ahead, saying that he was a religious man, not a superstitious one. 'Everything is ready,' he said, 'the whole project is on course. St Cuthbert himself has blessed it. Should I delay because of what happened four years ago?'

On August 11th, 1089, an earthquake had been felt all over England. It had shaken trees from their roots, buildings from their foundations and caused a great disturbance to rivers which rose from their beds and flooded large tracts of land. From that time, August 11th was generally considered an unpropitious date, to be avoided if you wanted to get married, buy a bull or seal a charter. The year

1089 was a year of ecclesiastical earthquake, too, when a great pillar of the church finally collapsed. After nineteen years of dedicated service as Archbishop of Canterbury, Lanfranc died, leaving the four year vacancy that Anselm was still hesitating to fill. But the ill-boding associations of the day were swept aside as William St Calais carried out, in a memorable ceremony, the laying of stones from which would arise a new cathedral and a lasting peace between England and Scotland.

Robert watched the proceedings from close up, being permitted to carry arms as far as the cathedral precincts. In the evening, not being in attendance at the feast, he took himself off to his lodgings where his sons were eager to talk about the excitements of the day. Then, late at night, when they were settling down to sleep, Count Alan summoned him. He was to come at once. Robert dressed and made his way through the sleeping city to the bishop's house where Count Alan and King Malcolm were staying as honoured guests.

'Ah, Robert, a great day, don't you think? Our baron-bishop knows how to make a splash.' Count Alan had evidently been drinking. Did he even know it was the middle of the night?

'Is something wrong, my lord?'

'Yes, I suppose, in a way, something is wrong. I have not been entirely open with you and now I want to put that right.'

They were alone in a small chamber. The only light came from tar brands burning on brackets in the courtyard below and a single candle in the room. Count Alan did not invite him to be seated and stood with his back turned, looking out of the open window.

'You are no doubt wondering what you have been doing all summer, riding back and forth with sealed messages in closed bags.'

'It is not my business to wonder, my lord.'

Count Alan turned, his face in shadow. 'Do you know the importance of what you have witnessed here? William St Calais has achieved a diplomatic coup by flattering Malcolm with this invitation.' He went to a table on which lay a parchment. 'The King of England is now offering to treat with Malcolm, to discuss the peace of Abernethy, the garrisoning of Carlisle and the restoration of lands. He has invited him to come south, to meet with him in Gloucester at the end of August. St Calais drew Malcolm this far south with today's spectacle. A very little persuasion is now needed to get him to Gloucester.' He picked up the parchment. 'King William has appointed me to escort Malcolm and guarantee his safety in England. I want you and your men to ride with me as part of my retinue. Will you do so?'

Again, there was the politeness of a request when no request was intended.

'When do you plan to leave, my lord?'

'Two days at most. Leave your sons with my steward. They will be well provided for. On the road, we need fighting men.'

'Do you expect trouble?'

Count Alan shrugged. 'Malcolm has enemies. As we all do.'

Robert felt there was something more. This burst of candour, cloaked as polite intimacy, was a mask over an averted face. The fascination of Count Alan was that, in spite of his affable exterior capable of arousing ready friendship, he was two-thirds unknowable and one-third downright baffling.

'One thing more,' he said. 'When we part from Malcolm in England, I shall have further business of my own. You will, I hope, stay with me to see it through.'

On the way back to his lodgings, Robert realised that if Count Alan had summoned him to give a clear explanation, as he claimed, then he had failed. He was not sure what he had just consented to, or why, though he did not feel that an unwilling consent had been wrung from him. He imagined that, in going south, he would be going home. As it turned out, the dramatic events about to embroil Count Alan would detain them both for many more months.

****

One day, Ranulf Flambard, in a rare moment of leisure, was sitting in a corner of his lodging at Windsor entertaining himself with some reading matter. It was a chrestomathy, a small collection of short Latin extracts about the lives of famous men. After some time, he rose, put it aside and wandered over to Firmin who was hunched over a writing table, hard at work at a copying exercise. Observing for a little while the concentration of his devoted acolyte, the pursed lips, the fixed eye, the studious husbandry of movements, he was seized with a desire to disturb it.

'Firmin, let me ask you a question. If you were a monk writing the life of a great warrior or holy man, how would you begin?'

'I don't understand, master,' said Firmin, putting down his pen. 'With a preamble, I suppose.'

'You would begin where they all begin, Firmin. You would begin with a lie. You would invent some fabulous story about a miraculous dream his mother had before giving birth. It would foretell a life of prodigy or sanctity. Alexander the Great, Julius

Caesar, the Emperor Charlemagne, St Dunstan, they all had imaginative mothers. Great symbolic dreams are what is needed, Firmin, everything else is easy to fit in after that. The life of a great man or a saint must be fitted out with the fabulous.'

'I see, master.' Firmin was thoughtful for a moment. 'You mean like a hole in a boat which sails through a storm and does not sink?'

'Exactly. I think Baldwin is writing a saintly life of Anselm and is preparing the way with miraculous stories.'

Firmin's shrewd face showed that he was absorbing this matter. 'But how will he recount the terrible scene that happened today? Do such things square with a saintly life?'

'Monks find means to square these things,' said Ranulf, 'where facts will not serve, they use allegory.'

'What's that?'

'It's a rhetorical obscurity. It's saying one thing and meaning another. It's a way of suggesting by comparison.'

'I don't understand.'

'Well, let me give you some examples drawn from your own experience.' Ranulf enjoyed his role as instructor. More and more he was feeling that Firmin was capable of being set to useful purposes if he was properly trained. Firmin had brains and showed signs of a superior talent, signalled by a desire to quit his uneducated state.

'You have often helped out at hunts, haven't you, you've been abroad in the early morning with the fewterers and brachmen. You know their dogs.'

'Yes, master.'

'Well, doesn't it occur to you that you can think of our noblemen and courtiers in terms of these dogs? All you have to do is use allegory.'

Firmin lent himself to the game. It was the sort of thing that made service to Ranulf endlessly entertaining.

'What, you mean brachets and raches, lymers and greyhounds?

'They all have their specific uses, don't they? Like noblemen have specific uses to the king?'

Firmin wrestled with the idea for a moment, applying all his apparatus of thought.

'I see what you mean, master. In that case, Robert Bloet is a lymer, a scenting dog with his nose in the air. A lymer is always on a long leash. He tracks a beast to his lair and harbours him for the huntsman.'

'Very good, Firmin, I'll make a clerk of you yet. Now, what about FitzHaimo and Tirel? If they were dogs, I mean, canines,' said Ranulf. 'What would they be?'

'Without a doubt, master, they would be brachets. Brachets work in pairs, relying on scent. They sniff the wind and betray hiding places. They are limited to moving game for the individual hunter. They are dogs with small abilities and ideas.'

'You see how easy it is? Now then, what about Count Alan Rufus and William St Calais?'

'Ah, that's obvious. They are greyhounds, noblest of the dogs, always found in the company of lords and kings. They hunt by sight. Unleashed, they are independent, tenacious, swift and loyal. They hold the fiercest game and will kill unless restrained.'

'Well done, Firmin, you have grasped the lesson admirably. Allegory, you see, can make dogs of noblemen and turn a "terrible scene" into a demonstration of saintly resolve.'

Ranulf heard voices in the bailey and saw that the king was getting ready to ride out. 'Off he goes again. To think, only a couple of months ago he was about to exit the world.'

It was July and the royal cavalcade had now reached Windsor where the king was holding court. That morning he had received Anselm and pressed him once again to accept the archbishopric. Once again, Anselm had resisted, pressing back with his demands. Not only that, he had let words of criticism about the king's profligate court pass his lips, stinging William to a fierce rebuke and provoking what Firmin had called a 'terrible scene.'

'What makes the man so contumacious?' asked Ranulf. 'Why hasn't Baldwin been to work on him?'

'But master, he said it would be a slow process. Baldwin reckoned it would take till Christmas. Till then the bull and the sheep will go round and round.'

Anselm had dug in his heels over the same issues as before: all the lands of Canterbury as they were under Lanfranc were to come to him without diminution and unencumbered by any claims. The king must take him as his principal counsellor; the king must recognise pope Urban II. Out of these molehills, Anselm and William made unclimbable mountains of difficulty.

'It really would not be impossible to find some common ground between them. It's their characters that clash. The trouble with Anselm is that he has no capacity for allegory, Firmin. Let that be a lesson to you.'

In addition to the wrangles with Anselm, the king had to confront the problem of Malcolm. Having heard from Count Alan that the Scottish king might be willing to negotiate, William began to turn his attention northward and a process was set in motion to draw Malcolm to Gloucester. Once again, the question of the king's marriage to Edith was raised. Since his near-death experience William had become mindful of a need to secure his line and, although the prospect of marriage dismayed rather than pleased him, he began to give ear to counsellors who strongly advised marriage; none more urgently than Ranulf Flambard. But, like Anselm in regard to the archbishopric, the king could hardly be said to show enthusiasm for the prospect and, even as he entered into negotiations, he was looking for a way out.

In a private interview at Windsor, one day in early August, Ranulf found the opportunity to press his argument.

'My lord king, unless you make a bid for Edith, someone will forestall you.'

'Flambard, you are forgetting that Malcolm is my sworn vassal. He cannot dispose of his daughter without my authority. If he does, he breaks faith.'

'But Malcolm considers these things trifling formalities, my lord. He considers himself a king and equal. That's why he wants to see you wedded to his daughter. A girl of English royal blood, my lord, descended from King Edmund Ironside. Think how that would marvellously add to your stock of public favour just now.'

'Face of Lucca! I'm weary of this badgering. Marry, marry, marry. I ask you, do I want a thirteen-year-old girl in my bed?'

'Forgive me, my lord, but marriage is not about your pleasure which will go on in its uninterrupted course. This is politics. And consider what politics is being done right now between Count Alan Rufus and King Malcolm.'

'What? You think they're up to something?

'Well, no, my lord, there is absolutely no evidence of that whatsoever. Still, it would take only a little imagination to sketch out a scenario in which Count Alan, with the agreement of Malcolm, takes Edith for his bride. I have no doubt that Count Alan is completely loyal. But that is no reason not to take precautions.'

'What do you advise?'

'Two things, my lord. When Malcolm comes to meet you at Gloucester, discuss his grievances calmly and with grace. But make sure that he renews his homage to you. That way he cannot dispose of his daughter without your consent. Secondly, before the meeting, travel down to Wilton. Take a peek at little Edith. It might help you to make up your mind.'

'Face of Lucca, Flambard! Only you would have come up with that.'

****

Meanwhile, at Wilton, a battle of royal and ecclesiastical wills was being fought, smaller in scale than that between Anselm and William but no less fierce. Edith's health had steadily improved through the month of July, but her emotional state was still giving cause for concern. Agnes and Aefled delayed their departure many times because Edith pleaded with them not to go and leave her entirely to the mercies of her aunt. The effect of the illness, and more particularly, the recovery was perhaps more marked on Christina than on the sufferer herself. It was obvious that God had first stricken then spared the child as a sign that she must be dedicated to the conventual life.

'I vowed her to God in my prayers and God spared her. Would you have me break my vow? She cannot go into the world. She shall be the bride of Christ.'

While Agnes tried to persuade Christina from this intransigent course, taking her off on walks and pointing out the impossibility of Edith pursuing the religious life, Aefled spent many hours talking to the child, answering her questions about marriage and pregnancy, childbirth and motherhood, with as much candour as she thought appropriate. At the risk of displeasing the abbess, she found herself having to deny or contradict some of the more strident opinions of Christina, opinions held by the nuns of the rule, shaped by the misogynistic theology of a church horrified by sexuality. As a result, Edith was confused and guilty about her own bodily processes. Christina had told her that menstrual blood was unclean, its poisonous effects having to be purged with penances and prayers. It was from this kind of teaching that Aefled had escaped during her own youthful tutelage with Isaac and now she brought her arsenal of critical argument to bear on Edith's predicament.

'The nuns are mistaken. The teaching of the church misleads them. The church is afraid of the carnality of men and women, but especially women. Ever since St Augustine developed the notion of original sin, the church has feared and loathed the female body. It preaches that Eve was the first sinner. It tells you that Adam fell from paradise because of her. But, Edith, my dear, when you find the courage to think: 'that is not so,' you suddenly feel very brave. And when you learn that many thinkers, even men of the church and theologians, have disagreed with Augustine, you realise that there is another way of looking at things.'

Conversations along these lines did much to console the troubled child, who was struggling into maturity in blind ignorance and fear. Her child's body, once so easy to inhabit, had become a fearful thing, fraught with poisonous hazards, a source of threat and sin. Then, just as Aefled felt she was making some headway, Christina moved to impose another set of sanctions. She had always dressed the child as a nun and often forced her to wear the veil. Now she kept her from the sight of visitors and would not let her receive private letters. This over-protective cloistering felt like yet more punishment for the offence of womanhood and kept Edith in a mood of despondency, even while her health returned.

'Why does my aunt treat me like this? I feel as though I have done something wrong. It's not fair. She has taken my things, my combs and bonnets, the little trinkets my mother gave me. Even Mary has to dress like a nun and she's only ten. I told the abbess, but she said I must obey my aunt.'

It was true that the abbess felt overwhelmed and outranked by Christina's royal status. Although such a worldly consideration was not supposed to affect the discipline of a conventual house, in which the abbess was in full authority under the diocesan bishop, nevertheless it did. No attempt was made to restrain Christina. As a result, a sad scene was often to be glimpsed in the evening between vespers and compline. Two lively, intelligent little sisters wandering around the cloisters, subdued, listless, spiritless creatures with waxen faces like doll nuns. But in spite of her mute and repressed appearance, a flame still burned in Edith. When Aefled asked her one day what she hoped for, the response was immediate, defiant and characteristic.

'The world,' she said.

Aunt and niece were set on a collision course.

In the meantime, Aefled sent anxious letters home inquiring after her own daughter and promising to return as soon as she could. She wrote a letter to Robert at Richmond, explaining her visit to Wilton, but, having no idea of his movements, she could not be sure he would receive it. Her visit stretched out from days to weeks and she became anxious about spending so long from home. On the other hand, she found a new source of interest in the fascinating person of Gunhild.

Like so many of the women at Wilton, Gunhild's status was equivocal in regard to the religious life. She had met Abbot Anselm years ago and passed so many hours in pleasant conversation with him that a friendship had grown up. They often exchanged letters in which she asked for spiritual guidance and he gave her counsel. In turn, he was impressed by her learning, her flattering marks of devotion to him and by her spirituality. Yet she was not a professed nun, had taken no vows before a bishop and did not wear the veil. She was spiritual without being pious, and while her face bore the marks of sorrow, there was tremendous calm in her eyes and movements. Unlike her warlike father, she seemed to cast an aura of peaceful assurance on those around her. Yet there was a suppressed energy in her voice and manner, a charge of passion not yet realised. Daughter of King Harold and Edith the Fair, she was sprung from a fabled love, a fact which never ceased to impress Aefled. Indeed, sometimes it was difficult to recognise Gunhild as the offspring of a legendary love story which recounted how Edith the Fair, or 'Swan-neck' as she was known, had wandered the fated battlefield of Senlac Hill, looking for the remains of her dead lover. Such stories were the stuff of legend, already seeming so distant that it was hard to connect them with the mere lapse of one generation since the Conquest. Sometimes, glimpsing Gunhild in the cloister at evening, Aefled thought she seemed surrounded by a dewy mist as though not quite substantial, not quite of this world but of a world that had long passed away.

Gunhild was highly educated, rather more in the Norman style than the English but spoke both languages with equal fluency, to which she added the Latin of a scholar. Highly regarded for her learning, she was also a rich heiress with widespread lands inherited from her mother. This, along with her personal accomplishments and equable disposition, made her, like Edith, a desirable marriage prospect.

'It seems that Christina is set against her niece's prospects,' Aefled said to her one day. 'She is on a course that will bring her into conflict with King Malcolm. Do you know what can be done to dissuade her?'

'Alas, Christina has her own way of going about things. She was once greatly disappointed in love. She fears the world. But she has been very good to me.'

'How long have you known her?'

'All my life. She was a friend of my mother's. I knew her when I lived with Queen Margaret in the days before her marriage to

Malcolm. Perhaps Christina is a little jealous of her sister who has achieved the status she herself desired. She is an unhappy woman, but I believe she acts from the purest motives.'

'That is not always enough.'

'Sometimes I think Christina is frightened of what she sees as Edith's worldliness. You must have noticed a precocity in the child.'

'Indeed, I have. Once, when I asked her what she hoped for she said 'the world' as though intending to shock. She is struggling into womanhood and finds no help in her aunt.'

'Edith is eager to follow the example of her mother. She wants to be a queen. She desires wealth and power and status. She knows that to acquire them she will have to marry. The truth is, love is of no interest to her.'

'That is wise. She will not be disappointed.'

'Oh, but don't you think love is the most important matter? To experience it once, just the briefest moment of passion, love of another, body to body, for however short or long a time, don't you think that is the fullest and best of human life?'

As she spoke, Gunhild grew animated; her calm eyes disturbed by some unguessed at urge.

'If I was offered the chance, whatever the odds, I would take it.'

It was the nearest thing to an outburst Aefled had ever seen in this endlessly self-possessed woman.

When asked how she came to be at Wilton, Gunhild was either evasive or really did not have a clear recollection. It had been after the death of her mother when she was still very young. Of her mother, she remembered little more than a voice and a caressing hand. She had never known her father who had died in the year she was born. Such smatterings of information were drawn with great difficulty from a woman who would speak easily about most subjects, except herself. Sometimes, in a mood of nostalgic regret, she would talk about her uncle, Wulfnoth, whom she had never known.

'His life has been so sad,' she said, 'sadder than mine. He was my father's youngest brother, handed over as hostage to Duke William in 1051 for Harold's good behaviour. After Hastings, of course, there was no chance of release. When the Conqueror died, nearly six years ago, we all thought he might be freed under the clemency of the new king. But he wasn't. By then, he had been a captive for thirty-six years and some said he had become incapable of independent life; that it was a mercy to keep him, provide for him, you know. When I asked to visit him I was told that there was no point, he no longer knew who he was.'

'Where is he now, Gunhild?'

'As far I know, he was conveyed to Winchester where he lives under the care of the Prior, Godfrey of Cambrai. The shell of him lives there, he himself has never lived.'

Aefled was aware that, in her talks with Gunhild she was hearing the last testimony of a survivor of another age. In conversations patched with the tatters of Harold Godwinson's ill-starred clan, she heard the remarkable accents of a fast-fading past speaking without bitterness but with the poignancy of what might have been. But she did not talk only about the past. At times, speaking about the future, she began to throw off her conventual obedience and became animated, almost defiant. 'There is something more for me, Aefled,' she said. 'I know there is another path for me in the world. When I get the opportunity, I will take it.'

Subsequent events were to prove that Gunhild indeed possessed the Godwin spirit. Breaking from all expectations she was going to make one last gamble against the odds, as her father had done, and seize for herself a desperate adventure, a final encounter with history before obscurity would claim her forever.

****

Towards the middle of August, William decided to take Flambard's advice and pursue a leisure trip to Wilton. August was the month of 'the grease time,' the fat season for stag hunting which ran from the 1st of August until the feast of St Peter's Chains on September 14th , when the king loved nothing better than to be out all day with his hunting cronies, firing arrows at the stags in the butts. That he was willing to delay this pleasure until after a visit to Wilton was a measure of how much his thoughts had turned to marriage. This, at least, was the hope of Ranulf Flambard who was appointed to organise and accompany the royal entourage. It was to be an informal journey and, as far as possible, a secret one. William relished a scheme in which Wilton, and all its inhabitants, would be taken by surprise. An unannounced visit, an impromptu journey and the adventure of untrumpeted travel appealed to the king's boyish fondness for pranks and japes which had never entirely left him. His party was comprised of the usual favourites, among them Robert FitzHaimo, Walter Tirel, Urse d'Abetot, as well as officers of his household, men at arms, grooms and servants, numbering some thirty riders in all.

'And the king is pleased to call this a secret trip,' observed Ranulf drily to Firmin whom he had smuggled into the party for the precise purpose of being the appreciative recipient of his satirical remarks.

Following a route from Windsor, their road skirted Basingstoke, turned south to Winchester, due west to Sarum and on to Wilton, three miles further to the south-west. The journey was expected to take three days.

Basingstoke paid no attention to the king, nor he to Basingstoke. A royal manor of about two hundred souls and a huddle of cottages around a market square, its greatest boast was the possession of three watermills. The main Winchester road lay just to the north, edged by strip fields which had been reaped of the Lammas harvest and extensive commons where the Basingstoke ruminants grazed.

The king was in excellent spirits. *How sweet,* he thought, to ride through this rich and fertile country on a pleasant August day. He was seized by unfamiliar feelings of appreciation for the natural world. Trees and hedgerows ceased to be a blur and defined themselves into interesting shapes with leaves. Dull, late summer leaves looked as fresh to his renewed senses as burgeoning spring leaves which he had failed to see this year and had never in all his life appreciated.

'Face of Lucca, Flambard! How fine a thing is health!'

How fine a thing, too, was kingship. Especially when it had been inherited reasonably smoothly. There had been trouble after the Conqueror's death, the inevitable rebellion, the sieges, the battles, the treacheries, most notably that of William St Calais. But once St Calais had been won over, this time for good, William had felt his position unassailable. And so it had proved, right up until his illness. That had shaken him. For the first time, he had begun to think seriously about the succession. Although primogeniture was not yet an established custom, displacing all other means of legitimately transmitting titled property, having an heir would undoubtedly ease the way to a new reign. Yet William, as only a third son and not even named as heir, believed strongly in luck and destiny. Things were fated. There was a predetermined working out, whether under God's dispensation or not. Probably not. Inevitability could not be moved by prayers. His imagination was informed by an almost secular view of chance and fortune which allowed him to take risks in battle and put a loose rein on his conscience. What luck, he thought, being only the third in line to his father, to have inherited a kingdom. What luck to be in excellent health, riding unceremonially through one of the richest parts of the kingdom on this fine August day. It had all been so different a few decades earlier when this region had burned while the Conqueror torched and battled his way to London to be crowned.

As the royal party took the north road and proceeded towards Winchester, Ranulf Flambard was having less gratifying thoughts. He had been hoping to dash off to Huntingdon, while the king was absent, to spend a few days with his beloved Aelfgifu or rather nights with her, the days would be spent with her husband, a fine broad-faced fellow, a solid Huntingdon burgher, whom Ranulf had specially selected for his complaisance. But, instead of enjoying these pleasures, he found himself having to wait upon the king in an enterprise he himself had devised. But did William really intend to marry?

The reputation of William II, formulated largely by hostile ecclesiastics, was unremittingly bad. He was accused of moral laxity, wasteful luxury and ungodliness. His court, they said, was racy, salacious, overrun with long-haired favourites. Boys seen entering his chamber, women in pairs on their way out. Night long carousings and every kind of immodesty, grossness and obscenity. Not only debauched but irreligious, even downright blasphemous. This was the clerical view. But Ranulf, who knew him better than most, suspected that William might be sexually passive, or lukewarm, getting his erotic thrills as much from hunting as from passing encounters. There was something orgasmic in the hunt: the breathless pursuit, the dying fall, the blood-soaked end. Flambard had never taken much pleasure in it but he made a point of participating as often as possible. No man would ever gain the full confidence of the king unless he joined him in the hunting field. That the king had passed up the August hunt was surely, thought Ranulf, an indication that his thoughts had, at last, turned to marriage.

At the end of the second day, they came to the royal city of Winchester and rode past the Norman castle to the west, still not yet rebuilt in stone, past the royal palace, restored by William the Conqueror, past the new Minster and the half-demolished remains of the old cathedral, and rode on to Wolvesey Palace, the bishop's residence, where the king could lodge at someone else's expense. Unknown to the king, Ranulf had sent a messenger ahead to alert Bishop Walkelin to the prospect of a swarm of voracious visitors so that the household would not be caught out. By the time they arrived, some efforts to prepare food and lodging had been made. The king and his chief attendants were given a suite of rooms in Wolvesey Palace, a rambling old wooden building not worth the name. Servants and grooms were lodged in the hostelry attached to the newly completed cathedral, upon which Bishop Walkelin had lavished all his devotion and most of his money for the last fourteen years. Walkelin was long past his prime, being in his mid-sixties. Appointed bishop in 1070, by the patronage of the Conqueror whose chaplain he had been, Bishop Walkelin had known the king from boyhood. He greeted him with genuine warmth and led him to the feast in the bishop's hall.

'Keep your eye on the table,' said Ranulf to Firmin as they joined the gathering of the bishop's senior staff and the king's household. 'The bishop has a predicament. Too much expense on a lavish feast will suggest that he is too rich; too little, that he is lacking in respect.'

Bishop Walkelin appeared at ease and made a speech of welcome. He was a dignified old man, short and inclined to stoop. Immensely learned in theology and an expert in administration, he had guided the ecclesiastical estates of Winchester with a sure hand for twenty-three years. He oversaw the treasury and the royal mint on behalf of the king with scrupulous honesty. His greatest project was the building of a new Minster which he had begun in 1079, launching himself on a long-drawn-out battle for money. It was not until William granted the bishop half a hide of land in the Isle of Wight, with license to search for and excavate stone, along with forest to supply the timber, that Walkelin had been able to make real advances in his building project. The king, who liked to be congratulated on his more liberal acts, nodded graciously when Walkelin thanked him.

'It is due to your generous gift, my lord king that the monks were finally able to move into the new Minster this very spring, towards Eastertide.'

'That would have been during my illness. Alas, this year, for me, there was no spring.'

Ranulf noted how the king was quick to get in a little reminder about his illness.

'We offered daily prayers for your return to health, my lord.'

William Rufus raised a goblet. 'And I drink to your health, my lord bishop and thank you for your hospitality.'

Ranulf wondered what was coming next. William was always at his most polite just before he struck.

'Did you hear that St Calais has just dedicated a new cathedral church at Durham?' said William, glancing sideways at his dignified host.

'I have indeed, my lord king. Our work of glorifying God through the raising of these magnificent new foundations is proceeding with such success it is likely to lead us into the sin of pride.'

'Or greed,' said the king. 'Certainly, the church is finding enormous sums from somewhere.'

Ranulf, who was sitting close to the king and could hear the conversation, had been wondering how long it would be before William turned to the topic of money. Flattering the bishop with complimentary remarks about the splendour of the table, William made a joke about there being 'no money left' in the Winchester treasury. Later, out of Walkelin's hearing, he whispered to Ranulf: 'When the good bishop dies, remind me to keep this see in my possession.'

Ranulf was finding the conversation dull and the evening altogether tedious when his eye was drawn to a figure sitting at the end of the high table, looking like a menial who had mistaken his place and inadvertently sat down with his betters. He signalled to Firmin, who was standing behind him.

'Find out who that is,' he said.

While Firmin went off to make inquiries, the king began to regale the party with old hunting stories and gave every impression of enjoying himself immensely, eating and drinking heartily though not to excess. In a short time, the decorous atmosphere of the bishop's palace gave way to the rollicking ambience of the court as the king's party grew noisy and boisterous.

After some time, Firmin returned. 'I couldn't find out who he is, but apparently, his name is Wulfnoth,' he said.

Ranulf studied the man. *So, the rumours are true,* he thought.

It was an hour or two before he found the opportunity to approach the object of his interest without attracting attention. He sidled along the table and sat himself in an empty seat next to the figure who was staring distractedly at nothing and seemed oblivious to the general conviviality. Dressed in a monk's habit from which stuck thin white limbs, he barely touched his food. He bent forward, elbows on the table, saying nothing to his companion whom Ranulf recognised as Godfrey of Cambrai, Prior of Winchester.

'Good evening Prior, good evening, Wulfnoth,' he said.

Godfrey looked round, but the other seemed not to have heard.

Godfrey shook his elbow. 'Wulfnoth, this is Ranulf Flambard, the king's minister.'

Slowly he turned, as if coming back from some far distance, lifted his face to Ranulf and smiled. Ranulf was struck by the youthfulness of the face, the innocence of the smile. It was the face of an old man who had never experienced the world. The empty-eyed face of a youth trapped in an unfamiliar place and grown old while looking for a way out.

At last, he said: 'Good evening, Ranulf Flambard,' in the low, whispery voice of a man who prayed much. A pitiable gentleness, a vague look, a ghostly voice, these belonged to the last surviving male relative of King Harold.

'You are in good health, I trust.' Ranulf was thinking he looked far from well.

Wulfnoth sent a glance to Godfrey, like a pupil looking to a master for encouragement or guidance. He seemed surprised at having to make a reply, at being the focus of someone's interest.

'I am well,' he said after some hesitation. 'But tired.'

'He attends all the offices,' said Godfrey as if in explanation. 'He rises for Matins at midnight and goes with the brothers throughout the day to all the canonical offices. He is an example to the monks.'

So, he has turned to the faith to keep himself afloat, thought Ranulf. Well, I suppose it brings peace of a sort. He was itching to find out more about this man, this unhappy flotsam from an English wreck, cast up on the shores of a Norman realm years later. But when he tried to turn the conversation to the king, who was at the far end of the table, Wulfnoth answered in an unexpected way.

'The king is not here,' he said. 'My brother is coming for me, then he will be king.'

As far as Ranulf could judge, during the conversation that followed, Wulfnoth thought he was still living in Normandy and still awaiting the return of his brother Harold to redeem him from confinement. He was fifteen years old, stuck at the age of his handing over.

'Is Hakkon with you?' asked Ranulf.

'Of course,' said Wulfnoth, 'he sits at my side.'

Godfrey of Cambrai had become Hakkon in the imagination of this poor bemused monk, a fiction that the prior was evidently used to indulging.

‘It helps him,’ he said. ‘God puts many thoughts into his mind, harmless thoughts that help him sustain a world to live in. It does not matter that his world is not quite real. It harms no one.’

Hakkon, long dead, was the nephew of Wulfnoth and Harold. As a young boy, he too had been given as hostage for Harold’s good behaviour, a pledge not to seek the throne of England. But after ten years of captivity, during Harold’s last visit to Duke William’s Norman court in 1065, Hakkon had been handed back and had returned to England.

Had Wulfnoth seen his nephew depart, with Harold and all the English sailors, sailing away in a high-prowed ship, bellied sail to the open sea, driving over breakers through the salt spray towards their waiting hearth fires? Had his heart been broken then? And did his mind break during the long decades of detention that were to follow?

‘You see how it is?’ said Godfrey. ‘Exile, prison, enclosure. Chains, sometimes, but there were periods when he was given permission to hunt or ride. The conditions of his imprisonment varied in response to the events in England. But he never saw any of his family again. Time stopped for him. Hastings never happened. He lives in an everlasting present, where Harold is always coming back and is always to be king. The only truth in his world is his faith. Christ is merciful.’

It was the saddest thing Ranulf had heard in a long time.

When it came time for evening prayers, Godfrey rose and took Wulfnoth by the hand. As he was leading him away, he said to Ranulf: ‘If at Wilton you happen to come across the Lady Gunhild, tell her I am taking good care of her uncle. He lacks for nothing. He has found, at the end of a long and wearisome life, a refuge in Christ.’

That night, when he told the tale to Firmin, the lad was moved almost to tears. ‘When we get back, master, you should send a donation to the good prior for the upkeep of this poor, stranded outcast.’

‘Well, well, Firmin, that’s a fine idea. You’ll make a clerk yet. Clerks are always ready to think up schemes for spending other people’s money.’

****

The following morning, the party set out towards Sarum, a modest settlement around a wooden castle built by the Conqueror in the shell of a Roman fort. Even its cathedral was unassuming, rather like Bishop Osmund who consecrated it in April 1092, then had the appalling experience of seeing the tower demolished by a lightning strike five days later. To William, it was of very little interest except as a route to the much larger settlement of Wilton. Leaving the majority of his party to wait at Sarum, the king, with a select entourage, rode the remaining three miles south-west to Wilton.

Even as the king neared his destination, Ranulf saw signs of failing nerve. 'Second thoughts,' he said to Firmin. 'He's having them. Study his face.'

Certainly, William's expression soured as he approached Wilton and the exultant mood of the previous few days seemed to leave him. Yet the scene was all sunshine and verdure, just the thing to appeal to the reborn senses of a convalescent who had been seized with a fondness for greenery. On a tongue of higher ground, rising above the confluence of the pure chalk streams of the Wylye and Nadder, studded all around with bright patches of rich pasture, the little town clustered around its market square, dominated by the ancient church of St Mary. It was the kind of scene that poets sang about in the cloudless songs of the south, songs peopled by noble lovers. But love seemed far from William's mind as Wilton Abbey came into view, a sprawling assemblage of conventual buildings with a new monastic church and cloister, girdled by walls inset with round-arched gateways built of glowing sandstone. The king knew it was one of the most important nunneries in the south, the richest female Benedictine house in England, famed as a centre of education and learning, attracting renowned scholars to study in a well-stocked library and mingle with visiting prelates from the continental houses. Never for a moment would the King of England have admitted to feeling intimidated by the place.

William approached the main gate and, finding the doors closed, dismounted. All his men followed suit and stood quietly in the August sunshine wondering what to do. For a brief moment, Ranulf thought the king might cut and run. Some men have a perfect knack of scotching enterprises before they are really begun. Ranulf knew this. He knew he was not one of them. He also knew that the king was.

'My lord,' said Ranulf, 'perhaps you had better send a messenger to the abbess, seeking permission to enter.'

'Face of Lucca, Flambard! You counselled this. What have you made me do? Go yourself and be quick about it.'

After speaking to a veiled nun through a grille beside the wicket gate in the great plain oak door, Ranulf was led inside, half-expecting the king to be gone when he returned.

When Aefled, looking out from an upper window, saw horsemen approaching the abbey she called Agnes to come and see.

'Who are these men?'

Agnes looked and gave a shriek of dismay. 'Call the abbess, call Christina,' she said, 'one of them is the king.'

They flew down to the abbess and found her already with Christina, taking counsel about what to do.

'We cannot deny the king entry,' said the abbess, 'the gates must be opened. Allow them to come into the courtyard.'

Down in the courtyard, they found Ranulf Flambard already inside, escorted by a nun. 'My lady abbess,' he said, 'the king and his knights seek permission to enter. I am Ranulf Flambard, the king's minister.'

The abbess gave permission and the king entered. As he did so, Christina went off in panicky flight to find Edith and hide her. She knew what he was here for and it terrified her. Grabbing Edith by the hand, she led her to a private room in the inner quarters where men were not allowed, covered her habit with a shapeless cape, rammed a cowl on her head and hid her face with a veil.

'What are you doing, Aunt? What is happening?'

'Shush, child. Do exactly as I say. Wait here. Do not stir until I return.'

What happened next was very simple but it would be the subject of gossip and inquiry for years. Letters would fly back and forth between people in the highest positions in church and state, reports would be furnished, an ecclesiastical council would be called, and conflicting views set out. Years later, controversy would still be raging over what happened at Wilton that day.

Finding that Christina was reluctant to produce Edith to the view of the king, Ranulf Flambard negotiated a harmless little scene. Since she could not insult the King of England by a downright refusal, he persuaded her to permit the king to view Edith from a distance, without her knowing. And so it was arranged that the king, after saying his prayers in the abbey church, would walk out into the cloister garth, as if to view the roses which grew in great fragrant bowers in the central garden. Christina would bring Edith into the cloister but no introduction would be made, no encounter would be permitted, no word would be exchanged.

This was agreed and, soon after noon, the king walked into the blazing garth where the sun struck down like a blinding sword. Clusters of roses, by turns dozing in the perfumed breeze then startled awake by the buzz of bees, nodded at him in the bright sun as if to say 'we know what you've come for.' He heard footsteps and looked around. Coming into the cloister from the west side was a tiny nun, led by the hand of a stern-looking woman. They were both wearing habits and were veiled. Eyes ahead, looking neither left nor right, they stepped along the arcade, past the entrance to the chapter house and entered the church by the southern door.

So this was what he had come for. This dressed doll was Edith, daughter of the King of Scotland, his prospective wife. A Benedictine nun, wearing the habit and veil, draped with a cape this hot day. But had she taken her vows? Had she been consecrated by a bishop? If she had, any attempt to remove her from Wilton would be a violation of the most sacred rites. More probably she had not. Why are they all so confoundedly mysterious? William studied a rose, flushed pink with an intense red centre, deep green leaves, sharp thorns. An image of Edith, that delicate little rose of Scottish fortunes, prickled all over with plots and schemes to compromise his northern territories. But surely, he thought, Malcolm would never let his prize commodity become a nun. She was too important in the game of alliances. Is that why he was coming south? To arrange a marriage deal, preferably with him but if not then with some other? Did Malcolm know what was going on at Wilton? If he did not, what a pleasure it would be to tell him. William thought that the stern-faced woman must be Christina, the child's aunt, Malcolm's sister-in-law, a woman notorious in her hatred of him, which was why she was staging this ridiculous charade. Did she think he was going to leap upon the girl, assault her, or carry her off? In a sudden reflex of offence, William took out his knife and cut off a rose at its head. A rose would be all he took from this convent. Damn you, Flambard. A wasted journey. But, as he strode towards the gatehouse, his chief feeling was of relief.

Ranulf's experience on that day was slightly more interesting than the king's. While the king went into the cloister, he was loitering by the gatehouse when he saw two rather fine looking women, about thirty years old, walking together and talking in intimate and serious tones. One wore a sober dress but looked every inch a worldly type, married perhaps, with children. Under a coif, her hair was loose, honey coloured curls threaded with the first signs of grey. The other, wearing a habit but no veil, had the bearing of a nun. Noticing him, they stopped abruptly but did not speak or run away. He approached them, wished them good day and announced himself as Ranulf Flambard the king's minister. 'Excuse me, ladies, I have a message for the Lady Gunhild and would be much obliged if you could direct me to her.'

'I am Lady Aefled, wife of Robert, Lord of Castle St Mary's,' said the handsome one he had assumed was married. 'This is the Lady Gunhild.'

Ranulf was intrigued. To encounter twice, in less than a week, figures from the same blasted family, people separated by time and distance, who had never known each other but the threads of whose lives had been spun out of the events at Hastings, seemed remarkable. As did the impressive lady who now greeted him. Gunhild, the daughter of King Harold, was a living connection to a past that was now almost mythical, so much had attitudes and people changed in the intervening years.

Ranulf flourished a bow. 'My Lady Gunhild,' he said. 'It is a pleasure for me to bring you news of your uncle. Last night, at the bishop's palace of Winchester, I spoke with Wulfnoth. He is in the care of Godfrey of Cambrai, who greets you and assures you that he is doing all he can for the care of your uncle.'

'Godfrey of Cambrai is a good man. Thank him. Tell him that I will pray for him and my uncle. Is he well, does his mind grow dim, as they say? Is he aware of me?'

'Alas, his mind is not strong. But his faith is. He goes to all the offices and is an example to the monks. Godfrey told me he is happy to dwell in the tranquil spaces that God has placed in his mind.'

'Thank you Ranulf Flambard. I am obliged to you for those words.'

Gunhild began to walk away, followed by her companion who lagged behind and turned to give him an intelligent, inquiring gaze, the kind of look that says 'I want to remember you.'

There goes an interesting woman, thought Ranulf. She would be worth getting to know.

On the way back to Sarum, the king raged at Flambard for dragging him on a pointless errand and subjecting him to the humiliation of being kept waiting at a gate. 'Face of Lucca, Flambard! You have made a fool of me.'

'On the contrary, my lord king,' replied Ranulf calmly. 'In point of fact, I have put a weapon in your hand. You now know the state of things at Wilton. This puts you at an advantage over Malcolm in the coming negotiations. You are also now confirmed in your own mind that you will not marry Edith. That means he cannot use her to bargain with you. You are also forewarned that some other prospective husband will be sought and that alerts you to look out for likely candidates. My lord king, I believe this journey has been of the very greatest benefit.'

****

Chapter Five

A Plucked Rose

Many people would be drawn into the events that were about to unfold at Wilton as a result of the king's visit. One day, the ramifications would reach as far as Anselm and draw him into a painfully personal dilemma. But for the moment he was fully occupied with the question of the archbishopric. A few days after the king returned to Gloucester to make preparations for the arrival of King Malcolm, Anselm turned up with a request to speak to the king. Thinking that he had by now fully accepted his appointment and had come to do homage prior to his consecration, William met him privately.

'The trouble with both of them,' observed Ranulf to Firmin, 'is that they both have principles. The king is a principled upholder of royal rights. Anselm is a principled churchman, or let's call him a cloisterman since he is a monk through and through. He's an intellectual, a defender of doctrines, a theologian. He's uncompromising, scrupulous, dangerously innocent and has the infuriating habit of correcting sin in others. The king, on the other hand, is practical, tenacious, has a sense of humour and a huge capacity for hypocrisy, all valuable political tools. Unfortunately, they inflame Anselm with the tiresome need to preach sermons. So, what are we to expect from the meeting today?'

'Very little, master?'

'Correct.'

'Shall I arrange a meeting with Baldwin afterwards, to sound out the true state of things?'

Ranulf and Baldwin met the following day when Anselm's spokesman was able to report that the private talks had been 'frank' but some issues were still 'unresolved.'

'In your view, what is to be done?'

'Well, it would help if the king did not keep referring to him as "my archbishop", thus assuming an inevitable acceptance.'

'But it is inevitable, isn't it?'

'Of course, but it will take time. In his mind, he is still Abbot of Bec and considers himself beholden to the monks there.'

'But they have released him, formally, from his obligations. He even sent back his staff and told them to get on with electing his replacement.'

'That is so. That is what happened in the real world. But Anselm's mind sometimes lags behind worldly events. It occupies a higher plane, you see. Did you know he is working on a new book? A refutation of all those rabbis and infidels who deny the Godhead of Christ. It explains by reasoned argument why it was necessary for God to become man. The *Cur Deus Homo* will answer by plain reasoning all the objections of those who doubt the Incarnation.'

Ranulf and Firmin exchanged a glance; even Baldwin now seemed to be losing the thread.

'Forgive me,' he said, catching their look, 'I know it is not important to you that such a book should be written. But believe me, it is important to us, and one day it will be of importance to the whole Christian world.'

'I don't doubt it. But, for the moment, can we concentrate on Canterbury?'

'Well, since we last met, the bishops and the monks of Christchurch have been putting pressure on him. Prior Osbern has written forcefully on behalf of the cathedral monks. They want him and soon.'

'Meanwhile, what is he saying to the king?'

'He accepts the king's offer to meet him halfway on the issue of the Canterbury lands. That is to say, he will have Canterbury just as it was at the time of Lanfranc's death. But then he also demanded the fiefs that Lanfranc had claimed but failed to recover, among them the city of Canterbury and the Abbey of St Albans.'

'No wonder the king was furious.'

'Then Anselm relented on the issue of the pope. He has dropped the recognition of Urban II from his list of demands.'

'Most pliant of him, since the king can hardly recognise anyone else. The king has lands in Normandy, he can never put himself in the position of governing territories which recognise two different popes. Anyway, that's only a detail. William Rufus will never let a pope's authority interfere with the affairs of England.'

'Anselm reminded the king that he made sacred pledges in March which were written out and placed in the cathedral. He has failed to act on them.'

'And never will. Anselm can forget that one.'

‘Lastly, he has dropped the demand to become the king’s principal counsellor on the grounds that it would involve him in the distraction of worldly affairs.’

‘And, of course, the post is already occupied.’ Ranulf did not add ‘by me’ but the words echoed silently. ‘Well, to sum up, we could say that the progress made is far from satisfactory.’

‘Nevertheless, it is progress. This is how it is done with Anselm. He is so afraid of treading wrongly that he hardly dares set his foot down at all. But, with faltering steps, he proceeds. He is in some ways like a blind man groping about in a dark world. The world of sin is obscure to him, he lives in the light of the eternal.’

If Ranulf had ever had any doubts, he now became convinced that Baldwin was preparing the way for a saint.

‘So, are we any nearer to having an archbishop?’ Ranulf asked the question but he was wondering whether all this effort was going to be worth it. Would it not be preferable to provoke Anselm to reject the position outright and start looking for a more compliant candidate?

‘As I said before, Ranulf Flambard, we will have him consecrated by Christmas. The four-year vacancy is a scandal that must be ended. I promise you, in December Anselm will arrive at the king’s Christmas court, here in Gloucester, as enthroned archbishop.’

But even if that turns out to be true, thought Ranulf, who is to say that they will get on any better after the consecration than before it?

Baldwin rose, thinking that the interview was over, but found himself being offered a cup of wine.

‘I know you are an abstemious man, quite properly,’ said Ranulf, ‘but I also believe you appreciate small pleasures. One of the good things about the recent improvement in relations with Anjou is this.’

He handed Baldwin a cup of the latest import and watched with satisfaction as he drank. ‘Let us celebrate our understanding. We work to the same ends, do we not? The efficient running of church and state.’

Firmin, who had launched himself on a full-blown apprenticeship in politics and administration, realised he had no idea where his master was going with this and sat himself on a bench in the corner to learn.

'I know how dedicated you are to your master, and I know that you, possibly more than any other, understand his position on religious matters.'

Baldwin looked up. He had not expected Ranulf Flambard, the most worldly of the king's ministers, to show the slightest interest in religious matters.

'One thing which I know is of great importance to Anselm is the matter of monastic obedience.'

'Indeed, he is a recognised authority on the monastic life. It is very dear to him. It is why he is so reluctant on the matter of Canterbury.'

'Well now, knowing your master's mind as you do, how do you think he would view the breaking of monastic vows? Suppose, for example, that a nun who had worn the veil decided to leave her convent for the purposes of marriage?'

Baldwin did not hesitate. 'He would condemn it. He would see it as a renunciation of a holy profession. The wearing of the veil binds irretrievably to the monastic life. To turn back from it would be to face damnation. In Anselm's mind, every step away from the cloister is a step further from salvation. He feels very strongly on this issue.'

'So now, I will put a hypothetical case. Suppose a man was persuaded upon a certain course of marriage but discovered that the object of his affections was, unknown to him, a nun who wore the habit and veil. What would Anselm advise him to do?'

'Without a doubt, he would advise a prohibition. He would advise the man to cease his suit, and the woman, to return to her convent.'

'And would he be likely to take into account the circumstances which led to the wearing of the veil?'

'It might make a difference in exceptional circumstances, but on the whole, I can confidently say that Anselm, believing the monastic life to be the highest form of existence and the true path to salvation, would always prefer to see such a resolution.'

'I see,' said Ranulf, thinking that on this issue at least Anselm might finally be of use to the king.

Equally, Baldwin left the meeting with the impression that Ranulf Flambard would prove to be of the greatest service to his master, since he was finally taking an interest in spiritual matters.

When he had gone, Ranulf asked Firmin to comment on what he had just heard.

'You are clearing the ground in case the visit to Wilton is held against the king.'

'And who is the person who might object to that visit most strongly?'

'King Malcolm.'

'Exactly. In a few days, Malcolm will arrive and his head will be full of plans to marry off his daughter, Edith. His preferred candidate will undoubtedly be William. Such a marriage would facilitate all his demands and ensure the good intentions of the king towards Scotland. Now, we know, but Malcolm does not, that the king has put himself decidedly out of the running. So who is the next most likely candidate? Who has spent the last two weeks with him, riding leisurely down from Durham with the psalms of a consecration still ringing in their ears?'

'Count Alan Rufus of Richmond.'

'The most powerful nobleman in England, the old companion of the Conqueror, the greatest magnate of the north, the man who holds the key to the border country. Now, the question that confronts us, Firmin, is this: Would Edith's marriage to Count Alan be in the king's interests or not?'

Firmin screwed up his face in puzzlement. There was only one important angle to any question, the king's. But to know what was in the king's interests, at any given time, and in a context of continually shifting alliances and endlessly variable contingencies, was never easy.

'You see, Firmin, the disputes between William and Anselm are largely trivial and inconclusive. They drift from one point to another without ever reaching an issue on which serious argument can take place. So they simply annoy each other and part. No harm done, everything is put off for another day when the whole process is begun again. But with men like Malcolm and Count Alan, the situation is very different. These are men whose disputes have magnitude, high seriousness, and involve the disposition of lives and fortunes. They play for high stakes and could, if necessary, back their positions with weaponry. So you see, Firmin, we must prepare ourselves to move to a higher plane of negotiation.'

'But master, I thought the king is ready to placate Malcolm on all the conditions he sought.'

'How can we be sure those conditions still hold? What changes have come over Malcolm's mind during his time with Count Alan? Let me tell you, the Count of Richmond might be fifty three, might have lost his glossy locks to streaks of grey, but he is a powerfully seductive man, to both men and women.'

Ranulf poured himself some more of his favourite Anjou and leaned up against the table.

'Perhaps it was a mistake to appoint Count Alan to escort the king. That was my doing, I admit it. But, naturally, I planted spies in the entourage who have been hurrying back and forth. Learn from that, Firmin, never rely on only one source of information.'

'And what have they been telling you, master?'

Ranulf did not answer. He paused for a long while, seeming to reflect on some particular knotty issue. Was he prepared to open his secrets to this ambitious, willing lad who was, nevertheless, in Ranulf's estimation, an innocent? At the very least, he was a young person without guile for whom he felt a great deal of affection. It's easy to say he's like a son to me, he thought, and most often that's a meaningless expression. But I have sons. Would I be prepared to apprentice them to this life or would I seek to protect them from it?

'Master,' said Firmin. 'I'm still here.'

Coming back to himself, Ranulf saw eagerness and anticipation in Firmin's face; youth, curiosity, a readiness for the life of activity and adventure. That was the trouble.

'You are a sprightly lad, Firmin,' he began. 'You have come a long way since I scraped you out of the dirt of Huntingdon, and you are deserving of higher things. But I must warn you that there is a cost. You have to ask yourself. How far can I go? At the furthest end in one direction is everything you desire: the power derived from knowing secrets, privileged access to distinguished people, the dignity of work well done, all the high achievements of royal service. This is principled and noble, easy to square with your conscience. But at the other extreme is something altogether darker, murkier, noisome, ignoble and cruel. It lies, usually, at the end of a long corridor or twisting stairwell, leading downward to some rank, fetid cell and a terrified prisoner who is always innocent. Here lie the things you do not want to do. So you must ask yourself some deep questions. Once you are set on the path, there is no going back.'

Firmin was astonished. He did not understand. Yet he felt that this speech had entrusted him with a great secret because, as much as it was a warning, it was a confession. But what had compelled his master to say these things, so unlike himself? In a daze, Firmin was still sitting silently on the bench in the corner when Ranulf left the room.

****

At Wilton, the king's visit had tempestuous repercussions. Now Edith fell out completely with her aunt. She railed and stormed, ripped the veil from her face, tore off her habit and strode about in a coarse linen undergarment saying that, since she was treated worse than the lowest menial, she would dress like one. Edith, who had seemed to Aefled a child of indomitable spirit, now showed that she had a temper to match the legendary rages of her father.

'I won't speak to her,' she said to Aefled. 'Don't let her come near me. She is trying to ruin everything.'

Aefled and Agnes tried to calm her, but despaired of the situation. It had undone all their good work in helping Edith recover from her illness and the emotional turmoil surrounding her first menses. It now appeared that the very thing that made her marriageable had caused the loss of the royal husband she so desired.

'Aefled, what can I do? Help me!' Despite Edith's pitiable pleas Agnes and Aefled were powerless to intervene. Aefled thought of Robert. Surely he might be prevailed on to ask his lord for some kind of intervention. Count Alan Rufus had influence with Malcolm. Should King Malcolm be informed about what was going on at Wilton? But she did not know where Robert was and was not even sure that her last letter had reached him.

Meanwhile, Christina was far from contrite. She believed she had acted in the best interests of her charge by keeping her out of the clutches of a man she regarded as a creature of unbridled lusts, a threat to all virtue and a minion of Satan. Christina was volubly self-justificatory and would not relent in her attitude to Edith.

'I made a vow to God. Edith was spared for a purpose.'

When the abbess and a delegation of nuns came to suggest a reconciliation, bringing Edith to embrace her aunt, a terrific scene took place with aunt and niece shouting that each had betrayed the other. The weight of convent opinion took the view that Christina was right to be protective of her niece, but that she was too severe, especially at a time when Edith was still emotionally distraught. But they also saw Edith as disruptive and disobedient, not the kind of material from which a Benedictine nun could be made. Their quarrels were reminiscent of the conflicts between William and Anselm, but in the latter case, the solution was always for one or other to withdraw. In the convent, that was not possible. The antagonists were thrown together day and night, exacerbating tempers and fuelling the conflict to such a pitch that Aefled and Agnes began once again to fear for Edith's health.

There was an intervention, of sorts, from a surprising quarter. In the middle of one of these heated rows, Gunhild suddenly came forward and took Edith away by the hand, promising to speak to her some words that would bring comfort.

'You can't comfort me,' said Edith. 'I swear to you, I will never be reconciled to my aunt. I will tell my father everything. Oh, if only he would come!'

They went to the room occupied by Gunhild who, because of her royal lineage, was given comfortable quarters. There was a cot bed, a table spread with writing implements and parchments, a chest with an image of a haloed Christ in a wooden frame above. The low window was open to a breeze from the garth, bearing the scent of roses. On a corner of the table, was a small box. Gunhild opened it and took out a beautiful silver brooch, set with precious stones. 'This was given to me by your mother,' she said in a gentle voice. Edith took it eagerly and held it to the light. 'I knew your mother when I was a child in her household, before she went off to marry your father. She was very kind to me.'

'I wish she was here, being kind to me,' said Edith, who had very little knowledge of either of her parents. They seemed like remote, glowing figures moving in a landscape of incomprehensible power.

'Perhaps I could take her place for a little while.'

Edith sat on the bed, swinging her legs, pouting.

'Christina took my caps and bonnets and my trinkets. How I hate her.'

Gunhild's expression was indulgent. Unlike the nuns, she was prepared to let hate have its free run through the soul of this girl and would not sermonise.

'Perhaps you should know that I hid the things she took. Look, they are here.' Gunhild reached into a little box under the bed and brought forth the child's treasures.

'Oh, you kept them! Did you steal them from my aunt?'

'Perhaps we ought to say I borrowed them.'

Edith gasped with delight and began to place them, one by one, on her head. There being no mirror in the room, or indeed in the convent, she had to look for her reflection in Gunhild's admiring eyes.

Sitting next to Edith on the bed, Gunhild removed her headdress, easing her hair into long unwinding strands. It fell about her shoulders and down to below her waist, great waves of light brown hair streaked with grey.

'I have had a letter,' she said, taking up a parchment from the table. 'It's from the man who will be the next Archbishop of Canterbury.'

Edith seemed disappointed. What possible relevance could it have for her?

'It's from Anselm. I met him once, years ago. Since then we sometimes write to each other. He helps me when I am unhappy and confused by the world. He calls me his sister in God. But that isn't what I meant to tell you. In this letter, he says that he has just left the king in Gloucester and is on his way to Canterbury. But while he was there he heard news that your father is, even now, travelling to Gloucester and will be there very soon. It is possible, Edith, that when your father has finished his business at the court, he will come to visit you here at Wilton.'

'Oh, if only he would! If only he would come and take me away from here, away from Christina.'

'But, Edith, even if he came and took you away, would you be happy to part from your aunt on such bad terms? After all, in spite of what has happened, she loves you and sincerely cares for you. She is frightened of the world and that makes her want to protect you from its dangers. Could you not find it in your heart to relent and forgive her?'

Edith paused in placing a cap on her head. 'Do you think I should?'

'You should do what you feel is right, Edith. That is the responsibility of a woman of courage and spirit. You are a woman now, who might enter upon a high station sometime in the future. Sometimes it is best not to leave bad feelings behind you. Christina has chosen her path, taken her vows and dedicated her life to the service of God. Your path may lie in a different direction. Once gone from here, you may never see her again. Do you not think it possible that you could be at peace with her?'

Believing that her father would soon come and take her away, Edith relented. And through Gunhild's good offices, a truce was arranged. Aunt and niece embraced, protesting that they forgave one another. Edith even consented to wear her habit, counting the days until she would be rid of it forever.

****

The first intimation that King Malcolm was nearing his destination was the appearance of Dunmore, Lord of Moray, with a formal message of greeting to the Norman king. He went first to seek out his old contact, Ranulf Flambard.

'He'll be here tomorrow, before noon.'

'How many mouths at board?'

'At least twenty for the feasting hall. Maybe fifty in total.'

'The king's suite can be lodged here at Kingsholm, the others in the abbey, inns and hospital. I don't want the townspeople put to any disruption. We had enough of that when the king lay dying. King Malcolm is in good health, I trust?'

'Never better.'

Since little more was to be extracted from the close-mouthed Dunmore, it was now a matter of waiting. Ranulf broke into a sweat when he considered how much was riding on this meeting. Perhaps the very peace of the realm itself. From his sickbed in March, William had given undertakings to Malcolm, which Flambard himself had glossed. But the king had given undertakings to Anselm, too, which he had now broken: those sacred pledges in the cathedral remained unfulfilled. Even Ranulf Flambard found it difficult to read the king's mind. Certainly, since his visit to Wilton, he had been more than usually obstreperous, boiling with bad temper and caustic remarks. The Scottish king might well be riding into a storm.

In the meantime, Firmin was in a sulk. Showing a perplexed face, he padded around, looking after his master's needs, but not responsive in the usual way.

'Why so glum, Firmin?'

He had been thinking about his master's unsettling words. How was he supposed to feel, what should he think? All his confidence had been undermined. He was so distracted by these feelings that he had even forgotten to ask his master what news the spies had been bringing from Malcolm's entourage.

'Are you having doubts?' said Ranulf when the lad did not reply.

'Master, I am confused. I think you were trying to tell me that I am not suited to this life.'

'Not at all, quite the contrary. But I want you to have a chance to examine your own mind. There is a cost, as I said. But that is very far from saying that the cost is not affordable. You might come to me and say "but there are always guards and soldiers and tough military types who operate in the dank, rank places. We are not involved, we can keep our hands clean." And to an extent, that is true. But you should also be aware of how far that is not true. You should see in your mind the hands of others at work on the bodies of those brought for punishment. You should imagine them as your hands, doing your work, at your orders. In that way, you will avoid the giving of jealous, angry or ill-considered orders and their consequences.'

'Master,' said Firmin, 'do you still have faith in me?'

'I think you have mistaken my meaning. Let me be open with you.' Ranulf paused, fixed Firmin with a serious gaze, and went on: 'Let me tell you that I have never conducted the king's business in such a way that I could not, in all conscience, one day, aspire to a high post in the church. After years of faithful service, my reward will be a lucrative post, a bishopric, perhaps. That would do me very well. But I must be able to bring my conscience before God on the day of my consecration without unpardonable shame. That is the end to which I conduct my affairs.'

Still puzzled, Firmin asked what Ranulf wanted him to do.

'I want you to do nothing that will jeopardise your soul, Firmin, because you are dear to me. You must remember that kingly service is precarious and favour may always be lost. The day may come when you will stand alone to face your conscience. Never lose sight of that.'

Satisfied that he had reassured and placated Firmin, Ranulf quickly forgot the episode. But Firmin remembered it long after as the moment when devotion to his master became his overriding rule in life.

The following day, the great noisy inrush of Malcolm's retinue swelled in the courtyard of Kingsholm. Trumpets blared, bridles jingled, there were shouts, cries and commands as the palace and the whole town reverberated to the arrival of the long-expected guest. Servants and attendants rushed to conduct the visitors to their assigned lodgings, to prepare food, stable the horses, unpack the king's effects and install them in the suite of rooms prepared for him. Count Alan Rufus, who had conducted the business of safely delivering the king, was given quarters in the castle while his men were lodged wherever space could be found in the adjacent buildings. Robert found himself crammed with half a dozen others in a sweltering stable loft. After their days on the hot August road, they stank so badly that they went out to find a spot where they could strip off, swim and splash in the cleansing waters of the Severn.

The next day, August 24th, was the feast of St Bartholomew, marked by a mass in the cathedral church conducted by Serlo, Abbot of St Peter's. This was to be the opening ceremony of the diplomatic summit of which the high point would be the formal meeting between King William and King Malcolm; England and Scotland meeting in amity with a view to resolving all the difficulties of their relationship. As the grandly dressed officials of the two courts filled the nave, standing bare-headed behind their monarchs, Ranulf could not suppress the thought that, of all the saints in the canon, St Bartholomew, who had been hailed by Christ himself as 'incapable of deceit,' was the most unlikely intercessor to preside in spirit over the coming talks. Two monarchs more adept at practising deceit could hardly be found.

The first sign that something was wrong came over the matter of protocol. At the end of the ceremony, when the kings were expected to meet before the altar and exchange a kiss of peace, William failed to acknowledge his counterpart and left the cathedral without having formally recognised the presence of Malcolm. It could not be anything but a deliberate snub.

Among all the symbolic acts of kingship, the kiss had a peculiar meaning. It was the climax in acts of homage and fealty, in reconciling enemies and restoring harmony. The kiss of friendship, given or withheld, could play a hugely significant role in public acts. That William had behaved in this way set off alarm bells among his ministers and Malcolm was visibly vexed.

'My lord king,' said Ranulf in a private interview later that morning to discuss the agenda of the meeting, 'was it wise to offend Malcolm at the very outset of these negotiations?'

'Was it wise for Malcolm to offend me before he even set out?'

Ranulf was nonplussed at this response, having no idea what the king was driving at. They were in the king's private closet where William had received him in a state of informal dress, wearing a loose robe without a girdle. His barber had finished shaving him, his hair was combed. Ranulf noticed how healthy he looked when scrubbed. William took an apple from a bowl and bit deeply into it with strong teeth set in a well-hinged jaw.

'Durham,' he said. 'Durham rankles. What was St Calais up to, inviting him to the consecration? It is my place to lead in the cult of St Cuthbert. My assertion over the north stems from it. The saint's relics are a means of upholding political power. Malcolm made a political statement in attending the consecration, seeking to challenge my dominion in the north. I have returned snub for snub.'

The king, who had never mentioned this before, took another bite from the apple and threw it away.

'Look here, Flambard,' he said. 'For thirty-four years Malcolm has been a menace on the border. He's a firebrand, a warlord, a hell raiser, a mere baron who has done me fealty in the past. I have been gracious enough to promise the hand of friendship and I will do so, but on my own terms. For I would rather have these matters settled in a court of my barons than treat with him as a king and equal.'

For once, Ranulf Flambard was wrong-footed by the king's mercurial temperament. He had not seen this coming and was momentarily perplexed.

'My lord king,' he breathed, 'are you going to refuse to meet him?'

The king's dressers came bustling into the closet and began laying out formal tunics and robes, fussing over their costly materials, smoothing wrinkles from damasks and silks. William raised his arms as they removed his outer garment in order to dress him in ceremonial attire.

'Do I look as if I am refusing?'

'Forgive me, my lord. May I ask what you wish?'

'Let Malcolm send me emissaries with his requests. I will consider how I might answer them. After that, if a meeting seems appropriate, I will gladly oblige.'

In other words, thought Ranulf with a crushing realisation, he is pulling out. Or at least threatening to. The instant he withdrew from the king he rushed to inform Dunmore of the king's vacillation. In turn, Dunmore alerted Malcolm who summoned his leading counsellors. By the afternoon, they had drawn up a list, not so much of requests, but of allegations and complaints about William's failure to keep his word. These were promptly despatched to Ranulf, who read them to the king.

'The peace terms of 1092 have not been implemented; no promised instalment of Malcolm's money fief has been paid; there has been no return of the lands compromised in the seizure of Carlisle. But the main request, my lord king, and the one that heads the list, is that negotiations of marriage with his daughter, Edith, should be brought swiftly to a happy conclusion.'

At that, William laughed aloud. 'Does he dare?' he said. 'But no, he cannot be aware then, that his daughter is a nun.'

A polite, but unhelpful, reply was sent to Malcolm's camp from the hand of Ranulf Flambard, desperately proposing a delay in negotiations since the king was taken with a sudden indisposition.

‘This is monstrous,’ he said to Firmin. ‘This is worse than the bull and the sheep. This is two intransigent bulls with their heads down and horns locked.’

When the response came from Malcolm, it simply repeated the previous demands in a more aggressive tone. William refused to budge, stating again that Malcolm’s concerns were legalistic and should be settled in a baron’s court. This was a calculated insult and Ranulf foresaw a reciprocal reaction. But the expected emissaries did not return from Malcolm with insults and threats. Instead, there was an intervention from an unexpected quarter when Count Alan Rufus appeared to make an appeal directly to the king. William immediately agreed to receive him with all honour in the great chamber of Kingsholm.

Count Alan Rufus, with his silver-streaked hair, his confident bearing and no-nonsense eye, was not a man who could be lightly dismissed, even by William Rufus in a bilious mood. He came striding ahead of a small delegation, including his brother Alan Niger and newly-promoted aide, Robert, who was making a rare appearance before the king and thinking how he must find a way of writing to Aefled about it. No doubt some Gloucester monk would charge him an exorbitant fee. It galled him to reflect that in the circles of magnates like Count Alan Rufus there were secular men who could read and write. Communications in the form of letters, charters, writs and bonds flew about everywhere and increasingly the courts of kings and nobles were made up of writers and readers of script. Ironically, at Gloucester, a centre of learning and government, the seat of royal ordinance, there was one half-educated man who showed no interest in reading: the king himself. And so, when Count Alan went to hand him the list of Malcolm’s demands, he simply said: ‘Please be so good as to read it out, Count Alan.’

William’s attitude to Count Alan Rufus was based on the respect of long and faithful service in defence of the northern borders, mixed with admiration of his personal qualities. Here was the type of man that women admired, men aspired to be and kings schemed to get in their inmost circles. Instead of reading from the list, Count Alan set it aside and spoke his own words.

‘My lord,’ said the Count, ‘the King of Scotland desires to know, plainly and with certainty, whether you will, now or in the future, be prepared to press a suit of marriage with Edith, his daughter. And I must also add, my lord king, so there is no risk of future allegations of deceit or misrepresentation, that if you desire no marriage with the said Edith, he intends to give her in marriage to me.'

The king hesitated for a moment but betrayed no flicker of surprise. Flambard, alerted by his spies, had warned him of this private agreement. What was surprising was that Count Alan was so open about it.

'And you, Count Alan,' said the king after a pause, 'what do you intend?'

'As your liegeman, my lord, I intend to serve you faithfully. It seems to me that a great cause of friction in the border country will be removed by such a union.'

'Count Alan, I fear you have been misled. Whatever Malcolm has been saying to you, whatever prospects he has been holding out, if they concern his daughter, they are worthless. Edith has taken the veil. Do you not know that she is a nun at Wilton? I fear that neither I, nor you, can marry the lady.'

Self-possessed though he was, even Count Alan was disturbed by this unexpected answer, while William sat with polished impassivity inwardly exulting in Flambard's brilliant suggestion. That trip to Wilton had put him in a position to refuse marriage himself and deny it to his vassal, thus preventing an alliance he had never wanted. At the same time, he could do it all without offence, for had it not been taken from his hands?

'Alas, as a nun she is inviolable. Who can overturn the holy rituals of the church, who can countermand the vows of religion? Perhaps King Malcolm ought not to persist with his suit here but proceed directly to Wilton and attend to his daughter.'

Later, when Ranulf Flambard gave an account of this episode to Firmin, he was uncertain how to present it. From William's point of view, it was a short-term triumph with the potential for long-term disaster. For King Malcolm, it had been a catastrophic failure since the only thing he could get from William was permission to return unmolested to Scotland. But King Malcolm and Count Alan were not about to accept an unsubstantiated rumour, nor would they change their plans without proof of William's claim. The only way to get such proof was to go to Wilton and check on the state of affairs, as the king had suggested. There, Count Alan Rufus would discover that what had at first appeared a disappointment to his marriage plans would prove to be the most extraordinary opportunity.

****

Since the reconciliation between Edith and her aunt, brokered by Gunhild, a tense quiet had descended on Wilton. Under hot August skies, the abbey seemed to be drowsing through the days of late summer. Bells rang the canonical hours to call the nuns to worship. Roses bloomed in the garth, casting their fragrance along the cloister walks. Agnes and Aefled began to think of returning home. But just as they were making plans to leave, a violent tempest was unloosed upon the sleeping abbey.

King Malcolm and his Scottish entourage, along with Count Alan Rufus, his brother Alan Niger, his aide, Robert, and a select escort of retainers, had ridden the hundred miles from Gloucester across the bare, dry North Wessex Downs, skirting the cone of Silbury Hill where men said ancient warriors were buried and over the scrub of Salisbury Plain to reach Wilton within three days of setting out. In that time, Malcolm's anger had not been assuaged. That the Norman king should humiliate him was bad enough, but that he should publicly broadcast a falsehood damaging to his daughter was insupportable. Provoked beyond endurance by the indignities of his treatment at Gloucester, he arrived in a mood of rage, resentment and the desire to be avenged. As everyone remarked who witnessed it, this destructive mood was the very worst in which to conduct a reunion with his vulnerable young daughter.

The visitors could not be denied entry, any more than King William had been, and were allowed to ride into the courtyard: men, mounts and arms, a vast masculine influx swelling into a quiet feminine space. The Abbess, senior nuns, Christina, Gunhild, Agnes and Aefled stood close together, at a loss to know what was happening until Christina recognised King Malcolm and stepped forward. Out of the corner of her eye, Aefled caught sight of Robert, standing beside a big grizzle-headed man she did not know. The instant their eyes met, communication flashed between them: 'Be silent, say nothing now, I will explain later.' In a moment, Malcolm was shouting at Christina, rushing forward and seizing her wrist.

'What is going on here? Where is my daughter?'

Christina pulled away. 'Never show violence to me!' she yelled. 'How dare you disrespect this holy house?'

'Holy house? A nest of schemers! What are you playing at? Who has started these rumours?'

'For God's sake, and the sake of these holy nuns, calm yourself! You don't know what you're saying. You are a king. Act like one.

Begin by asking permission of the Abbess to explain your business here.'

Momentarily brought back to his senses, Malcolm relented and let go of Christina's wrist. He then apologised to the abbess and, to show he had some understanding of the civilities of these occasions, sought permission to pray in the abbey church, requesting that Edith be brought to him afterwards.

While Malcolm was in the church, Count Alan and his entourage milled about in the courtyard, giving offence to no one. Again, Robert caught sight of Aefled, disappearing towards the cloister with two companions who seemed to be nuns. She looked round at him and smiled as if to say: 'I have much to tell you, but not now, not now.' What was she doing here? Why was she not at home? Since he had not received her letter, Robert knew nothing about the events of the last few months.

'Who were those women?' asked Count Alan, coming up to put a hand on Robert's shoulder.

'One of them is my wife, my lord.'

'Good God, Robert. And what is a wife of yours doing here?'

'I have no idea.'

'Well, go and speak to her, find out.'

And so, after six months apart, with scarcely a letter between them, Robert and Aefled met quite by chance in the same unlikely place. It was the first instance of what Aefled would later come to call "the strange mystery of Wilton", the first experience of the power that Wilton seemed to exert over interior lives and outward events. But for the moment their meeting, muted by decorum and the presence of others, felt like a happy coincidence. Aefled introduced Gunhild, describing her as a 'royal princess' which undoubtedly impressed Robert. When he discovered that her father was the usurper, Harold, his reaction was more grudging. But later he was able to report truthfully to Count Alan that he found the woman called Gunhild to be "dignified and gracious". At this, Count Alan showed a degree of interest and immediately commanded an introduction.

Meanwhile, the abbess was delaying Malcolm as long as possible so that Edith could be prepared. First, there were prayers, then she insisted on refreshment, served to all his men in the refectory by lay brothers from the monastery. Either by coincidence or choice, the refectory reading that day was from St Paul's Letter to the Ephesians: 'Let not the sun go down on your wrath. Let all bitterness, and wrath, and anger, and clamour, and evil speaking be put away from you.' If Malcolm heard these words through his seething rage, he omitted to act on them. The next ruse of the abbess was to conduct Malcolm to the library in order to show why the abbey had such a grand reputation for education. She pointed out the long low room where the oblate girls and secular wards took their lessons. Deeply bored, Malcolm was just about at snapping point when one of the nuns came to say that Edith was ready and desired to meet her father. The Abbess, feeling that Malcolm could do with a little more chastening delay, decided to talk about Gunhild and made a long speech praising her as 'a scholar, also a royal princess, a proper companion for your daughter.'

At this, Malcolm showed an interest, became gracious and inquired courteously about her, seeming at last to achieve some equilibrium of temper. Thus hopes were raised for an unimpassioned meeting between the trio of aunt, father and daughter, and all still might have gone well had it not been for one little item of clothing.

Ever since the quarrel with her aunt, Edith had been looking forward to the prospect of her father's arrival. But when she heard that he had entered the courtyard boiling with a temper so ungoverned that he appeared to attack Christina, she imagined that she herself was the cause of his anger. Having no knowledge of what had passed at Gloucester, she again felt blame for something that was not her fault. She was frightened of him even before she saw him and began to wish he had not come. Aefled and Agnes tried to explain the situation, but it was Gunhild who took her away and gave some well-meant advice on how to conduct herself in the presence of her choleric father.

'Dear Edith,' she said, putting an arm around her, fully aware of the high cost of being the daughter of a royal house, a cost which she had been paying all her life.

'Don't fear the king, he is not angry with you. Answer him respectfully, make no complaints against your aunt, pay tribute to the nuns, be gracious to all. Then he will see that you deserve the fruits of your privileged education. He will ensure that you are well settled in the world and married to a good man.'

'Gunhild,' said Edith, 'why are you not married? '

'My dear, I had no father to settle it. He died before I was born and there was no one to take his place.'

Edith began to weep. Now that she was about to confront her father, she wished he had not come. Wilton was the only home she had known, what if he took her away?

Gunhild let her weep, stroking her hair, watching the small form convulse with sobs. Here, at the centre of international diplomacy, political battles between kings and endless discussions between men, a little girl in tears was frightened to leave her home. Edith cried so much and rubbed her eyes so roughly that her face became red and puffed; her nose would not stop dribbling. When Christina saw her, she was horrified. 'Edith, you look a fright, what will your father think when he sees you? Here, this will cover it.' And she fixed a veil over Edith's face.

When everything was ready, Edith, wearing her habit and the hastily attached veil, was led into the chapter house where she would be reunited with the father she had not seen for half a dozen years. The scene that followed was unprecedented in the annals of Wilton. Those who witnessed it never forgot it. The effect of his daughter's appearance on Malcolm was instant and terrifying. He flew into a rage, called out that he had been betrayed, berated Christina and the Abbess for practising deception on him and tore the veil from Edith's face.

'My daughter is no nun!' he yelled. 'It's false, a lie! Who sought my permission? Who consulted me?'

Edith burst into tears again, terrified of her father's anger. She turned on her heel and ran out, flew along the cloister arcade and sought sanctuary in Gunhild's room where she threw herself on the bed and sobbed inconsolably. Again, it was Gunhild who took it upon herself to reassure the child.

'Your father is not angry with you,' she said. 'Just now, he is feeling angry with himself because he should have been more alert to your situation. And he is angry with King William. He feels the king has humiliated him.'

Edith wiped her eyes and sat up. 'What did the king do?'

'The king refused to see him, refused to negotiate, broke promises. Your father has some grounds for anger, Edith, my dear, but he is not angry with you. If he is angry with anyone, it's your aunt.'

Edith seemed pacified by this. It seemed to offer common ground with her father, putting them on the same side against Christina.

'Will my father take me away from her?'

'Yes, Edith, I think he will. Should you like that?'

'I don't want to leave you, Gunhild, or Agnes and Aefled, you have all been so kind to me. But yes, I want to go away from my aunt. She would make me a nun.'

Later Edith was persuaded to a second interview with her father, minus the veil. Both made an effort to be civil. Edith employed Gunhild's advice, made no complaint about her aunt, praised the nuns, displayed what she had learned during her time at Wilton and carried herself with dignity. King Malcolm, aware that some fatherly words were required, spoke gently, saying that she was the image of her mother, Queen Margaret, who was anxious to see her.

'Are you ready to come with me, my daughter, away home to your mother?'

The next day, still looking pale and crestfallen, not wanting to leave the convent but desperate to escape her aunt, caught up in conflicting emotions, sadness at leaving her friends, the hope of seeing her mother, Edith took her leave, embraced Aefled, Agnes and Gunhild, gave a grudging kiss to Christina, thanked the abbess and left with her father for Scotland.

Count Alan stayed on at Wilton, finding himself and his men lodgings in the town but coming to the abbey every day. He seemed particularly concerned that Robert should have every opportunity to visit his wife and even volunteered to accompany him, as if, by some strange twist, lord and liegeman had changed places.

After the third visit Robert said to Aefled, 'I wonder why Count Alan takes such an interest in us. Why does he hang about here? If he went back to Richmond, my service would be at an end and we could go home.'

'I would like to go home. Eleanor will be missing me.'

'A pity Count Alan is not of a like mind. What keeps him here?'

'But, Robert, are you the only one who doesn't see what's happening?'

From the moment Robert had introduced them on the first day, Gunhild had taken a liking for Count Alan. He, in turn, did not spare her the full glare of his charismatic charms. For his part, he was impressed by her self-possession, quick mind and extraordinary graciousness. She was the polished product of a privileged education, the best that Wilton had to offer. She was also of an age more suited to a man of fifty-three than the childish Edith had been. When he looked at Gunhild he thought it absurd that he had ever considered contracting a marriage with Malcolm's daughter. That plan, of course, was dead in the water. But, as he had discovered, Edith was not the only royal princess of an ancient English house to be lodging at Wilton.

Learning from Robert that Aefled was Gunhild's close friend, Count Alan asked to speak to her and a meeting was arranged with Agnes in attendance.

'We are both friends to Gunhild,' said Aefled to her husband's overlord, a man whose name she had known for years but had never expected to meet.

'What can you tell me about her?'

'Very little without her permission. That would be disloyal in a friend.'

Count Alan was impressed. This was a sparky wife for such a dull old workhorse as Robert.

'I can tell you that she is the most worthy lady I know. She is kind and sympathetic. She is highly educated, in Latin and Norman French, and can write in many styles. She is in personal communication with some of the greatest scholars in Christendom, but she has not taken the veil. She has made no vows, yet she is spiritual and gracious to all.'

'She is the daughter of King Harold, I understand.'

'Yes, the last child of the English royal line. If her father had lived and not, regrettably, died at Hastings, her life would have been very different.'

'Presumably, she inherited lands?'

It was a question she did not wish to answer. Aefled was in a difficult position and resented being used. She did not want to offend her husband's overlord nor did she want to betray the many confidences she had shared with Gunhild. If he desired to know about her inheritance, he must seek answers from her.

'My lord Count,' she said, 'I beg to be excused. Gunhild must answer for herself.'

Gunhild, it seemed, did answer for herself, gladly and at length, in many private conversations with Count Alan.

Every day he came to the abbey to spend an hour or two with her, walking and talking in the cloister garth. Soon Gunhild was looking forward to seeing him, then expecting him, then hastening to meet him. They walked and talked, often lingering by the roses, still pouring their fragrance on the late summer air, as they had when King William had hidden there to glimpse the bride he did not want. Now Count Alan and Gunhild loitered among the red August blooms, sharing their sweetness in warm looks and unspoken thoughts. Aefled could clearly see what was happening. Months ago, when they had first begun their friendship, Gunhild had said: 'Don't you think love is the most important matter, the fullest and best of human life?' If Gunhild really thought that, then it was likely she would risk everything for it. Her words came echoing back. 'If I was offered the chance, whatever the odds, I would take it.' Count Alan was offering that chance. There was no doubt that the formerly self-possessed Gunhild had fallen passionately in love.

On the day before he was due to depart, Count Alan plucked a rose to offer to her. As he did so, he pricked his finger badly on a thorn. He sucked away the blood, laughing that he had taken many wounds in his long life, but never before in the service of love. 'Look, it's the same colour as the rose,' he said, 'a perfect match, like us.' Gunhild thought, at last, she knew what happiness was. In a few days, Count Alan, so admired among courtiers, noblemen and war lords, even by the king himself, had found and won a noble love from a woman equally admired. He promised himself that he would treat it gently, respect it, treasure it, and if he could, nourish it with love of his own. It was a promise he was to keep to the end of his life.

When Aefled entered Gunhild's chamber that evening, she found her sitting at the writing table with a parchment in her hand, an image not of romantic love, as might be expected, but rather of studious composure.

'Gunhild, did you know Count Alan has been asking questions about you? Do you think that's right?'

'That's entirely right,' Gunhild smiled. 'In view of what he is proposing.'

'Gunhild, what's going on? What are you doing?'

'You see this?' she waved the parchment. 'It is a letter to the Abbess, to Christina and to the whole community, thanking them for their many benefactions to me. I will be sure to send them a large donation when my affairs are settled. I am going away, Aefled, I am going to marry Count Alan.'

'But, Gunhild, you've only known him a few days. Is this wise?'

'If, by wise, you mean self-serving and prudent, then no, it is not wise. Aefled, I am not spurning the spiritual life. I have been content here and would never willingly bring shame on the convent. But now I must try another way of living. Count Alan offers me that. When I'm with him I feel something I have never felt before. Aefled, consider, this is my last chance. The thrill, the gamble of a great adventure. Tomorrow I enter the world.'

****

Chapter Six

Enter Eadmer

The king's full travelling household descended on host towns like a Biblical plague. Early in September, before news of the events at Wilton had become known, the plague descended on Winchester. In contrast to the unofficial sojourn at the bishop's palace a few weeks earlier, this was a full-blown cavalcade of several hundred people sweeping into the quiet city with its inadequate resources. It was one of William Rufus's jokes that he never stayed in Winchester long because there was nowhere to stay. The old wooden castle was one of his least favourite places. For a royal city, the number of stone buildings was small and most belonged to the church. Far superior to any, was the great long-naved cathedral church, recently completed by Bishop Walkelin at huge expense which had exhausted his reserves. Even the bishop's official residence, Wolvesey Palace, would have to wait another thirty years before anyone would find the money to rebuild it in stone.

'Finding money is the chief occupation in life,' said Ranulf to Firmin as he looked over his accounts one morning in the first week of September. 'Even Anselm, the most unworldly of men, is preoccupied by every jot and tittle of the money fiefs of Canterbury.'

'Is that why he is here, master?'

'Well, he is not here for love of the king.'

Although not uncritically, Ranulf largely supported the king in his conflicts over money with the clergy. At least the king, in spending money, spread dribbles of income downward. Hunting alone generated hundreds of jobs, from whippers-in to horn blowers, fewterers to brachmen. Then there were scores of menial posts in all the various offices of the household, from the lowest who earned a penny a day, to the chandlers, stewards, butlers, and chamberlains on three shillings and six pence. Although royal travel sent shivers down the spines of elders and bailiffs, who saw their towns regularly trashed by brawling knights, it brought money in its wake, money readily grasped by the hands of local people. Coins were scattered down to the townsmen who organised supplies, women who did the washing or made running repairs on fabrics, boys who kept the harness, carters who packed and unpacked the travelling offices, the muleteers and ox drivers who hauled around the royal paraphernalia. These people were paid by the Despenser, grudgingly and at a strictly graded rate, but, more often than not, they were paid.

On the whole, middling ecclesiastics such as priors and abbots, tended to stay put in their monasteries, conserving what they had and adding to it by buying up neighbouring manors as cheaply as possible from debtors, or encouraging the ailing to bequeath lands at their death in return for prayers and benedictions. By and large, the hospitals and hostelries for pilgrims cost next to nothing, being run by the monks who were not paid, whereas shrines and reliquaries could be relied on to generate a steady income through the charging of entry fees and the sale of trinkets: little models of saints, phials of blood and tokens of pilgrimage. So, when Anselm dug in his heels over pecuniary matters, Ranulf found himself supporting the king. Fully expecting another stormy encounter between the bull and the sheep, he primed himself on the financial affairs of Canterbury and made sure he had a firm grip on the legal points that Anselm had come to Winchester to contest. As it turned out, the ever-surprising Anselm had another surprise in store.

King William Rufus, inwardly prepared for another quarrel, made every effort to receive the troublesome archbishop with as much cordiality as he could muster. Unfortunately, the day appointed for the meeting was September 9th, an inauspicious day, a day when William was likely to be more than usually irascible and driven. It was the anniversary of his father's death, a day on which he battled with the towering figure who had dominated his life and haunted his kingship with unmatchable examples. Conquest, diplomacy, power, undying fame, the old man had taken the crown in all, leaving William to operate in the shadow of greatness, measuring himself of little worth. He was not alone. All the Conqueror's sons suffered from complicated and destructive feelings in regard to their father but William, the only one who was defending a crown, was the worst affected and September 9th was a day he marked with particular combativeness.

'This long battle will wear one or other of us down eventually,' he said when Ranulf Flambard came to brief him that morning, 'and it will not be me. What are your sources saying?'

'My lord king,' said Flambard, 'I believe we might look forward to some progress at last. Baldwin tells me Anselm is preparing to take another step on the long road towards the archbishopric.'

'How big a step?'

'Shall you summon him, my lord, and find out?'

When Anselm entered, on the arm of Baldwin, with the little monk Eustace in tow, he did not seem in a belligerent mood. The anxiety of the last months, the tussle with conscience, the struggle between soul and duty, had visited his face and body with a wan shrunkenness. But his expression was unchanged and his eyes were still full of dauntless energy. However, when those eyes fell on Ranulf Flambard they seemed to burn with uncharitable resentment. Here was the man responsible for the king's intransigence, he believed, who encouraged him in licentious habits, or at the very least pandered to them. Flambard was said by many to procure creatures for the king's bed and misuse the influence of his office. Flambard encouraged mean and tight-fisted policies which curtailed the king's natural generosity. Whenever Flambard was around, King William tended to be at his worst: flippant, sarcastic and obstructive. The king's worst faults derived from Flambard who haunted him like an evil demon, such was Anselm's belief.

Fighting off these negative thoughts, he padded forward, stood before the king and waited for him to speak. William, seated on a dais in a high-backed carved chair with red and gold embroidered coverings, leaned forward.

'Welcome, archbishop, you are well, I trust?' William hoped that by constantly using the title and calling him 'archbishop' as often as possible, Anselm would become reconciled to it.

'I am well, my lord king. I thank you.'

'No inconvenient fire near your lodgings?'

Flambard rolled his eyes. This was typical of William who could never resist an inappropriate jest. Why did he have to mention it and get the meeting off on the wrong note? It was a completely gratuitous reference to an event that was said to have happened when Anselm was last in Winchester. He had been staying in a suburb of the city when a house caught fire near his lodging and spread quickly towards it. Everybody rushed about in fear but no one tackled the blaze. Someone called on Anselm to make the sign of the cross and thus ward off the fire. Anselm protested at first, deeming himself unworthy, but was eventually prevailed on to put forth the sign of the cross against the fire which immediately drew back and died down. Naturally, the story emanated from Baldwin, another of the wonder tales put about to prepare the way for his master's sainthood.

A pained expression passed over Anselm's face, but he refused to be drawn.

'My lord king, I greet you in the name of Christ and ask him to bless our counsels.'

'As, indeed, I do myself.'

'As you know, certain matters weighing on my mind have been put from me. The Duke of Normandy, your brother, has given his consent, as has the Archbishop of Rouen.'

'And the monks of Bec, I understand. You were especially attached to them. They have released you and you have returned your staff of office. So far so good. What next?'

'Your assurance, my lord, that I will receive the temporalities of my see. If you will give your guarantee, I am prepared to do homage.'

The king looked to Flambard, flaring his eyes in surprise. Undoubtedly, homage was a great step forward, which he would readily accept. But the financial detail was Flambard's territory and the topic for which he had been preparing. The 'temporalities' referred to those secular properties and possessions used to support a bishop or archbishop and his household. From them would be drawn the running costs and day-to-day disbursements required by the maintenance of a certain style of living. Canterbury had such manors scattered in many parts of the country in various dioceses. They were money fiefs, by and large, from which private funds were extracted. In preparation, Flambard had drawn up a list of them on a parchment which he handed to the king. 'I think, my lord that you will find all in order.'

After dawdling a deliberately cruel length of time over the list, the king rolled it up and smiled.

'I do not see that there will be any difficulty here.'

Perhaps Anselm secretly hoped there would be, so that he could go on delaying, but with the king's plain agreement there was no help for it but that he must keep his promise and do homage. To perform the act of homage was to concede on a point of principle. For the king, for Flambard and most certainly for Anselm, it was a matter of some significance, marking a considerable advance towards full acceptance of the office of archbishop. It must occupy the centre of formal ceremonial and public witness which, after further discussion, was arranged for later that day.

Then the king rose from his chair, descended the dais and embraced Anselm. The journey to Canterbury was not yet complete but a great step forward had been taken.

'It all went off without a hitch,' said Ranulf that evening as he reported on the event. 'A formal ceremony. Bishops and ministers in attendance. The king gracious, Anselm dignified. Whatever it cost him, Anselm has given fealty to the king. He has sworn an oath. Finally, Firmin, we have homage. There remains only enthronement and consecration then we can all sleep at night.'

'Master, is this the fruit of you and Baldwin working together?'

'Perhaps, Firmin, and yes, I haven't forgotten it was your idea. Baldwin has promised me to get him down to Canterbury by the end of September. Once there, you can be sure, Osbern and the monks will consecrate him. By force, if necessary.

'Why is the consecration of such importance, master?'

Spotting another opportunity to hold forth on a topic that greatly interested him, Ranulf replied: 'First, can you hazard an answer?'

Firmin could only offer a reasonable guess. 'Allegory?'

'Well, to a degree, yes, allegory and symbolism being much the same. One thing standing for another, in the broad sense; one meaning laid over another. Symbolically, or allegorically, if you will, the thing, or person, to be consecrated is ritually taken out of the profane world and dedicated to the service of God. A consecrated thing or person takes on a new meaning and is elevated to a new state. The new state is permanent and the rite of consecration can never be repeated. It is far greater than a blessing. A blessing will do for a mere abbot, but a consecration is a different order of thing. It is a sacrament of immense solemnity and power. Have you ever seen one, Firmin?'

'No, master, never.'

'Serve me well, lad, and one day I'll invite you to mine.'

****

Within a few days of each other, Edith and Gunhild had gone from Wilton, leaving Aefled and Agnes bereft and baffled. Aefled, in particular, was disturbed by Gunhild's uncharacteristic behaviour and, even though swept up in the romantic elopement, half-believing and half-doubting the possibility of happiness, she was inclined to think that Count Alan's arrival had been a great misfortune to her friend. For herself, with Robert now discharged from Count Alan's service and free to return to his estates, she looked forward to a few days of travel back to Castle St Mary's under his protection in the company of Agnes. By early September, she was home, reunited with her daughter and slipping back into a quiet provincial life. Then the devastating news reached them in a letter from Gunhild.

The first sign that all was not well, wrote Gunhild, came ten days after the elopement. By then, they were staying at a manor near Bury St Edmund's, occupied by Count Alan's tenants who bore the unlikely names of Ribald, Bodin and Bardulf. Gunhild was quickly discovering the strange composition of her lover's family. These men were his illegitimate brothers and their housekeeper was their old wet nurse, Orwen. To this unlikely group of people, Count Alan brought her until they could arrange to be married in the great abbey church of St Edmundsbury, of which he was a benefactor. Immediately afterwards they would set out towards their new life together at Richmond.

'I never regretted for a moment what I had done,' Gunhild wrote. 'Count Alan was kind to me, he showed me every mark of affection. We planned to marry as soon as I could establish my secular status. I was never a nun and had taken no vows. There would be no hindrance to my quickly passing into the married state. I knew the embrace of a man and the pleasure of the flesh, we lived together and he called me wife. He hoped at last to have children born from our love, the only love, he said, he had known. We were transformed by joy into new beings. Aefled, I attained the highest happiness for the briefest time. But now I am utterly distraught.'

The first sign of what was to come occurred when Count Alan was about to ride out one morning. As he took the reins from Bodin, who was holding the bridle, they both noticed that one of his hands was swollen.

'That's a great paw you have there, Count, but it lacks a fellow,' said Bodin.

It was true. One hand was enlarged and inflamed. 'Curious, it does not hurt,' he said and went about his business. That night when he returned the swelling had not diminished and, as he sat at supper in the beamed chamber of the manor hall, where Orwen waited on the men and Gunhild poured some of the local brew into wooden beakers, he complained of stiffness in the neck.

'It's age, brother,' said Bodin, 'or it's twisting your neck to look lovingly at your Gunhild. That's what's doing it.'

'It's the bolster,' offered Orwen, 'you've flattened it these nights together.'

Indeed, everyone was inclined to make a joke of it, at first. But over the next few days when the swelling did not subside and Count Alan became restless, Gunhild began to wonder what was wrong. Then he began to complain of feeling unwell, the swelling spread to his arm and he began to suffer painful contractions of the muscles.

'What can be done, Orwen? How can we help him?' she asked in rising panic.

Orwen suggested treatment with fennel. It was tried but had no effect. Some sort of toxin seemed to be spreading inexorably through his body, weakening him hour by hour. He became short of breath and complained he was suffocating. At this point, he was forced to his bed, something that he had resisted until then, being convinced that if once he lay down with the disease he would never rise from it. Orwen prescribed infusions of various mints, then poultices of honey and marshmallow, but nothing had any effect.

Although close to panic, Gunhild tried to appear calm as she sat at his bedside hour after hour watching the terrible progress of the disease through all his limbs. Now, for the first time, her thoughts turned to God. Was this a visitation of heaven's vengeance for her renunciation of convent life? Was this her punishment, to lose the last chance of earthly happiness which marriage to this man would give her?

That night, before the disease reached his face, closing his jaw and locking it so that he could no longer speak, he held her hand and whispered: 'Regret nothing, Gunhild. For a little time, we had a great love.'

Gunhild shook with grief. Hot tears rolled down her cheeks and fell on his swollen hand resting on the bed, the hand where the disease had started, the hand with which he had plucked the rose at Wilton, the hand which had been pricked by a thorn.

During the night there were violent spasms, endured silently for he could speak no word, and in the morning, he was seized with a convulsion and died instantly.

The effect on Gunhild was devastating. She sat by her dead lover the whole day without moving, speaking or eating. It fell to Orwen and the brothers to lay out the body and summon the only man who could manage this situation, Count Alan Niger, his brother and heir.

'Count Alan Niger has been good to me,' continued Gunhild's letter, 'and has done everything necessary for his brother's obsequies. He was on his way to Winchester to seek the king's approval of our marriage but came here within four days. He has offered me his protection even to the extent of marriage so that my future will be secure. Count Alan has been buried at St Edmund's with all due rites. And so his earthly remains are gone. In my distress, I have written to Anselm asking for spiritual guidance. I am desolate. I am broken by the world, Aefled, but it was the world I sought. Prayer is no consolation for me. Of all people, you alone will understand that.'

At the end of her letter, Gunhild added: 'Do not grieve for me, Aefled. God will lend me strength adequate for this trial. I will stay on here for a time before I decide what to do. I will write again.'

And that was the sad end of the passionate affair between Count Alan and Gunhild as it was revealed to Aefled. She put the letter away and wept bitterly.

When Robert heard of the death of his overlord, his first thought was about how it would affect him personally. All Count Alan's estates and tenantries had passed to Alan Niger so he would continue to owe fealty for his northern possessions to the same great family of Breton overlords. He imagined that things would continue more or less as before, affecting neither the service he owed, nor the income he made from the northern manors. But then, at the end of September, from out of the north, came more bad news. King Malcolm, having returned to Scotland, still reeling with outrage at his insulting treatment by William, gave vent to his anger by raising an army of Scots, disaffected Norman barons and mercenaries, and raiding into the border country. It was a full scale attack which spared nothing and no one, he burned villages, ruined crops, and gave full rein to widespread destruction and slaughter. Thus he sent a bloody message to the Norman king. 'No more pretence at talking. Come and fight.'

The immediate effect was to destabilise the border country, especially the great tracts of Cumbria under the lordship of Count Alan and the Northumbrian territories of Robert Mowbray, Earl of Northumberland. Count Alan Niger's inheritance was under threat and, being determined to defend it, he went north, leaving Gunhild in the care of Abbot Baldwin who lodged her in his house. There, she felt near to Count Alan and often went to kneel at his tomb in the south transept, bending over the place where he lay, hands clasped, lips mouthing prayers that would not come, a sight which drew looks of pity from the monks. Now utterly abandoned, without protection and living far from the people she knew, Gunhild gave herself up to the full force of despair. In this low state, she wrote a second letter to Anselm, a confessional letter, full of spiritual turmoil. She was reaching out to the only person who might offer comfort and solace, a man to whom she had written before in moments of crisis and with whom she had established a precedent for honest counsel. She told him all that had happened, assuring him that she had not spurned Christ, that she was never a nun but a woman who truly loved and was loved in return. Out of Christian charity and a desire to do right by his dead brother, she wrote, Count Alan Niger had offered her his protection. What should she do? She was weak, confused and feared to lose the love of Christ. This, and more, she wrote down on parchment from the abbey scriptorium and sent to Prior Osbern at Canterbury in the expectation that Anselm would receive it on his arrival there.

****

Meanwhile, the reluctant archbishop-elect was travelling to Canterbury at snail's pace, finding excuses for every kind of delay which Baldwin had to manage with every kind of tactful manoeuvre. It was not until the third week of September that he finally entered his diocese while Malcolm was ravaging the north and the king, failing to see what he had brought on himself, was fulminating against all Scots.

Welcoming him into the refectory at Christchurch on the evening of his arrival, Prior Osbern and the monks of the chapter house gathered to hear what he would have to say. Great things were expected from him as a renowned scholar and man of eminently holy habits. Prior Osbern had been eagerly pressing for his acceptance ever since the election in March and had written desperate letters urging him to come quickly. Many had high hopes of Anselm's incumbency which would see the prestige of Canterbury rise from its lapsed state to a new resurgent vigour. But that evening Anselm cried off giving a speech or entertaining the monks with an appropriate homily. 'I am tired, Baldwin,' he said, 'ask them to excuse me,' and he left, leaning on the arm of the little monk, Eustace. As it turned out, this phrase 'ask them to excuse me' might well have served in the coming years as his motto. For a man whom everyone expected to fill a vacancy, he was destined to be notoriously absent.

Within a few days of arriving at Canterbury, however, Anselm was stamping himself on the community. Once he had recovered his energies, he went on a tour around the various foundations, was introduced to the monks, sat with them at meals, discoursed freely about the rule and was prevailed on to give one or two of his famous homilies. In one of them, he likened himself to an owl, which some thought a fanciful comparison: 'Just as an owl is glad, when she is in her hole with her chicks, and just as she is unhappy when she is attacked and torn by crows and rooks, so it is with me.' Simple natural images peppered his talks with easy to grasp parables and everybody thought the glad owl was Anselm, safe and happy in Canterbury among his tonsured chicks, with whom he would stay and never venture out again among the rooks and crows of William's court. From such reassuring images, the monks took to heart as they set about the preparations for the long-delayed enthronement.

'Master,' said Baldwin one morning a few days before the ceremony was due to take place, 'there's someone I would like you to meet.'

Baldwin gestured the man to enter. He came forward, went on one knee and kissed Anselm's hand. He was of slight build, about thirty or so with thick sandy hair around his tonsure, a sprinkling of freckles around a fleshy nose and blue-grey eyes of startling ardour and ingenuousness.

'Welcome, young man, I greet you in Christ's name.'

'Master, this young man is Eadmer. He tells me he has met you before.'

Anselm turned his full benignity on Eadmer, smiling to cover the fact that he did not remember him at all. 'Tell me about yourself, Eadmer.'

'Master, I am from a poor Kentish family and I was brought up here at Christchurch by the monks. I met you on your first visit to Canterbury fifteen years ago when you were Abbot of Bec. I have never forgotten that visit. You spoke of Old English piety and defended the English Saints and the feast days of the English Church, whose worship was slipping from the minds of men under the new customs of the Norman church. You spoke so highly of St Dunstan, former Archbishop of Canterbury and now a holy saint whose body lies here in the church, master, that I and all the English monks felt that we had come alive again. Master, it is my dearest wish is to serve you.'

Although moved by the man's ardour, Anselm had no recollection of ever expressing these opinions. In fact, they were so far from his present views that he thought Eadmer was imputing to him something he had heard from someone else. In any case, he had no employment for him.

'Thank you, Eadmer,' he said graciously 'but I fear I can do nothing for you. It is my intention to keep a small household.'

'A small household, indeed,' countered Baldwin, 'in keeping with the monastic rule. But, master, an archbishop must, for all that, live in a certain style. To do otherwise brings discredit to the office.'

Somewhat surprised at this intervention, but willing to be guided by the judgement of others in affairs not connected with theology, Anselm said: 'What do you say then, Baldwin? Can we find a place for this keen young man?'

Baldwin, who had made the introduction for that very purpose, suggested that Eadmer had considerable skills in writing, note-taking and compiling and ought to be of use in the copying of the great work, still in progress, the *Cur Deus Homo.*

'Very well, let it be so,' said Anselm agreeably.

Although no one knew it then, this introduction would be of the greatest significance in all their lives. Baldwin, overworked and hard-pressed for time, found himself so occupied in managing the great man's affairs that he did not have time to write the work which would proclaim his master's sainthood to posterity. On the lookout for a keen scribe with ability but little independence of mind, he had fastened on Eadmer, an impressionable monk, a Canterbury man born and bred, and an ardent devotee of the new archbishop. And so, that evening, thanks to the efforts of Baldwin, a momentous meeting took place between a man on the way to being a saint and the man on the way to becoming his biographer.

Later, when they were alone, Baldwin gave Eadmer his instructions.

'I want you to write up his sayings and doings. I want you to keep a record of his travels. Make a note of everything, even your own impressions. You will have to live closely with him, observing all aspects of his life, as I do. Sometimes you will write down the information I give you. Is that clear?'

Eadmer nodded eagerly, like the young man everyone kept saying he was, though he was over thirty. And indeed there was a youthful, sometimes juvenile, aspect to his enthusiasms. But youthful fads are quick to fade, whereas Eadmer's earnest devotion to Anselm would last unflagging for many years.

Eadmer had not been in his new position long when a letter came for Anselm, brought by travelling lay-brothers from St Edmundsbury. Since Canterbury had some fiefs in that area, Eadmer thought it might be important and took it to his master immediately. But Anselm, ever ready to postpone unpleasant things and assuming that it would contain requests or complaints, left it unopened. And so Gunhild's letter was put aside until after September 25th the day on which, finally and to the utter relief of Baldwin and the harassed household, Anselm's enthronement finally took place.

The ceremony went off with all the pomp and seriousness that human ingenuity could devise around a man sitting in a seat. Or rather, in the case of Canterbury, two seats. Anselm was first installed on the diocesan throne, the *cathedra*, from which he would preside, as successor to Lanfranc and bishop of the see of Canterbury, over the oldest diocese in England. Then he was enthroned on the seat of St Augustine, founder of the English church, who had led the evangelical mission to England nearly five hundred years earlier. In a ceremony presided over by the Archbishop of York, the *prognosticon* was read out, a Bible verse found at random and believed to indicate the character of the newly sanctified prelate. The words which fell to his lot were from Saint Luke: "…he bade many: And sent his servant at supper time to say to them that they were bidden, Come; for all things are now ready. And they all with one consent began to make excuse." No quotation could have been more fitting. After five months of making excuses, of every kind of delay and obstruction, Anselm had, at last, come to where he was bidden.

As he sat, occupying the centre of the historic ceremony, Anselm thought about the peculiar Englishness of the rites. Whatever impression he had given Eadmer, the old English church had never been of interest to him. He was Italian and Benedictine in outlook, thoroughly steeped in Continental practices and had no understanding of the sensitivities of monks like Eadmer, aggrieved by the Normanisation of their long insular traditions. Perhaps Eadmer would prove to be of use in explaining some of this past, he thought, as he moved from seat to seat, feeling the solemn weight of mighty expectations descending on his frail shoulders. This is what he had fought against for so long, this was what he had tried to avoid. The words of David's psalm kept echoing in his head: "Make haste, O God, to deliver me, make haste to help me, O Lord." Even at this late hour, he began to wonder if he might still resist this horrible burden, escape the consecration and find a way to return to the peaceful obscurity of a monastery. Then he saw, glaring at him from the sea of faces in the nave, the most unwelcome of men. What was Ranulf Flambard doing here? How typical of William to sneak a witness into the solemnities, as if he expected a last minute evasion. How unfeeling to send this man who was always in the background of their disputes.

Knowing his presence would be unwelcome, Ranulf had tried to hide discreetly among the ranks of distinguished guests and found himself rather enjoying the proceedings. It was his great ambition one day to attain to such a state; an enthronment in a bishopric would crown a life of dedication to royal service. His eyes were on Durham, presently occupied by St Calais who was conveniently aged and could not last much longer. Durham was rich and the magnificent Romanesque cathedral presently under construction would not require repair or embellishment for years. In some ways, Durham was even more prestigious than Canterbury, since the local authority of the Bishop of Durham was almost equal to the king's. With a rank equivalent to that of an Earl, the bishop could appoint all his own officials and was entitled to summon and preside over a judicial court. Durham was, in point of fact, a quasi-independent fiefdom. Naturally, the occupier of such a post must be indisputably loyal to the crown, a man of proven worth and achievement, such as himself. But he frequently had to remind himself that, in the attainment of such a goal, he must be humble before the Almighty in whose ultimate dispensation, after all, it was.

At the end of the long and impressive ritual, when the newly enthroned archbishop was receiving well-wishers, Ranulf Flambard sought him out. He had no wish to spoil the archbishop's great day, but there were certain outstanding matters to be wound up. Displeased though Anselm was to see him there, he was about to be very much more displeased by the reason for his coming. The bishopric had been in royal custody for four and a half years, much of that time under Flambard's own supervision on behalf of the king. Revenue had been his particular concern and he had kept a steady stream of money flowing into the king's coffers. In addition, during the vacancy, William had created over ninety knights' fiefs on Canterbury lands to provide the horsemen who were now needed to repel the incursions of Malcolm. Ostensibly, the return of these fiefs had been agreed at Winchester, just before Anselm made homage, but in the rush to secure homage before he changed his mind, the matter had never been officially resolved. Flambard had come, like some dreadful figure from Anselm's worst nightmare, to serve a writ on him on the very day of his enthronement.

'I refuse to see that man,' said Anselm. 'I shall be drawn into the sin of wrath. He inflames me with uncharitable thoughts.'

So it fell to Baldwin to treat with Flambard during the days of the transference of the see, when the unravelling of complex affairs forced them to spend considerable time working together.

'Our trouble, Baldwin, is that your master is exactly the sort of character most likely to provoke the king. Violence or guile he can understand, or even outright opposition, as was the case with William St Calais who actually rebelled but was forgiven. But Anselm's habit of sleeping out an argument then suddenly waking up to make impossible demands, is infuriating.'

Ranulf Flambard spoke to Baldwin quite openly in this way and discovered that Baldwin understood this point of view even though he did not share it. In his opinion, saints were exceptional men who behaved exceptionally because they were pervaded by the Holy Spirit.

'You must understand that, in view of what is happening in the north, the king is in desperate need of knights, therefore their fiefs must be confirmed. They need to equip themselves and their horses.'

'But my master was assured that there would be no diminution of Canterbury lands. That he would have them just as at the time of Lanfranc.'

'Which is exactly the case. The fiefs I am talking about have been created from properties acquired during the vacancy. They represent no diminution. All we want is a legal settlement.'

'Hence the writ,' said Baldwin.

'Oh, that's a mere formality, think nothing of it. Just get his agreement.'

'You know, Flambard,' said Baldwin, 'it would be wrong to think that Anselm is an opponent of royal authority or of secular policies. He knows that such policies demand their own set of virtues; energy, for example, and practical wisdom, and these he can admire in the king. That is why he did homage a few weeks ago. But it must be clear that he did not accept investiture from the king. He would never contemplate paying money for his office, in the usual way of investiture. That would be an act of simony which is expressly against the pope's will.'

'Of course, I see that,' said Ranulf who knew that a demand for money would soon be on the way. 'This has nothing to do with simony. But a fact which Anselm has to acknowledge is that, from now on, he will find himself closely involved in the temporal affairs of the kingdom. William needs to raise cavalry and Anselm will need to reassure the knights that, when they go to war against Malcolm, their fiefs will not be compromised.'

And so the arguments between Anselm and William were carried on through their representatives. Tempers were not lost, nor insults exchanged, but, on the contrary, reasoned discussion allowed them to arrive at last at vague but acceptable compromises. The king's interests at Canterbury were wound up in a few days and there remained only one more step on Anselm's path to the archbishopric, the consecration. With assurances from Baldwin that it would happen in the next few weeks, Ranulf Flambard returned to Winchester just in time to hear the latest thunderclap of news from the north.

****

Even before his consecration, which he was determined to delay as long as possible, Anselm began to write letters under his new title of archbishop and was positively encouraged to do so by Baldwin.

'Now is the time to proclaim yourself, master, and enter into the full authority of your office. Let the world see that the shameful vacancy is ended.'

Still dragging his feet, Anselm set to work, but his interest was rather more in doctrinal and spiritual matters, or the finer points of Benedictine rule, than in worldly affairs. So the letters to the pope and to fellow bishops and archbishops in England and the continent, which should have been a matter of priority, were put aside for a more pressing issue. Religious duty, private counsel and, most importantly, the saving of a soul, seemed to him more deserving of urgency. And so, immediately upon reading Gunhild's desperate letter, he took up his pen to reply.

'Anselm, by the ordination of God, Archbishop of Canterbury, to his beloved sister and daughter, Gunhild,' he began.

There was only one course of action he could advise and that was a speedy return to the convent. In his view, Gunhild had a spouse in Christ whom she had scorned by running away, exchanging the purity of spiritual vocation for the impurity of carnal pleasure. Setting out to write in a consolatory and encouraging tone, he found it impossible to prevent a shrill note of panic, for he was convinced that Gunhild had risked eternal damnation by what she had done.

'It is impossible for you to be saved in any way unless you return to the habit and the life of a nun.' Her choice was stark, her position precarious, her soul at risk. To put off the habit and renounce the conventual life was a great sin. Almost beside himself with anxiety about the state of Gunhild's soul, Anselm did not mince words. 'Strive and shatter your heart, grieve deeply about your fall. Throw off and trample the secular dress you have put on and assume the habit of the spouse of Christ which you have cast off.'

Although sprinkled with kindly phrases to his "dearest daughter" and "my daughter", the letter was full of affrighted admonitions to return to the convent and throw herself on Christ's mercy. 'If you refuse to do this,' he ended darkly, 'everybody will be against you, and I and the Church of God will do what we know is to be done in such a case.'

The effect on Gunhild was disturbing and in no way consoling. She wondered if, in assuming the archbishopric, Anselm's views had hardened. Certainly, he sounded less lenient and forgiving than in the old days when their correspondence had been intellectually frank but always warm. Not knowing what to do, she remained at the abbey of St Edmundsbury, close to her dead lover, ground down by grief. Desperate for consolation, she took up her pen and wrote once more to Anselm, this time trying to justify her actions. The second letter disturbed him even more than the first since there was no sign that Gunhild was minded to return to the convent. Was she now adding the sin of disobedience to the long list of her transgressions?

'I still greet you and call you most beloved daughter,' he wrote in reply, 'because I do not yet despair of what I desire for you, namely that you may yet regain your senses through the visitation of divine grace and return to Christ.' He reminded her that he was her 'true friend' and was admonishing his 'sister and daughter' out of concern for her immortal soul. He decided to spare nothing in order to save her, even the harshest words. 'Your loved one who loved you, Count Alan Rufus, where is he now? He delighted you while alive, now he is rotting flesh and putrefaction. What if God had taken him away from this life as a punishment?' he asked. Or as a prevention from further wickedness? In his panic, he did not scruple to bring out the weapon of moral blackmail, targeting her most tender feelings towards Count Alan Niger, even stooping to making puns on his name.

'Why are you not afraid that, because of you, God may kill Count Alan Niger by a similar death, or—what is worse—if you are united with him, God may condemn him with you to eternal damnation? Oh, would that he be black to you and you black to him.' The blackness of sin and the name 'Niger' led Anselm to obvious and needless, if not obtuse, puns which he regretted later, but as he thought about these events, solicitude turned to panic and then to desperate and rather cruel admonitions. 'You know that I advise, beg, beseech and command you by the authority which permits and obliges me to do so, to resume the habit of monastic life and return to the grace of God.' Anselm would leave Gunhild in no doubt about the peril of her position. All dreams of a worldly life, of passion and love for a man of flesh and blood, were shattered, she must now think only about her divine spouse and a soul which was perilously close to damnation. In this way, dashing off equal amounts of love and consternation in tortured panic-stricken phrases, he laid out in the starkest terms what she must do. By now, thoroughly alarmed at the strange goings-on at Wilton, Anselm sent off a message to Bishop Walkelin at Sarum asking him to make inquiries into the affairs of the abbey and give a full account of what he found. Baldwin, in the meantime, dismayed by his master's inexplicable interest in such trivial affairs, was doing his utmost to nudge him towards the consecration.

****

King William Rufus often got angry but did not often throw things in rage. On the day the news came, in late November, he did. The hapless projectile, a silver goblet, planed straight towards Dunmore's head, spraying a trail of Anjou in its wake.

'Holy Face of Lucca! That damned Mowbray!' he yelled, 'that treacherous dog! He brings dishonour on me!'

This was not the reaction Ranulf was expecting, since the news that provoked this outburst was, from a certain point of view, eminently to the king's advantage.

King Malcolm was dead.

But it was the manner of his death which caused the goblet to fly at the head of Dunmore, who had brought the news. William Rufus did not fear open fight, in fact, he rather relished it, whether he was putting down internal rebellions or launching full-scale assaults against his brother on the Norman mainland. But any hint of treachery or low, murderous attacks or sneaking ambushes were not methods he could publicly countenance. Robert Mowbray, Earl of Northumberland, in league with his nephew, Morel of Bamburgh, had trapped Malcolm and a small party travelling to a rendezvous close by the swollen river Alne and killed him and his eldest son, Edward, who were rumoured to have been unarmed at the time. There was more than a whiff of dishonour in the affair. It coupled the king's name with an act of downright malevolence. What Mowbray had done bordered on *lèse-majesté*, for the killing of a king was a cause of great disquiet among kings.

For all his faults, endlessly castigated by monastic chroniclers, William Rufus prided himself on forceful and open dealing and enjoyed a reputation as a warrior of some ability and proven success. He took care of his troops, promptly ransomed prisoners and won sufficient glory to satisfy subordinates. He had even received the basics of a military education, being instructed in the famous handbook of soldiers, the *De Re Militari* of Vegetius. This was a treatise on how to organise a Roman army, of which some parts were still relevant, although many were not. What William had learned about how to confront an enemy in possession of camels and elephants was never tested in battle, but he did know that his father had adopted one important dictum from Vegetius: 'It is better to overcome the enemy either by creating famine, by raiding or by inflicting terror, rather than by coming to battle where chance, rather than heroism, usually affects the outcome.' So much for valour and glory. But William Rufus liked to think of himself as a Caesar, a magnanimous commander, rigorous in warfare but capable of clemency, a war leader not lost to all honour. Robert Mowbray clearly was, and this he took as a personal affront. What was Mowbray doing cutting down his enemy by stealth when he could do it openly and with honour for himself?

'How do we answer this, Flambard?'

'For the moment, my lord,' Ranulf replied without hesitation, 'not at all.'

In Ranulf's view, the death of King Malcolm was a godsend. All plans to march north to punish the Scottish king for his violent raids into English territory could now be put on hold. There would follow a period of uncertainty in Scotland which would weaken its power. Malcolm had never proved to be the loyal vassal and friendly neighbour that England had desired to further its interests. Perhaps now it would be possible to wrest lasting concessions from a successor. Ranulf advised caution, wait and see, letting things take their course until a clear policy would emerge. What a lucky stroke that William did not at this moment find himself married to Edith, whose value had suddenly plummeted. As for Mowbray, the king could bide his time and wait for an appropriate opportunity to strike against him. It occurred to Ranulf that Mowbray had been seeking revenge for Malcolm's plan to marry his daughter to Count Alan Rufus which would have meant a northern alliance in which

Mowbray would have been trapped. It was in revenge for this, Ranulf assumed, that Mowbray had committed his treacherous act. An act which had terrible repercussions for Edith's mother, Queen Margaret. Having lost her husband and eldest son, she fell ill, declined rapidly and pined away. Not long after the ambush, she died.

'My lord king,' said Ranulf in response to this news, 'the maid Edith is now an orphan. It would be right and just that you offer her protection. Let her come to England, to her aunt Christina at Wilton, perhaps. Be generous, my lord, offer to pay her keep, let her continue her education. In your wardship, she can be disposed in marriage where you will.'

The king was inclined to accept this advice on all points apart from Wilton. The news that Count Alan Rufus had abducted Gunhild from Wilton a few weeks after his own visit there, and that he would have married her without royal permission, had he not been prevented from doing so by dying mysteriously a few days later, filled William Rufus with distrust of the place. Besides, Christina hated him and would continue to poison the child's mind against him. And, after all, he had nothing to show from his own visit to Wilton, save sourness and a wilted rose.

'Flambard, I grieve for Count Alan. A man fit for admiration and respect. A loyal vassal and brave. What possessed him? What happened to him at Wilton? Did he lose his senses?'

'I can offer no explanation, my lord, either of his conduct or of his death.'

'Many say he was struck down by God for violating a nun.'

'Many say that, my lord, and there is a certain mysteriousness in the confluence of these events. In September, Count Alan is struck by disease and dies. In November, Malcolm is ambushed and killed. Within a few weeks of leaving Wilton, both men have encountered terrible fates.'

William Rufus gave a shudder. 'It's as though they have been punished for taking away from Wilton women whom God had called to his special blessing.'

Ranulf would say in after times that the king was genuinely moved by Count Alan's death and the reasons for it. For several days he was moody and downcast, seeming to absorb great lessons from this event. He made inquiries after Gunhild, wishing to know more about her whereabouts, the events at Wilton and the manner of Count Alan's death.

After an interim of gloom, the first indication that the king was recovering his spirits came one morning during a discussion of the king's illness and his return to full health.

'Since that brush with death I have never felt so well, Flambard,' he announced.

'It is indeed gratifying to see you strong and energetic, my lord. Do you consider that, in this renewed state of vigour, you might once more turn your thoughts to marriage?'

William's reply was swift and characteristic.

'Now, I ask you, Flambard, in regard to health, was marriage good for Count Alan?'

****

After replying to Gunhild's letter, Aefled spent an anxious period of waiting, feeling cut off from the flow of events and news. Since her visit to Wilton with its mysteries and excitements, her world had shrunk to the size of a small provincial keep, as damp and bleak as her spirits. She longed for news from the outside, from Gunhild in St Edmundsbury and Edith who had simply vanished into Scotland and was now an unprotected orphan with no settled home. What would become of that extraordinary child?

The immediate impact of these events on her life at Castle St Mary's was that Robert was once again called to the service of his lord. That lord now being Count Alan Niger, Robert found himself under orders to ride north where Niger was going to establish his presence in Richmond, stake his claim to the Cumbrian inheritance and fortify his borderlands against any further incursions from Scotland. Whenever Robert left for active service, Aefled was aware that he might never return. He was no longer young, now forty-seven years old, still fit for the saddle or for battle, hardy, solid and rarely ill. But, so had Count Alan been. When Robert left, at the end of November, to ride north into the teeth of winter, Aefled had no way of knowing when, or if, she would see him again. She kept Eleanor close under her eyes, anxiously wondering if, like little Edith, she might soon lose her father to a treacherous sword.

In Robert's absence, she relied heavily on Hugh, the steward, who had been at the castle for many years and knew every detail of the estates and their administration. But when Robert was absent he always made a point of involving Aefled. They worked well together and their long acquaintance had established trust between them; so much so, that Aefled could even tell Hugh about her religious doubts and how much she struggled with the faith.

'I find it impossible to believe all the things the church tells us to believe,' she said to Hugh one day. 'But then I feel fearful for my children because I cannot pray.'

'I'm afraid, my lady, that your doubts are the legacy of Isaac's teaching.'

Hugh had hit on the great truth of Aefled's life. Years ago a Jewish scholar called Isaac had come to England in the wake of the Conquest and, being attached to Robert's affairs, he had settled near the village. By chance, one of those astounding chances that occur in chaotic times, he had begun a friendship with Aefled's father who agreed that Isaac should give his daughter instruction in Norman French and Latin 'to make the village stronger.' In the early days, Isaac's teaching had been a source of freedom, opening her mind to strange new worlds. She had embraced it with passionate enthusiasm, thinking it gave her all the answers. Now she had grown up, had children and was encountering the harsh realities of the world, in which the consolation of earnest belief played the most important part in everyone's daily life and from which she felt excluded. This was the 'legacy' of which Hugh spoke.

Some years ago, Isaac had settled in London, where there was an established Jewish community in which he felt safe, and there her beloved teacher was growing old and infirm. But he had many Christian friends who enabled him to transmit letters and he wrote regularly to keep her informed of his affairs. By the same means, she wrote back to tell him about the children of the school, about Tancred, Maria's studious son, who seemed destined for the church and the English boys, Edward and Alfred, who were growing wild in their ways and were a constant source of worry. She explained that Maria, her friend and closest companion, had been abandoned by her husband, the undersheriff, Roger, who was living with a concubine on his manor at Ranulfstead. Maria, in turn, consoled herself with Arnoud, the constable of the castle with whom she had been in love for years. When Aefled had to summarise affairs at the castle in this way, she doubted that anyone could say that it was a disciplined, conventional household. 'I do not know what impression my letters make on you, Isaac,' she wrote in her last letter, 'but I fear it is not what you would wish. The source of all my pleasure remains my dearest Eleanor, she at least brings me nothing but joy. You would be pleased by her progress in learning for she far outstrips the boys.'

One day, towards Christmas, a messenger arrived at the castle with a letter. She hoped it was from Gunhild, from whom she had heard no word for several months, or from Robert to say he had arrived safely at Richmond. But being busy about some pressing affairs, she put it aside and did not have the opportunity to read it until late at night. Setting a beeswax candle close by, she sat in Robert's chair, opened the letter and began to read the unfamiliar script. It was in Latin, the classical Latin used in the east which Isaac had taught her, stylish and formal, evidently from the hand of a scholar. But it was not Isaac's hand. As she read the painful content, her eyes began to fill with tears. Dashing them away to prevent them falling on the manuscript she read on to the end and then began again as the terrible news sank in.

Isaac was dead.

At the end, she read: 'Peace be upon you, written by the hand of Rabbi Simon in London at the Poultry.'

Underneath he had written: 'almost with his last breath, Isaac wished me to tell you this: "Do not grieve for me. Take comfort from Lucretius. There is neither heaven nor hell, but simply the void and the atoms, to which I now return. Lucretius said: Nature resolves everything into its component atoms and never reduces anything to nothing. I, therefore, go from this life, but I shall not be nothing."

As she read these words, she saw Isaac's face and heard his voice again, calm, reassuring, wise. The years of their friendship came rushing back in memories intense with sadness and joy. He had been her teacher, guide, a second father and had understood her mind better than anyone in the world. She felt suddenly chill, as though a wind was blowing sharp and raw about her. She was losing those closest to her. Robert and her sons were far off. Gunhild and Edith had gone away into unknown places. And now Isaac, the great wandering spirit at the centre of her childhood, had departed for his home among the atoms.

****

Chapter Seven
Gunhild's Secret

True to his word, Baldwin succeeded in bringing about Anselm's consecration before Christmas. Three weeks before, on December 4th, just as the king's cavalcade was heading once more to Gloucester, the final act of the long-drawn-out drama was staged in Christchurch, Canterbury. In a ceremony led by Thomas, Archbishop of York, before a congregation of the most prominent bishops of England, including William St Calais, Osmund of Sarum and Bishop Walkelin, Anselm reached the end of a long, tormented journey into high office. Afterwards, Anselm and his entourage travelled to Gloucester where the details of the consecration became known.

'I would have liked to tell you, Firmin, that it all went off without a hitch. But, alas, I can tell you no such thing.'

'What happened, master?'

'Almost at the outset, a row erupted over the form of words. When Bishop Walkelin read out the writ of election, Thomas of York objected to the part where Canterbury is called the "supreme diocese of the whole of Britain metropolitan". Thomas protested loudly that he would not have York treated as less than Canterbury and that the word 'metropolitan' must be dropped. So there was an unseemly bandying back and forth while they came up with a different formula. Eventually, they settled on calling the Archbishop of Canterbury "primate of the whole of Britain". You see how much can rest on a single word, Firmin. That is why clerks and officials must always choose them with care.'

'These bishops seem every bit as obsessed with their dues and precedence as courtiers and nobles, master.'

'They are. And never forget they are barons, Firmin, who have made homage to the king. That's why William doesn't want that allegiance complicated by the recognition of a pope.'

Ranulf poured himself some wine and stood sipping thoughtfully.

'But did you observe how warmly the king welcomed him when here arrived here last week, thinking their disputes were at an end? Did you see how they walked about together like two old friends who had never had a tiff in their lives?'

'Master, I heard about it. And people are saying that the bull and the sheep have stopped going around.'

'Well, people say many foolish things.'

Ranulf set down his wine cup and went into a corner to relieve himself in a bucket set by for the purpose.

'But all that goodwill, Firmin, how long did it last? How long before Anselm was once again antagonising him with complaints? And do you know what their first argument was about?'

'No, master, I never heard.'

'Hair. Hair! Can you believe it?' Easing himself back into his breeches, Ranulf went over to Firmin and tousled his mop of unruly brown hair. 'This stuff that grows from your head.'

Anselm had long been troubled by the morals of the court and had complained to William about it. Most especially, he deplored the fashion among the young courtiers of wearing their hair long like girls.

'He says the young men mince abroad with their locks well combed, glancing about and winking in an ungodly fashion. These days, he complains, you never see shaved Norman necks at court, it's all tousled locks and fashions. He couldn't criticise the king directly, but it is William's long hair and fondness for fine clothes that he abhors.'

'Along with the rowdy company he keeps, master, his companions in drink and profligacy.'

'Profligacy? A fine word, Firmin, where did you get that from?'

'Anselm uses it a lot. And you must admit, master that it exists at court. Anselm is not wrong.'

'Well, yes, let's allow him that. But he is not going to reform the court with a sermon to a king who grows his hair long, wears fine apparel and sets the tone among his followers. We can deplore such types as Walter Tirel and Robert FitzHaimo, but the king gives them licence to behave as they do.'

'But surely, master, their great falling out wasn't over hair.'

'You're right Firmin. It was, of course, over money.'

At this time, when the king's projected offensive in Scotland had been indefinitely postponed, all his attention was turned to Normandy which he was trying to wrest from his brother Robert. An invasion was planned for early next spring, for which the king needed to collect money from every possible source. When Anselm offered to donate 500 pounds of silver, the king was at first pleased and ready to accept.

'I advised him to take the money,' said Ranulf, 'and he was prepared to do so. Then some of those long-haired types got to him, saying that tight-fisted Anselm ought to pay out at least a thousand, anything less was treating him with contempt. So William asked for a thousand, at which Anselm balked. There was a great row and the upshot was Anselm gave the original 500 pounds to the poor. So now bitterness festers once more between them. I think we will all live to regret the day we elected him archbishop.'

'What is Baldwin saying?'

'He says Anselm was concerned about offering a thousand pounds because that's the going rate for a bishopric. It would look as if he was paying for his office. He would be accused of simony which is something he holds in horror. And he has a point. But all this unpleasantness might have been avoided if approached in the right way. Unfortunately, when once Anselm and William come together, there will be dissension. And, to use your phrase, Firmin, the bull and the sheep will continue to go round and round.'

'In that case, master, it might be worth getting to know Eadmer. This new young monk is always at his side.' Even Firmin, at half his age, seemed like so many others to assume that Eadmer was young. Perhaps the gauche freckle-strewn nose produced this impression, or the credulous blue-grey eyes.

'Who is Eadmer?'

'He is the most recent addition to the archbishop's household, he follows him about everywhere, like Eustace used to do.'

'Eustace?'

'Don't you remember, master? When Anselm came to Gloucester during the king's illness Eustace was in his train. Through him, I was alerted to Baldwin as a useful contact.'

'Ah yes, I remember. So this Eadmer has replaced Eustace in Anselm's affections, has he?'

'Not only Anselm's. Master, I think Eadmer is the one Baldwin has chosen to write the life of a saint. Baldwin wants to write it himself but doesn't have the time, so he has found an impressionable young scribe to do it for him, someone who will be privy to Anselm's words and thoughts and comings and goings. He might prove a useful source.'

Ranulf was pleased by this information. Firmin was, as he had foreseen, proving most adept and trainable. Perhaps the time was not far off when he might be given independent work of his own.

'It occurs to me, if your report is right, that while this Eadmer enjoys some status of confidence and trust with his master, there remains at Canterbury a young monk who might be feeling, let's say, spurned, bitter and abandoned.'

'So, Eustace might still be useful to us, master?'

'Perhaps. But, first, get to know Eadmer.'

For the rest of the Christmas festival, while Ranulf did the rounds of his acquaintance, greasing his path with favours gained and given, calling in old debts and engaging new ones, Firmin set about courting Eadmer. At Gloucester, the households of the archbishop and the king were half a mile apart, the king lodging at Kingsholm and the archbishop at St Oswald's Priory. Firmin took himself off to the priory, hoping he might find Eadmer in his own house, as it were, and have a chance to observe him at leisure. A few attempts produced a familiarity with Eadmer's features, but no contact. Then one cold, sleety morning, Firmin was crossing the cloister garth when he spotted Eadmer making his way towards the *scriptorium,* carrying a bundle of manuscripts. When some of them slipped from under his arm into the slushy mud, Firmin scurried to pick them up.

'No harm done,' he said, wiping them against his jerkin and handing them back.

Eadmer looked at him with interest. 'God bless your charity, young man,' he said in English and made to move on.

Firmin was surprised and asked him if he was English.

'Yes, I am.'

'I am, too. From Huntingdon. My name's Firmin. I'm a clerk of the king's court. Aren't you Eadmer, the famous scholar?'

'Me? I'm Eadmer, but neither famous nor a scholar. Though I hope to be both, one day.'

And so the introduction was made. Before long, Firmin was told all about Eadmer's love of the old English saints and the high hopes he had of Anselm's support of the ancient church. In turn, Eadmer heard about Firmin's desire for learning and had taken him to the freezing *scriptorium* where rows of monks sat at benches, trying to keep their ink fluid by blowing on their frozen fingertips clasped around the pots.

'Do you write here?' said Firmin.

‘No, I write nearly every night sitting at a table before the archbishop’s fire, in his private chamber. I am very privileged and, I fear, all too unworthy.’

Firmin made a mental note of this. Being ‘all too unworthy’ was a particular pretension of Anselm and suggested emulation in his young disciple.

‘Do you write in English?’

Eadmer laughed, screwing up his freckled nose. ‘What would be the point of that? No one writes in English these days, more’s the pity.’

From there, it was a small step to win Eadmer’s confidence by getting him to talk about the glories of the Old English Church and the traditions which he was hoping Anselm would reinstate. On the point of Englishness, there was an immediate contact but, whereas Firmin felt no particular animosity towards the Norman overlords, there was a part of Eadmer that burned with resentment. He was sick of foreign priors and monastic officials riding ironshod over ancient practices, imposing an alien language and outlook on traditional English communities. For his part, Firmin had no such feelings. He had been born at the very bottom of the social heap, abandoned by family and left to fend for himself in the running gutters of Huntingdon. No matter who ruled higher up, he ought, by all principles of social convention, to have remained there. Instead, Ranulf Flambard, a Norman official on his way up in the world, had raised him out of the filth and saved him. Mulling this over later, Firmin could see that he shared fundamental similarities with Eadmer. They were both English and devoted to non-English masters who were pre-eminent in their fields. The great difference was that Eadmer believed his master to be a saint whereas Firmin knew Ranulf Flambard was greater than that.

‘Well?’ said the great man a few days later, ‘did you initiate relations with Eadmer?’

‘I did, master, in the way you said.’

There were, according to Ranulf Flambard, three essential moves in the process of initiating relations. The first was, put yourself in the way of the object of interest, the second, perform a service, and the third, to establish a connection. In going to the priory, picking up the manuscripts and discovering a common Englishness, Firmin had demonstrated the effectiveness of his master’s method.

Unfortunately, as it turned out, no further contact could be made because Anselm, bitterly disappointed by the king’s obduracy, left

Gloucester suddenly on the Feast of the Holy Innocents. In the late afternoon, after conducting the mass, all his household, including Eadmer, packed up and set out for his manor of Harrow, where he had been asked to dedicate a church begun by his predecessor, Lanfranc. Anselm and William did not meet again until early February at Hastings where the king was gathering his forces to launch a spring invasion of Normandy. By that time, the bull and the sheep were ready to go round again.

****

During the Christmas festival, and for several weeks afterwards, Aefled was frozen into her cold castle, missing Robert and her sons, cut off from news about Gunhild and Edith, feeling anxious and dispirited. She did what she could for the villagers, but it was pitifully little. Through the village boys, Edward and Alfred, she sent grain and ale to their families but this had only a negative effect. Special treatment made them feel the injustice of their situation. The English boys found themselves the unwilling recipients of hand-outs, while the families of Tancred, Ralph, Alan and the other Norman boys enjoyed plenty by right.

All the squabbles among the boys, either immediately or ultimately, derived from their Norman or English lineage. It was a phenomenon more marked and bitter the lower down the social scale it occurred. Children, the most powerless in every society, seemed to feel it most strongly. At the departure of her own sons, Robert and William, Aefled had hoped that things would settle down, since they had been among the chief offenders. But there were others only too ready to follow their example, among them the sons of one of Robert's retainers, lads of eleven and twelve years old called Alan and Ralph. Between these two boys and Alfred and Edward, a war seemed to have been declared.

In this predicament, faced with the failure of her school and the collapse of the hopes surrounding it, Aefled felt Isaac's death as a final crushing blow. She was in need of his counsel as never before and the letter from Rabbi Simon devastated her with an unfillable emptiness. She had kept all Isaac's letters in a box and spent many hours taking them out, rereading, remembering, shedding tears. At death, he said, he would return to atoms, be dispersed, filter out into the great spaces of the universe as mere particles returning home. But in her mind, he was still whole, fully present, his voice and face, the things he had done or said, as though a spirit bound them and he walked again.

In the death of Isaac, she felt a great collision of the beliefs that had informed her upbringing: Isaac's Lucretian materialism against the Christian doctrines of Godhead, Incarnation and Salvation. In a situation of bereavement, everyone around her would turn to God, sink to their knees in prayer or at least seek priestly counsel, as Gunhild had done in her letter to Anselm. Instead, she sought the company of those who remembered Isaac, especially Hugh who, many years ago, had saved him when his house was burned down by a vengeful chaplain. What should she reply to Rabbi Simon? Would a letter even reach him? Certainly, no letters could come or go until the roads were passable. No word was coming from outside and she had received no second letter from Gunhild. Wherever Gunhild was, all her dreams of 'the world' conceived at the height of summer in the rose garden at Wilton, had ended in the bleakest of winters.

Then one morning in late February, Hugh came with news of a visitor.

'Who is it, Hugh?'

'Lady Agnes, from St Sepulchre's.'

Eleanor, who had been sitting beside Aefled at her morning studies, leapt up eagerly and ran down to see her godmother who had ridden over from the convent on a mule, accompanied by a monk from St John's Abbey. They went below and found her dismounting in the bailey. She was wrapped up against the fierce cold with mantles, scarves and warm, kidskin gloves, looking every inch a lady of the court. When they had embraced and kissed and Agnes had asked the monk to put the mules in the stables, they bustled inside to the warmth of the private upper room where Aefled had been spending her lonely, melancholy days.

Agnes eyed the open box containing Isaac's letters and one small codex which was Eleanor's reading matter, hastily abandoned moments before.

'Godmother,' said Eleanor, 'I have made something for you.' She hunted around among the parchments then handed Agnes a quarter sheet on which was written, in the most careful Latin script, the opening line of the Lord's prayer.

'Mama said you would like to see how well I can do it.'

'Oh, Eleanor, that's very fine indeed. What a lovely gift!'

She exchanged a look with Aefled, both beaming with pride. Eleanor was just a month away from her eighth birthday, slight, well-formed, with long brown hair bound in tresses and large hazel eyes. After they had made a fuss of her and talked lightly of local affairs, Agnes said to the child: 'Eleanor, my dear, would you go down to the stables and fetch Brother Michael inside. Perhaps he would like something to eat.'

Only too happy to be charged with an important task of hospitality, Eleanor bounded away, eager to do anything her godmother wished of her.

'She is devoted to you,' said Aefled.

'Bless the child. That sweet round face of hers is a joy to see.'

'She has been a great solace this winter, a real comfort in my sorrow.'

When Lady Agnes heard about Isaac's death, she nodded sympathetically and said some suitable words although, not having known Isaac, she had no idea of the measure of Aefled's loss.

'Aren't you going to ask me why I came?' she said.

'I don't think I need to.'

'Have you heard anything?'

Aefled showed her Gunhild's letter. 'This is all I know.'

Agnes read it and put it aside. 'I had a similar letter a week ago. Terrible, isn't it?'

'I've tried to pray for her,' said Aefled.

'I very much fear God will defeat her spirit by testing a good soul too far. The irony is, she is truly a religious woman, as saintly as any I have met. But also eager for life, bursting with the will to live. I ask you, is it just to punish her in this way?'

Aefled did not answer.

'But, I have heard something of our other runaway.'

'You've heard from Edith?'

'Not directly, but a stranger who came to St John's brought news from London. Word is that, on the death of her parents, Edith fled to her Uncle Edgar Aetheling. I think she will be safe with him, at least for a time.'

'And who is King of Scotland now?'

'Malcolm's brother, Donald Bane. But many contest it, encouraged by King William who has a candidate of his own. It will probably mean war before long.'

'Poor Edith, an orphan among warlike folk, in an unfamiliar place with people she does not know. So young, Agnes, so small and alone in the great warring world.'

'Somehow Edith will survive. I have the very strong feeling, Aefled that our little Edith will prove to be someone of great importance one day. She will never be forced to marry against her will and that will enable her to remain a person of substance.'

'Is that what you are, Agnes, a person of substance?'

'What makes you ask?'

'Because you have told me many times that you are not a spiritual person and never chose the religious life.'

'I am a niece of Bishop Wulfstan but I'm not sure that makes me substantial. He offered me the shelter of a convent to escape from a greedy suitor. He found me the post here at St Sepulchre's, but it was never supposed to be permanent. I have never taken the veil and I would marry tomorrow if I had the right offer.'

Agnes threw back her head and laughed. 'People forget that ecclesiastical positions can be bought, or acquired or conferred in all sorts of ways. I have benefited from the system. St Sepulchre's has given me a home, an income and an occupation. I owe a great deal to my uncle.'

'He sounds a remarkable man. Tell me more about him.'

Just at that moment, Eleanor returned to report that Brother Michael was warming himself by the kitchen fire and had eaten a bowl of soup with a piece of rye bread.

'Mama,' she said, 'I saw Ralph fighting with Alfred again down by the gatehouse. Why do they fight so?'

'I wish I knew, my sweet, then perhaps I could stop it.'

'They seem to hate each other. They called each other horrible names. Then they started fighting.'

It was a state of affairs that grew worse by the year as the boys developed a sense of themselves and their place in the world. Geoffrey Rufus, the longstanding tutor, had struggled to instil Aefled's principles of mutual trust and regard. But now, as they were all reaching the age of ten to twelve years old, rivalry and aggression came to dominate their relations.

'Perhaps we could send the English boy, Alfred, to my uncle. He might make a monk of him,' said Agnes, only half joking. 'Wulfstan would show him how an Englishman can make a good life in the church.'

Eleanor was staring at her godmother with big round eyes, utterly fascinated by what she heard. This Wulfstan was someone who could take Alfred away, stop him fighting and make him a holy monk. These were marvellous ideas.

'Will Alfred be a monk, godmother?' she asked.

'Ah, my dear,' said Agnes, 'only if he wishes.'

By the time Agnes thought of returning home, it was already growing dark. The short day was ending in gusts of snow whipped by high winds. Being invited to stay overnight, she agreed and that evening went to supper in the hall where she met all the boys of the school along with their tutor. At first, she wondered what Aefled had meant by saying that they were wild and obstreperous because their behaviour appeared quite normal for boys of their age. They sat together and talked civilly enough when asked questions by the adults. She spoke to Alfred's mother, Gyft, who was evidently satisfied with her well-grown son and found no fault with him. Her other son, William, the same age as Eleanor, was good-natured and biddable. All the children were robust, healthy and excitable, except Tancred the dark-haired, dark-eyed son of Maria who seemed thoughtful, quietly self-possessed and mature beyond his years. In several conversations with him, Agnes discovered that his gentle exterior hid a passionate love of learning and he was not at all averse to the opportunities that a great monastic library would offer him.

Finding the household congenial, Agnes was easily persuaded to stay for a few days. At the end of that time, she had a better understanding of Aefled's concerns, having witnessed many instances of antagonism. Outbreaks of rivalry and resentment between boys brought up as brothers were not unusual, however, and did not happen only at the lower end of the social scale.

At about the same time as Agnes was witnessing fraternal discord among the castle boys, a far greater conflict was about to break out between brothers of the highest rank. Down at Hastings through February and into March, William Rufus sat waiting. Across the channel, Robert of Normandy was strengthening his defences. The royal brothers with their long-nurtured antagonisms and fierce rivalries were preparing for the latest round of family feuding.

****

A white-haired man with sea-green eyes stood before King William clutching his sailor's cap.

'What do you mean 'impossible to sail?' said William.

'My lord king, the wind is not in our favour.'

'You've been telling me that for days. Why do you come if you haven't anything better to say?'

'You asked me to report every day, my lord.'

'Well, don't bother in future. The next time I see you I want you to tell me that the wind is set fair and we can sail.'

The pilot bowed and withdrew.

'Holy Face of Lucca! How long am I going to wait, Flambard? And every day come more petitioners bringing me their tiresome requests.'

The king was referring to all those magnates of church and state who were to remain in England during the king's absence and were taking the opportunity of the delay to put in requests for favours.

Seeing the king's buoyant mood deteriorating daily, Ranulf Flambard hadn't the heart to tell him that Anselm had just arrived, late enough to avoid a private meeting before the ceremony due to take place the following day, February 11th, which they were both to attend. This was a significant day for the king, on which he would perform one of those rare acts which the clergy could unanimously applaud. In the morning, he rode out with a great bevy of diocesan bishops, a large crowd of clerks, barons and lesser laymen to the abbey of St Martin at Battle. There he met Anselm who, as Archbishop of Canterbury, carried out the dedication of the church which William's father had built to commemorate his victory at Hastings. The huge, boastful edifice mocked William with another stupendous feat of his over-reaching father, a symbol of all he himself could not perform or perform only in a lesser way. Nonetheless, he ensured the ceremony was despatched with the gravity the occasion demanded and acted the part of dutiful son. Thinking to please him, Anselm gave a speech in praise of the Conqueror, enumerating triumphs he could not match, while William sat glowering. Afterwards, determined to shine in one way or another, he made a show of granting rich lands in East Anglia to the abbey, along with churches, tithes and tenants. The day's proceedings were rounded off by a convivial banquet which went some way towards improving William's frame of mind before his coming interview with Anselm.

While the king was at Battle, winning favour with the clergy who were so pleased they granted thirty days remission from purgatory for all involved, Ranulf Flambard was trying to prepare for the next round of negotiations in informal discussion with Baldwin. They met in a small upper chamber, unheated except by a feeble fire in a basket grate. Ranulf shivered, but Baldwin, like all monastic Benedictines, seemed to be thoroughly hardened to the cold.

'Let's examine possible points of agreement, shall we?' said Ranulf after the civilities were done, wine poured, Baldwin refusing it, and Firmin standing alert behind his master, being instructed to listen and learn.

'Is there any matter on which Anselm will support the king?'

'Most certainly. He will support the king in consecrating Robert Bloet as bishop of Lincoln, a matter which, I understand, has been challenged by some of the bishops. I also believe Anselm's views coincide with the king's on the sanctity of conventual life.'

'You mean that Edith ought to go back to her convent?'

'That is his view.'

'And that is most certainly William's view, although for entirely different reasons.'

'There is also the matter of the lady Gunhild, shamefully abducted by Count Alan Rufus who was struck down by God after the act. The archbishop has written in the warmest terms to advocate her return.'

'And has she returned?'

Baldwin indicated with a gesture that this was not yet known.

'What is Anselm's view of the projected expedition into Normandy?'

'He is willing to pay the required aid, as a tenant-in-chief, but he views it as an unjust war. A frivolous and wasteful assertion of dominance over his brother with no clear objective.'

Here, Ranulf found himself agreeing with Anselm since, in his view, they all ought to be better employed than hanging about in Hastings, hatching an ill-conceived enterprise, waiting for a wind to carry them into probable disaster.

'But Anselm will make no criticism of the war,' said Baldwin, 'although he might criticise the king on more personal matters.'

Firmin swung his face to his master and smiled at the secret thought of another argument over hair. Ranulf glared back at him. Although these matters in retrospect were full of mockable idiocies, they were also charged with the gravest consequences for church and state.

'The archbishop is also anxious to receive the *pallium* from Pope Urban.'

'From a pope whom the king has not recognised?'

The *pallium*, a small piece of material four fingers wide, was of no interest to William but to Anselm it was the ultimate symbol of his authority. A narrow, circular woollen band placed around the shoulders with a short lappet hanging front and back, the *pallium* was a ritual vestment of obscure historical origin. Tradition dictated that an incoming archbishop must receive it within a year of his consecration, otherwise his assumption of office would be null. Perhaps Anselm was hoping that William would forbid a journey to Rome and that, failing to acquire the *pallium*, he would be free of a burden he had never wanted.

The more Baldwin talked, the less likely seemed an agreement. Ranulf was nervous. He felt a gathering storm. The king was in no mood to make concessions on the latter points and, although Anselm was making polite noises, he was evidently not giving ground on anything important. However, Ranulf felt it wiser not to alert the king to the results of his discussion with Baldwin. It was better not to sour his mind before the meeting. 'I don't want to poison relations at the outset,' he said to Firmin. 'Let the king encounter him in fresh hopes and a mood of benevolence. Besides, Anselm is capable of changing his mind at the last minute because he never works to a settled policy but rather as the spirit moves him.'

Even so, Ranulf was hopeful about the agreement between the king and the archbishop on the matter of Edith. Perhaps it was too much to call it an agreement, rather it was a coincidence of views arrived at from utterly different directions. An unlikely instrument in bringing about this state of affairs was a giant Scotsman, the most unsubtle of men, the glum and taciturn Dunmore who turned up at Hastings and made contact with Ranulf. Since the death of his liege lord, King Malcolm, for whom he had acted as agent at the English court, Dunmore, discovering that he had no place at the side of Donald Bane, had thrown in his lot with Edgar Aetheling, Edith's uncle.

'The trouble with Edgar,' said Dunmore, 'is that he wants to be friends with both William of England and Robert of Normandy and makes pacts that tend to cancel each other out.'

'Not an easy man to serve, I take it?'

Dunmore shrugged. 'I deliver his messages and take answers, it's not difficult.'

'So, what do you have for me?'

'Edgar Aetheling is anxious that his niece is protected. And the best way of doing this, he has concluded, is that she should live in England under the protection of William. He will agree that Edith is sent back to Wilton on the condition that William will pay her keep.'

Ranulf was delighted, a ripe fruit had just fallen into his hand, a proposal that exactly coincided with his own advice. Here was an arrangement that would suit the king, even if it had the drawback of costing him money.

'You must understand that, if he did so, William would be taking on a *de facto* wardship which would give him full control over her marriage.'

'That is understood.'

'And what does Edgar gain?'

Dunmore gave one of his blank, impenetrable stares and hunched his shoulders. 'He wishes to be free of the responsibility. The lady is demanding.'

'So, Edith is not behaving herself?'

'She wants a crown, and Edgar is in no position to give her one.'

'And he thinks William *is*?'

Once again, Dunmore shrugged. How such a shrugging man could occupy the post of negotiator was a mystery.

'You can leave it to me. I vouch that William will accept this proposal. Let her come south, let her return to Wilton, to her dear Aunt Christina. Let all be just as it was before.'

'And William will pay?'

'Most certainly. William will pay.'

And so the matter was settled between them. At the first opportunity, Ranulf got the king's consent and arranged the first payment for Edith's maintenance at Wilton.

When he heard about William's action in defending the sanctity of the religious life, Anselm was heartened. The king shared his view that a runaway nun, whatever her rank and circumstances, should return to her convent and apply herself to penitence. Surely this was an indication that William was not so secular or reprobate as was commonly rumoured. And so Anselm came to the meeting, the day after the consecration at Battle, full of hopes of working amicably with the king. Here was a matter on which they agreed, perhaps they could find others. Where they disagreed, God would shed the light of true understanding on a mind led astray by sin. Sin had been the subject of Anselm's Lenten sermon when he had spoken out against the lax morals of the court, especially the deplorable licentiousness and unmanly preoccupation with hairstyles and clothes so prevalent among the younger nobles. Though still smarting from this scathing criticism, the king, with his long hair combed and wearing a silk mantle with gorgeous embroidery, received him graciously in the hall of Hastings castle.

'I greet you heartily, Archbishop Anselm. I trust you have come to bless our enterprise.'

‘I have, my lord king.’

It was as if the court sighed with relief. For once, after so long, the bull and the sheep were in step, they were going to draw the plough straight, at last, working together for the good of the realm. To the surprise of all, the king called for a chair and had Anselm sit beside him, out of respect for his advancing years. And there they sat, pleasantly discussing their points of agreement in what appeared to be an astonishing rapprochement. But while the king never lost sight of political objectives, Anselm never lost sight of his apostolic zeal. Overconfidence, or misjudgement, drew him into a blunder.

‘My lord king,’ he said, ‘if you sincerely wish your enterprise in Normandy to prosper, you might well consider serious reform in the kingdom you leave behind.’

‘What reform do you have in mind?’

‘It has not escaped my attention that no general Council of Bishops has been held in England since you became king.’

‘Nor for several years before that. My father reigned without them, so can I.’

‘But is it not true that there is a woeful lack of leadership in the reformation of morals? A council would give guidance and help to secure Christianity in this kingdom where so many wrongs go unchecked.’

The king bridled. Here was a blatant implication that he needed assistance from the church in running his court. Anselm had said “kingdom” but William knew what was meant and confronted him with a direct question.

‘Suppose I agreed, what would you speak about in such a council?’

‘That most shameful of crimes,’ came the impolitic reply, ‘the crime of Sodom, not to mention luxury, lasciviousness, concupiscence, illicit marriages between close kin and other wicked crimes that go on daily about the court.’

Anselm seemed completely oblivious to the offence he was giving and continued in this vein, full of earnest and genuine zeal, as if he truly believed that an accusatory speech might reform the king. For his part, William began to suspect that he was dealing with the most dangerous kind of fool, a holy fool with whom it would never be possible to reach a political understanding.

‘Do you imagine I would be willing to call a council in which you would be free to say such things? I want to hear no more about it. Holy Face of Lucca! Is there not something upon which we can agree?’

Since those meagre points had already been discussed, Anselm fell silent for a time. The king yawned and looked around for Flambard, who was standing some way behind him with William St Calais and Bishop Walkelin. At the king's side, Robert FitzHaimo and Walter Tirel stood sporting their long locks and fine clothes, the very image of immoral courtiers.

'My lord king,' began Anselm after a while, 'there is another matter on which I would speak. There are in this land many abbeys bereft of their pastors where the monks give themselves up to luxuries for want of proper governance. I beg you to appoint abbots to these houses so that they may be saved from destruction.'

'Face of Lucca!' snapped William, by now thoroughly angered. 'What business is that of yours? I shall do what I like with my abbeys. Your predecessor would never have dared say such things to my father. I will do nothing for you. I will not grant you my favour because I do not hear what I should.'

The king rose, dismissing Anselm who finally realised that all his words were cast on wind and they parted on the worst possible terms.

Afterwards, when the king's favourite oath was heard echoing up and down the castle: Face of Lucca! Holy Face of Lucca! Firmin became curious about it.

'Master, what does the king mean by that oath? Why does he use it all the time?'

'Good question, young Firmin. Well, the Holy Face of Lucca, il Volto Santo, le saint Voult, le vo de Luche, whatever you call it, is a wooden image of Christ in the cathedral church of St Martin at Lucca. Ask Abbot Baldwin about it. He once went on a pilgrimage there and saw it. People say it was carved by an angel from the face of the living Christ. As you can imagine, it's an image of the greatest veneration and sanctity.'

'But why does the king use this oath so particularly?'

'Who knows what's in the king's mind? But I think he likes the contrast between the holiness of the object and the profanity of the occasion on which he evokes it. It allows him to be irreverent without being overtly blasphemous. But more importantly, it is an oath that would almost certainly have offended his father.'

The following day, Baldwin came sheepishly to ask if Ranulf thought anything might be salvaged from the wreck. Both were anxious that the king should not sail for Normandy leaving such ill-feeling between them.

'Is there, even at this late hour, some way back into the king's favour? My master is anxious to make amends if he has offended, though he can by no means see how he may have done so.'

'Can he not? But it's obvious, Baldwin. When the king said "I do not hear what I should" he means he did not hear the chink of money.'

But if Anselm was persuaded to offer money in the hope of returning to favour, it was now too late. Word came from the king that Anselm was not to wait to give blessing when he set sail, but to seek no further audience and leave Hastings at once.

The meeting, which had begun with goodwill on both sides and ended in a great falling-out, revealed the improbability that these two men could ever work together. The king, guided by policy, prudence and self-interest could never understand a man governed by conscience, scrupulosity and Christian virtue whose motives were annoyingly unfathomable. Even Baldwin, asking himself why Anselm did this or why he did that, sometimes saw no clear answer. Ranulf put it down to the bizarre logic of incipient sainthood, always sailing close to divine madness. One thing was clear, this meeting, as all previous meetings, did nothing but cause the greatest amount of dissatisfaction to the largest number of people for the least possible result.

The evening after Anselm left, Ranulf came back late to his lodging where Firmin was waiting. 'I've been at the *quai* talking to Stephen, the pilot. Do you know, he's the very same Stephen who steered the Conqueror's boat across to Pevensey all those years ago. I said: 'Were you heading for that bay, or was it just luck?' He said 'Just luck. But then, I'm always lucky. We could have hit the coast further east. It was a dark night and for a time we were becalmed, I even thought about turning back.' So you see, Firmin, I just met the man who made Hastings happen by not turning back.'

'Does he think the wind will turn soon?' said Firmin, unimpressed by the story.

'A couple of days, perhaps.'

'About time,' said Firmin, 'it's been almost a month.'

Ranulf, who was not due to accompany the king, being required to stay in England to raise foot soldiers and organise their transportation, was looking forward to a trip to Huntingdon and would be leaving as soon as the king departed. It was pleasurable to think of Aelfgifu's bodily charms, her decently-run house where he was always welcome, her companionable husband and the children who ran about the place, still too young to inquire deeply into their parentage. He was in need of a rest. It was almost a year since the king's illness and Anselm's election, a year of hectic activity and constant disputes. He had earned a rest. Taking off his mantle and woollen bonnet, he handed them to Firmin with a strange expression on his face, serious and amused at the same time.

'Down on the beach today, Firmin, I saw a remarkable sight.'

'What was that, master?'

'I saw a couple of crabs having an argument. Have you ever seen that? They shuffle sideways, come at each other obliquely, strike with a claw, retreat, shuffle sideways, then begin again. Does that remind you of anything?'

****

Events in Scotland were more chaotic than usual in the spring of 1094. Ranulf confidently predicted to Firmin, 'As soon as William leaves for Normandy by the front door, the Scots will start to rattle the back door.' Scotland sat atop the island like a permanent frown and trouble was always expected from that quarter. But for once, Ranulf, like so many others, misunderstood the real nature of the threat.

While a few internal Scottish dissensions spilled over into the border lands, the greater trouble came from Wales. Hardly had the king left for Normandy than the Welsh rose in mass rebellion, threatening the lush counties of Shropshire, Cheshire and Herefordshire. Insurgents were pouring into the marches, forcing the Norman lords to retreat to their castle strongholds where they had no recourse but to sit out the insurrection. Montgomery itself was under threat. The whole of West Wales, with the exception of Pembroke, was taken by a resurgent Welsh nationalism, reducing Norman power to a precarious hold on territory previously thought to be conquered. This seemed all the more remarkable because there was a distinct lack of notable Welsh princes who might inspire rebellions, the kind of charismatic leaders who specialise in defiance.

Since the death of Rhys ap Tewdwr, who had maintained the stability of his south Wales kingdom, defending it against baronial incursions, but equally preventing warlike Welsh forays into the marcher lands, a pivotal balance had been lost. Wales was going up like a tar brand and the marcher barons had been badly weakened by devastating lightning raids into the neighbouring counties. It was Welsh, rather than Scottish, trouble that would finally call William back from Normandy to face a year of trial and disaster, for which he would require a great deal of courage and resource, qualities which his monkish biographers continually denied him.

In the north, while Donald Bane was testing out alliances and making do with token measures, such as ejecting Norman councillors from the court of Scotland, there were, surprisingly, no major conflicts. Count Alan Niger's extensive assets in Cumbria and Northumberland remained relatively peaceful. Robert spent Christmas enjoying the bounty of Richmond Castle, whose monumental keep rose above its hilltop perch like a gigantic windbreak, sheltering the little town huddling below. Reunited with his sons, William and Robert, he found them in good health, well settled and full of admiration for the crossbow which could send a bolt through plate at 600 feet, even when in the hands of unpractised youths like themselves. They had spent the summer training in weaponry, learning about horse management, and having lessons in siege warfare and strategy. They threw themselves into whatever tasks they were given, hungry for experiences as long as those experiences did not include going to the schoolroom or to church.

'Wild, unruly, but with great passion for what they do,' said Robert in his first letter home, written by a paid scribe since both his sons were attending on their lord. 'There is no fighting here at present. Count Alan Niger has succeeded to his brother's estates without contestation. He is surrounded by yet more brothers, half-brothers, illegitimate brothers, all fiercely loyal.'

One sentence in this letter struck Aefled with a particular chill when it arrived at the end of March. 'Count Alan Niger intends to stay here and makes no move to come south. I shall stay until his plans become clearer.'

If Alan Niger was planning to stay in Richmond, what did he intend for Gunhild? Was she to be abandoned, forgotten, after all his promises of protection?

The letter was frustratingly terse, just like Robert in person, shreds of news pared down to the merest rudiments, in no particular order or degree of importance. 'All the surviving sons of Malcolm have gone south, excepting Edmund, the eldest. Rumour has it that King William will support Malcolm's son, Duncan, who has gone to Durham.'

Aefled found nothing of significance in this, she wanted to hear about Malcolm's daughter, not his sons. What had happened to Edith? Where was she?

There was no direct reference to Edith but Aefled found a mention of Edgar Aetheling, who was reported to have offered her his protection. 'Edgar Aetheling is up to his usual tricks. He is rumoured to be seeking King William's support for another of Malcolm's sons, his namesake, Edgar. In the north, Aetheling enjoys a reputation for backing madcap schemes, choosing the wrong side in rebellions and alternating between frenetic activity and indolence.' The letter ended with loving messages for her and Eleanor, prayers for health and advice for Hugh in the running of his affairs.

A few weeks after the receipt of this letter, the only message from Robert in months and unlikely to be followed by another for yet more months, Aefled was suddenly plunged into the forefront of a dramatic and controversial episode which would have tragic consequences. One morning, in early April, Hugh came hurrying to her chamber looking alarmed. 'My lady, there is a visitor below.'

'Who is it, Hugh. Is it Agnes?'

'No, not someone I know. She will not give her name but asks to speak with you urgently. She is accompanied by monks who say she has made a long journey and is in desperate need.'

Almost not daring to think who it might be, Aefled dashed down to the great hall. Eleanor, hoping that her godmother had returned, bounded ahead. 'Oh, it's not godmother,' she said in disappointment, standing on the threshold looking at an unknown lady, dressed in a green mantle, flanked by the earth-brown habits of her monkish escort. Overtaking her daughter, Aefled saw who it was and ran to embrace her warmly. 'Gunhild, thank God! You are safe. I have longed to see you these many months.'

'Did you get my letters?' said Gunhild when they had greeted each other, kissed, embraced, kissed again, introduced Eleanor, Hugh and the monks, ordered food to be brought and caused a general bustle.

'I had one letter, months ago. I have been worried all this long winter, not knowing what had happened to you.'

The monks warmed themselves around the fire in the hall where they all gathered, but Aefled noticed Gunhild kept her mantle warmly bundled about her as if suffering from the cold. Thinking Gunhild would be more comfortable in her private chamber, she gave orders for food to be brought and went up the narrow winding staircase behind Gunhild, with Eleanor leading the way.

'Are you ill?' she asked. Gunhild seemed breathless on the stairs, labouring her way up like a woman twice her age.

'Not ill,' said Gunhild, pausing for breath, 'just tired. Forgive me.'

Something was wrong. Aefled grew alarmed. This was not the Gunhild she had known, nor someone crushed in spirit. She was changed, certainly, like someone who has been broken apart and has settled back around a new centre of gravity.

Aefled's chamber afforded space and privacy. It was warmed by a glowing basket grate struggling to chase the chill from walls on which hung bright new *tapisseries*, one made by Maria which portrayed the archangel Michael with the face of her lover, Arnoud. Eleanor sat on the bed watching the strange lady as she removed her hood. She saw a tall, graceful woman, about the same age as her mother, with large, calm eyes in a sad face. When she took off her hood, long light brown hair streamed in waves over her shoulders and when she sat down in the offered chair it almost touched the floor.

'Are you still cold, Gunhild?' asked Aefled, seeing that she did not remove her mantle. 'I can have more grates brought if you wish.'

'No, it's not the cold,' said Gunhild. She seemed close to tears.

Aefled embraced her. 'I am so sorry for Count Alan's death,' she said. 'I have prayed for you. So has Agnes. We have both prayed for you these many months.'

It struck Aefled as odd that Gunhild had come seeking refuge at the castle, rather than St Sepulchre's where Agnes would have welcomed her. A convent was surely a more natural sanctuary for a woman of faith. The answer to that question did not become apparent until, after some time and with the greatest reluctance, Gunhild removed her mantle.

'This is why I have come,' said Gunhild, spreading her hands across her belly, 'to seek your experience and help.'

It was evident that Gunhild was heavily pregnant.

'Eight months gone with Count Alan's child,' she said in reply to Aefled's inquiring look.

'Why did you leave it so late to come to me? You took a great risk in travelling in this condition.'

'Oh, Aefled,' she said, 'I have taken so many risks this last year, one more hardly matters. You see how justly I am served?'

'Don't say that, Gunhild, you had a great love, don't regret it. In this child, your love will live.'

'I'm frightened, Aefled, I don't know what to do.' Tears, long held back, began to flow. In the relief of being safe, she gave way to a reflux of feeling, overwhelmed by exhaustion and the terror of what lay ahead.

Eleanor sat quietly watching the women, aware that something momentous was going on, something mysteriously feminine which she did not understand. She rose from the bed, went over and took Gunhild's hand, feeling sorry for the lady with the sad face and the plenteous hair.

'God bless you, child,' she said through her tears, 'God bless you.'

The next morning, Aefled wrote a letter to Agnes, asking her to come as quickly as she could so that they could plan how to care for Gunhild and bring her safely through her ordeal. Everything must be done for the safe delivery of this child, the child of Count Alan Rufus. As she was writing the letter, it struck her as one of the most extraordinary quirks of chance, or fortune or God's providence, that here, in Castle St Mary's, in her household, a child of royal blood would be born, the lineal descendant of the English royal line, the grandchild of King Harold.

****

Chapter Eight

Heartbreak

When the king departed for Normandy in mid-March, Anselm had already retreated to a little estate at Godmersham, one of the numerous Canterbury manors scattered about the kingdom. As archbishop, he held fiefs in Sussex, Surrey, Essex, Buckinghamshire and Oxfordshire as well as Kent, and he had it in mind to visit as many as possible, but Kent, being particularly well-endowed, detained him long.

The manors and fiefs were of two distinct types. Some financed the archbishop's personal upkeep and running of his household, others paid for the maintenance of the monks at Christchurch and the costs and upkeep of the buildings. Anselm did not know much about these matters and was not interested, beyond sticking to the principle of maintaining the Canterbury endowments as they had been at the time of Lanfranc's death. This was a simple idea which he could defend without feeling he was being dragged into the worldly pettiness of estate management. What did interest him, however, was the well-being of the monks and the good order and uprightness of all the communities that looked to Canterbury for spiritual guidance. In spite of being head of the foremost see in England with an income of more than a thousand pounds, he earnestly wished to set an example of frugal and humble living. Particularly keen to avoid the accusation of extravagance, he kept a small household, being some thirty people in all, a far smaller number than his successors would countenance. Even so, he was anxious not to impose hardship on any community by forcing it to sustain him for long. The need to shift around, in order to mitigate the burden on any single community, meant that he was constantly in a state of transhumance, a pastor moving his flock from pasture to pasture, browsing and passing on. From Godmersham he went to Orpington and then on to Petham, a rich archiepiscopal manor where, he claimed, he could maintain his household at his own expense.

But there were many who asked if this continual journeying was really necessary. Baldwin, Eadmer and other members of his staff found it caused them a great deal of work for little apparent gain. Why dodge and duck about the countryside for weeks on end, when there was a fine residence at Canterbury? Was all this activity merely a cover for a deep-seated reluctance to spend time in Canterbury itself? Was Anselm intentionally avoiding the monks of Christchurch and the scene of his enthronement? One evening Baldwin spoke to Eadmer about it.

'Don't you think it might be asked why, if Anselm holds the monastic life in such high esteem, he goes to such lengths to avoid it?'

'I have asked that question, but the master does not confide in me. It would be much easier if we could be settled at Christchurch. All this moving about is a dreadful trial. I have to pack and unpack all his writing materials at every stop. Ink, pens, knives, pots, boxes, piles and piles of manuscripts. He is constantly writing. Not only letters but that long work of his, supposedly a letter to Pope Urban, but it's turning into a treatise. I have to keep everything in order. It's a nightmare every time we move.'

'And you have your own writing,' said Baldwin, 'very important writing, the life of the great man. How is it coming on?'

'I certainly have no lack of material.'

'Well, be sure you put something in it explaining why he is avoiding Canterbury.'

'But I don't know why.'

'Does that matter?'

Whatever the real reason for avoiding Canterbury, Anselm was certainly lavishing time and effort on his new work. *On the Incarnation of the Word* had been begun two years earlier and he was only now getting around to finishing it. He planned to send it to the pope who would then invite him to come to Rome to receive the *pallium*. Such an invitation would force William's hand in allowing him to leave. After the last sharp encounter with William, the mere exercise of writing the work soothed his spirit and focused his mind on higher things. He was able to think of great universal issues of faith rather than the petty squabbles of the court. Why couldn't he get on with the king? Every time he went to a meeting he resolved it would be different this time. 'Our differences are not insoluble,' he said to Baldwin, 'the king is not a wicked man. Misled, perhaps, impious occasionally, ill-advised by that scoundrel Flambard and his long-haired minions, but not a wicked man. Why can't we get on?' Although he was a man entirely without arrogance, it never occurred to him that he, also, might be at fault.

In the opinion of many, an archbishop was only ever as good as the household surrounding him. He needed solid, loyal types who could take on the day-to-day organisation and management of affairs, leaving him free to do the work of the spirit and the intellect. Anselm, sixty-one years old and temperamentally unsuited to a great office which made him, in effect, an ecclesiastical baron surpassing in importance the highest of the king's advisers, was very much in need of such men and held himself blessed to have found them in Baldwin and Eadmer.

Baldwin was about fifty, a career cleric of proven worth in the administration of affairs, a practical, shrewd, effective negotiator, as Ranulf Flambard had discovered. Eadmer, a mere thirty-three, appeared and felt inappropriately young, but was not going to let his juniority demean him. He had been given a great role, he, a Kentish monk of middling birth who had spent all his life in Canterbury, had been appointed by Providence to fulfil an important task. Nothing, in his view, could be more important than communing with posterity. He had been chosen to write this life so that future ages would know what manner of man his master was. But though he would dutifully, faithfully, and as far as possible, honestly record the life of Anselm, he was also aware that he was making a record of himself. Although he was adopting the style of hagiographies, containing the conventional devices and expected phrases, the work could not fail to bear the imprint of his voice and eye. This is what I saw, this is where I was, this is what Anselm did, this is what he said. Here I am, telling you about Anselm, saying this, doing that, going there. Here I am, waving at you through my words. I am in the stories, the parables, my master's sermons, his conversations with the monks, I, Eadmer, witness to the miraculous, bound up in these words of pure wisdom, I, Eadmer, chosen to transmit them through the ages, to all you unseen readers crowding round to hear the life of a saint. Hundreds of years, a thousand hence, here I am, Eadmer, still talking; in this work, I go on living forever, always young, always writing, never coming to an end.

'Don't let this task go to your head,' said Baldwin one day. 'Don't forget, you have the greatest model of humility before you. Pride is a great sin and Anselm abhors all sin. In fact, I want you to put a little passage in the work on that exact theme.'

But it was only much later, after constant pressing by Baldwin, that Eadmer was induced to add to the finished work a section entitled: '*With what care he avoided the horror of sin.*'

Eadmer often resented the dominance of Baldwin and wished to have more freedom with the writing, but Baldwin was determined to exert control. So Eadmer had devised another project, one which he would have the freedom to shape as he chose. It was an account of Anselm's dealings with the king and the court, starting at the time Eadmer came into his service last year. It was to be a history of events in England as witnessed first-hand by himself and drawn from notes made on the spot. He wanted it to be his personal tribute to Anselm, setting him among the events and personalities of the times, recording the words, the letters, the sayings of his master as noted by an observant eye-witness, himself. He would give portraits of important people, the king, the barons, the bishops, describe their characters and doings, quote from their letters or their speeches verbatim and show how they impinged for good or ill upon the life of his master. Complementary to the *Life of Saint Anselm,* but distinct from it, he gave it the title: *Recent Events in England*. In this work, Eadmer would choose his own material, develop his own style and speak in his own voice. It would be his private realm, a secret vengeance on Baldwin.

One outcome of Anselm's constant hastening from place to place was that he was very difficult to contact. Messengers arrived for him in one place just after he had set out for another, letters went astray and every kind of business was delayed. Perhaps this was deliberate. Anselm did not want to conduct business and had no desire to be contacted. When his tenants complained about the war-levy or protested that they were oppressed by the monasteries, or when those who had urged him to accept the archbishopric now came forward with claims for favours, asking for church lands, horses or money, he was seized with a paralysing panic and passed everything on to Baldwin. Instead of dealing with these secular issues, Anselm took solace in writing his treatise, replying to letters, advising those who came to him on spiritual matters and generally playing the part of the monk he felt himself to be. He wrote to Bec, trying to make it up to the brothers there who still felt betrayed since he had promised never to leave them. He wrote to his friend Hugh of Chester, whom he had been visiting just before the ill-fated day when he had been elected archbishop. He wrote to Bishop Walkelin asking why he had not yet conducted an inquiry into the running of Wilton Abbey from where, in the space of a week, two high-born religious ladies had decamped last year. He wrote to the Bishop of Durham asking him to make enquiries about Edith and, very anxious at not receiving a reply to his last letter, he wrote again to Gunhild.

It was a matter of grave importance to him that his dearest daughter in Christ should return to the convent and take the veil. To do otherwise was to risk her immortal soul. The prospect of her damnation filled him with genuine terror and he found himself becoming more and more anxious about her. Then he began to be anxious about what he considered an inappropriate fondness for her. It was this very fondness that had caused him to write harsh letters, begging, urging, demanding that she return to the convent. The strident, unforgiving tone, the cruel harsh words, were directed to himself as much as to her. His fondness was so great that it was close to sin.

Years ago, when they had met, Gunhild had listened to his talk with such devotional attention that she won his heart. In those days, her grace and noble bearing and, most especially, her attentive hanging on his every word, had overwhelmed him like an avalanche plunging down the mountainside and spurting through the valley of his native Aosta. Why did Gunhild always bring Aosta to mind? He never thought of Aosta, the alpine town he had left when still a young man, never consciously. But it always came to mind when he thought of Gunhild.

At Aosta, he had been young, he had been passionate. He had fallen in love and been tossed about by raging instincts and violent emotions. At Aosta, he had done battle with the demons of desire. Even the name was like a sigh, a longing that must be renounced. Aosta was where he had fought with himself and with his father. Aosta had offered him, the son of a sinking noble family, a certain possibility of life: becoming a merchant, getting married, bringing up children, acquiring goods and bequeathing them in a neat will upon a reputable death. Leaving Aosta was leaving all that, seeking another road, taking up a staff, becoming a monk, writing great works of faith, becoming archbishop. But did he ever leave Aosta? Aosta was the place he carried inside himself, from which he could not flee, the stamp of his soul. Inner contemplation, self-examination, getting close to the forbidden passions of the deliberately unrecalled, always brought Aosta to mind. Soaring up to the high, cloudy mountains, plunging down into deep ravines, Aosta's sharp peaks, lush valleys, tumbling rivers and wild, sheer sides came strangely to mind in the plain, broad countryside of Kent.

Yet here they were, Aosta's passionate beauties, in all their sensuous glory, whenever he thought of Gunhild.

In this frame of mind, he wrote again, hoping the letter would reach her at St Edmundsbury. This one was warm, gentle and heartfelt; he grieved for her grief and condoled her loss. He dropped the commanding tone and wrote from an emotion newly awakened by memories of Aosta where once, on the glittering mountains, he had had a vision of heaven. This letter, which might have brought so much solace to Gunhild in her coming ordeal, fell victim to the perpetual disruptions of the household and was never sent.

****

Immediately after waving the king off at Hastings, Ranulf Flambard hurried up to Huntingdon, arriving just after Easter with Firmin and a small entourage in tow. It was time to give his official person a holiday, put aside business, throw himself into the domestic scene and enjoy a reunion with Aelfgifu. That, at least, was the plan. But the official person was not so easily put aside, partly because it was comprised of diverse and numerous roles, none of which could be wholly divested. He liked to think of himself as the king's chief minister but had no formal title and was not recognised as such by most of the barons, who remained jealous of their own privileges. His closeness to the king was a source of resentment to many, but closeness to the king was not an office with a chartered entitlement or a regular stipend, even though plenty of money came his way. Some called him the king's *placitator*, one who pleads, placates, appeases, and he certainly performed this role often enough during the endless contentions of the bull and the sheep. At other times, he was called *exactor*, the king's financial agent, but this was a description rather more than a post. He was not a treasurer, nor a judge, nor a chaplain, nor the holder of any other office formally appointed by the king. He was an adviser whom the king liked to keep close that was all. No official sanction attached to this role and it would last only as long as the king's favour lasted. What was he then, Ranulf Flambard? A low-born greasy-pole climber, a flamboyant, reckless place-seeker, an extortionate tax-gatherer, a one-time priest and keeper of the king's seal, a brilliant royal servant of thirty-four? He was all of these and nothing.

'The trouble with holidays, Firmin,' he said one day, 'is that they give you time to think.'

But Huntingdon was pleasant. The little town was a modest affair: one bridge, one road, a market not yet chartered, a wooden castle. It slumbered in the Cambridgeshire countryside, minding its own business and grateful for the fact that it had rarely had a visit from the king. The house that Ranulf had bought for Aelfgifu was in the centre of the original settlement, straddling the old Roman road. It, too, was modest, but not without ambition. It had a large ground floor chamber with a central hearth and adjoining offices in the usual style, but it also boasted several upper rooms, servant's quarters, a bakehouse and extensive grounds. It had once belonged to Ramsey Abbey and the story of how Ranulf had got hold of it was part of the story of the abbey's long decline. Like her house, Aelfgifu was modest and comfortable. She produced children and cared for them without any noticeable effort. There were three belonging to Ranulf and two to her husband, all under ten years old. Aelfgifu was a member of a wealthy Anglo-Danish merchant family, long settled in Huntingdon, whose ancestry was visible in her pale blonde abundant hair braided around her head, showing small shell ears, a glowing skin and fine blue eyes. She was all white bread and honey, Ranulf's favourite supper. In this bustling household, Ranulf and Firmin spent the months of April and May.

Back in his hometown, which he had left without a penny to his name, Firmin was beginning to feel, in a modest way, rich. That is to say, he had a small cushion against falling back into poverty. Ranulf paid him a tiny stipend which he saved, having all his board and victuals found. This enabled him to amass the great sum of one pound, with which he was itching to do good to his native town.

'Master,' he said one day, 'if you had a little spare money what would you do with it?'

'In my view, Firmin, money is never spare,' said Ranulf without hesitation. 'What does it mean, "spare"? Pointless, ineffectual, without purpose? Such a term should never be used about money.'

Ranulf loved his own railleries far too much and was aware of it. But Firmin was used to them and usually persisted until he got an answer.

'Well, if you want to do good with a little money, Firmin, there is no better way than to give it to the church. I doubt you have enough to endow a chantry or repair a gatehouse, but you could give in a small way, by sponsoring a local baptism for a poor man's son, say, or buying a phial of holy oil for the poorest church in the parish. If you want to invest the money and do yourself a little good, then the best thing is to buy yourself out of a spell in purgatory.'

Firmin did not seem impressed by any of these suggestions.

'I wanted to do something for the town,' he said.

'What for, in God's name? The best thing you ever did was to leave this town.'

'But only because you made it possible, master, taking me on when I had no one in the world to look out for me.'

The conversation rested there for a few days but Ranulf was privately touched by Firmin's gratitude and his desire to emulate him. The trouble was that Ranulf had not acted out of a principled love of doing good or the virtue of generosity. He had acted on pure impulse, a whim, no more. At a time when he was in need of one, he had spotted the possibility of a cheap servant and snapped him up. All the devotion, talent and efficiency had been felicitous extras, discovered later. And now, he thought, with a slight twinge of conscience, he thinks I am a man of good works. How the king would laugh!

The king would not laugh, however, at Flambard's delay. The fact was, he was not in Huntingdon to take a holiday. Before he had left in March, the king had charged him with one of the most important and innovative tasks of military organisation since the Norman invasion. It would be his responsibility to do something that had not been done on a matching scale for years, not since King Harold had done it before Hastings. Ranulf Flambard was going to raise the *fyrd*. He wasn't just going to raise Norman knights and vassals from the shires, he was going to raise the *fyrd*. The word itself had a kind of majesty, an aura so resplendent that the Normans kept it in its original form. Even they heard in it the echo of ancient battle valour, saw the glint of shield walls and iron jaws squared in the face of Viking savagery. The *fyrd* were the foot soldiers of the English kings and it was William's intention to raise them, rally them to his banner and send them against his brother in Normandy. This is a measure of how quickly the world moves on, thought Ranulf. Twenty-three years after the Norman conquest of England, the Norman King is going to raise English footsoldiers to fight against the Normans in Normandy. What a splendid irony. This was the operation he had been entrusted with during the summer. He was to raise twenty thousand men of the *fyrd,* English thegns and farmers, men of the fields and labourers, train and organise them, muster them to Hastings, plan their transportation and be ready to send them to William before winter set in. It was a monumental task and, to prepare for it, Ranulf read a little history.

The *fyrd* was a way of raising an effective militia from the countryside. It had worked spectacularly well for King Alfred when he had to keep an army in the field against fast-moving Viking marauders and it worked because of the way it was financed. In professional armies, where men undertake a stipulated period of service for which they are paid in properly graded salaries according to their rank, when the supply lines are professionally administered so that food and weapons are never in short supply, and when the organisation is supervised by paymasters and all is under financial control from the centre, as for example, in the Roman Army, then the link between a man and his individual upkeep is relatively unimportant. But the great armies of the Roman world no longer existed in Europe and, even though one might learn a little bit about tactics and strategy from Vegetius, the military world about which he was writing had long departed. In the savage and violent times of the Danes and Vikings, when England's Roman order had been ripped apart, the *fyrd* had supplied a much-needed way of raising fighting men and sustaining them through campaigns without wrecking the agriculture of the land they were fighting to defend.

In King Alfred's day, every burgh, or settlement, sent a certain number of men to fight but held back an equal number of men to maintain the labour of the fields and police their own villages. This meant that communities would not be denuded of active men at times of harvest or in the face of bandits and thieves. A certain number of men of each social rank would remain in the villages to feed and defend the remaining population. Those men who went away to train and fight would do so in the knowledge that their homes and fields were protected. Thus, by halving the number of individuals raised in any particular locality, one doubled their effectiveness. This was exactly the kind of practical strategic planning that appealed to Ranulf.

A second ingenuity of the *fyrd* was to connect each man to a resource of keep and pay for the time of his service. Ranulf liked this clear-eyed approach as he believed it would be useless to appeal to English labourers to fight on the basis of abstract values, such as loyalty or duty. A man needed means for himself and his family, he needed sustenance and pay. So, under the *fyrd,* each man was attached to five hides of land. This land would support him, pay him and sustain his family while he was away. Each hide would pay 4 shillings, thus a man supported by five hides would be provided with a total of 20 shillings, half for keep and half for pay. This was the system Ranulf intended to apply in order to raise troops without costing the king a penny from the royal coffers.

There was, of course, one major drawback. Men raised in this way were not professional soldiers. However well fed and well paid they were, they were not trained to the same degree as the knights and vavassours of the feudal system, whose main purpose in life was to participate in war. But Ranulf had a plan of audacious ingenuity, a way of using an ancient system for the introduction of a novel scheme, turning it into a shrewd money making enterprise. If he could bring it off, William would have all the troops he needed, coffers full of cash and, on the other side of the deal, not one of the English foot soldiers would be forced to fight against his will.

In May, the groundwork plans were laid, and a team of clerks and assistants set up. One of the upper rooms of Aelfgifu's house became a sort of bureau from where letters were sent to the sheriffs of the southern counties, calling on them to select men from their localities and organise the hidage subsidies. Muster stations were organised along the roads to Hastings, depots from where groups of men, having assembled from the surrounding country, would set out to march down to the ships. Ranulf planned to spend late summer travelling to oversee this work and to be present himself at Hastings for the embarcation in early September. It would be then, at the very last stage, that he would put into his plan into effect. A plan that would bear the unmistakeable marks of Flambardian resourcefulness and effrontery.

****

While she was at Castle St Mary's in late May, awaiting the birth of her child, Gunhild received a letter from Bishop Walkelin of Sarum. It was brought by Agnes who was anxious to maintain the fiction that Gunhild was in retreat at St Sepulchre's. Agnes ensured that all the letters sent and received by Gunhild should go through her and be transmitted only by travelling monks. Very few knew about her flight from Wilton, although those few were some of the most notable people in the land. But no one, except her most intimate friends, knew about her pregnancy. It was most necessary, Agnes believed, to protect Gunhild's reputation so that if she ever wished to return to Wilton in the future her good name would not be sullied. Aefled and Agnes did all they could to shield her by offering seclusion at Castle St Mary's, while at the same time allowing her to maintain correspondence with the outside world through St Sepulchre's.

There was frenetic activity at the keep in the days leading to the birth: Agnes, constantly coming and going between castle and convent, Aefled busy with the household and the preparations for the lying in, Maria and Gyft helping out wherever possible. Maria liked to spend time with Gunhild, often playing her rebec and singing the lovely songs of her native Sicily. It was Maria's particular sorrow that she had never been able to conceive a second child. Now thirty-seven years old, she despaired of ever having another baby and she looked on Gunhild's condition with mixed feelings of envy and protectiveness.

'It's so kind of you to play for me,' said Gunhild one morning after listening to a sad song of parted lovers. 'These tearful laments suit my mood.'

'Tell me about Count Alan,' said Maria.

'I knew him for the briefest span of time, yet long enough to know that I loved and was loved. But this child, Maria, what is to become of this child?'

'God will have a purpose for him, Gunhild, as he has for each of us.'

'Anselm says that there is no worse disobedience to God than shirking that purpose. He fears I am damned, Maria, because I left the convent. But how can I be damned when I am so obviously blessed?' She stroked her swollen belly and felt the baby move inside her which made her smile. 'Don't lose hope, Maria. Look at me, I'm thirty-three years old, only a few years younger than you. Miracles do happen.'

The women never spoke of their fears. To have a first baby this late in life and in such harrowing circumstances was a terrible risk, they all knew it. Aefled, with all her experience of childbirth and midwifery, was extremely anxious. Even in the normal course of things, death hovered very near every birthing bed. Any distraction was a relief, so when Agnes came with the letter for Gunhild, she handed it over, hoping it might bring cheer to the mother-to-be.

It did not. Bishop Walkelin's letter brought news of the death of Uncle Wulfnoth. Gunhild's last surviving relative was gone. Describing the last days of the broken old-young man, Walkelin explained that he did not suffer but went out quietly as if from a place in the world he had never quite occupied. A prisoner from the age of fifteen, never tasting independent manhood, he had been a child all his life, baffled and betrayed by court politics, trapped in the machinery of statecraft which he did not understand. 'He went to God in the gentlest manner on the feast of St Elwin,' wrote Walkelin. 'We buried him here in Sarum the following day when the monks sang his soul to rest in the most beautiful litanies. He was great among us, much beloved and honoured for his gentleness.' Bishop Walkelin enclosed a little parchment written in the hand of Godfrey of Cambrai, the prior, who had looked after him so fondly in his later years. It was an epitaph of his own composing. In it, Godfrey gave him the dignity of his old title, Earl Wulfnoth, and celebrated his simple manners and honourable judgments while recalling the terrible ordeal of his life. He wrote about "the boy and the old man" as though they were one being, "caught up in human bonds", the bonds of kinship and the bonds of imprisonment which entangled him in an incomprehensible fate, but ultimately bound him to God.

It was a moving tribute, over which Gunhild shed many tears. The last male relative of King Harold was dead but, inside her, she felt King Harold's grandchild moving imprisoned, anxious to be free. The strange pitch of these conjunctions, beginnings and endings, death and birth, confinement and freedom, cast Gunhild into a melancholy mood for several days. Wishing she had not received the letter, Aefled sent her daughter to comfort her. Eleanor was at an age to find immense interest in a woman's swelling belly. Why is it like that, what does it feel like, how does the baby get in, how does it come out?

One day, when Gunhild seemed in a talkative mood, Aefled broached the subject of Count Alan Niger. 'Have you heard anything since he went north?' she said.

'No.'

'Don't you think you should have?'

'I don't know what to think. He has probably forgotten all about the promises he made to me. They were made in an impulsive moment, perhaps I should not have taken them seriously. He offered protection, I thought he meant marriage. He acted honourably. I can't hold him to anything.'

'How do you think he will respond to news of his brother's child? Suppose it is a boy, will he view it with favour, or not?'

'I doubt it will be of much significance to him. Count Alan Niger won't be jealous of this baby, if that's what you mean.'

Gunhild was now only days away from the birth which was to take place in Aefled's chamber. It was on the upper floor with windows both east and west so that it was more airy and light than most other rooms. A few steps away along a corridor was a private oratory where the women could say their prayers. Sometimes the chaplain, Geoffrey Rufus, would say a mass. Aefled prayed that he would not be needed on the day of the birth, for his only role would be to administer an emergency baptism or the last rites, but she kept him on hand in case Gunhild should want to make confession before her confinement.

The next letter that came for Gunhild was not from Anselm as she had hoped, desperate as she was for some word of forgiveness. But the many forgiving words Anselm had written, words which would have consoled Gunhild in the midst of her ordeal, had fallen victim to the disorder of the archbishop's household and had never been sent. Instead, the letter brought news from another long-silent source. It was from Edith.

After the high level discussions at Hastings in March, Edith had been granted her wish to return to Wilton where she arrived at the end of April, exhausted and chastened by the experiences of the last eight months. One by one her male relatives had disappointed her, failing to treat her as she demanded, neglecting to house her as befitted her rank, ignoring her plight. Her father and brother had been murdered in a treacherous attack, her mother had died soon after of a broken heart. The prospects of a great marriage dwindled to nothing as suitors scurried away. No longer the daughter of a king, her only attractions lay in her bloodline and her person, though these were not inconsiderable. Uncle Edgar had offered protection, but though he promised much he delivered little; she found herself being dragged about the countryside, in constant discomfort and sometimes in actual physical danger, as when she had to make an escape by boat in a storm. It was an abrupt awakening to the realities of a violent world and within a short time she had begun to look on Wilton with a very different eye. Even Aunt Christina's sharp edges softened in hindsight as she remembered a secure and orderly way of life which had not, she now realised, been altogether insupportable.

So Edith's indomitable will had set to work upon Edgar Aetheling, who had finally been persuaded to make an arrangement with King William. In consequence, she was now an official royal ward, dependent on the king's bounty for her maintenance and under his protection. Since it was unthinkable that the King of England would maintain her in anything less than a dignified state, she could look forward to a reasonably comfortable life at Wilton. If ever the king should attempt to renege on his promises, by withdrawing his protection or cutting her maintenance, he would have Anselm breathing down his neck with sermons about keeping one's word. To have secured the agreement of these two battling parties on just the very issue that most suited her desires was success of a sort. In a sense, from a position of weakness, Edith had triumphed. But the triumph was short-lived. Back at Wilton, under the control of her Aunt Christina, without Gunhild or the interesting presence of Agnes and Aefled, she drooped with dullness.

'What does Edith say?' asked Aefled, seeing Gunhild put the letter aside with a regretful smile.

'Edith is an impossible child,' said Gunhild. 'Read the letter and tell me what you make of it.'

Aefled discovered that, like Edith herself, it was full of demanding love. 'Come back to us, Gunhild,' she wrote, 'my Aunt Christina adds her voice to mine. We are bereft of your gracious company, your kindly strength, your practical wisdom, you are the counsellor of all our troubles.'

After that appeal, probably sincere although overblown, Edith went on to relate events at the convent. 'Bishop Walkelin has been appointed by Archbishop Anselm to inquire into the abbey's affairs. Two archdeacons, William of Canterbury and Hambald of Salisbury, have been here several times asking questions about the events of last summer. They will learn only what is fitting for them to know. The abbess and my aunt have them in hand. They are asking about you, Gunhild, my dearest friend, but we have had no news of you these many months.'

Then Edith changed key and got on to the subject that really interested her, the scandal of Gunhild's elopement. 'My aunt says you went on a pilgrimage and are now in retreat. Oh, Gunhild, I know that is not true. Something marvellous happened to you. Was it a vision of divine love that took you away from Wilton in an ecstasy last summer? Through what travails of the spirit have you laboured, dearest Gunhild? I long to know.'

Then, towards the end, like the child she was, Edith forgot to be sophisticated. A few lines shone innocently, translucent with undisguised feelings. 'Please come back to us, Gunhild, Come back and tell me your stories. It is wretched here.'

Aefled shared a smile with Gunhild: 'An impossible child, indeed.'

'Strange, there is part of me that longs to go back. It's what Anselm and the bishops want. It's what the king and the church want.'

‘The only thing that matters to me,’ said Aefled. ‘Is what you want.’

‘All I want now is a safe delivery.’ Gunhild held out her hand as if suddenly afraid and seeking comfort. ‘I think it’s time.’

Gunhild took confession with Geoffrey Rufus and prepared her soul for the coming ordeal. Three experienced women helped her through the agonising hours: Aefled, Maria and Gyft, all mothers of healthy children. Maria prayed. Gyft wore rosemary sprigs in her cap to ward off evil spirits. Aefled read aloud to her. Between contractions, Gunhild lay back listening to the ‘Life of St Anne.’ It was a fine May evening but, in spite of the sunlight warming her back, Aefled felt a chill.

Gunhild did not at first complain. But whatever was going on in her body was matched by emotional torments: guilt at leaving the convent, fear of divine judgement on the child, regret for sins committed, but no regrets for the brief love she had known. She fought inwardly against the curse of Genesis: ‘In sorrow thou shalt bring forth children,’ by swearing that she would never, never be sorry for what she had done. Her brief summer of love with Count Alan Rufus was a bright, untouchable thing and she would never regret it. Nevertheless, from time to time she cried out that she was going to die and begged them to stop the pain. Aefled, Maria and Gyft had seen it all before and did not become alarmed until sunrise when there was still no baby in Gunhild’s arms. Then it was midday, then evening. Gunhild was exhausted.

Aefled only realised what was wrong when she found the baby was not being delivered in the usual position. Instead of a patch of wet hair, indicating that the head was on its way, there was the soft roundness of tiny buttocks. This was a frank breech, which meant that the legs were flexed at the hips and extended at the knees with the feet up around the ears. Still, Gunhild’s dilation seemed able to cope and with a few more pushes in time with the contractions, the bottom came forth. But it was slow, painfully slow. Then, after an agonising delay, the body slipped out, the head between the feet, the tiny face covered in blood and viscous fluid, a fully formed beautiful baby that made no sound. At this point, Aefled panicked, but she had enough presence of mind to blow air into the tiny nostrils. She felt for a heartbeat, signs of breathing. They were there. The child, a baby boy, was alive, but he gave no cry and his limbs hung limply. Gunhild fell back in the bed, semi-conscious, exhausted. Aefled took the opportunity to wash the baby in tepid water with lint wads and wrap him in woollen coverings to keep him warm but did not swaddle him. She wanted to see his limbs move, she wanted him to cry. At last, there came a feeble sound, one or two puffs of air, a little croak, but not the lusty sound of the usual new-born.

Gunhild stirred and reached for her baby. 'What is it?' she asked.

'A beautiful boy,' said Maria.

Gyft was making signs of the cross and twiddling her sprays of rosemary. She knew as well as Aefled that something was very wrong.

'Thank God, oh, thank God,' said Gunhild over and over. 'Can I hold him?'

She reached out her arms and Aefled lodged the baby in them. He lay there, silently, limbs flaccid, unmoving. Slowly Gunhild realised what her friends dared not tell her. Geoffrey Rufus came to baptise the child so that he would be accepted into the community of the faithful. He was given the name of his grandfather, Harold. He breathed but did not stir through it all. His tiny perfect mouth worked around inaudible sounds, his eyes opened once or twice and shut on nothing. Gunhild held him close and sat in an agony of silence through the few short hours of her son's life. Afterwards, when they took the little body away, darkness seemed to close in on her.

Days became weeks. Neither Maria nor Aefled nor Gyft could find any way to comfort her, to bring her round, to lead her back to the world. Even Agnes, arriving from the convent with another letter and a prayer from the nuns, along with some consolatory reading, could get no spark of response from her.

'Give her time,' said Aefled. 'For this ill, there is no remedy. Healing must be slow.' Aefled thought then about Mother Ethel, the old healer who had practised her wise crafts in the village for decades and had died in the winter of 1086. Mother Ethel used to be a great respecter of time's healing ways. But did time really heal? Had time healed the wound of Hastings? Wasn't time itself rejecting the continuity that Gunhild's child represented? The last of Harold's line was buried at St Mary's and time stamped on his grave.

Gunhild stayed on at Castle St Mary's all through the summer, slowly recovering. Aefled, Maria and Agnes, along with Eleanor and, occasionally, Gyft, tried to amuse and distract her but it took many weeks before she regained her health and was able to reflect seriously on her future. What was she to do? To Anselm's fierce advice to return to Wilton, King William had added his voice. After all, what was a suitable policy in regard to Edith would do equally well in regard to Gunhild. Let these wayward women return where they belonged. Edith had written again begging Gunhild to return and there was no reason why she should not do so. No one except the small population of Castle St Mary's knew about her pregnancy and confinement. These matters need never come to light. Whatever would be written in the annals of Wilton or in the monastic histories about this episode, it would not include any reference to these events, so wholly beyond the understanding of monks. No chronicle would ever tell Gunhild's story. The way was open to return to the religious life. She told herself that she had never rejected that life, indeed she had led it with sincere conviction for many years. What had happened had not been a rejection, had not been any decision of the mind or will, had hardly been deliberate. It was something altogether miraculous, she thought, inexplicable. Count Alan Rufus had wooed her with a rose, releasing the heady perfumes of desire, love and passion into her soul. In such circumstances, who would not have gambled with fortune, who would not have fallen in love and ridden into adventure? Gunhild had wanted the world and it had wounded her, crushing her with the weight of two unconsolable losses. Now the cloister beckoned, not simply as a shelter from a rejecting world, but as a revived vocation in which she could defeat time by seeking the immortality of salvation.

Painful though it was to leave the castle where her little boy was buried, and to part from the friends who had shown her such affection, Gunhild left Castle St Mary's at the end of September. She would travel only a few miles, to St Sepulchre's where, with Agnes and the sisters, she would prepare herself to return to the religious life. From there, in a few weeks' time, she would travel back to Wilton where Edith was awaiting her arrival. They kissed and parted. Eleanor was in tears, Aefled and Maria nearly so. Only Agnes, who had come with a few Benedictines from St John's to escort her to the convent, tried to smile. Gunhild looked slight and pale as she sat on her mule. Lost, terribly distant, like someone woken from a lovely dream into a bleak day and unending mourning.

****

Chapter Nine
Raising the *Fyrd*

Above a cliff to the west of Hastings rose a hill on which a castle had stood for thirty years. One day, in late September, Ranulf Flambard was standing with his back to the castle, gazing out to sea. Seagulls wheeled and drifted overhead, uttering their mocking cries. Occasionally, one would land and stare coldly at him as if inquiring what business he had there. The wind was westerly, warm, moderate. It was good sailing weather and the boats lay moored offshore, ready to take the troops across. There was no natural harbour, just a jetty, a little *quai*, enough for a few fishing boats to tie up safely. Hastings and the sandstone beds on which it lay were exposed to the full force of eroding wind and waves which had already eaten away the Roman town, and would, one day, probably do the same for the surrounding cliffs. Some years, the locals said, you could just stand and watch the cliffs falling.

One day the castle would go. Not that it was much of a place in Ranulf's view. It might be the first castle built by William the Conqueror in England but it was not a major military stronghold, nor a principal royal residence. William Rufus and his entourage stayed there when passing through Hastings, but it was cramped and poorly maintained. Ranulf Flambard preferred the little run-down cottage he had sequestered last year, close to the sea. He liked the fish stink and the yarns of the old seamen. Breton traders, Norman carriers, old Flanders tars and English fishers were brought together through the commerce of the sea which gave them a common bond, a fund of stories and a maritime language all their own. He liked to walk on the beach, spotting the shells, jellyfish and strange plants which were washed up there, along with the occasional body. Although he was a creature of palaces and towns, Ranulf was drawn to the sea with its restless, borderless acres. The sea was full of symbols and matter for reflection; one might be more spiritual by the sea, he mused, than in a monastery. After all, hadn't God's spirit first moved upon the face of the waters? Ranulf breathed the fresh salt air and felt a pale autumn warmth on his face. The boats were ready and the sea was calm. There was only one problem, where were the troops?

Firmin came climbing down from his lookout post on the eastern cliff. From there, he could get at least a partial view of the road. He shook his head. They weren't coming.

'It's not going to be today, master.'

'What's keeping them?'

'You were told 'a few days' and it's only been two. They'll come tomorrow.'

Ranulf hid his anxiety. The king had charged him with the task of raising twenty-thousand men of the *fyrd* but he had only raised half that number. Nevertheless, ten thousand men was a considerable force for which William ought to be grateful since his affairs in Normandy were not going well. The king had not been able to extend his foothold in Upper Normandy and had managed to compromise his position in Lower Normandy. Robert Curthose, his brother and long-time opponent, had forged a working alliance with Philip of France and together they were making William dance about and look incompetent. Having failed to organise the scattered powers of his Norman liegemen and knights, William was finding that his ambition was outrunning his military strength. But there was one important matter on which he could call himself successful.

His brother Henry, for so long trapped in the tension between his elder brothers, sometimes supporting one and then the other, had come out on William's side. They had parleyed and had been reconciled. They had exchanged the kiss of peace and Henry had promised to raise money to further the campaign. When he heard this news, Ranulf had the distinct impression that a new force was entering English politics. Henry was more shrewd than William and better educated. Less bellicose, he preferred diplomacy to battle; he was also less direct, more cautious and duplicitous and, although possessing a ready wit, he lacked a sense of humour. The youngest of four brothers and five sisters, Henry had not received a great deal of parental attention and had at one time been destined for the church.

On their father's death, Robert Curthose was chosen to inherit Normandy and William was indicated, though not named, as successor to the English throne. Henry got no land from his father's will, even though he had managed to rush to the paternal deathbed at St Gervais in time to put his case. Instead, he was granted a vast amount of money, some said five thousand pounds, which tight-fisted Henry had hardly diminished over the intervening years. While William was profligate in every way, Henry was thrifty with money but liberal with his amorous favours. Notorious for his rampant sexuality, he had affairs with women of every degree: noblewomen, servants, ill-watched royal ladies at foreign courts, even buxom farm girls when he was on the march. He was well on the way to fathering a tribe of royal bastards.

'Has anyone counted them?' Ranulf said to Firmin when they were discussing Henry later that evening. 'No, but I dare say you could trace his journeys over the last ten years by plotting his nurslings on a chart. Now, we hear, he will soon be rutting among the London dames. Believe me, Firmin, this cock let loose among the court hens will be a fine sight to see. Then Anselm will have something altogether different to complain about.'

'It may be, master that Anselm would get on better with Henry than with William.'

'It may be. If Anselm is constitutionally capable of getting on with anyone.'

Yet for all his prolific procreation, Henry had remained unmarried. Ranulf suspected that this was an astute calculation about the succession. If by mischance, or design, some adversity should befall William, then Henry would need to act quickly in making a bid for the throne. One of the most important means of acquiring baronial consent for an opportunistic grab at the crown would be to make an appropriate marriage. Ranulf was sure that Henry was thinking in such terms and even suspected that he had someone in mind, someone whom his brother had rejected only a year ago. Ranulf remembered how he had nearly written a letter to Henry at the time of the king's illness, in March last year. It would have been an offer of support in case the king died. But he could not bring himself to write it. Henry was politically shrewd and undoubtedly the best candidate to succeed but he had one major drawback, he had no love for Ranulf Flambard. If Henry ever became a dominating force in English politics, Ranulf would surely find his own circumstances suddenly plunged into serious decline. So he prayed for the continuing health of William Rufus whose favour had made him a man of substance. He hoped he would not lose that favour. He hoped the troops would come tomorrow.

Firmin took off his tunic and laid it carefully over a wooden rail. Ranulf watched him, waiting for him to give it a customary brush with his hand to remove the Hastings dust. The tunic, along with a warm winter mantle lined with fleeces, had been acquired by Firmin while in Huntingdon and he wore them proudly since they were the result of his own hard work. Ranulf watched the little performance, pleased to see that the lad had come to his senses. Having desired to do a good deed to his native town by spending his spare money in a generous act, he had instead bought these items for his own use. Ranulf approved. Firmin had overcome a charitable urge and taken thought for his own comfort, an indication of sound moral instincts kept in check by self-interest. Indeed, his young apprentice was making such steady progress towards becoming really useful that Ranulf thought he ought to be spared the more menial tasks of emptying piss pots, carrying water and taking care of their gear. Perhaps it was time to look around for a Hastings orphan to step into his role since he was so obviously destined for promotion. But that could wait until after the troops came.

Not long after dawn the following day Firmin hallooed and leapt down from his lookout post. He had seen a dust cloud at some distance, a reddish haze in the early morning sunlight. It was raised by the tramping feet of thousands of men making their way to the fields outside the town where they would be encamped and fed. Firmin pointed frantically in that direction as he came running down to Ranulf who was standing in the same spot as yesterday, looking out to sea.

'They're here, master.'

They descended to the bailey and went through to the constable's quarters. He was in the garderobe so they waited until he came out, a paunchy man with short grizzled hair and a square face. Ranulf had already sought, and gained, his collaboration for the ceremony that was about to take place. Soon afterwards, the constable went out and gave orders to a group of workmen. 'Set out the tables.' With a nod, he indicated where they should be placed. 'Plenty of room,' he said, 'so they can stand peacefully in line. No crowding, no pushing. You two,' he pointed to two garrison soldiers, 'choose some men to keep order here.' The constable then returned to Ranulf and, after a little discussion and some toing and froing among the soldiery, three money chests were brought from the strongroom and manhandled down the steps. These wooden coffers with hinged lids and metal reinforcings were placed on the trestle tables with their lids open like gaping mouths. They were empty.

'Right, Firmin, bring me the lists of the burghs.'

Ranulf had waited a long time to put his plan into action. It carried risks, but then so did every ingenious administrative experiment. Firmin saw a redoubtable glint in his master's eye and wondered what he was up to. It had not escaped his notice that there were not enough boats moored down at the seafront to take more than a few hundred men across. So what was his master going to do with all those troops massing in the fields around Hastings?

By the time everything was prepared and Firmin returned with the lists, the first of the English troops were filing into the bailey under the watchful eyes of the constable's guards, and forced to line up at the tables, snaking all the way back to the gateway. They were organised in burghs, men from each town or settlement grouped together. From the lists, Flambard knew how many men had been sent from each locality. Since each man was provided with twenty shillings from his burgh, for pay and sustenance, Ranulf was looking at the parade of a great deal of money before him.

When he saw the lines of men stretching out from each of the three trestles and was satisfied that they were now ready for what he had to tell them, Ranulf climbed up onto one of the tables and stood surveying them with a not unfriendly stare, raising his hands for quiet.

'My name is Ranulf Flambard,' he said. 'I am a minister of the king.' The orderly lines of men regarded him in parched, dusty silence. 'Let me ask you,' he went on, 'is there one of you here who would not rather be in his fields right now, getting in the harvest? Of course not. But, as brave and loyal subjects of the king, you have come voluntarily to offer yourselves to fight for him. On his behalf, I thank you.'

The men looked around at one another, at Flambard, the soldiers, the tables and the chests. One thing they had not reckoned to receive at Hastings was a speech from a Norman official in fluent English.

'You must know that the king values his loyal English subjects and has no desire to spill your blood. He is willing to put a proposition to you. If you agree, not one of you will go to Normandy, not one of you will lose his life.'

At this, there was some murmuring. Nearly all the men had said goodbye to wives and parents, children and families, expecting to be detained in Normandy through a long campaign, fighting for some barely comprehended objective in a foreign land with every prospect of being killed in battle or dying of disease. They looked questioningly at one another, at the guards, at Flambard. What were they doing here, lining up in this peculiar way listening to the words of a stranger standing on a table with open coffers at his feet?

'I am here to tell you that the king has no will to force any man to fight. Any man who wants to return to his home is free to do so.'

Again, a murmur of incomprehension ran through the snaking lines. Heads turned, men spat. They were restless, baffled and suspicious. Were they being tricked by this Norman speaker of English? Firmin feared that his master risked losing their attention by not coming to the point.

'Master, speak more directly to them in simple language. They don't trust you.'

Ranulf nodded and, sensing that Firmin was right, took the advice.

'You each have twenty shillings from your burgh,' he said as plainly as possible. 'Ten shillings for pay and ten for keep. Now, this is what the king offers. Every one of you can leave here today and return to your home with ten bright shillings in your pocket. For you, there will be no war, no hardship, no fighting. All you have to do is to deposit the other ten shillings in one of these chests.' Ranulf indicated them one by one.

'Of course, if you would rather keep all the money you are free to do so, in which case you will be put aboard a ship and sail for Wissant tonight. You have a simple choice.'

It took some time for the full implications of what Ranulf had said to sink in. But once they understood what was being offered there was a ripple through the lines as men readily stepped forward, pressing and pushing one another in their eagerness to throw their ten shillings worth of coins into the chests.

The entire performance was enacted many times over the two following days before all the recruits were dealt with. Every time the result was the same. An eager rush to dispense their ten shillings and get away from Hastings as fast as possible. Never was a tax so easily raised, or in such an atmosphere of relief. By the time the last of the conscripts came through the bailey, it was nightfall on the third day. By then, two chests were full and had been sealed and removed. As Ranulf had expected, only a few refused to accept the terms. Men of barbarous temper or natural inclination for warfare, real fighters with no families or men on the lookout for an alternative to back-breaking labour, these were the ones who made their way down to the boats, clutching their twenty shillings. By the time they sailed out later that night, Hastings was again almost deserted.

The plan had gone better than Ranulf could have hoped. Three chests, each so heavy that it took two mules to shift it, packed with coin for the king, lay ready for shipping. A rough estimate suggested that Ranulf had raised as much as four thousand pounds for the royal treasury, possibly more.

'So you see Firmin,' said Ranulf, toasting their work in his favourite Anjou, 'everyone wins. The king gets money to pay for mercenaries, properly trained knights, not like these raw field hands we've had through here these last days. Proper fighting men. He will have cash to pay bribes or buy off the opposition in Normandy and ransom his own captured nobles. And he will have ready money in hand to buy food and weapons.'

Firmin absorbed this explanation, frowning.

'And did you carry out this plan, master, purely from loyal motives?'

'Purely, Firmin, how can you doubt it?

Just how much Ranulf kept for himself, Firmin was not to know. But a few days later he would receive a small disbursement. 'For services to the king.'

'And so the Englishmen go back to their villages to greet their wives and children, to kiss the old brow of a patriarch and consider themselves blessed. What could be better? An all-round success, wouldn't you say?'

'But what will the king say, master?'

'The king is always ready to extract maximum profit from any situation. Be assured, Firmin, the king will be satisfied. We have been about God's holy work today. We have saved simple men from certain death. Has Anselm ever done as much?'

****

Following his practice of doing nothing for long periods and then doing something inappropriate, Anselm was gearing up to confront the king again.

'But, master,' said Baldwin, 'the king's campaign in Normandy has not gone well. He will not be in a receptive mood. Perhaps we should delay our visit.'

Baldwin was against the idea of going to see the king at Gillingham because, in his view, Anselm's determination to press the issue of the *pallium* would result in yet another fruitless confrontation. Besides, Anselm's motives were unclear. Did he want the *pallium* so that he would feel secure as archbishop, or did he merely want to press for it in the hope that the king would refuse it and, by default, grant him the thing he really wanted, release from the burden of high office? Baldwin sometimes wondered whether Anselm himself really knew.

In January 1095, the king had returned to England after spending Christmas stranded at Wissant, waiting for favourable sailing weather. In spite of Ranulf Flambard's subsidy, his campaign had not been a success, although it had made him more than ever determined to bring Normandy under his control. After a hurried compromise with his brother, Robert, whose dukedom he was one day resolved to acquire, he took ship, landed in Hastings, then rapidly crossed the country from east to west in order to confront the rebellions in Wales. He was now at Gillingham in Dorset, waiting for a break in the weather so that he could go to the aid of Hugh d'Avranches, the Earl of Chester, who had riskily placed his overweight, gouty body in the way of Welsh insurgents.

While the king had been away, Anselm had continued wandering about Kent, avoiding Canterbury, writing his treatise, penning letters and receiving complaints from the Christchurch monks who wondered why he was ignoring them. He was now back at the manor of Godmersham, stoking the fires against a raw and icy winter, trying to keep warm. Baldwin and Eadmer were sitting with the master in his private quarters. Although flames roared up the flued chimney, they were wrapped in blankets. Outside, snow covered the ground and buildings, drifts were piled against the hedges, people and birds scarcely stirred, sounds were muffled. Eadmer's chilblained hands could not write, though he kept his ink pots warm by the fire. He had a cold in the head and his only contribution to the conversation was to disturb his companions from time to time with coughs and sneezes.

'We must not fear the king's temper, Baldwin. Whatever rage the king visits on us does not reduce the rightness of our case,' said Anselm. 'No adversity should turn us from the path. '"Fret not thyself because of evildoers," says the Psalm. We must not be cheated of the glory of the lord.'

'What do you mean by that, master?' said Baldwin, leaning forward to stoke the fire.

'Church Councils, I have asked for them. The *pallium*, I have explained my case. The pope, I have urged recognition. The return of the Canterbury fiefs, I have pressed for them. All these things are in dispute, yet they can be easily settled. God will show us the way. Did not God show the way to Gunhild, my dear sister in Christ, leading her back to the sanctified life? And to Edith, now in the protection of the king? God enlightened the king on that matter and led us to agreement. I have no doubt He will do so again.'

Baldwin sat thinking that if these were spiritual matters, they wore the heavy disguise of worldly affairs. But then Anselm saw everything through the prism of spirituality. He did not have real arguments to defend, except in the realm of theology. There he could be as sharp as a blade. But in secular matters, he was incapable of perceiving a contrary point of view if it belonged to a man of whom he disapproved. In his relations with the king, of whom he thoroughly disapproved, he was reduced to a succession of moods, sulks, whims, adverse reactions and Biblical quotations.

Eadmer punctured the conversation with an almighty sneeze.

'Do you have a fever, young Eadmer?' said Anselm. 'You must ask Brother Gervais for one of his infusions.'

'This might be a sign that we should delay our journey,' urged Baldwin. 'It's winter and the roads are full of dangers. It will be hard on your people, master. Better if we all stay here until the thaw.'

'By then, it will be too late. Besides, bodily discomfort is the refining grace of monks. We must be stronger than our flesh.' This was said with some energy, even determination. Then Anselm sighed and added: 'But, perhaps you are right, Baldwin.' He drew his blanket around his old shoulders and listened to the wind keening outside. It would be good to stay. Even in front of the fire, he felt the edge of winter. He was dreadfully weary, tired of wandering. If he had known how many years of wandering still lay before him, he might have resigned on the instant. But the desire to make a success of his office was still not extinguished in Anselm. However many disappointing meetings he had with the king, he always clung to the hope that the next one would be different. And so, a few days later, on the Feast of the Epiphany, they set out for the royal manor of Gillingham to meet the king.

When William heard of their departure on that date, he made a joke about Anselm, Eadmer and Baldwin being the Three Kings bringing gifts of trouble, annoyance and bad feeling. Soon after arriving at Gillingham, Baldwin sought out Ranulf Flambard. Both men were anxious that relations should not descend into a protracted stalemate that would wreck the work already done. When he heard that Anselm was intending to press more strongly for the *pallium* and permission to go to Rome to receive it, Ranulf's spirits sank. Nevertheless, since he was unable to stop it, the meeting went ahead and resulted in predictable impasse. Neither the king nor Anselm would concede the point. Afterwards, Ranulf and Baldwin met again to comment on the proceedings.

'Does he not realise that asking William to grant permission to receive the *pallium,* is tantamount to asking him to recognise a pope? The king is firm on this point. He will not suffer his hand to be forced. Whenever Anselm asks for such permission the king's first question is always: 'Which pope?'

'Unfortunately, my master is convinced that if he is to operate as archbishop and uphold Canterbury's rights, he must secure the *pallium*. This is not to say that he is an enthusiastic papalist, he isn't. But since he has already recognised Urban, and since there is no party in England willing to recognise Clement III, Anselm sees no good cause for the king to hesitate.'

'The king hesitates because he enjoys being free of the interference of Rome and because Anselm is too importunate. The more William is pushed, the more he pushes back. The trouble is, no one but Anselm is in a hurry on this matter. I think I can guess the reason why.'

Baldwin pursed his lips and nodded. He knew as well as Flambard why Anselm was riding this question with spurs and whips. Anselm did not care if he lost his office in consequence of provocation of the king. Indeed, he would welcome it.

Flambard poured some wine from an earthenware crock into two goblets and handed one to Baldwin who placed it, untasted, beside him. Seeing this, he made a silent bet with himself. He would get Baldwin to loosen up and drink some wine before this meeting was over.

'But,' he went on, 'does Anselm have any conception of the position in which he is placing the king? He is backing him up against a wall where he will have to make a stand. Doesn't he see that?'

'I fear that the master's moral judgement of the man colours his understanding of his kingly role.'

'More's the pity,' said Ranulf, doubting that any progress was going to be made unless there was a serious concerted attempt by all the bishops and barons to force some kind of acceptable compromise.

'Our trouble is,' said Ranulf, 'both men are defending rights and principles. Just not the same ones.'

Baldwin nodded sagely in agreement.

'Even though they are as different as any two men can be, they are also, in one unique particular, very similar. Do you see what haunts the minds of both these men and sets them on a path of conflict?'

'I don't follow,' said Baldwin.

'What haunts their minds, what drifts ghostlike through all their thoughts, is a fundamental ruling figure. A figure they desire both to please and to escape from.'

'I take your meaning,' said Baldwin. 'The figure of the father.'

'Exactly. Why will Anselm not budge from the principle of maintaining Lanfranc's inheritance? Because Lanfranc is his father, his predecessor, both at Bec and Canterbury, his guide, the man from whom he sought love and respect, to whom he devoted all filial feeling. Anselm is afraid of not being worthy of Father Lanfranc.'

'I myself have thought so, many times,' said Baldwin, impressed by Flambard's insight. 'But is the same true of the king?'

'Oh, undoubtedly. William is haunted by that great name, isn't he? The Conqueror. An impossible exemplar. An uncomfortable legacy. Feeling inferior goes with the inheritance. The Conqueror ruled without recognising a pope after Gregory died in 1085, he freed England from papal interference and got control of all ecclesiastical traffic between England and Rome. In other words, the Conqueror had full management of the English church. This is what William is fighting to preserve and why he, too, is desperate to be worthy of the father. Ironic, isn't it? They are so far apart, and yet, so similar?'

Having established a point on which they both agreed, they fell silent for a time. Ranulf drank his wine and they sat wrapped in their thoughts. The shabby Gillingham lodging glowed feebly in the light of a few candles. It was as sparsely furnished as a monk's cell and, at that moment, as full of profound reflection. When they spoke, their breaths curled in the cold air. With his love of puns, Ranulf regularly talked about 'Chillingham' since his lodgings there were the coldest he had known.

'What do you advise?' asked Baldwin after a time. 'Will the king meet with him again, or shall we delay a further interview?'

'What we must do,' said Ranulf, 'is change tack. We must promote the idea of a high-level meeting. A full-blown summit, involving all the most powerful men who have an interest in these issues. We must avoid these constant scenes of head-butting between the king and Anselm.'

'Widen the discussion, you mean, but wouldn't that also widen the dissension?

‘Perhaps, but it might just reveal positions on which true argument can take place. How long would it take you to sound out the bishops?’

‘A month, perhaps.’

‘Well then. Let’s prepare the way for a great council, say, sometime in Lent. By then, the king will be at Rockingham. In the meantime, I will sound out the barons.’

Flambard drained his goblet, refilled it then stood turning the cup in his hands watching the swirling liquid with a pensive frown.

‘By the way, it would be as well to plant this suggestion in your master’s mind. Let him brood on it a little, then get him to write to the king asking for a plenary Council at Rockingham. In the meantime, I will work on the king. When Anselm finds the king willing to agree it will seem as though his request has been met.’

Baldwin nodded in agreement and Ranulf raised his goblet.

‘To the bull and the sheep.’

Baldwin lifted his cup and drank.

****

After Gunhild’s departure, Aefled and Agnes clung together in grief for their friend. They spent many hours talking over the events of the last two years when Gunhild had gambled with fate, found and lost a great love, given birth, suffered the death of her child and gone back to Wilton to take up her old life. But what sort of life could it be? What awaited her now but endless remorse? Gunhild’s journey out of Wilton and her tragic return gave them matter for reflection as they tried to understand how these events had been willed by a just God.

Agnes stayed on at Castle St Mary’s until winter when the roads closed, leaving them remote, cut off, grasping at every tardy drift of news as it flurried down to them among the snow falls and sleet showers. They heard of the king’s campaign in Normandy which achieved little. They heard about the meeting between Anselm and the king at Gillingham which achieved even less. The name of Ranulf Flambard filtered into their conversation, a name brought to their attention by Arnoud, Maria’s lover, who had heard of the raising of the *fyrd* from some clerks in Earlsham who had been involved in mustering the local levy. Agnes was particularly taken with the name of Ranulf Flambard. ‘Flambard’ was an unusual patronymic, one obviously forged to fit a style of person.

‘There are many ways to “flame,”’ said Agnes, when they were discussing him one morning. ‘He might have red hair, perhaps.’

‘Then they call you “Rufus”. It takes only a few red whiskers or the merest tinge in certain lights to earn you that name. Look at the king. He’s more brown than red. Look at Count Alan, poor Gunhild’s lover, how much red hair did he have? These are silly names, attached to people for lazy reference by unobservant monks.’

‘So we can assume that “Flambard” does not have red hair. Then the name must derive from some burning in his nature. Is he an ardent lover, perhaps? Or a torch who brings light to the king’s council, or a dangerous fire brand who scorches all who come near?’

‘Or a man destined for hellfire?’

‘Come on, Aefled. Even you have to admit, it’s a seductive name.’

‘Would it surprise you to know that I have met him? Two years ago. He was with the king at Wilton. He spoke to Gunhild. He didn’t have red hair.’

‘Good God, Aefled. I had no idea. Tell me about him.’

‘There’s nothing more to tell. He spoke to Gunhild about her uncle, that’s all. Oh, I wish Gunhild would write!’

Since going away after the death of her child, Gunhild had been silent. Robert was mute, too, although one short letter came to say that he was in London in the service of Count Alan Niger who was doing great things for her sons. She longed for more news but Robert was so dependent on third parties to do his writing that he tended not to bother. Or, when they came, his letters were disappointing because his unsubtle, laconic nature could barely distinguish vital news from unimportant gossip. Every winter it was the same. Cut off from the outside world, Aefled became discontented and restless, longing for spring, longing for the prospect of a journey.

‘I want to go to London,’ she announced to Agnes one morning.

‘Whatever for?’

‘Do you remember the letter I had from Rabbi Simon? I never replied to that letter because I cannot see any way of delivering it.’

‘Well, can’t you write to Robert and ask him to inquire?’

‘Robert wouldn’t like that. He was always against my association with Isaac, although he tolerated it for many years.’

‘There, you see, Robert is not a bad husband, is he?’ said Agnes absently. ‘He’s tolerant. Best of all, he’s absent. That gives you a degree of freedom and spares you the strain of constant pregnancy and childbirth. In consequence, you have kept your health. You're lucky, Aefled, believe me, I could settle for a man like Robert, given the chance. I don't aim to be a prioress all my life.'

Aefled laughed uneasily. When Agnes spoke in her provocative way about men and marriage, she was in flagrant defiance of church teaching. Should her state of mind become known to her bishop or her words reported to his court, she would be at risk of dismissal. Agnes knew it but seemed careless of the threat.

'Go on, write to your tolerant husband,' she urged. 'Get Robert to deliver your letter.'

It would have amazed them to know that Robert had already made a visit to the Jewish quarter at Poultry. Nothing could have got him into such a place except obedience to his overlord and it was on Count Alan Niger's orders that he had gone among the strange, unknown people who haunted the narrow alleys, wore bizarre clothes and showed by their polite but defensive treatment of him that they lived in awkward association with their Christian neighbours. One gloomy Saturday in February, he went to search out a man called Joseph who was well on his way to becoming chief Rabbi of London and was widely known, even among the highest in the land, including Henry, Count of Cotentin, brother of the king. When he inquired after Joseph, Robert was directed to a large wooden building at the end of a lane and told to wait outside.

'You can't go in,' said his guide apologetically, 'you wouldn't like it.'

The structure was a synagogue, or rather two synagogues huddled together, one for men and one for women. It was attached at one side to a strange square building which housed a bath. The *mikveh*, used exclusively in religious ceremonies for ritual immersion, was hidden away under a squat tower with what looked like a little bell tower on top, built of wood and thatch, as were all the surrounding buildings over which it loomed.

Staring up at it, annoyed at being kept waiting, Robert felt entirely out of place, as if he had entered a part of the city that had detached itself and floated away into a foreign land. And then, suddenly, from out of the synagogue came a stream of men wearing black and white shawls and pointed hats. Robert stood like a post as they swept by him, followed by a crowd of women, heads covered, walking in chattering groups. He was on the point of leaving when a man approached and said he was Rabbi Joseph. He was tall, bearded, with bright dark eyes and a gracious manner. When he spoke, everything he said, in the unmistakeable accents of Rouen, reassured Robert that Count Alan had not sent him on a fool's mission. Here was a man with whom a Christian could do business. Robert was not the first to be impressed by Rabbi Joseph who enjoyed courtly connections and a reputation for fair dealing. For some time there had been an understanding between him and the king's brother. It was rumoured that Henry's five thousand inheritance, invested by Joseph, had doubled in value, making him rich enough to be dangerous. When Henry had promised to raise money in London for the king's Normandy campaign what he had meant was that he would borrow money from Joseph. And one of the agents Henry was employing to conduct the transaction was Count Alan Niger. Thus the agency was passed down to Robert who found himself in the presence of a lean man, getting on in years, with longish, grey-streaked curls, an enigmatic smile and soft-spoken courtesy. A man who baffled, impressed and repulsed him at the same time.

'My lord Robert,' said the Rabbi, 'I understand you are the representative of the Prince Henry, brother of the king. I welcome you and will be ready to act in all things to the credit of his royal house. I have his instructions.'

It was polite, polished, bland, ingratiating and not quite true. As far as he knew, Robert was not Henry's "representative". Finding nothing to say, and keeping his distance as they went, he paced out the short walk to the counting house in Poultry Yard and followed Joseph inside to wait while he drew up the agreement on a small piece of parchment.

'The first payment will be made at the end of this month of February. If you will come, or send, or instruct one of your servants, the coin can be conveyed at very little notice. Will that be agreeable?'

Robert nodded, his eyes glancing around the room. There were small windows set high in the walls. There were trestle tables and counters, some with abacuses and weighing scales, others with parchment and writing implements. There were sacks stacked in corners, valuable shipments of imported seeds, powders for dyes, crushed lapis, amber and ambergris, bales of exotic materials, jars of wine and honey. The place was a treasure house, a cave of wonders, yet it was dusty, cobwebbed and gloomy, as if abandoned. From the outside, it looked like an ordinary hovel in an ordinary alley in a disreputable part of London.

'We mustn't attract attention,' said Joseph, seeing Robert's thoughts etched on his face. 'Either to ourselves or our habits and beliefs. We just do what we can under the law and fit in. Nothing secret or underhand is done, but nothing is seen. We live cut off. It breeds rumours, but that is the only way.'

'You mean, you never go out of here?'

'Rarely and never without a permit. In this little area, we can be safe. Henry has guaranteed it.'

'How long have you been working with him?'

'Many years. We have always received fair treatment at his hands. If he was king…' Joseph stopped abruptly, his dark eyes twinkling, waiting to see what response he got from Robert.

'If he was king—what?' pressed Robert.

'If Henry was king…well. It was close to happening two years ago when William nearly died. All the Jews of Poultry were ready to acknowledge Henry. Perhaps others, too. Nobles, barons, bishops. Perhaps Count Alan Niger? Perhaps yourself? But it was God's will to keep William on the throne. We leave all to God, whose workings are great and impenetrable. But, one day, if Henry…'

'If Henry…?'

'In my view, in our view, there would be better laws in the country. If Henry was king there would be a charter, he has promised it to many men, including us. A charter that would set out just laws and proclaim liberties. A charter that would seek to undo the abuses of his brother's reign.'

'And you believe these promises?'

'I do. Perhaps you think me a fool to trust the word of a great man, especially one who wants to borrow money. But Henry has given proofs in the past that he will stand by his word. That is why Count Alan Niger serves him and that is why, I suspect, you do too.'

Robert took the parchment and looked it over, pretending he could read. Once again, he was shamed by his ignorance of writing. Even a Jew, an enemy of God, he thought, can belittle me in this.

'This will have to be agreed by the Count.'

'All is in order. He will agree.'

'Why are you so ready to raise money for William's wars when all along you are wishing for his death?'

'We are not wishing it. But it would be foolish not to prepare for it. William is childless and shows no will to marry. Death can strike at any time. Who knows what is to come?'

'But he is young and may live for many years.'

'As is Henry. But all is in the hands of God. Your God and our God, they are not so very different. Neither are our aims. That's why we can work with Henry. He has sworn never to act against his brother, never to begin a reign in bloodshed or treachery, only to wait upon the will of God, as we all must do.'

Afterwards, Robert's first impulse was to find a scribe and write immediately to Aefled. He needed to tell her about this astonishing visit. Later he reconsidered. It might not be wise. Had he stumbled upon a plot? Was Henry actually planning a coup? Surely not. What he had heard concerned only vague feelings, wishes, rumoured promises. These were not treacherous in themselves, at least at the level of private conversation. And yet the visit may have been a way of instructing him, or testing him, or preparing him. For what? One thing was certain, by sending him into Poultry to collect a promise of payment, Count Alan Niger had sealed Robert's service to Henry as surely as if he had just taken a binding oath.

****

Rockingham Castle. A foursquare, rock hard fortress, built by the Conqueror. It was a fitting venue for a momentous event. But Firmin was puzzled.

'Why choose the chapel for the meeting tomorrow, why not the great hall? You can get more people into the great hall.'

'Quite so, Firmin. But we don't need numbers. We need concentrated minds.'

Ranulf Flambard was in a good mood. At Rockingham, the king's first minister at last felt himself decently housed. A small apartment overlooking the inner bailey and a private garden were at his disposal. From the window, Ranulf could see, beyond the curtain walls, a great hunting park stretching into the broad expanse of Welland Valley.

'The king loves to hunt here. The forests are stuffed full of deer and boar and many other of God's creatures who will yield their lives to his shameless bow.'

'Do you disapprove of the king's sport, master?'

'It's a curious thing, Firmin, but I find myself in agreement with Anselm on the matter. Baldwin tells me he feels a particular affinity with small hunted creatures and makes little edifying sermons on their fates. I should like to hear one.'

From a study of his master's face, Firmin could not be sure if this was the expression of a genuine wish or a throwaway irony.

'Incidentally, Firmin,' he added, 'while we are here I want you to renew your acquaintance with Eadmer.'

The day appointed for the opening of the Rockingham Conference, Sunday, 25th February, dawned crisp and clear. From daybreak, the castle chapel began to fill with the worthiest men of the realm, bishops, barons, counsellors and ministers. An air of excitement buzzed among the concourse with all the expectancy of a scandalous court case, as though Anselm was about to be tried on a treasonous charge. Eadmer stood beside his master, armed with nothing more than sharp eyes and a capacious memory, intending to take mental notes to write up later. A full written account, unbiased and impartial, was what he always aimed at and what, out of passionate partisanship, he continually failed to deliver.

Eadmer watched William St Calais, Bishop of Durham, leading out the assembly of bishops looking like a thunderous prosecutor with a water-tight case, although his official brief was merely to chair the conference. He liked a legal battle and had once honed all his forensic skills in his own defence at the time of the succession crisis of 1087 when he had backed Robert Curthose and was charged with treason. On principle, William St Calais never owned up to a fault and, when faced with the full force of King William's damning charge sheet in the court at Sarum in 1088, he had reacted defiantly, even insolently, refusing to acknowledge the charges in a case that pitched him against one of the greatest prosecutors of the age. On that day, no less a dialectician than Lanfranc himself had appeared for the crown. St Calais argued him up and down, saying that the court had no competency to try a bishop. Lanfranc replied that he was not on trial as a bishop but as a baron who had broken his fealty oath, whereupon St Calais appealed to the papal curia, a provocative gesture which angered the king. As a result, he was punished for contumacy. All his fiefs were forfeited and he was forced to surrender his castle. He took ship for Normandy where he became an adviser to Robert Curthose. By this process, he had been effectively split in two, the baron was punished, unpropertied and exiled, the bishop was still notionally presiding over his diocese of Durham. This might have finished some men, but St Calais was irrepressible, manipulative, clever and bold. He never gave up and was determined to be reunited with the other part of himself in England.

That moment came when the warring brothers had one of their periodic reconciliations in 1091, at which a general amnesty was issued. The bishop was reunited with the baron, he recovered his fiefs and, on September 11th, 1091, finally re-entered Durham. From then on, William St Calais was one of the king's most loyal vassals, someone who consistently supported him in all his disagreements with Anselm. This controversial, many sided man was the one who, in the royal court at Rockingham, during three February days in 1095, acted as prosecutor and leader of the bishops against their own premier archbishop.

After meeting privately with his councillors, the king entered the chapel and took his seat in the nave below the altar. He wore a simple belted mantle of wool, a gesture towards the renunciations of Lent. By dressing in this way, William forestalled the example of Anselm who was wearing a plain Benedictine habit without any embellishment. The chapel fell silent as all eyes were drawn to the two protagonists who were already, without a word being said, making statements.

With a blank-faced nod, William invited Anselm to address the meeting. Leaning on a staff, Anselm rose and launched himself into a long recapitulation of their falling out at Gillingham, giving his version of the dispute. Anselm wanted the *pallium* from the pope. William recognised no pope. Furthermore, William had clearly stated that if anyone sought to take from him his right of recognising a pope it would rob him of a prerogative and was tantamount to treason. Anselm told the gathered bishops and nobles that he was seriously exercised about where his first duty lay. It was the old question of God or Caesar. Having submitted to Urban he could not go back on it. Equally, he could not receive the *pallium* from a pope whom the king had not recognised. Where did his first duty lay? With the king who had prevailed on him to become archbishop, or with the pope who alone had the power to authenticate the office? From William's point of view, if Anselm gave obedience to a pope without his authority he was in breach of his allegiance to the crown and guilty of *lèse-majesté*. So things had been left in a state of perfect impasse at Gillingham and so they were taken up again at Rockingham.

Anselm spun out an interminable morning by arguing that at the time he had recognised Pope Urban, he had been Abbot of Bec in Normandy and not under allegiance to the king of England. He then went back to the circumstances of his election in March 1093 at the time of the king's illness. 'It was known at that time that I had recognised Urban. I made it clear I would not renounce my allegiance to the Apostolic Father and yet there was strong insistence, by many of you here that I should take up the office.'

After a long session of picking over the minutiae of past disputes, Anselm addressed the full assembly, his voice quavering with the pressure of his dilemma: 'To me it is a terrible thing to disown the Vicar of Christ. Terrible, too, to transgress the allegiance I have made to the king. All you abbots, bishops and barons called here today, do me the grace to advise me in this matter.'

The barons were displeased by this appeal which was likely to trap them in infinite degrees of error. Heads turned and eyes looked to the king who sat motionless, a strained expression on his face. He could not relent one jot on the principle of papal recognition, but he was not unaffected by Anselm's dilemma. The old man was flailing in a trap of his own making. For once, William was beyond jesting, beyond even gloating. Looking at the bench of bishops, he wondered how they could sit upright, being so spineless. They hardly dared look at Anselm, as if shamefaced at their own feebleness. It gave him no pleasure to see the old man treated with disrespect. William was remembering how Anselm had enjoyed the respect of his father, respect which, God knew, was given to few and did not include himself.

'I pray and charge you all,' went on Anselm, 'that you look diligently into this matter and, after the most careful consideration, advise me what I should do. I cannot breach the obedience I owe to the pope. Yet I cannot offend against the allegiance I owe to the king. I, therefore, appeal to the wisest heads in the kingdom—advise me on this matter. Lighten my burden by giving me the help of your advice.'

At this, the king rose and ordered the bishops to take themselves off to consider their advice in an antechamber while he and his advisers went to dinner. Joining him at the meal, Ranulf observed that the king seemed preoccupied and when he made some innocuous remark about the quality of the food, William said he could barely taste it.

'My lord king, are you indisposed?'

'I am well, Flambard, but troubled. I could wish things were not as they are.'

'We all do, my lord.'

'When I was grievously sick at Gloucester he came and gave me absolution. I opened my soul to him. That creates a bond, Flambard. When I thought I was dying, I held out my hand to him. He held it and I felt…I don't know what to call it. But I do know that, in all his life, my father never took my hand with such complete kindness.'

While the king dined and the bishops conferred, Anselm sat on in the cold chapel, abandoned by all but Eadmer and Baldwin. They tried to tempt his appetite but he refused all food, saying he was in a state of penance and would not eat till evening.

Poignant though Anselm's appeal had been, it cut little ice with the bishops. They now began to employ the non-committal replies that were to be the hallmark of their group response. In a very short time, they were back with their answer, delivered by William St Calais.

'The advice you seek rests with yourself,' he said. 'We know you to be wise in God and a lover of goodness. So why, in the name of the Almighty, do you need advice from us?'

Robert Bloet, Bishop of Lincoln stood forward. 'If you would put aside every other consideration and devote your whole mind to the service of the king,' he said in a milder tone, 'we would be very willing to go to the king where he is at dinner and put your case again.'

Disappointed that they were reluctant either to advise or support him, Anselm assented and the bishops went away to disturb the king's dinner. The outcome was that William cancelled the rest of the day's proceedings and ordered Anselm to return to his lodgings and come to court again in the morning. Then he went out with his hounds in the afternoon, glad to be unburdened of the matter.

'Day One, Firmin, and nothing to report,' said Ranulf that evening. 'Did you meet up with Eadmer?'

'I did, master.'

'And?'

'His account will be damning of William St Calais and won't exactly flatter the king. Eadmer believes there is a plot to depose Anselm from office and send him into exile.'

'Which is probably what Anselm wants.'

'But not what Eadmer wants. He wants to go on being the biographer of a saint and the close companion of an archbishop. It gives him status.'

'Eadmer hasn't done badly for a no-account English lad, has he? Secretary, associate, assistant to an archbishop and the keeper of his chapel. Not bad for an undistinguished youth of moderate talents.'

'And those moderate talents are stretching to another great work, master. Eadmer's latest resolve is to write a series of studies of the old English saints. St Wilfrid, St Dunstan, St Oswald and so on. He complains that the Norman church has no respect for the past. He told me that he could never forget when Lanfranc swept all the saints' relics out of their sacred resting places and bundled them into the north transept of the cathedral. He said it was an insult to the old church and he would never forget it. He feels his slighted Englishness very deeply, master.'

'Well then,' shrugged Flambard, 'he's heading for a lifetime of frustrated ambition and wounded pride.'

At the beginning of the second session on Monday, 26th February, which was conducted in William's absence, the bishops reaffirmed their refusal to support Anselm and an argument ensued. Realising he was going to get no help from the quarter he most desired it, Anselm went in person to the king. William listened and then declared that Anselm was to renounce obedience to Urban and in future act in all things only in consultation with the royal will. This was provocative. William was pushing him, seeing what he could get, employing harassment and bullying as legitimate weapons. William was ready to push him to the brink, but not over it. Here in a sharply etched form was a vital issue of power which would be tested again and again over the coming centuries. The struggle between royal and ecclesiastical prerogatives would embroil men for years, refining itself in precedents, legal instruments, agreements, contestations, battles and martyrdoms. And it would inscribe itself permanently into Anglo-Norman affairs at the very moment the king recognised a pope. Even while knowing that he would have to do so eventually, William fought against it with as much determination as Anselm fought against a renunciation. What might superficially appear as a matter of little significance was, in fact, a crucial issue of the times.

When William Rufus, King of England, from his fairly secure throne on the western edge of Europe, looked out towards the continent he could see, up and down Christendom, kings, dukes, princes and counts falling one by one to the domination of the church. Henry IV, the Holy Roman Emperor, Alfonso VI of Spain, Robert Guiscard, Duke of Apulia, had faced threats of deposition or suffered the imposition of the Roman Mass, or been strangled of their rights of investiture. In several cases, discussion had become argument, argument outright battle and many had gone to their deaths trying to solve the issue of whether a king could make a pope or a pope could make a king. In that very year of 1095, Pope Urban was riding a cavalcade of popular acclamation on a tour north of the Alps. Throughout France, Clement's former adherents were coming forward in steady succession to submit themselves to his rival's authority. Urban, a priest of the warrior class with the ruthless instincts of a castellan, was being recognised in Normandy and the independent fiefs of northern Europe as the legitimate pontiff. Whole swathes of continental Europe had pledged allegiance. England could not stay outside the game much longer, which made William all the more determined to skewer Anselm while he had the chance.

When the bishops reinforced the king's demands and advised him to accept, Anselm dug in his heels, refused and begged for an adjournment. Whereupon William St Calais went to the king and advised him to pronounce a judgement, thus turning the conference from an advisory conclave into what it had always threatened to become—a trial.

In public session, William St Calais then charged Anselm with polluting the fealty he had sworn to the king and seeking to despoil him of the greatest of his prerogatives, papal recognition. Dumbfounded that the bishops, whom he had called upon in a humble spirit for advice, could behave in this aggressive way, allowing the wolfish St Calais to heap him with calumnies, Anselm sat head bowed, leaning on his staff as charge after charge was reeled off, each one like a whiplash or a step along his own private via dolorosa.

The upshot of this tirade was unexpected. Suddenly the mood of the court changed. Bishops and barons alike swung towards sympathy with Anselm. He had been placed in a cruel dilemma, he was defending a principle which they could understand, he was not in any real sense a traitor, he was being subjected to intolerable bullying, his behaviour was quiet and dignified. St Calais realised he had overreached his brief and was creating a backlash against himself. Men with long memories were dredging up visions of St Calais in 1088 and did not like what they saw. That the Bishop of Durham should, in public session, browbeat the Archbishop of Canterbury was more than many of them could stomach and they began to shout him down. But St Calais did not end before he had made his point with forthright succinctness: 'If you offend the king, Urban can do nothing for you, but, if you are reconciled to the king, Urban can do you no harm.'

Once more, Anselm repeated his unshakeable position. 'I utterly refuse to abjure obedience to Pope Urban.'

At that, St Calais threw up his hands and swore.

When Anselm, seeing that the day was rolling on towards evening, asked for an adjournment, St Calais, along with a train of exhausted bishops and some barons, went straight to the king to confess their failure. Unlike Anselm, William did not feel in need of advice.

'He is seeking to rob me of my sovereignty by making Urban pope in this realm before I myself have recognised him. It is the thing I hold of chiefest worth, the thing that sets me apart from all other princes, a prerogative I derive from my father who alone held sway in this realm from the day of his conquest till the day of his death. Until he abandons Urban, he is no oathman of mine.' It was another calculated push, perhaps to the brink, but even now William was not prepared to see him fall.

When the king's outburst was reported back to Anselm he listened attentively and looked resigned. But when he spoke it was to say something momentous. In words resounding with the clash between worldly pragmatism and doctrinal conscience, he stated an unalterable position, one that would have immense repercussions in the titanic battles to come.

'No one can prove me false to the oath and allegiance I owe my earthly king because I refuse to abjure allegiance to the pope. To anyone who tries I will answer in the name of the Lord.'

With these words, Anselm marked the stand that many of his successors would take. Seventy-five years from now another Archbishop of Canterbury would be bloodily struck down in his cathedral for this very principle. On hearing his words, bishops and barons looked towards one another realising they had just received a threat. What till then they had not clarified as an idea, now became one: an idea that put kingship as the sovereign authority of the state at risk as never before. An Archbishop of Canterbury could not be judged or condemned by the king or the court or any human being except only the pope. Was the king to have an equal in his own realm? It was unthinkable.

Stunned and momentarily distracted by the issue of a challenge they hadn't seen coming, the bishops and barons united in calling for an adjournment, which was immediately granted. It being now night, everyone dispersed to his lodgings.

'Day Two, Firmin, and I have the distinct impression that something has occurred, although I'm not sure what.'

'The barons were trying to turn it into a trial, master, but Anselm called their bluff.'

'A conference, a trial, it's becoming whatever one wants it to be. But it's certainly not the thing that Anselm was expecting, Firmin, a source of sound advice. The bishops hesitate, the barons prevaricate, the king bullies and Anselm sticks to his narrow point.

One thing's certain, the king cannot afford either to condemn Anselm or remove him. It's quite a day, isn't it, Firmin, when the king cannot do just as he likes?'

When the barons went to William that night to report on the day's session, he was incandescent.

'Holy Face of Lucca!' he thundered. 'Is this the best you can do? Well, wipe the slate and start again. I tell you, I am not going to have someone equal to me in my kingdom.' Now he found himself in Anselm's position, needing advice and not getting it. 'If you knew he had such a good case, why did you let me start the suit against him? Come on! Give me some advice! Because if you don't get on with it and condemn him, then, by the Face of Lucca, I will condemn you.'

Ranulf had rarely seen him so furious but suspected that there was more than a little over-acting in the part. When word of this dramatic scene got back to Anselm, he panicked and asked for a safe conduct to a ferry port, which was denied.

'Why would he go into exile, master? Anselm can't really believe that the king would harm him.'

'Of course not. But from the moment he was elected Anselm has been seeking a way out. Exile would not be disagreeable to him.'

'Would the king agree to exile, master?'

'You can be sure, Firmin, that although the king desires nothing so much as to be free of this constant wrangling, he would not like Anselm to go travelling about the courts of Europe giving utterance to his opinions.'

'So what does the king want?'

'What he wants is a quiescent archbishop who would pay large sums regularly to the royal treasury. And that, I'm afraid, is not in my power to give him.'

'Then why have you been closeted with two of his sharpest operators these last few days? I saw you, master, talking with Gerard Chancellor and William Warelwast, the king's most slippery fixers. Master, something's afoot. What's going on?'

'Why, Firmin, how observant you are!' said Flambard with a smile. 'Something is 'going on' as you say. You'll have your first clue tomorrow.'

When the proceedings resumed on the third day, Tuesday, 27th February, both sides realised they had gone too far and recoiled from the brink. After long discussions between the bishops and barons and representatives of the king and archbishop, a truce was hammered out. It would last until May 20th and its undertaking was that, if no final peace had been made by then, William would grant Anselm safe conduct to the sea. Without any suspicions about this sudden volte face, Anselm accepted the truce with such rising spirits that he began to have benign thoughts about William, telling his household that the king was only a young man who sometimes stumbled into faults but was capable of reasonable decisions and even generous conduct. He could not have known that William, on the advice of Ranulf Flambard, in collaboration with Gerard Chancellor and William Warelwast, had hatched a plan to forestall his resignation or flight from the kingdom. A plan that aimed to defeat him by putting into his hands the very object that had brought about the Rockingham Conference, the prize on which Anselm had set his heart and his conscience—the *pallium.*

****

Chapter Ten

The Problem of the *Pallium*

Count Alan Niger stood in the south transept of the cathedral church of St Edmundsbury and watched his men straining at their grim work. It was late afternoon and dark. Some of the monks held torches, being allowed to assist but not take part. Ropes squeaked over a pulley, echoing eerily among the arched vaults. Slowly the object was raised, covered and bound to a wheeled board. The first stage of the homeward journey of Count Alan Rufus had begun. His remains, not the relics of a saint but of a man who had died in the fullness of a late-flowering love, were to be removed to St Mary's Abbey at York. Count Alan Niger, with the backing of the monks of St Mary's, had taken it upon himself to supervise the first stage of the translocation. With him in the nave on that cold dark afternoon at the end of February, was Aefled's long-absent husband.

Robert blew on his hands and paced back and forth, wishing to be gone. Digging in graves and disturbing the dead filled him with superstitious dread. He had heard tales of coffins cracking open, bodies splitting apart, gaping for their departed spirits. He saw ghostly shadows in the leaping light of the torches thrown across the great Norman pillars, souls disturbed by the brutal opening of a last resting place. This was not the sort of work he relished but he was a fealty man of Count Alan Niger and turned his hand to many tasks.

In reward for his services, Count Alan Niger had prevailed on Henry to take Robert's sons into his service. This was a significant advance in their fortunes since they were now attached to a royal household. In return for this favour, Robert had pledged extended service to Count Alan and had become responsible for the exhumation and the initial stages of the onward journey of the coffin. Once the work was complete and the body of Gunhild's lover was on its way north, Robert would accompany Count Alan to London where he still had unfinished business.

It was a testament to the count's decency that Gunhild had not been left out of the proceedings. Even before they left Richmond, he had written to her, seeking her agreement to the removal of her lover's body and she had replied in a manner that moved him and made him want to see her again.

'There, I interred him under the supervision of Abbot Baldwin, and there he has lain these many months. There, I spent days grieving for the man who had given me a snatch of happiness and shown me the greatest and best manifestation of the worldly life: passion of the body and joy of the heart, shared with one single beloved person which gives to life a touch of beauty and a glimpse of God. I pray you, my lord, take him home with my blessing.'

Later in the letter, Gunhild opened her secret to him. 'From our love, I bore a child whom God did not spare, a weakly child who lingered a few hours and carried off all my hopes when he died.'

And she ended: 'Let my beloved be laid among the monks of St Mary's to whom I send greeting.'

Was there ever such a woman? thought the Count when he had read the letter. Why didn't I marry her? Later, he said to Robert: 'When we have finished our business in London, we will go to Wilton.'

This plan, which threatened to entrammel him in many more months of service without any clear aim, was at first resisted by Robert. He made objections, saying that his own affairs demanded attention and it was time he went home. But Count Alan Niger was every bit as persuasive and charismatic as his brother and overbore all his excuses. At last, when his hesitation threatened to annoy the count, he relented. He could not risk losing the favour of a nobleman of his stature, one who had placed his sons in Henry's household and made himself, effectively, the liege man of a royal house.

Henry, Count of Cotentin, brother of the king, could play a waiting game. And he knew what he was waiting for. Although he was the youngest of the four sons of the Conqueror, he was the only one born after his father had gained the throne. As the son of a king, he aspired to be one but, in February 1095, when he was raising money for his brother's war in Normandy, such a prospect seemed remote. Since the death of his father, Henry had shuttled between his brothers, upsetting first one then the other, begging from one then the other, trusted by neither, close to neither, ducking between them, turning up on one side or another as a nuisance, an embarrassment, or a threat. Now, here he was, in February 1095, an ally of William against his elder brother and slightly more comfortable there than anywhere. Henry had convinced himself that he was backing the stronger of the two, certainly the more amusing, though not the more generous. It was Duke Robert who had granted him lands in the Avranchin, which included the great abbey of Mont St Michel, and Cotentin, from which he derived the title of count. But he had to pay an enormous sum in ready cash and was forced to do homage to his brother. Now he would seize the chance to make Robert pay for the humiliation and perhaps squeeze him out of power altogether. Henry calculated that in the final struggle between his two elder brothers, William would come out on top, leaving only one rival in the field. It was a long game but Henry was well-practised in the art of waiting. At twenty-eight, he was fit and lean as a greyhound. He had amassed money and had a good working relationship with the London Jews. He was no glutton for food, though his sexual gluttony caused many to sniff. He was of average height, generally considered good-looking with dark hair, kept neither long nor short so as not to identify with either the court intimates of his brother or the old style Normans of his father's generation. His sense of humour was more subtle than William's and he avoided antagonising churchmen with inappropriate jokes, but a sardonic wit lurked behind his polished manners. He had the skill to please, having all his life been forced to live by ingratiation. Such were the details about Henry that Aefled's husband gleaned from Count Alan Niger as he prepared to meet the man.

Henry sat with his booted feet up on a stool, leaning back against the wall. In anyone else this might have seemed like lounging but Henry was alert, listening to the conversation and observing his companions, Robert, Count of Meulan and his brother Henry, Earl of Warwick, Robert FitzHaimo, Nigel d'Aubigny. Robert Bloet stood to one side with the bishop of Hereford, discussing the news from Rockingham. Henry stood up and went towards a window to look out across the river at the great tower on the opposite bank, begun by his father and now almost complete. On a sunny day, the walls would gleam smooth and white, but today a drizzly gloom wrapped it in a grey cloud. Still, even from the narrow window of the abbot's house, it loomed, stark and impressive against the muddy sweep of the Thames. Wherever he looked, wherever he travelled, there were signs of his father's presence. Even under his feet. He was standing in the abbot's hall in Bermondsey Abbey. Many years ago his father had granted the royal manor of Bermondsey for the building of an abbey and he often used it as a London bolt hole when passing through the city.

'Are you sure they're coming?' said FitzHaimo.

'They'll be here.' Robert Bloet, Bishop of Lincoln, went to warm his hands at a feeble fire in a basket grate.

'Here,' said Henry, hauling out some logs from a stack and throwing them across to Bloet, 'let's have some warmth while we wait for the clerks.'

Henry's emphasis on the word 'clerks' measured his annoyance at being kept waiting. But these were no ordinary clerks. They were priests, his brother's emissaries, about to embark on an urgent mission and Henry had been tasked to speed them on their way with a subsidy from the king and permits to leave the realm.

Eventually, two men turned up in the courtyard with a small train of servants and baggage, looking as if they were about to set out on a long journey. Their arrival among the group of powerful men at the abbot's house in Bermondsey that night was the result of deep discussion in high places. Firmin had been right to suspect his master of cooking up a plan in the last days of the Rockingham Conference,

At the instigation of Flambard, William Rufus had contrived an inventive method of forestalling the archbishop's obstructive practices. Anselm had made a fuss about the *pallium,* making it clear that, until he received that little bit of material, there would be no acceptable solution. He would go on insisting on his recognition of Pope Urban, posing a challenge to William's sovereign right to recognise a pope. So Rockingham had ended in deadlock. Then Ranulf had come forward with a plan. Why not send someone to Rome to get the *pallium,* bring it back to England and deliver it safely into the hand of Anselm before the date on which the truce expired?

'Why not?' said the king. 'Face of Lucca! Flambard. Because the pope would never agree, that's why not. Besides, there's not enough time.'

'My lord king, I assure you there is time enough if things are thoroughly planned and well managed. Three weeks to get to Rome, three to negotiate, three to return, nine weeks in all. March, April and the first two weeks in May. Ample time, ample. But we must have canny, shrewd, astute, adaptable men who will know how to work on the pope.'

'Do I have such men about me? Well, Flambard. Who do you suggest?'

And that was how Gerard Chancellor and William Warelwast were appointed to the task of calling Anselm's bluff.

Without ceremony, the two men were hustled into the hall where the chest was handed over along with the documents.

'The boat is ready,' said Henry, 'it will take you down to King's Borough. You can land there on any tide. A ship is waiting to take you across.'

'My lord,' said William Warelwast, 'may we take food and drink?'

Some food was brought and wine in goblets. 'It's a filthy night,' said Robert Bloet. 'Eat and welcome. But don't delay.'

The two men ate standing, downed their drink and listened to the last words of advice from Henry. 'In your negotiations, seek out the Bishop of Albano, his name is Walter and he is Urban's legate.'

'My lord,' replied Gerard, 'it may very well be that, in order to acquire the *pallium,* we may ourselves have to recognise Pope Urban.'

'You will have to use your own judgement. That is why the king has chosen you. Be subtle with your words. Don't write or publicly proclaim anything to which you can be held.'

The two men nodded. It was by such practices that they had earned the reputation of the craftiest clerks in England.

Henry clasped each in turn by the hand. 'Get the *pallium* and return before the expiry of the truce. You will be well rewarded.'

They were hurried out into the gloomy evening, now growing dark. Torches lit them down to the river's edge and their baggage was stowed on board. Then the rowers pushed off and they glided silently out into the full brunt of the tide which caught them and swept them on their journey.

When Henry and his companions returned to the abbot's hall, they found Count Alan Niger and Robert waiting.

'Richmond,' said Henry warmly. 'I want to thank you personally for dealing with Joseph on the matter of the king's loan.' Henry always referred to Count Alan Niger as 'Richmond' and to his brother as 'the king.' These habits of reference clearly distinguished Count Alan Niger from his dead brother and deliberately distanced himself from William. 'The king' was a term without emotion, formal, distant and effortlessly respectful.

Richmond introduced Robert as the man who had dealt with Rabbi Joseph and secured the promise of a loan. Henry gave him a tight smile. 'So, at last, I meet the father of the sons. My steward says they are fine boys, spirited but tractable, eager to learn.'

It was one of Henry's winning qualities that he could remember even the most obscure people, their names and one or two facts about them.

Robert gave Henry the agreement written by Rabbi Joseph and watched him as he looked over the document, closely examining every word. Even simply checking a debt bond, Henry gave the impression that nothing escaped him.

'The first payment will be made at the end of this month of February, my lord,' said Richmond.

'Who will you trust to fetch the money?'

'I will, my lord,' said Robert, stepping forward, thinking to draw favourable royal attention to himself. 'Joseph knows me.'

'Good,' said Henry, apparently satisfied. 'Deliver it here. I myself will take it across to Normandy. We can begin raising troops by the end of Lent.'

Henry then questioned Richmond about affairs in the north while Robert observed the two men who had bound him to their service. His discontent was slight. Although he wanted to go home, he was aware how far his advantage lay in associating himself with these two powerful men. He found himself in a situation that more than matched his ambitions. He had no desire to grow greater. But what about Henry, he wondered. How great did he desire to grow?

Almost without meaning to, Robert found himself spying on them, listening to their conversations, watching their movements. But even though he had ample opportunity to observe and overhear, he could find no evidence of a plot. Neither Henry nor Richmond showed any sign of animosity to the king and never uttered a word of criticism against him. As a man of little imagination, Robert began to doubt himself for harbouring unsubstantiated, fanciful suspicions. He blamed Poultry. It was there his mistrust had first been aroused. He should not have given ear to Joseph and his deluded talk of some future charter if Henry should become king.

****

After the Rockingham Conference, Anselm had withdrawn to his manor of Mortlake, convinced that the truce was nothing more than a momentary cloak for further oppressions. Mortlake was a manor belonging to the see of Canterbury, once held by Archbishop Lanfranc and, by removing to it, Anselm thought he was reinforcing his staked claim to Lanfranc's inheritance. It was immensely wealthy, an asset of 25 hides, a church, two mills, a fishery, 33 ploughs, meadow and woods for 55 hogs. In addition, it possessed the rents from houses in London and Southwark and the tolls from Putney. But the material riches of this domain gave him no pleasure. In low spirits after the heel-digging exertions of Rockingham, Anselm drew his inner circle about him: Baldwin, Eadmer, Eustace, his closest clerks and chamberlains and the few monks who attended him from Canterbury. Of them all, he relied most on Baldwin.

'Be of good cheer, master,' Baldwin said to him one day in early March. 'The stand you made at Rockingham will resolve itself into recognition of Pope Urban in England. The king will have to concede eventually.'

'I could wish it was by his goodwill, in a spirit of happy agreement. Are we not all Christians? I would rather love the king than fight with him. I could wish to be a loving father to him. But he strays from me.'

'Master, you are the pilot of the Christian church in this land. God will show him that.'

For the first week after their arrival in Mortlake, Baldwin tried to inject a buoyant mood into the Archbishop's shrunken household as they sat out the tedious days till Whitsuntide and the expiry of the truce.

'What then?' asked Anselm, gloomily, 'what new villainies will the king invent?'

As it turned out, the king's villainies did not wait till May. Within a couple of weeks, a message came for Baldwin in the form of a private letter from Ranulf Flambard.

'In view of our past discussions,' he wrote, 'I feel I should warn you that the king is about to make a move which, as you may imagine, I have not counselled. The king proposes to banish you and arrest some of your master's household. Do not be alarmed, the action will be of limited duration, since you can be assured that I will not allow such a state of affairs to persist. The king has been led astray by villainous reports against you and the vengeful whisperings of some barons. Give me time to work. I would advise that you make no protest, that you quit Mortlake and lie low. In a few weeks, the king will repeal this ruling and you will return. I trust we will continue to work together in the future.'

Readied by this warning, Baldwin was able to prepare Anselm for his imminent absence and in the few days leading up to his arrest, he did all he could to secure his master's comfort and instruct the household in how to conduct themselves when the king's officers came. 'There must be no unseemly resistance,' he commanded. 'Do all things becoming to the dignity of the archbishop.'

And so the arrest went ahead without opposition or trouble of any sort. But not without shock. Anselm was so shaken by the loss of his closest adviser and dearest friend that he took to his bed for several days afterwards.

'He'll recover,' said Ranulf when he heard this. 'I never saw an old man more vigorous.'

Ranulf and Firmin were by then in their lodgings at Westminster where the king had gone after the Rockingham Conference. In contrast to Anselm, William was in jaunty spirits. His head was full of plans for a magnificent new hall at Westminster, a building of mind-numbing size, a vast hall which would be a monument to his reign, surpassing any other in beauty, magnificence and splendour. It would put the great white tower his father had built down river in its place. It would be the statement of his reign, a proclamation that he had matched his peerless father. Already in touch with masons, craftsmen, sculptors, woodcarvers, embossers, joiners, carpenters, who came and went with little models or sat closeted with him for hours, his head was buzzing with ideas, visions, possibilities. In Flambard's view, there was one insuperable problem. Where would he get the money?

Firmin was sitting at a table, his lips pursed in concentration. He was writing, a skill he was acquiring by arduous labours. Over the past two years, he had progressed sufficiently to take on basic aspects of the role of secretary. Firmin had copied out the letter to Baldwin, one of the most important tasks Ranulf had given him and one of which he was enormously proud. But the content of the letter continued to puzzle him.

'Master, why did the king banish Baldwin?'

Ranulf, who was reading by the fire, put down his parchment and studied the young face of his apprentice.

'Well, Firmin, some people might say it's a coded message for Anselm. "Seek better advice." Baldwin has been counselling him through the whole Rockingham conference and before that at Gillingham, so the king sees Baldwin as the source of Anselm's intransigence. But I think it's a message for Baldwin. "Take better care of your master's interests. Lead him towards compromise. If not, look what I can do."

'But isn't that like pushing someone over when he's nearly out of the door?'

‘Perhaps, but think about it. The Rockingham Conference was one gigantic tussle among advisers. Whatever happened there, good advice was always going to be the casualty.’

‘So the king, not happy with Baldwin’s advice, has banished him on his own initiative?’

‘Now, Firmin, whatever makes you think I did not counsel Baldwin’s banishment?’

‘But, in the letter, you said you had not done so.’

‘No I didn’t. I said, “as you may imagine”. Baldwin is free to imagine what he likes.’

‘But why, master?’

‘It was necessary to bring about Baldwin’s absence for a little while.’

Firmin persisted. ‘But why?’

‘Keep watching, Firmin. You’ll see why.’

After a brief stay in Westminster largely spent discussing his vainglorious project with artisans and craftsmen, the king removed to Windsor where it was his intention to prepare for a summer campaign in Wales. Military action on both fronts, Normandy and Wales, was a daunting prospect, requiring huge efforts of organisation in men and money. Yet William was thirsty for action. His fame was not going to be enhanced by constant wrangling with his archbishop. But, while desperate for success in other fields, he had not forgotten Anselm. From Windsor, William ordered Anselm to remove from Mortlake and go to his manor at Hayes in the hundreds of Elthorne, a village of five score households within easy reach of Windsor.

Anselm was by now thoroughly shaken up by recent events. At a loss without Baldwin, feeling persecuted by the king, his household barely managing to keep itself together, he now had to settle into another temporary home.

‘Why does the king torment me so?’ he wailed on seeing the dilapidated state of the Hayes manor, stranded in a sea of mud like an abandoned ship.

Eadmer, who had now become his chief companion and adviser, saw all Anselm’s sufferings as a validation of his principled fight for God’s cause. And he received corroboration of this view from the most trivial incidents, such as the one that happened while they were journeying from Mortlake to Hayes. It was immediately seized by Eadmer for his book and enshrined under the glorious title: *De liberatione leporis* or ‘How a Hare was Set Free.’ Unlike Firmin, Eadmer had a natural taste for allegory. He was aware that God had designed allegories in all parts of his creation, endowing the world with levels of latent meaning recoverable to mankind. He knew that allegory was a referential system of symbolism where every element referred beyond itself to something meaningful in a Christian universe. For him, it was obvious that God would design allegories to shine forth the sainthood of his master. Even the smallest incident might be the humble vehicle of divine allegory.

It so happened that, on the journey to Hayes, some boys of his household, running ahead with their dogs, chased a hare which they had come upon in the road. As they were pursuing it, the terrified animal headed straight to the horse on which Anselm sat and sheltered, trembling, between its hooves. Seeing this, he drew his horse by the reins to keep it still. So it was that the wretched, unhoused Anselm turned himself into a place of refuge for another victim of persecution. The dogs came around, snuffling. Anselm told the boys to haul them off. The hare sat still and would not move. Some of the boys began to laugh, never having seen such an unusual sight, made even more hilarious by the fact that it was the Archbishop of Canterbury, the second greatest man in England, who was giving refuge to a cornered hare under his stationary horse.

'Don't laugh,' said Anselm, 'don't mock the poor creature. He does not laugh. His enemies stand all about him. He looks for some helping hand. Shall we sneer at suffering innocence?'

With this, Anselm slackened his rein and the horse went forward, allowing the hare to dash away unhurt, running towards the fields while Anselm watched him flee to freedom with a look of longing.

That night, when Eadmer came to write up the episode, he went all out for allegorical and symbolic embellishments. By making Anselm deliver an impromptu sermon on the torments of the soul, he unpicked the latent meaning. When the soul leaves the body it is surrounded by evil spirits, ready to seize it and hurry it off to everlasting death. The hare is the soul. The devils are the hunters and dogs pursuing and tormenting it. The soul looks around in great alarm, seeking some help. But the demons laugh and mock, rejoicing at its sufferings. Eadmer worked long into the night like an alchemist altering the structure of matter. When he had finished, a brief, actual occurrence had been transformed into a perennially edifying Christian story.

There was no allegory in what happened next at Hayes. Only one level of meaning could be found in the arrival, one after another, sometimes together and even in small groups, of most of the bishops of England. It was another royal scheme to keep him constantly on the *qui vive,* in a state of uncertainty, perplexed and unsettled. Robert Bloet of Lincoln, the bishops of Hereford, Winchester, Sarum, bishops of the great southern dioceses, descended on the hard-pressed manor of Hayes and began to besiege Anselm with advice as to how he could restore himself to the king's favour. It was now only a couple of weeks until the expiry of the truce and there was a taut sense of time running out. But it would have been a mistake to think that, without Baldwin's presence, Anselm would submit easily to co-ordinated browbeating. There was a steely side to him and the more the bishops pressed and cajoled, the more strongly Anselm resisted.

The bishops' advice was unanimous and predictable. There was only one way out of the king's disfavour. Money.

'A gift in exchange for pardon is not such a poor deal.'

'You refused the king's request for money before. You gave five hundred pounds to the poor which should have gone to the royal coffers. For two years he has exerted himself to accommodate you. Now he expects some return for your obduracy.'

'Believe us when we say that William will reward your generosity with the largesse of his favour. The king is magnanimous.'

That word again. Anselm had not thought of it for a long time. Great-souled. That was what men said of him. Where did it come from? Why that word among all others?

'Archbishop,' said Robert Bloet, 'the king is more than ready for a reconciliation, but you must show yourself contrite.'

'Since when is contrition found in a chest of money?'

Anselm became angry. They were insinuating that he should pay for his office, luring him into the old offence of simony which he had condemned outright on numerous occasions. When they explained they weren't urging him to pay for his office, merely for the king's pardon, he stopped them by raising his hands and calling in a loud voice for silence.

'Unless I can obtain the king's peace and co-operation freely, I will have none of it. I will never stoop to buying that which is owed me. I will never pay money for the king's favour. If this is not pleasing to the king, let me leave the kingdom, let me go to Rome and receive the *pallium,* as I urged at Rockingham.'

From this position, they were unable to budge him and Anselm sent them away to consider his response. Eadmer, who had taken up an advisory capacity in the absence of Baldwin, saw through the plot.

'Master, they thought to make you easy prey by banishing Baldwin. But I assure you, if he was here now, he would counsel you to stand firm and not retract one step of ground.'

Eadmer was right. In desperate need of funds for his numerous ventures, the king was making one last ditch attempt to extract money from a source that had freely flowed to him for four years. Convinced that he was entitled to some compensation for the last two years of wrangling, William was entertaining regrets as he wondered what course events might have taken had he not fallen victim to that inconvenient illness. Would Anselm have become archbishop, or would he have remained where he was, obscure and contented, the humble abbot of Bec?

When the bishops returned, they realised that Anselm was in no humble mood and not ready to compromise. On the contrary, he was inclined to be reckless. Since all along he had been prepared to surrender his office, he could not be threatened with the loss of it. With great dignity, he made his final position clear. There would be no payment. He would not cease his suit for the *pallium*. He was accountable only to God. Let them go to the king and inform him that, upon these planks of policy, he, Anselm, was prepared to sit with folded arms.

Recognising their efforts were in vain, the bishops went away to report to the king. The upshot was, within a few days, Anselm received an invitation from the king to meet with him at Windsor.

****

One dank day at the beginning of March, Robert found himself back in Poultry to collect the money for Henry. Riding through the streets of the Jewish Quarter, with two armed men beside him, he noticed for the first time a singular lack of dogs. Most streets in most towns were full of dogs as well as pigs, goats, sheep and numerous animals nosing, browsing or snuffling hungrily for offal and waste, leaving piles of dung behind. These streets were unusually clear. A man could almost walk in them without ruining good shoes. Little things about the place began to penetrate. People went about their business with a brisk air. Everyone was busy. When it rained lads were assigned to sweep the water into ditches. It was all so different from what he had heard. There seemed to be little habits of orderliness quite lacking in most towns he had seen.

Dismounting, he walked his horse to Joseph's counting house and told his escort to wait. Inside, Joseph met him.

'Lord Robert, welcome, welcome. All is ready.'

He was shown the chest which contained Henry's contracted loan. He opened it and raked through the coins with his fingers, checking that there were no stones, a common cheat.

Joseph winced at the insult but made no remark.

'Good.'

Joseph took out a document and made a note of the amount and date. Then he signed the contract Robert had brought and handed it back.

'While I'm here,' said Robert, putting it into his jerkin, 'where would I find a man called Rabbi Simon? He was a friend of Isaac, the scholar who died recently.'

'Rabbi Simon? Oh certainly, he lives a few streets from here.' Joseph was immensely intrigued by this request but, since Robert seemed unwilling to enter into conversation, he asked no questions.

Leaving the chest under the supervision of the guards until he had paid his visit, Robert received some directions from Joseph and set off on a mission of his own. He made his way along several streets all looking much the same, fronted by two-storey structures of which the lower part was a store or warehouse or artisan's workshop. The different kind of wares on display gave variance to an otherwise uniform street façade. Rabbi Simon's place was a copyist shop, dedicated to the copying of sacred texts, commentaries and religious works of all sorts. Here, it did not matter that Robert could not read. No Christian could read these works. Unless, that is, he had studied Hebrew, Aramaic, Coptic, Greek and other languages of the east. He stepped into an interior lit by lamps since it was a drizzly early March day. Men sat writing at a number of tables. Parchments hung up on lines across the room. Ink making was going on in one corner. The whole place mocked him with his own ignorance of this skill.

Robert was so preoccupied with his own business that he was unaware of the anxiety he was causing among the occupants. They looked at him with mixed fear and suspicion, hesitating to speak even among themselves. Long experience of living under sufferance, here in London and among Normans in Rouen, where most of them came from, made them cautious and mistrustful of all outsiders.

'Rabbi Simon?' he said.

A man came forward. He was small, well set, with a beard, long black hair and twinkling eyes in a good-humoured face.

'Who asks for him?'

'I do.'

'What can I do for you?'

'Perhaps we should go somewhere private.'

Puzzled, but willing to oblige, Rabbi Simon led him into an inner room, even darker than the workshop, and gestured him to a seat. Robert had never seen a place like it. It was filled from floor to ceiling with shelves intersected vertically with wooden planks so that the whole thing looked like the place where pigeons roost. Each cube of space was filled with parchment rolls. Roll upon roll, the whole length of the wall and its entire height, all around the rectangular room.

'Please,' said Simon, 'speak freely.'

'I'm here on an errand for my wife,' Robert found himself saying. 'Years ago she knew Isaac the scholar. He died recently. I want you to tell me about the manner of his death.'

This question evidently puzzled Simon and he hesitated before replying.

'Isaac was a great scholar. He loved to talk. He could argue all night, even right up to the end.'

'Rabbi Simon, my wife would be glad to know about his last days.'

Finding this the oddest request he had ever heard, Rabbi Simon agreed. 'What do you want to know?'

'Did he ever mention the name of Aefled?'

'Aefled? Indeed, he did. He called her "the most intelligent of women". He loved her like a daughter. He spoke about her until the very end. He regretted that he could not see her to say goodbye and asked me to write to her so that she would not be disturbed by his sudden silence.'

'Aefled is my wife. She would be obliged to know how he died.'

'I see,' said Rabbi Simon. 'Then tell her Isaac made a good end. He died peacefully in his sleep. He was ready. He did not suffer. He went out of life as he had lived, fearlessly keeping faith with his philosophy.'

Robert stood up. It was enough. For himself, he had always detested the intimacy and intellectual closeness his wife had shared with Isaac, a Jew, an infidel, a menacing presence, a dangerous thinker. But now that Isaac's death had freed him from a life-long resentment, he could be greater than his instincts. It cost him little, after all, and would give Aefled the precious gift of knowing she had been remembered.

'My wife would wish me to thank you, Rabbi Simon, for your trouble in this matter.'

It was a stiff sort of thank you, grudgingly given, but the best Robert could manage in a situation he found testing to all his long held prejudices.

****

When at Windsor William preferred to stay in the former palace of Edward the Confessor rather than in the draughty old motte and bailey castle his father had built on a hill above the burgh. He purposely neglected his father's stronghold, spending no money on it. Edward's old palace offered an escape from the perpetual shadow of his father, the man against whom he was always forced to measure himself and always find himself wanting. The ancient sprawling pile with its chapel and hunting lodge nestled its sedate wooden frame on the south bank of the Thames. Encircled by expansive royal estates taking in swathes of Berkshire countryside, it offered some of the best hunting to be found. But in the third week of May 1095, William Rufus was not out hunting his prey. He was waiting for his prey to come to him.

While he waited, he was enjoying one of those brief moments of his reign when affairs were going well. His brother, Henry, had gone to Normandy with money to buy mercenaries and was already employing these resources with some success against Duke Robert. Scotland was momentarily quiet, being distracted by internal disputes, and although Wales continued its resentful insurgencies, plans were in hand for a campaign of reoccupation. There remained only Anselm to deal with and Anselm was on his way, travelling innocently towards an entirely altered state of affairs.

One night in the previous week, William had been roused from his sleep by Ranulf Flambard, standing over him with a lamp.

'My lord king,' he said, 'they have come.'

'Face of Lucca, Flambard! Who have come? Can't it wait?' The king stirred, flinging his arm over his eyes, revealing the tousled head of the youth beside him in the bed.

'No, my lord. Rouse yourself, they are below. Your emissaries to Rome. Warelwast and Chancellor. They are below, my lord.'

Ranulf Flambard's plan was coming to fruition. A plan of considerable impudence and daring was nearing its end and a high stakes gamble was about to pay off. He did not want the king sleeping through his moment of triumph.

In the great beamed hall of the old palace, the king found not two, as he expected, but three travellers at their supper in front of a roaring fire which had been lit to dry them from a drenching on the road. They had the whiskered, hurried, bedraggled look of men who have been riding up and down Europe against the calendar for weeks. In spite of their drowned appearance, Gerard Chancellor and William Warelwast were in the best of spirits. They had returned to report total success in their enterprise. It was no small achievement to journey to Rome, negotiate for the *pallium* and return with it to England before the expiry of the deadline. For this feat, they were congratulated by William and would, before long, be ensconced in lucrative bishoprics. However, there was one slight drawback. When the *pallium* arrived in England it was firmly attached to the papal legate.

The third traveller at supper rose and stepped forward to introduce himself as Walter, Cardinal Bishop of Albano. The king greeted him with stiff politeness, looking questioningly at Flambard as if to say 'who gave permission for a papal legate to enter my kingdom?'

'My lord king,' said Warelwast, 'we had no choice. It was either Albano and the *pallium* or no *pallium* at all.'

The situation was delicate. A legate could not be officially present in England until William had recognised as pope the man whom he represented. But since Chancellor and Warelwast could not separate Albano from the *pallium,* they had been forced to break the rules and bring him along anyway. So they had hustled him incommunicado through Dover and Canterbury so as not to alert the Christchurch monks, and rushed him to the royal court at Windsor, arriving there about an hour before Ranulf woke the king. It was close to Whitsun with a few days of the truce yet to run.

'King William,' said Walter of Albano, proffering a kid skin pouch decorated with the curial arms. 'This, I believe, has been the object of much contention in your kingdom.'

And so the *pallium* came into the hand of the king, not Anselm. William stared at the pouch a long moment before opening it, knowing that he was now in a commanding position. He could, if he wished, eject Anselm and bestow the *pallium* on a new archbishop of his own choice. The little piece of cloth, which he took forth and held in his hands, no more than four fingers wide, impregnated with immense symbolic significance, now had the potential to swell to the size of a gigantic blanket and smother Anselm's career in an instant.

It was not long before William learned, to his immense satisfaction, that Urban was willing to do a deal with him. In return for recognition of his claim to the papacy, he would grant the king all he wanted in regard to the royal customs and rights that had been in dispute. Then, during the ensuing negotiations with Walter over the next few days, it became apparent that further concessions would be made. Urban was prepared to promise that no papal legate should henceforth be sent into England without the king's express command. Even more importantly, it was agreed that no archbishop, bishop, monk or clerk in England should receive or send papal letters without the king's authority. 'Am I in bed?' said the king, 'I must be asleep and dreaming.' In a few days, more progress had been made with the Bishop of Albano than in the previous two years with Anselm.

Anselm arrived at Windsor on the day before the truce ran out. The king, along with as many bishops and barons as were able to assemble, with the Cardinal Legate in a prominent position, gathered to watch the final scenes of the long-drawn-out drama. Anselm came into the chamber, leaning on Eadmer's arm, his pastoral staff in hand, wearing his archiepiscopal robes.

'That was the first clue we had,' said Ranulf afterwards, discussing the day's performance with Firmin. 'He was not going to resign.'

In fact, he would not need to resign. Some way into the discussions it became apparent that part of the agreement made through Albano with the pope was that William must confirm Anselm as archbishop.

Since William had never actively sought Anselm's deposition, simply a way to work with him, his consent was readily given. In his view, archbishops were tiresome as a class and there would be battles with whoever was chosen. For all Anselm's faults, the king had never personally disliked him. Sometimes he was even inclined to feel sorry for him as a man whose humble instincts were completely at variance with the role he had been called on to fill.

When it was explained to Anselm that Cardinal Albano was the papal legate of Urban II, a look of beatific astonishment came over his face.

'You will rejoice to know,' said the king, 'that I have recognised Urban II as pope in this realm. From now on there need be no lack of clarity as to where your loyalties lie.' William limited himself to this mild reproof, but as he proceeded through the terms of the papal compromise he could not prevent himself crowing over the resounding success of this piece of diplomacy. In short, the pope had made a settlement with William behind Anselm's back. Urban had recognised William's customary rights and ancestral prerogatives: investiture, papal recognition, freedom from papal interference and the control of all ecclesiastical traffic between England and Rome. Not a single letter from a single monk would pass across the channel without the king's say-so. This meant that William had the full management of the English church in his control. It was the position his father had enjoyed. In return for the recognition of Urban as pope and Anselm as archbishop, William had achieved the thing dearest to his heart—never to reduce by one jot the full enjoyment of his inheritance. Far from it, the recognition of Pope Urban made his enterprise in Normandy more likely to succeed since he was now on an equal footing of papal favour with his brother.

Only one more matter had to be settled to achieve perfect peace, the conferment of the *pallium.* But Anselm once again confounded expectations.

'He refused,' said Ranulf, 'can you believe it? He refused, utterly, to accept it from the king's hand.'

'He refused it, master? Surely not even Anselm…'

'It's true, Firmin, though barely believable. When it was offered to him, there in full view of the court, the bishops, the Cardinal Legate and the assembly of barons, Anselm made his stand. He refused to accept it on the grounds that it was not in the king's but in St Peter's gift. To accept it from the king would be tantamount to recognising the royal right of investiture, something he has refused all along to do. So, then he was asked if he would accept it from the pope's representative, the Cardinal Legate, Walter of Albano. No, came the reply, he would not.'

'What can he possibly hope to gain by refusing?'

'Who can say? Some ineffable object of his own dreaming, probably. Or perhaps he was making a last-ditch attempt to retain some purchase on the issue of Church Councils.'

'What do you mean, master?'

'Anselm once asked the king for permission to hold Church Councils, ostensibly to address reform of the clergy, but really to lecture the king on improving his morals. Well, that's dead in the water, now, Firmin. No council can go ahead without the express sanction of William. Since he will never give it, Anselm will find himself powerless to act on behalf of the church. That's why he dug in his heels over the *pallium.* But, Firmin, I think he knew it was pointless, even then.'

Anselm was beginning to learn, as he was to learn again and again, that popes are rulers who prefer to negotiate with other rulers through their own confidential agents, squeezing out local men who have little understanding of the big picture of papal policy.

'You could see Anselm's disappointment in his face,' said Ranulf. 'After all those impassioned defences of Urban, he realised the pontiff had sold him out.'

'What did he do?'

'He maintained his position not to receive the *pallium* from the king. But I think there was a moment in the proceedings when Anselm realised that William was not, and had never been, his enemy.'

Ranulf was referring to the moment when Anselm, realising all was lost, appealed directly to the king's one quality he had always doubted, his magnanimity.

'My lord king,' Anselm sighed, 'advise me how I may in all conscience receive the *pallium*, for I think only you truly understand my predicament.'

Momentarily disarmed, momentarily moved, William looked at Anselm, disappointed and at bay, and saw again the humble priest who had held out his hand to a dying man in a gesture of complete kindness.

'Anselm, archbishop, spiritual father,' replied the king, 'let us put our long antagonism aside. All may yet be mended.'

The whole court heard this exchange in awed silence.

'It was as if we were overhearing a private communication of seraphs,' said Ranulf, 'they were so changed. I really wouldn't have been surprised to hear a heavenly choir singing "holy, holy and holy."'

In full view of the court, Anselm and the king had embraced. For an instant, they had shared the pulse of something greater than their own agendas. Mutual goodwill, a conviction that all would be well, surged between them.

'So a compromise was reached?'

'Indeed, it was. The spirit of compromise sprouted wings and flew above our heads.'

'And what was concluded, master?'

'Walter of Albano has agreed to place the *pallium* on the high altar of Canterbury Cathedral.'

‘But Anselm never goes to Canterbury.’

‘You may be sure he will go to Canterbury now. There, at a special ceremony, he will retrieve the *pallium* from the high altar. Perfect, isn’t it? Perfect! He will, as it were, take the *pallium* not from the king, not from the pope, not from St Peter, but from God himself.’

And so it was done. On Sunday, May 27th, Cardinal Legate Albano, bearing the pallium in a silver casket, accompanied by the monks of Christchurch and the neighbouring Abbey of St Peter and St Paul, surrounded by a great crowd of rejoicing monks, relieved courtiers, exhausted bishops and bemused townspeople, placed the *pallium* on the high altar of Canterbury Cathedral. Incense swung in thuribles, litanies were sung, prayers were offered and Anselm, symbolically barefoot but wearing his mitre and robes, episcopal ring on his finger, pastoral staff in his hand, looking every inch an ecclesiastical potentate, walked down the nave, up the steps and raised the *pallium* from the high altar to a swelling acclamation of relief. And there, to witness the long-delayed moment when Anselm finally entered into the full role of archbishop, was Baldwin, newly restored to his master’s side.

After two years and two months of battling back and forth across the realm, from the disputed election at Gloucester through countless arguments at Winchester, Canterbury, Hastings, Gillingham and Rockingham: two years of misunderstandings, appeals, claims, protests, threats and the odd reconciliation, the bull and the sheep finally settled their differences and began to draw the plough in a straight line. How long it would last, no one could say.

****

Chapter Eleven

What Was Said at Wilton?

At the beginning of April, after weeks without news, two letters came. One was to Agnes at St Sepulchre's. The other was to Aefled at Castle St Mary's, brought by a travelling lay-brother. Any bit of news was to be seized on avidly. Aefled hoped the letter might be from Robert. At last, after all these months, she would learn where he was, what he and the boys had been doing, and when they were coming home. There was none of that. As usual, her taciturn husband was miserly with his news. 'All is well,' she read. 'The boys thrive. I remain in the service of Count Alan Niger.' But, along with the usual greetings, prayers for her good health and loving phrases about "too long parted", there was one sentence that stood out like an unexpected peak in a desiccated plain of news. 'I am going to Wilton in May.' That was it. No explanation.

'Why is Robert going to Wilton?' asked Agnes when she came a few days later with the news that she had at last heard from Gunhild.

'It must be to do with his service to the count,' said Aefled.

'How strange to have two letters coming almost at the same time, both mentioning Wilton.'

Eleanor, who had been having a morning lesson with Aefled, stood listening to the women's talk. After a time, she came to sit beside her mother and put her head in her lap, as if suddenly tired.

'When's papa coming home?' she said.

'I don't know, my sweet, he doesn't say.'

'He has been away so long. Will I know him?'

Aefled felt the same about her sons. Would she recognise Robert and William now? It was two years since they had gone away, two years in which they must have grown and changed and been formed by knightly training into beings she might not know. They had lived in the great Richmond stronghold of Count Alan Rufus, travelled through the wild terrain of the north, been present at the consecration of the foundation stones of Durham's new cathedral and moved among the greatest nobles of the high Norman elite. How would all this experience stand up against their early education? She had tried to instil in them the best habits of mind and urged them never to reject their English heritage. For that reason, they had been instructed in the language and brought up with ordinary English village boys who were now themselves showing awareness of their unequal status. She had wanted her sons to be the pioneers of a new way of living in England, combining two distinct heritages into a unified pattern of Anglo-Norman conduct. This had been her aim for the boys, too broad, too high, too unrealistic, she now acknowledged. In a way, she feared to see them just as much as she longed to see them. It was impossible to guess what they had become.

In the meantime, she turned her thoughts to Eleanor, now ten years old, tall for her age and in good health. Her unbound hair was a great drift of soft brown curls. If Aefled set herself to number the excellences of her daughter, she would be at it for hours, but there was one criticism she might make, which was rather of herself than of Eleanor. In spite of her education, Eleanor was ignorant of the world. She had barely left the keep in all her life except for trips to St Sepulchre's and the occasional visit to Earlsham priory church. Aefled used often to think of Edith and the dangers she had encountered because she had not been prepared for the adult world. This failure, thought Aefled, was surely a moral weakness on the part of the nuns, a neglect of duty by all who had surrounded Edith, most especially by Christina, her aunt, who had failed her utterly, leaving her exposed to hysterical fears and disabling terrors so violent that she had been laid low on a bed of sickness.

But then Eleanor said something that made Aefled think that she had picked up a little worldly knowledge from the sad ordeal of Gunhild and the heart-breaking loss she had suffered in that very room last year.

'Will Gunhild have another baby,' she said, 'will she find another man?'

Agnes and Aefled exchanged a look but failed to give an answer.

'What does Gunhild say?' asked Aefled.

'She greets us both as her sisters and longs to see us again,' said Agnes, taking out the letter. 'She asks after Eleanor and calls her "my sweet shared daughter". She is recovered in health. As for her heart, she says, "I handed God a broken thing, snagged on the brambles of the world and he is mending it".'

'That's sad,' murmured Eleanor from her nest in Aefled's lap.

Agnes was looking for a particular line in the letter. '"Consolation comes late and slowly. I ache sometimes and long to see you, my dear friends".'

'Does she mention Edith?'

'Yes, here.' Agnes read aloud the passage. "Edith is closed and calm, but she bears the scars of her experiences in Scotland and the death of her parents. As she nears her sixteenth year, she shows interest in political matters but is often low in spirits. She has been disturbed to learn that someone is writing the life of her mother, Margaret, proclaiming her a saint. She herself is beginning to write in a most alarming way, not saints' lives, prayers, or letters to spiritual advisers, but poetry in a most unsuitable style. Sometimes I am anxious for her".'

'I wonder what she means by that,' said Aefled.

So long awaited, these two letters produced only disappointment. Hidden purposes and mysteries, created by an insufficiency of detail, made them anxious to know more.

Later, when Eleanor had gone with Maria to oversee the pantlery, Aefled gave voice to her fears.

'I don't want Eleanor to be kept in ignorance like Edith. Poor Edith, she was left too long without an understanding of her own body and heart. I must prepare my daughter so that she won't be frightened as Edith was. The day is not far off when Robert will begin looking about to negotiate a marriage for her.'

'I know what we must do,' said Agnes. 'We must take her to Wilton.'

'The place which caused Edith such suffering? Why would we do that?'

'No, the place where Edith learned much about the ways of men and the world. With you to guide her, she will not be left in pitiful ignorance, as Edith was. But, think of it, Wilton will allow her to mix with noblewomen, royal women, and yes, damaged women. She will learn a great deal about the ways of the world. She will see Gunhild again and be able to learn directly from her about her experiences. She will find Edith an exciting companion and she will be reunited with her father there. Can you not see that Wilton is the answer?'

Aefled thought about this proposition for a long while, hesitating to make a decision yet feeling that Agnes was right. The nunnery of Wilton was a sanctuary from the world but also a place where worldly intrigue and interests intersected with the spiritual life. It was a place of renown, a centre of learning and a way-station in so many lives. Why should Eleanor not derive benefit from a visit there? And she herself was yearning to see Gunhild and Edith. Besides, if they went to Wilton and stayed until Robert came in May, they could all travel back together. Eventually, she was so well persuaded by the rightness of this idea that letters were sent to Gunhild and to the abbess promising to be with them at the end of April.

****

Wilton at Whitsuntide was a place of solemn gaiety. The frugalities of Lent were over, Christ had risen from the tomb, salvation's promise was renewed and now Pentecost marked the descent of the Holy Spirit upon the Apostles and all who followed in their footsteps. Whitsun was a time of white. White blossoms of elder and hawthorn decked the cloister arches, the first white roses were in bud in the garth and the nuns dressed in white to walk the bounds of their precincts. Edith, too, wore white and sang the Pentecostal psalms among the nuns who filled the chantry. When they bowed their heads they were like rows of snowdrops. Edith observed them from under her lashes, fastening her cold blue eyes on Aunt Christina as she tried to feel the Holy Spirit moving her soul to forgiveness. But it was hard to dislodge the great lump of resentment that got in its way. There were still battles between them, less violent than formerly since Edith had better control of her feelings. In Scotland she had learned to eat the raw meat of humiliation with its after-taste of blood. That taste was gone. She was now in possession of a strong sense of herself and, although Aunt Christina still had the power to annoy, she no longer had the power to crush. Certainly, Edith's status in the wardship of King William, who had undertaken to pay her expenses so long as she was at Wilton, gave her a certain independence and allowed her to continue her education. So she spent her days in relative peace, nursing her ambitions, refusing to take the veil.

News from Scotland, maintained largely through her Uncle Edgar Aetheling, gave her little cause to hope for any change in her circumstances. Donald Bane had succeeded her father in 1094, lost the throne, taken it again against an army supported by William Rufus, and was now hanging on to it while the pretender, Edgar, the fourth of her six brothers, was seeking to wrest it from him with the help of Uncle Edgar Aetheling. Her marriage prospects varied with this volatile scene and there was little she could do but wait, hope and pray, holding herself ready for the time when a glorious future would open before her.

On their return to the convent, Gunhild and Edith had renewed their friendship after the disasters of their brief sorties into the world and had become very close. At first, Gunhild seemed well in health, able to take an interest in the communal life of the convent. She wrote to Anselm again, asking forgiveness. She wrote letters to the monks of St Mary's, York, which were read aloud in the chapter house there.

But the exhumation of Count Alan Rufus went deeper than the six feet of Suffolk earth in the nave of St Edmundsbury. She began to dwell on the implications of disturbing his body and regretted having given permission for it to be done. She could not rid herself of the sense that Count Alan had left her again. He was gone where she could not follow, where she could not imagine him, a place she did not know and had never seen. It was partly to overcome this aching renewal of loss that she wrote to the monks of St Mary's, trying to keep some connection to him by requesting particular prayers on certain days at stipulated times. She hoped that by saying these prayers at the same time as the monks of St Mary's she would be close once more to her lover. After a while this became an obsession and when Gunhild started to rise for Matins and Lauds in the middle of the night and at dawn, the nuns became anxious for her health and went to Edith, asking her to intervene.

Edith, the younger by some years, began to take the lead in their relationship, trying to console Gunhild in her terrible sorrow. She became pale and thin, looked ill and listless and often broke down in tears. When Aefled and Agnes came at the end of April, they found her in bed, too weak to get up. But ten year old Eleanor, full of spontaneity and innocence, rushed to her, threw her arms around her, burst into tears, wept freely and murmured, 'I am your shared daughter, please have the strength to love me.' From that moment, it was widely observed, there was a discernible improvement in Gunhild.

The spiritual life of the convent centred on the *Book of Hours* with its eight sections containing prayers, psalms, hymns and other devotional material around which the cycle of worship turned. Gunhild measured out her days according to these holy offices, constructing a daytime routine around prayer and work, but she was forbidden by the abbess to rise for the night offices on the grounds that it would damage her health. Edith, by contrast, spent less time in observance of the offices and more time in her own comfortable quarters, writing.

Aefled sought her out. 'What are you writing, Edith?' she asked one day.

Edith seemed startled by so blunt a question. 'I write metrical exercises in French and Latin,' she said.

'Can I see them?'

Edith evaded the question by saying that they were uninstructed and primitive, too poor to show. Disappointed, but unwilling to press the point, Aefled began to ask her about her experiences in Scotland.

'They are too painful,' said Edith. 'I prefer not to talk about them.'

Aefled began to see what Gunhild had meant when she had described Edith as 'closed and calm.' It seemed she had put up armour around herself and would allow nobody near. Nobody that is, except Eleanor. Eleanor became an indispensable companion to both Edith and Gunhild. They enjoyed walking with her, showing her the lakes and fish ponds of the abbey, taking her round the weaving and sewing rooms where the nuns embroidered beautiful copes and banners and the lay sisters wove or spun wool from the abbey sheep. She was shown the processes for producing wine, ale and honey. This active, workaday side of abbey life seemed to delight her as much as the liturgy and daily offices, towards which she had begun to show a strong inclination.

One evening while Eleanor was at prayers, Aefled found herself walking alone with Edith in the cloister garth. It was the twilight of a showery spring day. Striking between parted clouds, a thick, viscous light honeyed the sandstone walls and shone on the wet flags. Dripping roses, clustering in fragrant masses, released their perfume on a mild breeze. Vespers had cleared the precincts, no one came or went. They walked in silence until Aefled realised that Edith was crying.

'What ails you, my dear?'

'I feel so alone,' said Edith between sobs. 'So alone.'

Aefled put her arms around the sobbing girl and kissed her.

'The nuns despise unhappiness,' said Edith, shaking her head. 'They say it smacks of wilfulness. Insufficient obedience to the will of God. My Aunt Christina says it is a selfish indulgence.'

'I disagree,' said Aefled. 'I don't think you should blame yourself. If God ordains all, he has ordained your feelings and they are valuable in his sight.'

Edith wiped away tears with her sleeve.

'Why do you feel alone, surrounded as you are by people who care for you?'

Edith looked around as if to check that no one else was listening, then lowered her voice to a whisper. 'Someone is stealing my mother,' she murmured, 'taking her away from me.'

Aefled did not know what to reply but simply took her hand and waited for her to go on.

'Someone is writing her life as the life of a saint, to make her the pure image of devotion, to take her from me and give her to the church. The church steals women to make them chaste, to make them models of piety. To drain them of mind and blood and passion. But my mother lived in the world, loved a man, gave birth to children, governed a household, shared in the rule of a kingdom. She was not a saint. She was what I long to be.'

'Do you write these ideas in your metrical exercises?' asked Aefled, suspecting that here was the cause of the 'poetry in a most unsuitable style' that Gunhild had mentioned in her letter.

'Yes, how did you know?'

'When I was your age I wrote in such a style. Poems and stories that said what I felt, not what the church taught me to feel.'

'Do you regret it? Is it wicked?'

'Not in the least. I don't regret a word of it. Nor should you. It is a way to be free, to be yourself. It harms no one. And God, who understands all, forgives all.'

'Lady Aefled, I'm so glad you are here,' said Edith with something of her former directness, 'only you would speak to me in this way.'

****

Count Alan Niger, who was becoming known as 'Richmond' since there was no longer any need to distinguish him from his brother, reined in his horse and sat staring at the view ahead. It was the view King William had seen two years earlier when he had made his abortive journey to Wilton. Running alongside the Nadder, obscured on one side by mature willows reflected in the waters, the sprawling pile of Wilton glowed in the afternoon light.

'Do you suppose we'll be welcome?' he said, looking back at the great party of riders who had reined up behind him. 'There are so many of us.'

'I cannot say, my lord,' replied Robert.

In the normal course of things, the party would not have been so large. Even though many men had been left behind at Sarum, there were some dozen escort and hangers-on, most of whom belonged to the Count of Cotentin.

'What's the matter, Richmond,' said Henry as he came riding up, 'lost your nerve?'

'Perhaps we should send ahead and alert the nuns. They may be frightened at our approach.' He was thinking particularly of Gunhild.

After some discussion, it was decided that the main party would wait while a messenger was sent ahead to inform the abbess of their arrival.

Henry dismounted and lounged at the foot of a tree. Robert thought that he lounged the way other men tense themselves for action. He relaxed like a cat, always secretly alert, his eyes missing nothing. Even now, Robert did not know why Henry was here. He had joined up with them in London, having just returned from Normandy where he had carried out his brother's wishes in delivering the Poultry money to William's Norman sympathisers. After two months of activity, including an unsuccessful attack on Rouen, he had slipped back across the channel to report to his brother, anxious to keep himself in sight and in favour. Too late, the king had already set out for Nottingham. Instead, Henry met up with Count Alan Richmond and decided to accompany him to Wilton, saying he had a mind to meet the lady Gunhild, of whom the count spoke with such admiration, though Robert had a suspicion that Henry was working to a plan of his own. Whatever the case, here he was, Henry, Count of Cotentin, brother of the king, son of William the Conqueror, stretched out on the grass beneath a tree waiting for the abbess to give her permission.

Wilton was not unused to prestigious visitors. The controversial visits of King William and King Malcolm within a few weeks of each other in the summer of 1093, had entered the realm of Wilton anecdote. In the abbey's unofficial mythology, many stories were being embroidered around the snooping king and Edith's hot-tempered father. Hoping to avoid any similar scenes, the abbess deputed Christina and the almoness to receive the men and keep them at prayer in the abbey church while she herself took Richmond and Henry on a tour of all but the private sanctuaries. Richmond submitted to these formalities with good grace but after a time Henry became bored and made his escape to prowl about alone. Passing through a little courtyard draped with ivy, he stopped at a ground floor window, open to the May sunshine. Looking in, he saw a very young woman, sitting at a table writing. Her head was bent low over a parchment and she appeared completely absorbed in what she was doing. Her hair was unbound, uncovered and fell in smooth red-tinged waves down her back. He saw in profile, a round cheek, a neat mouth, pursed in concentration and a charmingly pointed nose. When she looked up, he saw a pair of watchful blue eyes, intelligent, circumspect, perhaps even cunning.

'Go away,' she said.

Henry was about to start on some of the mannered phrases he had picked up at his sister's court at Blois, but thought better of it. Those eyes, he thought, would look right through any kind of floss.

'Forgive me, I have no wish to disturb you.'

'You are disturbing me. And now I have lost my thought. It was beautiful, too, and had taken all morning to come.'

'Why so long?'

'It had to come in metrical form. It was a dactylic hexameter, a perfect line.'

'Is that why it was beautiful?'

'Not entirely. It was about my mother. Oh, why am I talking to you? Go away.'

Amused by this curious encounter, Henry went away. He had no idea what a dactylic hexameter was and did not care. More mystifying was why such a meaningless exchange should actually interest him. It struck him that he had never had such a droll encounter with a woman in his life.

On a far higher emotional note, was the meeting between Gunhild and Richmond which took place in the cloister at vespers. He saw her before she saw him. She was paler, thinner, than he remembered, somehow less substantial. She wore the Benedictine habit but no veil. A string of questions ran through his mind. Had she taken vows? Had she thought of him? Would her wounds be opened again by seeing him? Would she agree to what he was going to propose? He knew the answers almost before she turned and saw him. She came towards him in ready steps, eager but controlled, to take his hands and greet him, raising them one by one and kissing them. 'Dear hands,' she said. 'Dear kind hands.'

'They were not kind,' said the count, 'they let you go.'

'They were generous. I will always owe you the greatest gratitude.'

They walked along the cloister's open arcade and made their way out into the garth. This was the garden in which Count Alan

Rufus had dug up her heart. There at the centre were the lush staked bushes, drooping with white petalled roses, hiding their fatal thorns.

'They were red then,' said Gunhild in a voice low with regret. 'In May, they are white for Pentecost, in August red roses bloom. Blood red. We lingered there. He gave me to believe he loved me and I leapt willingly into that belief.'

'Gunhild, I should not have left you. I intended to do right by you.'

'You did. You gave me protection in my plight. You never judged me. You never gave your word on anything and so you never broke it. If I assumed too much, I am sorry.'

'Perhaps I should not have come. I was moved by your letter. I did not know you were with child.'

'If the child had lived everything would be different.' Tears came into her eyes as she took his hand and led him towards the roses.

'He stood there and plucked a rose. As he did so, he pricked his finger on a thorn. It bled a little but he sucked the blood away and laughed. It was then that the illness began. I swear it. It was then. Within a few days, he was dead. He died for plucking a rose.'

Count Alan Niger was not a man given to sentiments or regrets. The death of his brother had never hurt him. Rather it had given him practical but manageable inconveniences until the time when he secured his inheritance. It was only now, through Gunhild's loss, that he began to feel his own. A nephew, a close born male heir, a rare thing among the Richmonds and, even rarer, of royal blood. Could he replace that lost boy with a child of his own in a union with this exceptional woman? Could he still say what he had come to say?

Gunhild placed a finger on his lips.

'My life is here now,' she said. 'God has led me back where I belong.'

'Is it what you truly want? To take the veil?'

Gunhild hesitated, steadying a resolve which wavered momentarily in the face of real affection. 'Archbishop Anselm wrote to me that it is only in the embrace of Christ that I will find happiness. At first, I resisted but now I see that he is right.'

Gunhild did not tell him of the fear that Anselm had planted in her mind in words of terror and threat: 'Are you not afraid that because of you God may kill Count Alan Niger by a similar death…'

Fearing her damnation, Anselm had spoken out with the importunate voice of orthodoxy. But another voice was speaking to her, in the pulse of her veins, in the beat of her heart, in the ill-fated blood of the Godwins. A family doom, snatching at dreams and plans, seizing victory from worthy hands and sweeping away the possibility of earthly joy.

'So you will stay here and take the veil?'

Gunhild nodded, unable to speak.

She was certain. By taking the veil, she would stand between this man and the vengeance of God.

****

For the second time, Robert and Aefled found themselves meeting by chance at Wilton, but it was not until they found themselves alone later that evening that they could finally begin to fill in the missing portions of their long separation. For once, Robert had substantial news. Count Alan Richmond had come to Wilton to ask Gunhild to marry him. And Henry, Count of Cotentin, had accompanied him to Wilton.

Aefled, who had not yet seen Henry and had no idea he was present, was astonished.

'Why has he come?'

'He doesn't say.'

'Where is he now?'

'I suspect he's wherever Edith is.'

'Christina was looking for Edith a moment ago. Robert, do you think they are together?'

'Very likely.'

'He's come to proposition Edith, hasn't he? The king rejected her, maybe that makes her all the more attractive to him.'

'His mind may be running in that direction. After all, he has two unmarried brothers without legitimate heirs.'

Robert then told her what he had heard from Rabbi Joseph in Poultry about a 'charter' he had promised to the Jews if he should ever become king.

'Do you think Henry is plotting something against his brother?'

'I doubt it. Henry's sly. He's subtle and duplicitous. But that's no calumny. You could say the same of William, or Flambard, or any other great man. But I think he's playing a long game with high stakes in view.'

'Robert,' said Aefled with concern, 'are our sons safe in his household?'

'Quite safe. Don't forget, Henry is now openly tented in William's camp and more favoured than he's ever been. Besides, Henry has taken up with Count Alan who is a loyal oathman to the king. If he's planning anything, it will be for the long term.'

That evening, before the men were due to travel back to Sarum, Aefled was introduced to Count Alan Richmond and Henry. She found Richmond remarkably civil and winning. Henry, too, was polite and gracious. When he was introduced to Edith under the watchful eye of the abbess, he gave no sign of having met her before even though he had been secretly closeted with her for over an hour. Aefled noticed Edith's eyes shining at Henry with all their craft and ambition, though her manner was distant. During the evening, Henry became expansive, voluble, charming, even winning Aefled's good opinion by praising her sons.

'My steward tells me they are fine lads. You must come to London one day to visit them.'

'That would give me great pleasure, my lord.'

Robert listened to this exchange, feeling, as he always did with Henry, that there was some ulterior purpose in everything he said and did.

Later, as they were getting the horses ready in the courtyard, preparing to ride out, Robert remembered the things he had not had time to say to Aefled that day, among them his visit to Rabbi Simon. Since there was no urgency in the news, he let it go and in time, would forget it. It was typical of Robert that he would both, do and undo, a good deed.

'I'm going back to London with Count Alan,' he said. 'When I come home I will bring the boys with me.'

Aefled held the bridle as he mounted. 'I pray you will. God keep you, Robert.'

He leaned from the saddle to kiss her forehead. 'How long are you planning to stay here?'

'A few weeks, then I'll return with Agnes.'

'Well, don't let Eleanor pick up a taste for convent life.'

As he rode out, Aefled called after him: 'Will you be home for Christmas?' but her words were lost in the clatter of hooves on the courtyard stones.

The ride back to Sarum was short and filled with silences. Count Alan Richmond made no comment about his parting from Gunhild, at once so final and so full of unfinished tenderness. Henry said nothing about his meeting with Edith. If he had latched on to Richmond's party in order to pay suit to a prospective bride, he showed no sign of it. But he rode away with the distinct impression that the trip had been worthwhile. An indication, if he had known it, of how much his fortunes were about to rise. In the ongoing conflict with Normandy, it had always been a gamble to have taken William's side. But, in a surprising and unforeseen way, that gamble was about to pay off.

****

'Now then, Firmin, I am going to pose you a question and I want you to think carefully about it. Answer me this. What is the alternative to securing Normandy by conquest?'

Firmin thought for a moment, wondering what his master was driving at. He relished the spontaneity of these questions which suddenly confronted him with new puzzles. Ranulf used them like a mason's mark on stone, the signature stamp of his workmanship.

'Think about it, Firmin. How would you come to possess Normandy without fighting for it?'

'Through inheritance, master, it's the only other way.'

'Disallow inheritance and conquest. How would you acquire Normandy?'

Firmin shook his head. 'There is no other way.'

'Yes, there is.' Ranulf strode across to the window and stood looking out towards the Thames. 'You buy it.'

'Buy Normandy!' Firmin's mouth fell open. 'It can't be! There's no sum in all the world that could do that.'

'Yes there is. Ten thousand silver marks to be precise.'

'But surely, master, no one in Christendom could find such a sum.'

'I dare say no one in Christendom would even contemplate it, except William. And he is not only contemplating it, he is resolved to do it. You see, Firmin, there is not a thing that money cannot buy if you have enough of it.'

This venal conversation, which took place in January 1096 while William was holding his Christmas court at Windsor, was the curious result of a movement of the Holy Spirit in a most unlikely quarter. In response to the preaching of Pope Urban at Clermont in November, when princes and rulers were urged to lay aside their differences and make war on the heathen, Robert Curthose had decided to answer the call and become a warrior of Christ. Nothing less likely or more harebrained could be imagined and Ranulf momentarily wondered if the rumours had muddled the name. Some other Robert was meant—Bellême, perhaps, or Mowbray. They both had good cause for penitence. But no, it came confirmed from William who heard it straight from his brother's mouth. Robert Curthose had been bitten by the bug of zealotry and would be off to foreign parts as soon as he could raise the cash.

The broad picture of papal policy, which had trapped Anselm in the episode of the *pallium*, had expanded to encompass, not just the Roman church, but the neighbouring realms of eastern orthodoxy, in particular Constantinople. The young Emperor, Alexius Comnenus, desperate for reinforcements to protect his Christian frontiers and fearing for the survival of Constantinople itself, had appealed to Pope Urban for aid. What was to be his response? Pope Urban, French nobleman and instinctive castellan that he was, could not duck the issue. Were Saracen hordes to pour into Constantinople, capital of the first Christian emperor? Were infidels to go on ruling in all the sacred places, especially Jerusalem? Thus it was that, on the 27th November 1095, Pope Urban had preached an impassioned sermon at Clermont, setting loose a response that even he had not anticipated. At its core, was a simple message—fight and be saved. The words rang through the Auvergne, Burgundy, France, the Holy Roman Empire and eventually Normandy, setting off a reaction of unforeseen eagerness, not just in the warrior class and nobles, but in the lesser knights, manor lords and simple peasants. Here was a way to gain everlasting life.

'If any man sets out from pure devotion, not for reputation or monetary gain, to liberate the Church of God at Jerusalem, his journey shall be reckoned in place of all penance.'

Suddenly men had in view heroic work of universal importance, a new road to the city of God, a guaranteed way to salvation. And roads filled, men were on the march, lords mortgaged their estates to raise the money. They set out overland or by sea, in cavalcades and on foot, with prayers on their lips while priests blessed them on their way; great ribbons of marching people who had cut up their cloaks and jerkins to make crosses to be worn as proud badges of a new-found fervour. An original appeal for military aid from Constantinople had transformed into a tide of Christian fervour, aimed at nothing less than the reconquest of Jerusalem. And among those swallowed up in this extraordinary pandemic of enthusiasm, to such a degree that he was ready to mortgage his entire dukedom, was Robert Curthose, Duke of Normandy.

The details were to be worked out in the months running up to Easter 1096 and conducted through the offices of the abbot of Dijon. It was not quite a sale, as Ranulf had implied, but a three year lease. In return for 10,000 marks of silver, William would gain freehold custody of the duchy for three years, ostensibly managing it until his brother's return. Since Robert was going to leave no wife or child behind, having no legitimate heirs, William would then be in a strong position regarding the succession. It seemed highly unlikely, to Ranulf, to William and most of the English barons that, given his previous combat history, Robert Curthose would ever return from his madcap adventure.

'In which case, Flambard,' said William when discussing it with his chief financial adviser, 'it will have proved to be a sound investment.'

'My lord king, it is true that 10,000 silver marks is less than a quarter of your ordinary annual income from England, yet such a sum cannot be raised without much difficulty.'

'It's not so difficult. We will make exactions on the church. Up and down the land churches are crammed with plate and gold ornaments, silver vessels and caskets of relics, books of the gospels overlaid with precious jewels, great money chests. Face of Lucca, Flambard! Abbots and bishops are sitting on fortunes. We will ask for donations. After all, this money is destined for a holy cause, a crusade preached by the pope himself. Surely the clerics and prelates will rush to support so good a cause.'

At this, William smiled, knowing that the reaction to any such appeal would be quite the reverse. 'Begin with Anselm,' he said, 'the Archbishop of Canterbury should be allowed the opportunity to lead by example. We have six months, Flambard, six months to raise the sum.'

'Why so short a time, my lord?'

'Robert will want the money by September so that he can get through the pilgrim route to Rome before the Alpine passes are blocked. We have the summer to make good our promise. Start with the church, then the Jews, after that begin filling vacancies at an increased fee, then require a voluntary donation from the barons. If they refuse, exact it. After that raise taxes. Six months, Flambard. See that it's done.'

Thus the king had declared his will.

'Behold me, Firmin, and behold my pitiful fate. I am the one who must do it.'

‘Master, how will you do it? It’s a bigger job than raising the *fyrd*.’

‘Bigger, yes, but for the same end. To pour money uselessly into Normandy. And we will proceed in a similar way. We will establish a writing office and send out letters. Communication is the key. We must think of tone, wording, pitch, presenting our demands as invitations to participate in a great cause. We must play on consciences and religious feelings, spinning away like busy spiders, entrapping men into our collecting web. Don’t forget, Firmin, there is no end to the gullibility of mankind if managed in the right way.’

‘Quite so, master, but, all the same, many will resist.’

‘Well then, we will have to threaten, cajole, urge, plead—and if we don’t get what we want, we will have to frighten the manor reeves who will screw the money from the poor.’

‘But, master, what authority will we have for this? Will the king issue written documents commissioning it? Will there be agreements and contracts? Or is it all to be done word of mouth? Is this plan sound?’

‘By God, Firmin, those are clerkly questions!’ Ranulf went over and rubbed Firmin’s great mop of hair, making it stand up. It was an approving, affectionate gesture but Firmin had outgrown it. He had some right to respect, he thought, because he was now very good at his job.

‘The plan is completely unsound, Firmin. Apart from the utter folly of making war half a world away, the whole thing is a precarious tissue of interfamilial promises, brotherly assurances and informal undertakings. There will be no charter to back it, probably because nothing like it has ever been undertaken before. And it’s not just two brothers we are dealing with, but three.’

‘How does it involve Henry?’

‘In return for Henry’s support, William is prepared to be generous. Complete adherence to William’s cause, on oath, will bring him two more Norman counties: Coutances and Bayeux. And besides, while Robert is away putting the fear of God into the heathen, Henry will do very nicely in a quasi-official role, holding Normandy for William. He will maintain order and collect the ducal income, no doubt creaming off a tidy sum for himself. If Henry behaves himself, he could do very well out of the deal.’

‘Is there any reason to believe he won’t behave himself?’

‘None that I know of—yet. He kept himself pretty fragrant during the Mowbray rebellion. He might genuinely be a supporter of the king. Though William, of course, will only trust him so far.’

'Master?' said Firmin, dragging out the word into an interrogative. 'You know that once, some time ago you told me to keep in touch with the little monk, Eustace, who used to be a clerk of Anselm?'

'I remember.'

'Well, I did so, although he never proved useful. Until now. Recently he informed me that the abbess of Wilton has received an unexpected visitor of very, very high rank.'

'How high?'

'Royally high.'

'By God! So Henry has followed his brother to Wilton, has he? Two dogs sniffing about in the same yard. And does Eustace say what happened on this visit?'

'Apparently, the abbess thinks that Edith and Henry were alone for a short while and that they had a private conversation.'

'How did he get this information from the abbess?'

'From reading a private letter she wrote to Anselm.'

'Ah. Poor old Anselm. Everyone abuses him, even his own sly little menial. Isn't there a phrase in the Gospels somewhere on exactly that theme?'

'There is, master. You often hear it about the court. "And a man's foes shall be they of his own household." It's from Matthew.'

'Ah, that's it exactly. "And a man's foes..." If you don't look out, Firmin, I will have to carry you around like a chrestomathy, you are so full of pithy matter and quotes for all occasions.'

'Shall I encourage Eustace, master?'

'Certainly. Try to find out more about this secret meeting. I think it's time to interest ourselves in Henry's affairs.'

****

After the ceremony at which he received the *pallium*, Anselm had remained at Canterbury for a few weeks during which time his relations with Walter of Albano, the papal legate, became strained. Eventually, they had parted on bad terms: a rift that was very much approved by William who resented the presence of a papal legate in his kingdom. Relations between the king and archbishop were at this period unusually calm and remained so during the Christmas court at Windsor where Anselm presided over the religious observances. In his sermon, he steered clear of controversy and both men were optimistic about their future partnership. And so it remained until their differences broke out once more over the issue of money.

One of the first letters despatched from the office of Ranulf Flambard in the matter of the Normandy mortgage was addressed to Archbishop Anselm and eventually caught up with him on his estate at Hayes. Having fled from Canterbury at the very first opportunity, the primatial household had resumed its old habit of never remaining in one place for long although, by the time the letter came, they had been frozen at Hayes for three weeks. There, one morning in February 1096, Anselm was sitting reading the letter in his private office wrapped in a blanket, close to the fire. Baldwin was writing at a table, Eadmer stood behind at a lectern, reading from a psaltery. Eustace came in with a gust of raw air, drawing a sled piled high with logs and began to feed the fire.

'That's goodly work, Eustace,' said Anselm, 'you make light and warmth for us.' Eustace felt demeaned by the kind of praises that would satisfy a menial and squirmed with resentment. Ever since Eadmer had come on the scene he had felt himself slipping further from the master's sight. Nevertheless, when Anselm looked up from the letter and began waving it about to call them into a circle of attention, Eustace was not excluded from the gesture.

'There is never any good news that comes from Flambard,' he said. 'How William can keep such a man about him exceeds my understanding. I shall never forget how he served a writ on me on the day of my enthronement.'

Baldwin stopped writing. 'That letter then is from Flambard?' Baldwin, who had worked with the king's minister and had developed a different view of his qualities, was suddenly attentive.

'What does he say, master?' Eadmer scented material for the defamatory picture he was constructing in his great work of the king's unpopular minister. Eustace was all attention but made no remark.

'It is, of course, a plea for money. But the reason is quite unlike any that has ever been broached to me or that I have ever heard of.'

No sermon of Anselm could have held the little circle quite so rapt or expectant. All eyes were on him as they waited for him to go on.

'Robert Curthose has listened to the Pope's appeal at Clermont. He proclaims himself sickened by war and feuds in Normandy, ruined by wasteful expenditure and bowed down by a sense of his own sin. He is to go to Jerusalem.'

Anselm put the letter aside. 'How much easier it would be to work with Robert than with William. At least, he has spiritual purpose and the interests of the church at heart.'

‘But what does the letter say?’

‘It says that the Duke of Normandy intends to go on campaign to Jerusalem for which purpose he will make over the sovereignty of Normandy to his brother, William, for a term of three years in consideration of a money payment.’

‘So Flambard’s letter is asking for money?’

‘Indeed, as I said. He insists on the rightness of the cause. He invites me, as a longstanding supporter of Pope Urban, to lead by example.’

‘But master,’ said Baldwin, who was thoroughly acquainted with the papal address at Clermont, ‘this is not good news for us. Pope Urban’s preaching has begun by inspiring a righteous cause but it will end with great despoliation throughout the Roman church.’

Baldwin’s practical mind stood aghast at the drain on ecclesiastical resources being proposed. In his view, mass movements of people were dangerous and hardly ever achieved their objectives. He could foresee much damage. On the one hand, William would use Robert’s warlike venture as a means of bettering his own position by extorting money from the church. On the other hand, the church itself was being called on by the pope to support all the pilgrim warriors, by guaranteeing their land and revenues while they were absent, and raising money for their expenses. Baldwin could see great streams of revenue pouring away from the church as abbots, priors and even some bishops became infected with the mania of war. Sometime later, Baldwin had clear proof of this development. Hearing that the abbot of Cerne had begun urging his monks to go to Jerusalem and was preparing to go himself, he prevailed on Anselm to write to Osmund, Bishop of Sarum, ordering him to stop any monks from leaving. Anselm did so. Whereupon, Osmund wrote back to say that the Abbot of Cerne was so far gone in zealotry that he was in the process of buying a boat and had put down thirty shillings on it. Advising the abbot to re-examine his state of mind, Osmund had seized the boat.

When the king’s demand came to Anselm, Baldwin found his master uncharacteristically supportive of the king’s need for money.

‘I must extend a helping hand in so proper a cause,’ he said.

These were still the halcyon days of good relations between himself and William. He thought he had gained a paternal role from the reconciliation at Windsor last year. He looked forward to being able to guide the reprobate king into better ways and effect real reform in his personal moral habits. He even cherished the hope that the intransigent monarch might eventually be persuaded to accept Church Councils.

'How will you respond to Flambard's wicked demand, master?' asked Eadmer, hoping for some useful condemnatory phrases which could be worked into his text.

'It is not wicked, Eadmer, even though Flambard is its source. He is about the king's business. But how shall I answer this?'

Anselm answered it by journeying to Canterbury and taking up residence in the monastery of Christchurch. There, much to Baldwin's surprise, but with the approval of the chapter house, he took from the treasury of the priory church, partly in gold and partly in silver, the sum of two hundred silver marks, equivalent to one-fiftieth part of what the king needed. 'If fifty of the wealthiest foundations in England make such a donation,' said Anselm, 'we can supply Robert's needs.'

'Aren't we rather supplying William's needs?' said Baldwin.

'Here is a case in which they are barely distinguishable, my friend. Without the money, Robert cannot go on pilgrimage. With the money, William purchases himself a dukedom. We are caught between them, Baldwin. But we must try, if we can, to prevent an increase of the intolerable burdens on the poor.'

Once back in Canterbury, Anselm began to involve himself in the life of the monks, something he had always claimed was his true vocation. He instituted a few reforms, made some appointments, but failed to do anything about recognising the old English saints or forms of worship, much to Eadmer's disappointment. He carried out routine episcopal duties, filled minor vacancies and followed the king's campaigns in the north, in Wales and in Normandy. At a time when the kingdom was plunged into frequent turmoil and William was threatened on several fronts at once, Anselm kept his head down, bearing himself with discretion, awaiting the time of peace when he would once again be able to press the king in regard to church reform. All this was duly reported back to Flambard by Eustace.

As the months of spring passed into early summer and the list of names grew, it became clear that Robert Curthose was only one of an army of distinguished princes, dukes, counts and greater and lesser nobles who were throwing themselves behind Pope Urban's appeal. In Robert's party alone, were cousins, kinsmen and men of his clan: Stephen of Aumale, Stephen Count of Blois, Robert Count of Flanders, Alan Fergant Duke of Brittany, the counts of St Pol and Mortagne.

Great swathes of northern Europe were to be denuded of their rulers and a great proportion of the warrior class, shaking up the administration of these provinces to such an extent that few would escape its effects. A massive programme of victualling, arms and supplies would produce a leaching of rents, foodstuffs, horses and fodder across the Mediterranean to sustain the vast numbers of warriors and pilgrims on the march. A quartermastering operation of quite staggering proportions would be necessary if the operation was to have the least chance of success.

Incessant appeals to God in chants and prayers, hymns and sermons, were furnished by the accompanying clergy. The church of Normandy was to lose two out of its seven bishops: Odo of Bayeux and Gilbert, bishop of Evreux. In Robert's entourage, went his chaplain, Arnulf of Chocques. Some of these men were not much younger than Anselm himself, now sixty-three years old.

As the list of names grew, numbering churchmen as well as laity throughout Europe and the Mediterranean, including Norman lords from Apulia and Sicily, the scale of the movement became evident. Something uncontrollable had been set in motion and was carried along by a furious pressure of its own, something astonishing, portentous, unprecedented. But Ranulf Flambard and Baldwin of Tournai, men not by nature given to zealotry, watched the great awakening of Christendom with growing alarm. On this matter, they were in perfect agreement. Their way of doing things was by steady, painstaking negotiation resulting in small incremental advances. In their view, this wild enterprise was from first to last misconceived, wasteful and reckless.

****

Chapter Twelve

The Property Deal

When her family came together in December to spend Christmas at Castle St Mary's, Aefled discovered that her premonitions about "not knowing" her sons were justified. The boys were now fourteen and twelve years old, youths who had seen something of the world, mixed with noblemen and courtiers and now found life in a provincial keep in the depths of winter wretchedly dull. Stiff behaviour to their mother, politeness lacking the eager warmth she so desired, made it clear that they wanted to be elsewhere, indeed were longing to be gone. They spent a great deal of time outdoors seeking the company of male companions, especially Arnoud, the constable, who was an excellent horseman. They were out on horseback most of every day, and when they weren't riding, they were in the stables or practising with arms.

All the lessons that Aefled had tried to teach seemed to have been forgotten. Everything she had been striving for, her high aims of moulding noble natures against the grain of entrenched prejudices, had not outlasted the first trip home. She had hoped that, by following her system of education, the castle boys would mix and mingle freely, establishing friendships across the divides of lineage and status. But her sons' new experiences seemed to have erased these lessons. Aefled's great sadness during that Christmas season was the discovery that she had failed. She thought of Isaac. How right he had been to say that prejudice and arrogance on one side and resentment and grudge on the other could not be overcome in one generation. Her sons were growing up and were well aware of their entitlements. Worse, they showed traits of the Norman arrogance that Aefled secretly loathed. This was most apparent in their behaviour to their old companions and playmates, the English boys, Alfred and Edward. But Aefled had no idea of the real situation until one aggressive incident resulted in violence.

The four boys were together at the stables one morning where they had been sharing the work of grooming and feeding the horses. Deciding to ride out, Robert told Alfred to fetch his saddle.

'Get it yourself,' he said. 'I'm not your serf.'

'Get me my saddle!'

When Alfred refused to obey his order a second time, Robert struck out at his former playmate with the loose reins of a bridle he was carrying.

Alfred clapped his hands to his stinging face and felt blood oozing from a welt.

'That'll teach you,' said Robert.

The blow reverberated around the keep, taking on symbolic significance. This was a reflection of the great social divide, the one Eadmer suffered from, the one Firmin was overcoming as he sought to rise in the service of Norman officialdom. Bloodlines and lineage were just that, lines, lines which could plot or unplot your course through life. They were restrictive but not insuperable, as many advancing English careers bore witness. But Alfred and Edward, having been encouraged from infancy by the false sense of equality fostered in Aefled's school, found them insupportable. With the advent of the favoured sons of the household, they became more dissatisfied with the kind of future they were facing. Their education had fitted them for more than toil or servitude and they reacted passionately against demeaning treatment.

When Gyft, Alfred's mother, saw his bleeding face and learned what had happened, she took her complaints to Aefled. While fully aware of the problem, Aefled felt powerless to do anything. A few words to Robert and William had no effect, they only listened to their father and he was not about to defend the sensibilities of boys of no degree. And so, in the spring of 1096, catching the fever of a stirring world, Alfred and Edward ran away. They disappeared overnight and could not be found after a week of searching. Rumours circulated they had gone to join a pilgrim train heading south to Hastings with the intention of reaching Rome. They were among many to be flung from the course of their lives by the great new purpose engulfing Christendom and, although they had never heard of Urban and had no idea of his preached message, they were caught up in the wake of the movement like pebbles in a tide. A tremor passed through all levels of society, shaking loose the fervent, the war hungry, the least attached and those with nothing to lose.

During that winter season, too, Aefled was worrying about Eleanor. By the end of their stay at Wilton, the previous summer, Eleanor had become attracted to the religious life. It seemed that what she had witnessed of Gunhild's tragic loss of her baby, and what she had heard of her experiences with Count Alan Rufus, had furnished Eleanor with a negative view of love and marriage, and turned her against the worldly life. To Aefled's dismay, when the time came to leave Wilton at the end of August, she had protested, saying she wanted to stay longer with the nuns. At Aefled's urging, Edith had spoken out with her strong views.

'It is a fearsome thing to dedicate yourself to God,' she told Eleanor. 'A life of denial, obedience, abnegation. Marriage is the better option. Seize life, live in the world. You are lucky, you have a mother and father who will plan a grand marriage for you. Mine are dead. I must make my own way.' Edith fully intended to do just that. With her sights set high, she was confident enough to reject lesser suitors. When, the previous year, a proposal had come from the immensely powerful magnate, William de Warenne, Earl of Surrey, whose family held large estates in England and Normandy, she made a show of being tempted by the offer. Certain pledges, made through his steward, promising dowry lands and money fiefs and other generous inducements, gave Edith an indication of her value and simply made her more certain that she could aim higher. So Warenne's suit had been dismissed after a cruelly lengthy period. Edith rebuked herself for having drawn it out so long but felt no harm had been done.

At that time, not long after the visit of Henry, Edith was summoned one day to the abbess and asked directly what had occurred between her and the king's brother. Had they been alone? What had he said to her? Had he made any proposal about the future? Edith denied that any such meeting had ever taken place or that any plan had been proposed. She was adamant almost to the point of rudeness. 'I will not be questioned,' she said.

'You will be questioned, Lady Edith.' said the abbess. 'You are the daughter of a king, but not of a reigning monarch. You are now beholden to the King of England. Do you have any idea of the seriousness of the situation you are in? If Henry has made any proposal to you, if he has broached the question of marriage, then it must be a matter of the greatest interest to the king. If Henry has drawn you into a compact, an understanding, an agreement of any sort, it is your duty to tell us.'

Edith denied everything and went on denying everything until the abbess, unconvinced, was silenced. Then Aefled, Agnes and Gunhild were urged to use their influence to dislodge the truth from the girl. But Edith's icy calm and self-control could not be dented. She would say nothing except to utter opaque remarks about being worthy of her mother, Queen Margaret. Eventually, the abbess, feeling it was her duty to alert the highest ecclesiastical authority, had written to Archbishop Anselm.

And so the departure from Wilton had left many unresolved questions hanging in the air. A change had occurred in Eleanor. Edith was hiding secrets. Wilton itself was a mystery. Although she had spent many months there, Aefled felt she still did not know the place. But somehow the place knew her. As it had known Gunhild. She thought about Gunhild's profound encounter there with her own desires and passions. Wilton had shown her a truth about herself, flung her out into a world of hurt and grief, then caught her up again, this time for good. Wilton had loosed Edith's instincts in an involuntary arousal of desire and was tempting Eleanor with the first stirrings of religious vocation. Wilton's mystery, she thought, went beyond spiritual orthodoxy into something occult and latent. It was a place of confrontation and discovery, where anything could happen and often did.

In this frame of mind, Aefled had come home to Castle St Mary's to face a troubled Christmas at the keep. Robert brought the news of Pope Urban's sermon and spent Christmas wondering if his overlord, Richmond, would decide to take up the Holy Cross and go on crusade.

'Do you think that Henry will go?' asked Aefled one evening when they were discussing it alone in their private apartment.

'No, not Henry. He will take the opportunity of gaining favour with his brother. William will need him in Normandy once the duchy comes into his hands.'

'But if Henry is so staunch for his brother, why do you suppose he was secretly talking to Edith?'

'Henry is a man who finds women irresistible. He may have been amusing himself.'

'Amusing himself! But she's no more than a child. Strong and canny, I grant you, with a will and determination beyond her years. But still young enough to be drawn into error.'

'Worse than error. If Henry filched a promise of marriage behind the king's back, they would both be acting treasonably. In that case, the only assumption to be made is that Henry is plotting something against his brother. And yet I would swear he is not.'

'Something happened,' said Aefled, musingly, with a distant look in her eyes, 'something happened there. Something that could only happen at Wilton.'

'What do you mean?'

'Wilton has a strange power over people. At Wilton, things are not as they are elsewhere. Did you not feel it?'

Robert shook his head.

****

'Holy Face of Lucca! Flambard, a paltry sum.'

Such was William's reaction on learning of Anselm's donation towards the purchase of Normandy.

'But, I trust, my lord king, you will be pleased to accept it.'

William nodded. 'I will accept it. You may tell him so. Thank him. Humour him. Anything, so long as he keeps from court and does not plague me with requests for Church Councils.'

'Granted the donation is paltry, yet to his credit, he has been making efforts to raise knights from his fiefs for your Welsh campaign.'

Ranulf thought he might put in a good word for Anselm whose ungenerous response was at least not downright refusal.

'The Welsh, the Welsh,' said William. 'What use is the great bulk of Hugh d'Avranches if he cannot stand in their way?' He was referring to the Earl of Chester, a powerful marcher lord, a man of titanic physique, huge appetites and martial reputation who was, in spite of these great qualities, failing to keep Welsh nationalist fury in check.

'I'll settle with them when I have got hold of Normandy. How far are we from our target?'

'Still some way, my lord. But there is no doubt that William St Calais has benefitted your cause by his most opportune death.'

'Indeed, Flambard, the bishopric of Durham has become vacant with perfect timing.'

At just the time William was in urgent need of money, Durham had fallen into his hand like a soft, ripe plum, oozing cash. An immensely rich see, perhaps even richer than Canterbury with vast lands and tenantries throughout the north, supplied a steady stream of revenue which would now revert to the royal coffers. The vacancy of Durham represented a significant source of income and

William was determined to hold on to it. In regard to the personal ambitions of Ranulf Flambard, however, the death was inopportune. He had long aspired to a bishopric, most particularly Durham, but by falling vacant at a time most advantageous to William, this most delicious plum would not come into his hand, if it ever did, for a very long time.

In his more pragmatic moments, Ranulf Flambard knew that his qualifications for high ecclesiastical office were rather like Anselm's donation—paltry. It was true that he held a few minor preferments, among them the deanery of Christchurch Priory at Twynham in the diocese of Winchester, where he was building a new church. Such provincial projects, however, were not a stepping stone to a great ecclesiastical career. More useful was his membership of a group of influential Norman clerics in London who belonged to the cathedral clergy of St Paul's, on whom he was counting to propel him one day into the ranks of the episcopate. In this way, he hoped to lay the groundwork for a splendid second career in the church once he had become expendable as a minister of the king.

But at present, he was far from expendable and knew it. William relied on him more and trusted him further than his own brother. Despite his recent reconciliation with Henry, there was little trust between them. Flambard, on the other hand, was always dependable, always there, capable, inventive, ready with a plan, adaptable, efficient. If anyone could bring off this immense task of raising funds, negotiating, organising and carrying through the enterprise to secure Normandy, it was Flambard.

They were talking in William's private quarters at Rochester Castle where the king was holding his Easter court. Rochester was the seat of Anselm's old friend, Bishop Gundulf, who was invited to give the Good Friday sermon and celebrate the paschal mass. William was even prepared to listen to Gundulf's longwinded praises of Anselm out of ancient affection for the bishop. Years ago, soon after coming to the throne, William had appointed Gundulf to build the new stone castle at Rochester, an enterprise he carried out with efficiency and economy, winning William's respect which he had retained into old age. But now the old bishop was bent and frail, his face an unilluminated parchment, his sermons rambling. Perhaps he would not last much longer. Perhaps another rich bishopric was about to fall vacant.

William was seated at a table with open manuscripts scattered on it, rifling through letters that had come his way.

'Why don't my clerks deal with these?' he said tetchily.

'They do, my lord king. Then they give them to me. I deal with what I can but occasionally, my lord, some of these papers must come to you.'

'Well, read them to me, Flambard, I cannot be looking at these tiny scratchings all morning.'

Flambard picked up the first document and read: 'Emissary from Dijon.'

'What do you think of this abbot,' said William, 'is he up to the mark?'

He was referring to the grandly titled Abbot Jarento of Saint Bénigne, a monk of Dijon, the intermediary sent by Robert Curthose to finalise plans between himself and William for the transfer of Normandy. A swarthy Burgundian, round-faced and ponderous, his rotund and amiable exterior hid a razor-sharp, scholastic mind.

'My lord king, having taken the measure of the man, I believe we can do business with him.' Flambard did not mention that, included in the 'measure,' were several casks of the best Burgundy wines which went some way towards lubricating the negotiations.

By the end of the Easter Octave, discussions were complete and arrangements were made for the transfer of the Duchy of Normandy to William's custody at a ceremony to take place in Rouen in September. At that time the full amount of ten thousand silver marks, mostly in coin but also in the value of supplies, would be handed over by William in person. He would then bid farewell to his brother and Robert would depart on the risky venture from which no one expected him to return.

Before all this could happen, there remained the matter of raising the money. Ranulf Flambard and his bureau of clerks, tallymen and agents were working long hours to realise the vast sum of the pledge. The church was the main target but had to be squeezed, pressed and threatened at every turn as abbots, priors and bishops, went to desperate lengths to hang on to their wealth. When Ranulf preached the example of Anselm and the treasury plate he had taken from Canterbury, they answered with equally paltry sums, often with outrage, resentment and, occasionally, threats to write to the pope.

In April, Flambard set out for London with Firmin and an entourage of canonical lawyers, clerks, agents and henchmen, to effect the king's command. Planning to fill some of the lesser vacancies by offering them to whoever could pay the highest price, he wanted to consult his clergy friends at St Paul's about likely bidders. Then he would invite the Jews of Poultry to show their loyal support for the king's enterprise. Arriving in London on a blustery spring day, Ranulf rode through the barbican of the tower, the great stone keep on the banks of the Thames, angled into the Roman walls. Strange to think that this impregnable royal palace was the work of that same Gundulf, Bishop of Rochester, who had just delivered the Easter sermon. A mind that had once conceived the design of this gigantic military fortress now ran on resurrection and eternal salvation.

Flambard and his household lodged at the tower in a suite of rooms often occupied by royalty and this became his central station for the sending out of requests and receipt of monies. Firmin, who was rapidly rising in his master's service, was deputed to oversee the running of the office. He had his own writing table and his own set of tasks, but as yet no formal title. It was his job to keep close records of donors' names, amounts given and a running total, regularly updated. He was one of the seven key holders to the great chest of coins. So much was being amassed in so short a time that the great chest was supplemented by barrels, each holding one hundred pounds. By the middle of summer thirty barrels were stored in the tower vaults, safe behind a battery of locks, bolts and guards. Firmin was entrusted with one of the keys to the vaults. If asked, Ranulf would most certainly say that he trusted Firmin as utterly as one man can ever trust another. Even so, he kept a close watch on him and on everyone else who had possession of keys or entry to the vault. One day, when Firmin was caught going outside the tower without permission carrying a suspicious leather bag, the guards brought him to Ranulf. Confronted by a guilty-looking, hangdog Firmin, Ranulf felt a pang of something like grief go through him. Please God, let it not be. Not Firmin. Not my lad.

'Master,' he said, 'I can explain.'

Ranulf's heart sank. This is how the guilty ones always begin, he thought.

When the bag was searched it was found to contain only a piece of blank parchment, a set of writing implements and a small Latin psalter.

'Where did you get that?'

'Master, it's true, I borrowed it from the chaplain.'

'Stole it, you mean?'

Firmin nodded. 'Just for a time. I was going to give it back.'

'Why did you want it, even for a short time?'

'Master, I am still perfecting my Latin. I go to whoever will teach me, usually a clerk not of your entourage, sometimes a local priest, here it is a clerk to the chaplain.'

'You mean you stole the chaplain's psalter so that his clerk can teach you out of it?'

'Yes, master. I did not want to tell you. I wanted you to think I am further forward than I am so you would give me greater tasks and think well of me.'

Ranulf was so relieved by this explanation that he could have hugged the mop-haired aspirant to his bosom.

'Well, Firmin, I don't think ill of you for having ambitions and working hard. But I shall think ill of you if you get caught again.'

Soon after this, one day in early June, Henry sent a message across the river from the Abbot's house in Bermondsey where he was staying, inviting Ranulf Flambard to feast with him in the abbot's hall. It was not an invitation to be declined so, the following evening, he had himself rowed across the river with Firmin and two clerks of his household. For once, he was caught by surprise and had no idea why he had been summoned or what Henry was planning. In spite of further inquiries, he had not been able to find out any more information about Henry's visit to Wilton or what had happened between him and Edith. Even though in recent times Ranulf had encountered the king's brother about the court and had a nodding acquaintance with him, Henry was an unknown force in the world of political intrigue. Remembering the allegorical game he had once played with Firmin, fancifully turning courtiers into dogs, Flambard wondered what kind of dog Henry might be. Certainly not a lymer on a leash, nor a brachet, for he could not be paired with an equal. Nor a greyhound bounding in full view like Count Alan Rufus and William St Calais, bold runners both, now run finally to ground. Henry was too subtle in his gambits, too devious. He did not seek to outpace but to wait and pounce. Like a cat. That was it. A sly creature of subterfuge who would rub himself against your legs then claw your eyes out. Ranulf was rarely baffled by the motives of men, but Henry baffled him. Sitting opposite in the boat as they were oared across the high running waters, Firmin threw him a questioning look.

'Don't ask me why, Firmin. And don't speculate. We obey a summons, that's all.'

The abbot's hall was a beamed chamber of modest proportions with glazed windows. A long trestle oak table with benches at either side was laden with dishes enough for the ten or a dozen men seated at it, along with two or three ladies. Henry was sitting in the abbot's seat on a raised dais at one end, looking every inch a king, thought Ranulf.

Henry rose and greeted him warmly, holding out his hand. Ranulf saw a paw which had just been licked clean by a rough pink tongue.

'Ranulf Flambard, welcome. And welcome to your people,' he said eyeing Firmin and the clerks. "People" put them in their place. Their place was not at the table but with the other servants in an antechamber. Ranulf glanced around at many faces he knew well. Men of the court, mostly staunch oathmen to the king, among them Count Alan Richmond, Robert Bloet, Robert FitzHaimo and Walter Tirel. He recognised Roger d'Avranches, the steward who ran Henry's household. One face was unfamiliar, it belonged, he learned, to Richard Redvers, a vassal poached from Robert Curthose and now one of Henry's closest companions. Flambard thought him slimy, a man on the make, catlike and sly like his master. Although wine flowed, the evening passed off without drunkenness or controversy. In fact, much of the talk ran on ecclesiastical matters and though some criticism was made of Anselm, none was made of the king. Ranulf wondered whether this decorous ambience was due to the presence of a few women, the wives of Henry's vassals, invited as company to Henry's latest paramour. *Why are we here?* wondered Ranulf all evening. It can't be to talk politics. What is he up to? Why this sudden extension of civility to myself? Even now, in spite of all his misgivings, Ranulf had no grounds for suspecting Henry of plotting against his brother. On the contrary, it was in Henry's interest to remain staunchly loyal to William and help him raise the money that would put Robert of Normandy out of the way.

The meal was served by squires of Henry's household, sons of noblemen and retainers, among them two sprightly lads called Robert and William. But it was not until later in the evening that Ranulf realised that one of the women was their mother, an Englishwoman called Aefled. A handsome woman with honey-coloured hair sprinkled with grey, held back from her face in a coif from which some curls escaped. With the distinct impression that he had seen her before, he introduced himself.

'Ranulf Flambard,' she said. 'Indeed, we met at Wilton three years ago. You brought a message for the lady Gunhild, from her uncle. I am Aefled, wife to Robert of Castle St Mary's.' She indicated her husband, who was standing near the entrance to the antechamber, talking to Richmond.

So the whole family is here, thought Ranulf, quite an outing.

'Your sons are fine young men.'

'You see them there?' she asked proudly. 'They are in the service of my lord Henry, training to become knights.'

'Does that please you, Lady Aefled?'

'Why should it not?'

'Because they will become Norman knights without a trace of English in them.'

Aefled was taken by surprise. How could this man have seen so deeply into her private anxiety on such a brief acquaintance?

'Don't be alarmed,' said Ranulf. 'It may surprise you to know that I have some interest in English affairs. One of my most trusted clerks is English. An orphaned boy from Huntingdon. Keen, well-witted, thirsty for education, ambitious. A remarkable product of Anglo-Norman co-operation. There should be more of it.'

Ranulf, whose interest in English affairs stretched all the way to taking ten shillings from every man in the *fyrd*, had instantly caught Aefled's attention. In spite of the disreputable stories she had heard about him, this man was impressive. Humorous, goose-grey eyes that missed nothing, a pleasing way of talking, a posture of relaxed calm overlaid with total self-control endowed this tall man with a charming allure.

'Shall you return to Wilton, Lady Aefled?' asked Ranulf.

'Perhaps. I have friends there. I long to see them.'

'You mean the ladies Gunhild and Edith?'

'Yes, they are pressing me to visit them with Lady Agnes and my daughter, Eleanor. I think I shall.'

'But something holds you back?'

'I fear for my daughter. I fear she is becoming attached to the religious life.'

'You do not approve? You think the married life is better for a girl?'

'I think it better that she does not make such a decision until she is truly able to understand all its implications. I do not agree with childhood dedications. I do not agree that oblate children should be offered to the church before they have attained full understanding.'

'But do you not think it saves them from the afflictions of the world?'

'To give an ignorant child to the church seems to me an act of cruelty. The religious life must be entered in full maturity, in full knowledge, with full consent. Only then, I believe, can it be acceptable to God.'

It was Ranulf's turn to be impressed. He had rarely heard such outspoken views. How easy it would be, he thought, to allow this fascinating woman to divert him from his path of questioning.

'Please convey my sincere greetings to the lady Gunhild and to Lady Edith. Perhaps you have received letters from them?'

'Not for some time.'

'The Lady Edith, do you believe she is one to seek the religious life? Is she happy at Wilton?'

Now Aefled was on the alert. Ranulf was angling for some information on Edith, undoubtedly in connection with the visit from Henry. So Flambard knew about it. But, of course, Flambard knew everything; had spies and informers everywhere, so Robert said.

'The Lady Edith is entirely happy at Wilton,' said Aefled abruptly.

She excused herself and hurried away, anxious to escape from a dangerous, charming, presence to which attached the high fame of a scurrilous reputation. Traduced by monks, trusted by the king, loathed and liked in equal measure by the barons, adored by a small circle of family and servants, Ranulf Flambard was as unsettling as the flame for which he was named, now warming, now scorching, now destroying all in its path. How easily she might be drawn into an attraction for this man who was not only one of the most influential ministers of the realm but seductive, roguish, many-faced, whose presence sent out a *frisson* to which she was not immune. To be held enchanted in an enigmatic, probing conversation with Ranulf Flambard was tantamount to a flagrant adventure. She escaped, shocked at her feelings, ashamed that with the next breath she might have compromised not only Edith but herself.

Later, when the meal was over and the guests had split up into little groups, Henry approached Ranulf and drew him aside.

'No doubt you are wondering why I asked you here, Flambard,' he said.

'Indeed, my lord.'

'It's quite simple. I want to do you a service. I want to save you time and effort.'

'How might that be, my lord?'

'I hear you are about to start raising money from the Jews in Poultry. I want you to be aware that I have treated with them in the past and have a good relationship with their Chief Rabbi. My agents will raise the money in Poultry.'

So that was it. He had received a warning. Leave the Jews alone.

Henry was jealous of his connections with the Jews, to whom he had vaguely promised benefactions should he become king. Over a period of years he had worked hard at establishing good relations, which gave him access to immediate loans. It was a position he was prepared to defend, even to the point of making friendly overtures to the king's first minister whom he distrusted and disliked. Ranulf Flambard must be prevented from learning about the promised 'charter,' setting out the liberties and rights that Henry would grant the Jews should he ever become king. It was a vague and sketchy promise, given at a necessitous moment when he was in desperate need of cash, without substance or any plan of action to back it. Even so, Henry knew that Flambard would denounce such a promise as plain treason to the king.

As he was rowed back across the river that summer's night, Ranulf had the distinct feeling that he had been spat at and clawed. Whatever the reason, he had been warned in the clearest terms. Don't set foot in Poultry.

****

All summer the money flowed in steady streams, from the church, from the barons and, when Henry had delivered on his tacit agreement with Flambard, from the Jews. By the end of July, thirty barrels were stored in the vaults alongside the original great chest, amounting to some four and a half thousand silver marks. But there was more to do.

'Now we come to the hardest part, Firmin.'

'What is that, master?' Firmin knew very well what came next but he played up to the role his master wanted, the part of the faux naïf questioner, the foil upon which Ranulf could scintillate his various humours.

'Now we come to the castellans, the possessors of minor honours, manors, villages and towns, the local lords who will unleash their reeves and bailiffs on the people. We have squeezed from those who can pay, now we squeeze from those who can't. This is the bloody handiwork I warned you about, Firmin, though the only stain on our hands will be ink. But what can I do? The king must be served.'

Ranulf was misrepresenting the case, as he knew full well. In fact, strong distinctions between church money and secular money could not always be made. Where abbeys and bishoprics owned land, they also owned the places where people lived. For example,

Abbot Baldwin, who had attended William in his illness three years previously had not only made St Edmundsbury a hugely wealthy abbey but had built more than three hundred and fifty houses in a town that yielded resources in rents, market tolls and dues from the population of skilled artisans: brewers, shoemakers, robemakers, tailors and cooks, who supplied services to the brothers of the monastery. With all these resources at his disposal, and aware of the sum of Anselm's donation, Abbot Baldwin, in a spirit of rivalrous pride, surpassed it. But it was the people, not the abbey, who paid.

And so the work went on, at many removes from the centre, in the villages and manors throughout the countryside, the work of extortion and oppression as the king's unwilling subjects were invited to empty their purses in his cause. At Castle St Mary's, as in many lesser estates, the reeve went with armed bailiffs to impose new levies and invent ways to confiscate property in cattle, timber, fisheries and whatever else might be deemed convertible into cash. But then came the news, almost too late to be of service, that the price had been reduced. Robert, Duke of Normandy, found himself so unalterably committed to a departure in September that he would be ready to accept a lesser sum, perhaps as little as seven thousand marks.

While these things were going on, Anselm was quiescent. As he travelled around the dependent houses of his diocese, his mind was far from the king's purpose. It was focused on monastical matters, the filling of minor posts, the consecration of bishops and on the great work he was striving to complete. The *Epistola de Incarnatione Verbi* was hammered out over many years but never to his satisfaction. It was not a work he wanted to write, but rather a response to provocations by detractors, most especially Roscelin of Compiègne, a French theologian who enjoyed goading him with criticism. At this time, the acceptance of the archbishopric weighed heavily on him; he could not concentrate and found no peace. He was still looking for a way out. Every so often he would renew his approaches to the king for the granting of Church Councils in letters which William ignored. On the surface, their relations were static and Anselm had not given up all hope of working amicably with the king, sometimes even writing warmly in his defence, praising his energy and practical wisdom. But he was like a fish flopping on shore, out of his element, unable to swim anywhere but in the calm waters of monastic life. Having given his donation, he paid little further attention to the king's current enterprise of buying up Normandy. That Robert should want to go on crusade he found admirable but had little understanding of the political and financial arrangements that would make it possible. When, on his travels, he noticed a column of smoke rising from a distant village he thought merely of hearth fires and cooking pots, not of punitive raids or intimidations.

All this time he continued to be dogged by complaints from Canterbury. Anselm's raid on the treasury plate, although ostensibly approved by the Christchurch brothers, had offended many who now began to regret having given their approval. They felt robbed. The sour little monk, Eustace, still nursing grudges, was active in stirring up disaffection in the chapter house. Reluctantly, Anselm travelled down to Canterbury to arrange a compensatory grant to the monks from his archiepiscopal estates. It was a subsidy of thirty pounds a year, too little, too late. This arrangement was typical of Anselm's way of doing things, causing the greatest amount of dissatisfaction to the largest number of people for the least possible result. By September, he was back at his manor of Hayes, taking refuge from the quarrels of monks. Even his greatest contentments, the calm regularity of Benedictine rule, the companionship of his brothers in Christ, the concentration of study, were lost to him. He longed to escape. When he heard that the king was down at Hastings, preparing to go aboard for Normandy, Anselm thought about going to confront him, to ask for Church Councils yet again, or perhaps, what he now most desired: permission to leave England. But he lacked the resolve and did not go.

In the middle of September, sixty-seven barrels of silver were removed from the tower vaults, loaded onto carts and, under heavy escort, taken down to Hastings where they were met by the king. Sixty-seven barrels of one hundred pounds apiece plus the great chest, containing in total nearly ten thousand marks, were put aboard a number of boats, each carrying armed marines, weapons, supplies and horses. No chances were to be taken with a cargo that amounted to the entire expendable wealth of a kingdom. With the king at Hastings were assembled some of the most important men in England, those who would stay and those who would go with the king. Ranulf Flambard, along with Robert FitzHaimo, Robert FitzGerold, Robert Bloet, Urse of Abetot and Bishop Walkelin were to stay. They were to make up a regency council of justiciars who would rule during the king's absence. Among those who would go with the king were his brother, Henry, the Counts of Maine and Alençon, Robert of Meulan, Richard of Clare, Roger Bigot, chancellor William Giffard and a number of lesser lords and chamberlains. Days went by while favourable conditions were awaited. The old sea-captain, Stephen, was set to sniff the breeze, study the skies and read the sea's moods. Masses were said, prayers offered, blessings given. God himself was called upon to protect the irreplaceable money ships. If lost, all William's hopes for Normandy would be sunk with them.

It was with the greatest relief that Ranulf waved goodbye to the ships one late September morning. They were taking away the arduous labours of the summer, the long toil of organisation, the responsibility of collecting, guarding and transporting a sum so vast that it could buy a dukedom.

'Thank God,' he said. 'At last, a little peace, some rest. Let's go to Huntingdon, Firmin.'

****

In Rouen, the money was handed over. The brothers embraced, exchanged the kiss of peace, swore to abide by the *concordia* agreed between them, sat side by side at the grand farewell feast and parted on the best of terms. Soon afterwards, Robert Curthose left by way of the pilgrim route for Rome which would take him through the Swiss Jura to Lake Geneva, through Lausanne, Montreux, Martigny and the Great St Bernard Pass to Aosta, Anselm's birthplace, then on to receive Urban's blessing in Rome before setting out for the Levant. With him went many of the great lords of northern Europe and their followers. Vast numbers were on the march, including women and children, hangers-on, the desperate and unhoused. Facing deprivation, disease, inadequate supplies and harsh conditions, a great trekking stream of massed humanity was on the move, carried away by religious enthusiasm for an enterprise from which few would return.

William stayed in Normandy and celebrated the Christmas of 1096 in Caen. It was now that he had the full sense that he had 'come into' Normandy; that he was, if not Duke, at least the ruler of the duchy with legitimate title to govern. This sense was deeply impressed on him by an unexpected stroke of fortune. Abbot Gilbert, the abbot of Caen's great Benedictine foundation, L'Abbaye aux Hommes, where William's father, the matchless Conqueror, lay buried, came to him one night with some of the monks from his monastery, carrying an iron-bound wooden chest on a stout oak pole.

'My lord king and lord of Normandy,' he said, 'there are in our keeping some precious relics of your father's reign which you might like to see.' The abbot gestured his monks to open the chest which took so long that William began to lose interest. When at last the contents were revealed, however, he was struck with wonder. All he could say was: 'Holy Face of Lucca! I thought they were lost.'

The conqueror's crown, his sceptre and rod, a cup of rock crystal, a golden candelabra, all perfectly preserved, glistening in the light of the torch-hung hall, lay on a bed of damask and silk. When William had done staring, Abbot Gilbert expressed a willingness to part with these treasures on the payment of a certain sum. After all, he said, it would be irresponsible to give them away when they represented a great value to the abbey. Astonished that the abbot had the gall to ask for money when he should have given these heritable items freely as a gift, but desperate to have them, William agreed to pay. Somehow he still had spending money, even if it had to be scraped out of his courtiers' pockets. He bought the sparkling regalia of gold and crystal from the abbot and they were handed over.

At the Christmas court that year, William wore his father's crown, carried his sceptre and rod, feasted by the light of his father's candelabra and drank from his rock crystal cup. These objects had not been seen in public since the death of the Conqueror, almost ten years before. They had been of no use to Curthose, who was not a king and had no right to a crown. But William was a king and he seized them with covetous desire and wore them with defiance. The parade of his father's regalia was a public statement that all aspects of the paternal regality were now incorporated in him. William could count himself equal with his father. He had governance of England and Normandy, jurisdiction over the church in England, control of correspondence with the pope and the promise of no interference from papal legations. These prerogatives had been jealously defended by William *père* and now William *fils* had matched him. Who could now say he was a lesser king? He had taken another step closer to his father, or rather to closing the gap between outward filial duty and the real antipathy he felt for the great dominating colossus of his life who had thrown a shadow over everything he did. He had spent all his life escaping from his father, but in the wearing of the symbolic regalia he could conquer his father's ghost and lay to rest his life-long self-doubt. Typically, he marked the moment with a jest, saying, 'My father is worthy of this son.' But, in the absence of Flambard, there was no one by to laugh.

By Easter 1097, William was back in England, making plans for the Welsh campaign. Ranulf Flambard met him at Windsor and they travelled to Hereford to put spirit into the lacklustre marcher barons who blamed their want of success on the mediocre quality of the fighting troops. Poorly trained, ill-equipped, unseasoned, these men, the second and third generation after the conquest, were without real fighting experience. Men like Count Alan Niger and William St Calais, the old soldiers from Hastings, were long past their prime and dying off. That spring, Richmond, the former Count Alan Niger, was one of them. He had been travelling back to his estates in the north, with Robert and his sons, when he was suddenly taken sick. After a few days, he seemed to recover and they set out on the road but had only gone a few miles when he gave a cry, struck his hand to his chest, then keeled over in the saddle and fell dead to the ground. Robert escorted the body back to Richmond where Count Alan Niger was interred beside his brother. And so the two lovers of Gunhild lay side by side in the monastery of St Mary's at York, which they had helped to found. It fell to Aefled to break the news. At the end of May, she was back at Wilton with her daughter and Lady Agnes.

Whitsuntide at Wilton with the white roses blooming in the garth, May blossoms strewn about the cloisters and white-robed nuns chanting their beauteous litanies, was an enchanting scene at odds with the bleak task she had come to perform.

Gunhild took the news badly. Somehow, while Count Alan Niger lived, something of her old love persisted. With his death came the opening of unhealed wounds, despair and ache. 'While he was active and full of life, my old love lived. I was awake in the world,' she said. 'Now all is sleep and night to me. I have become a ghost, like Wulfnoth.'

'But Wulfnoth found strength in faith,' said Aefled. 'God gave repose to his soul and a tranquil spirit. Can you not find such peace, here, at Wilton?'

Even as she said it, Aefled knew the answer. Wilton was not where you found peace unless peace was already in you. Wilton found you out, turned you inside out. Unless God was already manifest in you, you did not find him there.

What Edith found at Wilton was manifestly not God. She had grown into a tall, fascinating young woman. Now seventeen years of age, her features had composed themselves into a semblance of beauty but not beauty itself. Neat pouting mouth, sharp nose, remorseless eyes, an imperious step, graceful movements, she held herself in high regard and expected high regard from others. But she could also be disarmingly sweet, as she was with Eleanor who hung on her every word and imitated her manners.

In that Whitsuntide of 1097, Edith was waiting. She had always been waiting for the grand portal of destiny to open wide to her, not knowing what lay beyond. But, since the visit of Henry, she knew. All she had to do was keep silent and wait. But her silence thundered through Wilton, beat clangorous in the ears of the abbess, baffled all who made inquiries and piqued Aefled with curiosity. From Gunhild, who had spent the intervening months in her close company and was thought to have received private admissions, nothing could be wrung. Besides, Gunhild was weak, easily tired, worn out with grief. The news about Count Alan Niger, struck down by a vengeful God, caused her inconsolable anguish. She took to attending all the offices again, seven times a day, from Nocturn to Compline, kneeling on the stone flags, standing for hours in prayer, renouncing food and drink, spurning the comforts of the body, searching, searching for repose of spirit which never came.

'What can we do for her?' asked Aefled.

'There is nothing we can do.' Agnes thought her case hopeless. 'She is dying of grief.'

And so it proved. Within a few weeks of their arrival, while the May blossoms were still in bloom and the white roses had opened in their full glory, Gunhild took to her bed, frail as a petal, her handsome face ravaged by sorrow. At her bed, Aefled and Agnes watched in weary vigil as the last child of King Harold slipped away. Eleanor came and went, weeping for her lovely idol, the noble lady who had first interested her in the religious life. On the night she died, Edith came and stood in the doorway with a candle. She did not weep but stood looking at her companion with a steady gaze, her blue eyes seeming to etch the scene in her mind as if to preserve it forever. She stood waiting, waiting, as she had waited for years and as she would wait for a few years yet, waiting for a future to open, a life to fade, things to happen, the world to turn. That night Edith ceased to be a child. At the moment Gunhild died, she extinguished the candle and walked away.

Anselm was deeply saddened by the news of Gunhild's death and he prayed for the soul of his sister in Christ whom he had loved and tried to save. She had, as he desired, returned to her convent but, as the abbess wrote in her letter, had not been able to find her way back to God. Memories of her fall from grace stirred his own dissatisfaction with a life increasingly worldly. Before he could rightly speak in defence of the church, he, too, needed to find a way back to God. Wherever he looked, he saw churches and monasteries sunk in disorder, despoiled of possessions, ill-led by corrupt abbots and priors: a king who, setting his face against Church Councils, presided over an immoral and ungodly court. Accordingly, that Whitsuntide he presented himself at the king's court at Windsor, determined to press his demands for reform.

'Look lively, Firmin' said Ranulf when he heard news of Anselm's arrival. 'Our days of peace are about to end. Send for Baldwin.'

In a private meeting, Baldwin revealed that his master intended to pursue the old demands.

'But doesn't he realise William will never concede? He cannot have churchmen dictating to the court. Church Councils take authority from the king. Such a request will be refused.'

From Baldwin's expression, Ranulf saw that there was more. 'My master is disturbed in spirit, unable to work. His relations with the monks of Christchurch are strained and he feels he cannot lead the church as he should. He feels, he says, unable to bear fruit for Christ in this kingdom.'

'My commiserations to your master, Baldwin, but I do not see what I can do. What has caused this deep unrest? I thought, after his long silence, he was happily reconciled to his high office and ready to work alongside the king.'

'But the king will not allow him to do the work he feels called on to do. Anselm has said that he looked for a time of peace and beholds only confusion.'

'But that is just his way of speaking. What is really behind this discontent?'

Baldwin spent a moment studying his hands.

'My master received a letter.'

'From the king?'

'The king said that he was far from pleased with the knights Anselm sent from the Canterbury fiefs. He said they were not fit, not trained. He complained in the severest terms. Was this the sort of letter to write to the Archbishop of Canterbury? After months of silence on church matters, after ignoring Anselm's pleas for Church Councils, the king writes to complain about the combat readiness of knights!'

'I advised against that letter,' said Ranulf. 'He was angry when the Welsh campaign foundered for lack of seasoned troops.'

‘Then, adding to the indignity, the king demanded that he make reparation. You can see, Flambard, how my master must view this as egregious provocation.’

When the king and Anselm finally met that Whitsuntide in King Edward’s old palace of Windsor, it soon became clear that the peace of the last year had simply given occasion for fresh complaint and, while William had strengthened his position through his recent acquisition of Normandy, Anselm’s position had become intolerable.

‘My lord king,’ he said pleadingly, ‘give me permission to seek advice from the Holy Father. Allow me to go to Rome.’

‘What advice can he give you that you cannot give yourself? The pope can do nothing for the English church. A man as wise as you, Anselm, is better able to help the pope than the pope to help you.’

When Anselm came from the meeting with the king, he said to Baldwin: ‘He will not grant my request now, but he will do so another time. I shall not cease to ask.’

That, indeed, turned out to be his sole policy, to keep on asking until the king was worn down. From that time they never met but Anselm made the request and was always refused. William wanted neither reform councils nor a delinquent archbishop wandering about Europe proclaiming his failings far and wide. For his part, Anselm wanted the pope to free his soul from the burden of an unwanted post and restore its liberty to serve God by allowing him to fade back into the contemplative life. That the pope could deliver none of these things hardly entered his mind. As he saw it, the only way he could leave the burden of the archbishopric was to leave England.

****

On the death of Richmond, Robert’s full allegiance transferred solely to Henry, and he spent the greater part of 1097 travelling with the court in the service of his lord. Anxious to impress his brother, Henry was bent on sealing his fraternal alliance by sharing William’s passion for the hunt. In the summer, they went to one of the king’s favourite lodges, Brockenhurst in the New Forest, a vast hunting area, carved out by the Conqueror, lying south and west of the ancient capital of Winchester. Even in sport, William always used to be vying with his father’s ghost, driving himself hard through long days in the field. But that summer his companions noticed a change, as if the acquisition of Normandy and his father's regalia had assuaged his thirst to excel, as if he was no longer striving to match himself against his father's reputation, as if he felt, for the first time in his life, an energy and mastery that made him easy in his kingship. He showed more interest in the technicalities of the sport and less in the slaughter. When he rode out with Henry at his side in the hot August days of the 'grease time' he appeared gratified, confident and in excellent spirits.

The hunting field drew on a vast body of servants for its functioning. Huntsmen, foresters and parkers to manage the forest, verderers who exploited the *vert*, the timber and other resources of the woodland, fewterers and lymerers, beaters, and marksmen for killing off any animal wounded by a poor shot. The king was attended by noblemen, some of them shamelessly on the make such as the members of the Clare family, Gilbert Fitz Richard and his brother Roger; some powerful old stalwarts like Robert of Meulan and his brother Henry Beaumont; others who pushed themselves into the field out of a desire to please, such as the cupbearer William D'Aubigny. And then there were the close companions, men he could trust. Among these, Ranulf Flambard, Robert FitzHaimo, Walter Tirel and William of Breteuil. The hunting field was the king's court outdoors where favour was sought and places were jostled for in the unceasing competition for royal attention.

Of the different types of hunting: the 'formal' hunt which consisted of following a pack of hounds on horseback, the 'casual' hunt which consisted of an unorganised pursuit of whatever prey presented itself and was largely a training in military field-craft and the more elaborate 'stable' hunt which consisted of shooting dismounted at driven deer, William's favourite was the last. Typically, the day would begin at dawn when the beaters and dogs were sent out. Armed with short bows drawn with the arm, the hunters would make their way to the shooting field placed deep in the chases of the forest. Along the route, a barrier was placed to halt the fleeing stags, harts if roe deer and bucks if fallow deer. There the terrified animals, finding their escape blocked, would fall to the arrows of the shooters at the butts.

Robert and his sons attended Henry on many of these excursions. At Brockenhurst that August, his sons learned the finer points of dog-handling as they went out before dawn with the fewterers and lymerers. Robert was assigned the job of transporting the kill from the butts to the hanging sheds. By now, he was firmly attached to the service of Henry, believing him to be a loyal supporter of the king. Having observed him closely over many months, Robert had seen no sign of plotting nor heard any word of discontent. But it is not easy for an uncomplicated man to spot complications in another and many men of the court, including Ranulf Flambard, still had misgivings, considering him a tenacious self-seeker who needed watching.

But many courtiers found Henry in certain moods to be exceptionally agreeable and entertaining. He was excellent company at the feasts which followed the hunts, drawing to his side several of the king's companions, including Walter Tirel and Robert FitzHaimo, two long-standing favourites. One evening when the company was well gone in food and drink, Henry began to talk about the dangers of the hunt, where accidents were not uncommon. In his own family there were several such incidents. Richard, the bastard son of Duke Robert, had been killed only the year before on a New Forest hunt when an overhanging branch had caught him in the throat. Thirty years before, another Richard, the victim's uncle, the second son of the Conqueror, had been shot by a stray arrow and died at the scene. Such stories were often told, but Henry seemed to relish them.

'You never can tell,' he said, 'when your time will come.'

'Face of Lucca, Henry!' William replied, 'Why harp on such a theme? Death comes when it will.'

'But to be taken off suddenly, unshriven, laden with sins. Does that not seem terrible to you?'

'Leave all that to Anselm. That's his territory.'

On another occasion, when William had left the feast to relieve himself, Henry drank rather too much and began to boast of his amorous affairs, confessing that he was greedy for the love of women, that he had peopled the realm with bastards, that, if he couldn't match his father with deeds, he could match him in the spreading of his seed. In the raucous bonhomie of masculine company, disarmed by drink and urged on by his companions, Henry came close to letting slip what had happened at Wilton.

'Unlike my brothers,' he said, 'I intend to marry.'

'Is that what you spoke about to the Lady Edith at that secret meeting no one talks about but everyone has heard of?' Roger Fitz Gilbert, as far gone in drink as Henry, was careless in this remark.

'It might be.'

Ears pricked and the room went quiet. Henry looked at the faces of his companions, knowing well that what he said next would be reported to William within moments. He saw Ranulf Flambard staring back at him with pretended indifference. How Flambard would like to catch him out in an unguarded confession.

'Yes, I spoke to Lady Edith about marriage,' he said, noting the various reactions to what promised to be an astonishing confidence. What was he going to say, what secret was he about to let loose in that susceptible company? He paused a long moment while they hung poised, waiting for his words, eyes darting, mouths like fish, suddenly sober, expectant.

'I told her that, when I marry, there may be a place for her in my wife's household.'

Many thought that he was not as drunk as he seemed.

****

Chapter Thirteen

The Cat Pounces

'What I hate most about hunting, Firmin, are those boorish post-hunt feasts,' said Ranulf one day soon after they had left Brockenhurst for Windsor.

'Why do you go to them, master?'

'For the simple reason that absence attracts attention. Knives are sharpened at such affairs, especially by Henry's cronies. Since he came on the scene, I feel myself slipping. I have no protection save the king's favour and that, Firmin, is a shallow thing.'

'Why this mood, master?'

'In a word, Henry. The back-archer, the scratcher, the sly creature of subtle tread. He unsettles me. He has jumped into the king's lap and lies there, purring. If only he was as translucent in his dealings as Anselm. One policy, one idea, one plea. "Let me go to Rome".'

Soon after the court had returned to Windsor, Anselm had renewed his request. The king had refused, but this time asked him to come to Winchester in October where the matter would be discussed again. To arm himself for this meeting, Anselm called a council of bishops to explain his present course of action and ask them for advice. He was, he said, determined to go to Rome, his very soul depended upon it and, if he could not go with the king's permission, he would go without it. At this, they made it clear that Anselm would not be encumbered with their support, claiming that, while he was a saintly man far above them in virtue, they were worldly men whose first allegiance was to the king from whom their offices and patronage derived. Far from backing his request to go to Rome, they accused him of reneging on his promises. When he had taken the *pallium* from the high altar at Canterbury it was a public acceptance of his office, endorsed by the pope and without conditions. Now he was trying to attach retrospective conditions over the issue of church councils. The bishops explained that the king viewed this as plain obstinacy which would be met by plain refusal. Unperturbed, Anselm thanked them for their frankness and, without altering his position one jot, went to Winchester to answer the king's summons.

Early on the day appointed for the meeting, Bishop Walkelin of Winchester walked up from his palace of Wolvesey bending over his stick as if his conscience was weighing him down. Old, tired, feeling he had not long to live, he regretted that he had not supported Anselm at the meeting in August. Even though he did not agree with his demands, it went heavy with him that the primate of England had found no one to stand with him against the king. But Walkelin had known William for years, had been chaplain to his father and had received bounties from his hands, as when he was granted land in the Isle of Wight for the building of his great new Minster. He admired Anselm and respected William, he could see both points of view, hurtling along like two solid bodies on the course of inevitable impact. Arrived at the Conqueror's old palace where the king and his court were lodged, he went into the royal chapel and said a few prayers, asking God to look kindly on the coming discussions, then took his place in the great chamber among the assembled barons and bishops who had come to hear Anselm's latest petition. He knew, as well as anybody there, that the archbishop's position was perilously close to treason. By constantly pressing for leave to go to Rome, and by threatening to go without the king's permission, he was putting a higher value on his allegiance to the pope than to the king.

'The king thought he could argue him out of obstinacy with sound arguments,' said Ranulf afterwards. 'But you can't argue with a man who has no arguments. Anselm just keeps striking on the same anvil until the opposition is flat. But the king stands to gain in one important respect. If Anselm goes, the king will seize the Canterbury revenues. Although he cannot be unmade as archbishop, he can be deprived of his income. But who would have thought it would end like this?'

'Has it ended, master?'

'I believe it has, Firmin. The bull has unyoked himself from the sheep.'

'And will the sheep leave England?'

'Finally, Firmin, after one of the bitterest encounters of this long contest, he has got what he wanted. Never has anyone battled so hard to go into exile. The king gave him a safe conduct to Dover and eleven days to quit the kingdom. But then he said that although he could go, he would not be allowed to take any property with him, adding that a royal official would meet him at Dover to tell him what he could take out of the country. Anselm replied that he would go on foot and naked rather than give up his determined course. That was quite a dramatic moment, Firmin. I wonder if the little monk, Eadmer, will put it all in his book.'

'So Anselm is to go, master, and all his household?'

'Indeed. A pity, I will miss these episodes of high excitement.'

'So they parted in enmity?'

'Strangely, no, not enmity. Anselm went to the king and said he would have preferred to go on better terms, with mutual goodwill. He commended the king to God and asked him to accept a blessing. William was moved, deeply moved, even shaken. He said: "I will be glad of your blessing, Father Anselm," and embraced the old man. Then the king bent his head and Anselm made the sign of the cross over him.'

Hearing the sounds of horses in the courtyard, Ranulf looked out of the window. Below he could see Anselm getting ready to go into exile. Torches flared in the cold October night. Baldwin was giving orders in a subdued voice. Eadmer, who had never left England in his life, leaned against a wall like a dug-up sapling. The old man, wrapped in a thick blanket, stamping his feet to keep warm, looked like a wanderer stranded on a vast empty shore.

'What has he done?' murmured Ranulf. 'What does he think he has achieved? Four years, Firmin, four years since he was acclaimed at William's bedside. Well, I suppose if nothing else, he has proved us wrong. The great irony in all this, Firmin, is that Anselm is, by nature, a deeply obedient man.' Ranulf's breath smoked in the chill air. 'So, off he goes, down to Canterbury to take leave of the monks, and then swiftly to Dover, before the king changes his mind.'

As it happened, the king did not change his mind, choosing instead to inflict one last indignity on his recalcitrant archbishop. It came in the form of William Warelwast, the very same man who had brought the *pallium* back to England and thus prevented his earlier attempt to leave. Anselm got to Dover on the day before the expiry of the deadline set at the Council of Winchester and there waited for the weather and tides to turn favourable. At last, on November 8th came the signal from the sailors that they were to embark. All their luggage was brought to the shore, bags and crates full of the personal belongings of his household which included Baldwin, Eadmer, a few monks who had chosen to go with him, minor officials and his servant, Adam. It was bitterly cold and a strong wind was blowing. Then, along the shore strode William Warelwast with a party of grim-faced officials. No one could have been more repugnant to Anselm at that moment, except perhaps Ranulf Flambard, one of the very few men who actually regretted his going. And indeed it might have been Flambard who came that day, as the king had appointed. But, having no taste for such a task, he pleaded an indisposition and declined to go. Thus the odious mission was delegated to a man without scruple.

As William Warelwast approached along the shore, Baldwin went to confront him.

'What is your purpose here?'

'I am charged by the king to ensure you take nothing from the realm that ought not to be taken.'

'What do you mean? You see here the wretched baggage of men going into exile. What do you think we are taking, except our personal effects?'

'Since your master is sneaking away like a thief, we had better check that he is not a thief. Canterbury plate, for instance, gifts for the pope, papers, illicit letters from discontented clerics, the king's coin.'

'How dare you say such things! Get out of our way!'

Baldwin, furious at his contemptuous manner, tried to push him aside but found his way barred by henchmen.

Anselm stepped between them with raised arms, anxious that violent scenes should not accompany him into exile.

'Do you have gifts for the pope?' said Warelwast accusingly.

'My only gift to the pope,' replied Anselm, 'is my obedience. Why have you come to torment me?'

'The king has ordered a search of your baggage.'

Anselm signed to his companions to be patient, stood aside and pointed to the luggage on the beach.

'Then, in God's name, search it,' he said.

Warelwast's mailed heavies opened the bags and chests, rifled through them one by one, throwing Anselm's household chattels onto the sand, not caring what was lost or spoiled. It was a humiliating insult, made more severe by Warelwast's particular brand of cruel punctilio. But it was the final one. Although Anselm was to live to return to England, Anselm and William would never meet again.

****

The year 1098 began in unusual calm at the English court and Ranulf Flambard found himself curiously dull in spirits, as if the departure of Anselm had robbed him of a source of energy. News came of two more departures at the turn of the year, one of which affected him rather more deeply than he would have thought possible. On the 29th of December, Abbot Baldwin, the king's physician for many years, died at St Edmundsbury. Then old Bishop Walkelin, wan, bald and spent, died on January 3rd, in his diocese of Winchester, worn down by William's constant demands for money and the responsibilities of overseeing the royal mint. The great work of building the new Minster had exhausted his energies and emptied his coffers, and in his last years he struggled against the increasing indebtedness of the abbey. When William sent a requisition for 200 pounds on Christmas day while he was celebrating mass, he felt the end coming. A loyal, decent man, a builder, an administrator, a strong buttress in government, he was, like the best of his type, completely ground down between the millstones of duty and conscience. Perhaps that was what affected Ranulf most deeply. He remembered when Walkelin had received William during their 'secret' visit to Wilton in 1093, how he and his saintly prior, Godfrey, had looked after the poor wretch, Wulfnoth, and sweetened his last years with dignity.

The death of Walkelin was, of course, rather well received by William, who could now look forward to exploiting the abbey's revenues, but Ranulf was surprised by his own reaction. Not grief, certainly, but a sense of ending, the feeling that good men were passing. Perhaps it was the little verse, sent by Prior Godfrey, which stirred uncharacteristic feelings. Godfrey often churned out well-intentioned, hyperbolic epitaphs on the recently departed, but the tribute he paid his master was simple and sincere. 'January the third snatched you away and the indivisible triad lifts you above the stars,' he wrote. 'You were a staff for the lame, a guiding light for the blind and while you fed the many you starved yourself.'

After reading it, Ranulf remarked that such men as Godfrey proved that God had not yet entirely abandoned the church.

The year was wild with rumours of wars and death, prophecies of plague and tempest, forebodings of poor harvests, warnings about catastrophe in the far-off crusading armies. A strange star appeared in the south-west and the ray that stood from it shining south-east seemed to be very long. Men said that such a light had been seen in the days of the Conqueror, a sign of calamities, disturbances and unnatural happenings. Hermits sprang from their cells, claiming to have seen disasters in their visions. One or two even made their way to court to proclaim that the king's days were numbered. William quipped: 'Do they take me for an Englishman?' mocking the English propensity for superstition and the credibility of fools who listened to the ravings of snoring monks and old women who had bad dreams.

At Wilton, Aefled was ignorant of such stories. She had stayed on after the death of Gunhild, in deep mourning with Agnes and Eleanor. Hearing of Abbot Baldwin's death, she remembered how he had sheltered Gunhild in her time of loss, allowing her to stay in his house and receiving Count Alan's body to be interred in the sacred precincts of the church where he had built a magnificent shrine to the martyred king, St Edmund. Edith and Eleanor became close in their grief. Both had loved Gunhild in their different ways. They spent time together and Edith helped Eleanor to write a prayer for the repose of Gunhild's soul. Eleanor's education was advancing rapidly at Wilton, which was another reason why Aefled was reluctant to leave. Edith was teaching her Latin composition in various styles, improving her French, giving polish to her manners but did not, in any way, instil her with a desire for the religious life.

One day in the spring of 1098 Edith and Eleanor were writing in Edith's private chamber. In a good hand, Eleanor had written an exercise of consolation to a bereaved relative. It was the sort of thing a lady of high birth might be expected to do.

'Very good,' said Edith, reading it over. 'You have a plain style, just the thing to hide artful sentiments. You must understand that letters are rhetorical devices aimed at an effect. Noble ladies should never lose sight of the ultimate object of the letter. Is it to console, urge, persuade, deter, seek help? Everything must be fashioned to the objective. Honesty has no place.'

Eleanor was fascinated by this sort of talk. Edith had not lost her old habit of saying the thing that should not be said, although she had learned that no such matter should ever be put in a letter.

'But I am not a noble lady,' said Eleanor.

'Ah, but you might be one day. If you learn your lessons well, you will attract favour in high places and your parents will arrange a good marriage for you.'

At thirteen years old, the age Edith had been when they had first met, Eleanor was not yet preoccupied by thoughts of marriage. But now that she had revised her opinion of the religious life, finding that, without the encouragement and example of Gunhild, it had few attractions, she began to view marriage as an interesting possibility.

'Lady Edith, why do you not marry?'

'I am a ward of the king,' she said.

'Won't he let you marry?'

'He would prefer I didn't, at least for now.' As Edith said this, she turned to Eleanor with a flame in her eyes, as if she was burning to say more. She was constantly battling to maintain silence on a matter that she would have preferred to shout from the rooftops. She had needed all her considerable self-control to refuse to answer the abbess's questions, rebuff queries and ignore pointed remarks. Letters from Anselm had got nothing from her. She wrote back opaquely, models of rhetorical art. But long experience of hard treatment, at her aunt's then at her father's hands, then at the tumultuous court of her Scottish uncles, had honed her natural skills of dissimulation and she managed to appear exactly as she wished, calm, patient, submissive to the will of others.

'Who would you marry if you could?' said Eleanor oblivious to Edith's turmoil. 'As the daughter of a king, would you like to marry a king?'

'Of course, Eleanor. Who would not?'

'William Rufus is not so old, why not him?'

'That was thought of years ago and dismissed. Eleanor, stop this questioning and get on with your writing.'

'Isn't it true that William Rufus has no heir, except his brothers?'

'Yes, it's true.'

'Henry is young and good looking, isn't he? Do you remember when he came here?'

'Of course, I remember.'

'There was such a noise about him spending time with you. They all say he spoke of marriage. Is it true?'

Edith, who had turned back to her writing with a pen poised in her hand, froze. How did the child know all this? Was it possible that, after so much self-control, so long a silence, this innocent questioning child could break down her reserve? Unbidden thoughts of a promise given, of secret whisperings in a summer night, Henry's face close to hers, shook her awake from a slumber of denial.

'Yes,' she said. 'He spoke of marriage. But not in the way you think. And you must promise not to say anything. It must be a secret between us. One day, Eleanor, when I am in a position of power, I will have the power to do you good. You shall come and live with me and I will find a noble husband for you. Would you like that?'

Eleanor said yes, she supposed she would. And there the matter rested.

Towards the end of spring when Aefled and Agnes were preparing to return home, Agnes fell ill. Within a little while, she took to her bed, struck with fever, loss of appetite and stomach pains.

'What ails you, Agnes?'

'Can you not see?'

Aefled could see. She had suspected for some time that Agnes was in a crisis of disappointment. All her life, she had harboured longings to escape from the religious life by marriage. Now approaching her fortieth year, she felt herself slipping away from youth. Her bounteous hair, clear skin and wide eyes made her seem younger, but inside she had already grown old and was giving up hope.

Aefled tended her, read to her, trying to raise her spirits. But it was a shadow of Agnes in the bed, her bold energies had dissipated in a sudden gushing away of all desires. Aefled could not combat the superstitious feeling that her life was bound up in some obscure way with Agnes. All the exciting things that had happened to her in the last few years had happened because of Agnes: her visits to Wilton, her friendship with Gunhild and Edith, seeing King Malcolm and King William, being introduced to Ranulf Flambard, her visit to London, all these had been brought about, either directly or indirectly, through her friendship with Agnes. It was unbearable to see this source of energy, high-spirits and deep affection slipping into dullness and despair.

In the midst of this crisis, good news came from Scotland which materially enhanced Edith's status. Uncle Edgar Aetheling had launched a fruitful expedition against Donald Bane and succeeded in putting his nephew, Edgar, Edith's brother, on the throne of Scotland with the aid of William. In a fiercely fought battle, the only type of battle possible in Scotland, Donald Bane was driven out of the country and young Edgar installed on the throne as a client king of William Rufus. Unusually, William did not require Edgar to render any service or payment for his assistance in acquiring Scotland. On the contrary, William promised to make Edgar a payment of 60 shillings a day for livery whenever he visited the English court. Edith's brother was now king of Scotland and Edith's guardian, King William, was in formal alliance with her family. She had become, almost overnight, the most important marriageable lady within the Anglo-Norman sphere. If Henry was behind the king's largesse, or had any involvement in urging or bringing about this state of affairs for purposes of his own, no one knew for sure, except perhaps Edith. But on this matter, at least, she was not about to speak. Ranulf Flambard, however, saw unmistakable feline marks scratched over the whole project.

'So the cat has licked the cream of Scotland,' he said to Firmin. 'And goes purring about the king's legs.'

'You can't be sure of that, master. Henry was not even in Scotland.'

'You're right. But, by God, this one plays a long game. Ask yourself, what long-term benefits are to be reaped by a Scottish deal that elevates Edith? And who is planning to reap them?'

If Edith knew, she sat silent at Wilton, soon distracted by services for the dying. Agnes gave up and died in the summer, having been ill for the best part of four months. Aefled took her death badly, having lost her closest friend. Memories came flooding back, sometimes in jumbled dreams, sometimes in waking reveries when she relived the moment of their first meeting.

It had come about in unusual circumstances when Aefled was in the late stages of pregnancy with Eleanor at the beginning of 1086. Feeling low in spirits, Aefled had decided to seek religious advice from the Prioress of St Sepulchre's and had written a letter to ask for some prayers of grace and spiritual advice. Expecting a reply full of wise counsel in response to her plea, Aefled had been surprised to receive a visit from the lady herself.

'I cannot find my way to God, can you help me, Lady Agnes?'

Agnes's response was disarming. She smiled and said she thought it unlikely.

'It was said by a learned man, whose name I forget, that one should seek advice in all one does, but not the advice of all. Then again, in Ecclesiastes we read: "let your advisers be one in a thousand." But I very much doubt that I am one in a thousand. I am barely one in half a dozen. My own way to God has been full of blocks and stumbles. To be frank, it still is.'

Aefled always recalled her surprise at this admission. Surely a Prioress must be serene in faith, unshakable and full of good counsel. Yet, here was Lady Agnes confessing her own inadequacies within a very short time of meeting. With such revelations, a friendship was begun and did not end till Agnes breathed her last on Midsummer day.

****

While rumours raged in England the king spent most of 1098 in Normandy, travelling to receive homage from those of his brother's barons who had at first refused fealty. Unfinished business in the Vexin and a siege at Le Mans kept him busy till September, then he travelled through Pontoise and Conches, undertook another siege at Chaumont, and finally made his way back to Rouen through Pont-de-l'Arche in time for Christmas. Ranulf Flambard, who had remained in England as one of the chosen justiciars, spent this time issuing writs on the king's behalf, signing charters and raising money for the wars in Wales, none of which enhanced his popularity.

'Firmin,' he said one day. 'I am ready to give up. I labour in the vineyard. Who has laboured more than I? But it yields only vinegar.'

'Perhaps you need to go to Huntingdon, master. You always feel better afterwards.'

'But that is to pursue a sinful life, Firmin. A life of scandal with my Aelfgifu. A married woman and bastards. I know what the monks are writing about me.'

'It's not scandalous when you care for them and do right by them, master.'

Ranulf nodded, eager for these sagacious words and appearing to dwell on them.

'I have always desired high ecclesiastical office,' he said as though confessing a fault. 'I would discharge my duties with proper Christian humility. You believe that, don't you?'

Although addressed to Firmin, whose good opinion he truly desired, it was really a question to himself. In one of his periodic fits of self-questioning, Flambard was in the process of examining his own conscience.

In October, William had a narrow escape when the pope issued a threat of excommunication against him for the expulsion of Anselm the previous year. Having, by then, travelled almost to the heel of Italy, it was Anselm himself who pleaded in defence of William at the Council of Bari and the threat was dropped.

'Why did Anselm do that, master?' said Firmin, registering an astonishment that was shared by the barons and bench of England.

'Who can tell?' said Ranulf. 'Perhaps he is still trying to act the father, for old times' sake.'

Christmas came and went. William returned from Normandy and at Pentecost held court for the first time in his newly refurbished palace of Westminster. A crown wearing ceremony took place on May 29th which William used as an occasion to impress a distinguished visitor, Edgar, the Scottish king, brother of Edith. Having come south to swear fealty and render public thanks to William for helping him to the crown, Edgar was appointed to carry the sword before William at the great feast to celebrate the inauguration of Westminster Hall. It was meant as an honour, but the touchy Scots lords took exception to their king playing the role of sword bearer and saw it as a deliberate insult. On the whole though, the presence of Edgar went unnoticed. Indeed, he was not a notable figure, looking more like a clerk than a king, small, slight and pale. The impressive stock of energy and vigour bequeathed by Queen Margaret and King Malcolm to his three elder brothers, seemed to have exhausted itself in this fourth son. Neither could he be favourably compared to his formidable sister, the fiery Edith. Little attention was paid to his presence at Westminster and no one remarked on his absence when, not long after the ceremony, he left the court.

It was then, just at the time when Ranulf Flambard's energies were flagging, that the king invigorated them by giving him the gift he most desired.

'Face of Lucca, Flambard, you have long deserved reward from me. No one has worked harder for my interests, or laboured so long for my honour. You shall be my new Bishop of Durham.'

At last, Ranulf Flambard got the bishopric he wanted, the former seat of William St Calais, whose great new Romanesque church, begun in the year 1093, was rising high up on a rocky promontory above the Wear. The king was giving him the ripest plum in his basket of bishoprics, the palatinate of Durham, a semi-autonomous fief of vast wealth and resources. Finally, he had an official role and an office that could not be easily lost. However, the word 'giving' did not properly describe the transaction. William demanded, and got, one thousand pounds for the vacancy. But Ranulf Flambard was more than satisfied. For over ten years he had toiled in the king's service without the status of any formal office. He had made himself an indispensable financial agent, coming up with inventive solutions to the king's constant need for money. He had acted frequently as the king's justiciar, witnessed innumerable charters, raised money for the king's campaigns and done his best to manage relations with Anselm. Now his long overdue reward had been granted. The archbishopric of Durham spectacularly vaulted him into one of the highest ecclesiastical posts in the land. Authority, wealth and prestige were his. He did not even have to wait long for his consecration since the absence of the Archbishop of Canterbury was no obstacle to his assumption of office. Durham was in the province of York and so it was Thomas, Archbishop of York, who performed the consecration at St Paul's in London on June 5th 1099.

Firmin had never seen his master in clerical dress, much less mitred and sitting on a throne being anointed with chrism. When Ranulf rose from his seat, coped and decked, wearing the ring of office, carrying the pastoral staff and bearing himself with dignity, Firmin thought he looked just like Anselm. Through it all, his master wore an expression of dread seriousness and he remembered how Ranulf had once explained to him the awesome sanctity of the ritual, how it had the capacity to set apart and make sacred. Would the consecration change his master, he wondered, hoping it would not. In spite of the dignity of the ceremonial, however, Firmin felt a chill. Thomas of York hurried through the poorly attended ceremony. Clerics outnumbered laymen and the nave was almost empty. Few courtiers attended, certainly none of Henry's cronies. Evidently, not everyone was pleased by this appointment. When the ceremony was over, only a few attended the feast, most dispersed quickly. If the new Bishop of Durham was disappointed, he gave no sign and presided over a lacklustre evening with defiant goodwill. When Firmin joined him later, he looked worn and spent. His spirits remained low for several days afterwards, as if his unerring political instinct had discerned that the great upward step he had just taken was one step nearer to a great fall.

In July, the king went to Brockenhurst, an unfortified lodge with minimal defences and few locks or guards. Here he could relax among his trusted intimate circle, feasting in the evenings and spending days in the hunting field. Not that all business was suspended. There were still times when he needed to consult Flambard who was ordered to accompany him to Brockenhurst. Although no enthusiast of the hunt, Flambard went, eager to keep an eye on Henry, still basking in the glow of his brother's favour. The king's hunting companions, Walter Tirel, Robert FitzHaimo, William of Breteuil, Robert of Meulan, Urse d'Abetot, seemed to be drawn into Henry's orbit, spending as much time with him as with the king. Flambard noticed how they cut their hair short in the style of the 'old Normans' as if distancing themselves from William's entourage in order to establish an intimate circle around Henry. He would catch sight of them from time to time, closeted together or standing around in suspicious huddles. Once, after a day's hunting, he spied four of them drinking together in a small antechamber and approached down a corridor. Walter Tirel rose from his seat and shut the door in his face.

Ranulf Flambard was not a man to be ruffled and was not personally vain. When he took offence, it was usually on behalf of the king. The incident alarmed him but, without evidence, amounted to no more than insolence on their part and suspicion on his. If only he could insinuate someone into their private meetings. But they were careful, circumspect. They went softly on cushioned paws, taking their orders from the cat.

At Brockenhurst, everyone was familiar with the king's habits and the pattern of his days. What time he rose, what time the handlers departed, the order of going into the field, the course to the butts, the individual stands. All these things were well-known and it was unusual for the king to deviate from his customary arrangements. Ranulf put a watch on Henry and set Firmin to question his servants, but turned up nothing useful. Perhaps he was mistaken. He began to wonder if his personal dislike of Henry was causing excessive and wrongful doubt. Meanwhile, William showed continuing indulgence to his brother and they spent good-humoured days in the hunting field during the 'grease time' of August. But late in the month, their sport was prematurely interrupted by news from afar, unexpected news, news that went ringing around Europe.

Jerusalem had fallen to the Christian armies. Against all likelihood, the holy warriors had triumphed. But it was not until September that the first rumours came of the Battle of Ascalon. Suddenly, William and Henry were confronted by the worst possible turn of events. At Ascalon, Robert, Duke of Normandy, had covered himself in glory. He had not only survived, he had achieved military fame, he had earned remission of all his sins and he was coming home to claim his dukedom.

Unaware of this development, Edgar travelled down to Wiltshire to visit his sister, latest of a trickle of royal visitors to Wilton. In a matter of a few years, the summer months had brought the King of England, his brother, Henry, Malcolm, King of Scotland, and now Edgar, his reigning son, all knocking on the gates of the abbey to be received with varying levels of feigned pleasure.

Edith did not feign. She was genuinely pleased by the arrival of her brother. It gave her an indication that Henry was capable of fulfilling promises. She needed reassurances that she had not been forgotten, recognition that she still had a part to play in the affairs of two kingdoms. It also gave her the opportunity to show off and dazzle Edgar with her southern refinement and manners. They were strangers however, and as strangers they took time to get beyond the stiffest formalities. Neither felt able to be frank with the other. And so Edith, used to straight talking but having no good impression of close kin, kept control of her tongue. Edgar stayed at the abbey for several days, coming each morning for a conversation with his sister.

Eleanor watched his comings and goings with interest. After the third visit, she said: 'He seems well enough but he does not look like a king.'

'What does a king look like?'

'Tall and grand with a crown. When my mother saw him, she took him for a squire. He looks so young.'

'He is twenty-four.'

'That's not young.'

One day Edith asked her brother whether their Uncle Edgar Aetheling, was a reliable supporter of William Rufus.

'I believe he is obliged to the king for your upkeep these last years,' he said. 'But he tries to position himself between William and Robert Curthose, seeking friendly relations with both.'

'What about the other brother, Henry?'

'Henry? I don't think he considers Henry in the same league.'

'Isn't it remarkable, brother, that you, the fourth son of a king, should become our father's successor? Have you not considered that Henry is the fourth son of the Conqueror?'

'What are you saying?' Edgar's voice frowned.

'I'm only pointing out that remarkable things happen.'

'Is it true that Henry visited you here? That he spoke with you?'

'Yes.'

'Did he speak of marriage?'

'Is that why you have come? And what if he did? William doesn't want me. He only wants to keep me here and make me a nun. But, brother, I am not a nun. I wish to have my place in the world.'

'What might that be, sister?'

Edgar was so obviously trawling that Edith almost laughed. As if, after all these months of silence, she was about to let slip her dreams and desires to this ungainly youth.

'A place that would do honour to our noble mother, Queen Margaret. I have written poems about her life. Do you want to see them?'

Getting nowhere with Edith, Edgar started questioning Aunt Christina but found she knew nothing. Her hold over Edith was broken. Since the death of Gunhild, the only person who could make peace between them, aunt and niece barely exchanged a word. Although she was aware of Henry's visit, she had no idea what had passed between them.

'Edith no longer confides in me,' she said. 'But I believe she would do anything to pursue her own desires. Edgar, be warned, there is nothing she would not dare or do to secure a grand place in the world.'

'Aunt, be frank with me, what "grand place" do you mean?'

'I don't know. All I know is that she is capable of anything to get her way.'

'If Henry is plotting something against his brother, what are the implications for me? William has made me king.'

'You must ask your own ministers. Ask Edgar Aetheling. I don't doubt they will tell you that, though William made you king, he was strongly counselled to do so by Henry. Don't you see? Henry is preparing the way for Edith. First sister to a king, then wife.'

Edgar was shocked and filled with panic, feeling he ought to do something at once, but not knowing what to do.

Aunt Christina put her hand on his arm and gripped it with force. 'Do nothing,' she whispered, 'find out nothing, report nothing. Let things go on as they must. Henry is no threat to you.'

****

Far away on the other side of the Mediterranean, William's other brother was in a position to unleash a much more substantial threat. Robert Curthose was poised for a triumphant return to his dukedom. He could now claim to have participated in a miracle. The Holy Sepulchre was again in Christian hands. It was a turning point in the order of heaven and earth. Now every man who had fought under the banner of the cross partook of the glow of heavenly favour. Especially bright was the glow of those who had done the greatest work in the centre of the field at Ascalon, capturing the Fatimid camp and treasure; among them Robert of Normandy. Once the dust had settled, the foremost warriors of the new order made their way back to Constantinople, where they immediately plunged into a riotous round of celebrations. After receiving rewards from the Emperor, Alexius Comnenus, and with a stash of money large enough to buy back his dukedom, Robert Curthose spent a few hubristic weeks bathing in the afterglow of fame before setting out for home.

At last, he stowed his treasures aboard ship, crossed the Ionian sea and came into Apulia where he was welcomed at the court of Geoffrey of Conversano, Lord of Brindisi. Boasting that he was related to the Counts of Sicily and the Dukes of Calabria, Conversano made much of his distinguished visitor, treating him as if he had singlehandedly overcome the Fatimid Empire. It just so happened that he had a daughter, Sibyl, of marriageable age and was determined to snap up a notable son-in-law. Robert was no fool. He knew that his mere survival would cause offence at home. He was supposed to conform to probabilities and die. His return to Normandy would be considered an affront, worse, a threat. If he should, after so long a bachelorhood, return home with a bride and the possibility of an heir, scotching all William's prospects of permanently controlling the duchy, if he should, moreover, return with a marriage settlement sufficient to repay the 10,000 marks in silver, he could expect short shrift from his brothers. But the longer Robert dallied with Sibyl, the more he was drawn into a marriage of huge significance for the Anglo-Norman world, the less he cared about William. Months went by and Robert made no move to leave. Conversano's grip grew tighter. Sibyl played her part and was not unpleasing to him. At Christmas, 1099, he was still in Apulia and marriage was a distinct possibility.

In England, William celebrated Christmas unaware of these dangerous developments. He was certain that, even if Robert was to return against all the odds, he would have no money to redeem his dukedom. Even if the Emperor had heaped him with treasures, there was plenty of opportunity on the road between Apulia and Normandy to dissipate a fortune. He was more likely to arrive penniless. In the improbable circumstance of Robert being able to repay the loan on the nail, William would find ways to prevaricate. He felt secure enough. Even so, much of 1099 was spent in Normandy putting down the last remnants of rebellion at Le Mans, making treaties, pushing back the French, marching through Maine, Touques, Bonneville, Lillebonne, impressing his authority through successful military actions and diplomacy. Pope Urban obliged him by dying in July, which left him free to deal firmly with recalcitrant Norman bishops.

When he returned to England at the end of September, he felt, for the first time in his life, that he was returning from a secure duchy to a secure kingdom. At thirty-eight, he was the same age his father had been when he won a kingdom at Hastings. He was king of one of the richest realms in Europe, he had a grip on Normandy.

After nine disorderly years, orderly administration had been achieved. William's secretariat was producing crisp instruments of government. Jurisprudence was being strengthened and could be left in the control of the most reliable bishops and *vicomtes*. He had gained a reputation for military success and command in the field that made some observers compare him not only with the Conqueror, but with Caesar. William held his Christmas court that year in Gloucester at the palace of Kingsholm where, six years before, he had been dying. Like a king, he had taken the place of his father and, like a ghost, he had risen from death. But death was closer than he could have imagined. As winter turned into spring 1100, King William II entered his last year.

Holy Sunday in the year 1100 fell on April 1st. The Easter court was held in Winchester, Bishop Walkelin's old seat. William had not appointed a successor to the vacancy, exploiting it as another source of revenue. He was also, on the advice of Ranulf Flambard, keeping an eye on the royal treasury. Henry, whose relations with Flambard were by now openly hostile, kept close to the king. With a resurgent Robert on the horizon, the brothers united in a mutual protection of interests. Throughout the spring, the news of Robert Curthose grew more and more alarming. Robert was about to marry, Robert had married, Robert was coming home with a shining reputation and a pregnant bride. The news affected Henry even more than William. While William felt at his most secure, the youngest brother, the boldest, the least scrupulous and most devious of the three, stood to lose. He held castles and estates in Normandy and would not consider giving them up. As late as Easter, Henry was ready for anything, keeping all options open and prepared to act opportunistically, instinctively, to his own best advantage. But in July, when word came that Robert was likely to reach Normandy at the end of August, Henry knew that time was running out.

It was not until the court was at Westminster at Whitsun that Ranulf Flambard, feeling himself squeezed from the king's intimate counsels, first voiced his suspicions to the king. Treading carefully, aware that William thought himself in harness with his brother, pulling together in the face of Robert's imminent return, Ranulf went about it in a circuitous way. But William was primed and cut him short.

'Face of Lucca! Flambard. You have let personal animosity cloud your judgement. Henry has warned me that you are trying to undermine him. He believes you are jealous, that you are starting up rumours to prise him away from me.'

Nothing, it seemed, could dent William's new-found security. Without proof, Flambard had no case and desisted. Unlike Anselm, he would never push a quarrel. Henry's long game was paying off. Safe in William's lap, the cat had been purring away with fabrications, lies and falsehoods. William had stroked him and listened. The king warned Flambard to keep away from Henry, not to follow him, not to provoke him and not to set his men to watch him.

'I would rather you could be friends,' said William. 'But as things stand now, with Robert coming back to stir up Normandy, I need to keep Henry close. You see how it is, Flambard? You, I trust. I can let you go. Henry, I don't trust, he must stay. Besides, you are Bishop of Durham. Go north for a few months, establish yourself there, shake up the monks, check the finances. Face of Lucca, Flambard! It will do you good.'

When the king went to Brockenhurst in July to prepare for the "grease time", it was in the company of Henry and his cronies, Robert of Meulan, William of Breteuil, Walter Tirel and Robert FitzHaimo. In his entourage, Henry took Robert of Castle St Mary's and his two young sons. This time, Ranulf Flambard was not invited to accompany the king.

'That's it, Firmin,' he said. 'Whatever happens now, I have become expendable. Take note of this lesson. The condition of all achievement is insecurity. Insecurity on the way up, insecurity on the way down.'

'Master, are you in danger from the king?'

Flambard picked up a parchment from the table and began running his eye over it, as if to distract himself from a question he did not want to answer. Should he voice his thought? A thought so terrible that he hardly dared utter it, even to himself.

'I am in danger, Firmin, but not from the king. Nor am I in as much danger as the king himself. I fear, I very much fear…'

As if suddenly activated by a command, Firmin turned and began to clear his writing table, putting the pens, knives, ink pots and parchments in a wooden box. Then he went to the chest where he kept his smart new mantle, took it out, brushed it down and folded it neatly.

'What are you doing?' asked Ranulf.

'Packing for a journey, master.'

But they did not go to Durham. To ensconce themselves so far north at a time of uncertainty would be imprudent. Flambard was not popular there. Having so newly come into the bishopric, he had no established body of loyal supporters to call on. Instead, he decided to go south, down to Twynham in Hampshire, ostensibly to inspect the building of his priory church but really to be close to the sea. Since Henry had ejected him from the king's circle, he must consider his options and be ready for anything. If his worst fears were realised, he would be in the greatest danger. Taking Firmin, a small household staff, his moveable chattels and personal funds, he decamped to the coast. There, in close proximity to fast sailing ships and a sea racing with currents, he could look out upon broad, foam-tipped horizons and wait upon events.

****

On Thursday, 2nd August, William was at his hunting lodge looking forward to a day of sport. It was his habit to rise early but that day he was unusually late in rising and decided to delay going out until after his dinner. Robert's sons, who had gone out at dawn with the fewterers, came back to ask what was the cause of the delay. Robert told them that the king was at dinner, but that Henry was determined that the day should not be lost. 'Go back and wait with the handlers,' he said, 'the king will come soon.'

William dined rather well in the company of his brother and his closest companions, among them Walter Tirel, Robert FitzHaimo, Robert of Meulan and his brother Henry Beaumont. Afterwards, just as he was pulling on his boots to go forth, laughing and joking in his customary way, a local smith arrived with six arrows, saying he wished to offer them as a gift to the king. Taking them in both hands, William looked them over, tested them for weight and balance and, praising their craftsmanship, took four for himself and gave two to Walter Tirel who was standing beside him. 'Here, Tirel,' he said, 'you are a deadly shot, see what you can do with these.' Walter Tirel took them, looked at Henry and put them in his quiver. Just as the king was finally on the point of departing, a monk came from Gloucester with letters from the Abbot which Henry took and put aside. 'Don't let business delay us,' he said. 'You can deal with them after the hunt.'

Henry led the way outside to where the horses were waiting to carry them into the forest as far as the butts. When they entered the woodland, they sent huntsmen off in different directions to drive the game towards the waiting archers, as was usual. Other huntsmen were detailed to stand behind the individual members of the royal hunting party in order to fire at the deer at the same time as they did.

This was to enable the aristocratic hunters to claim the kill, even when they had missed, but mainly to ensure that no wounded animal escaped into the undergrowth. Meulan, FitzHaimo, Breteuil and Henry went off to their separate stations with their huntsmen. The king and Tirel took up position at their butt. By the time the deer were heard racing into range, they were alone, save for two marksmen standing behind Tirel and the king. Attendants with the horses were some way off and concealed from one another by the foliage. At this point, any words spoken would be in a whisper.

It was by now late afternoon. Out of the dazzling light of a low sun, a deer passed within bowshot of the king. He fired and wounded it. Shading his eyes against the blinding glare, William looked round for the marksman who should have shot and finished it off. There was no one there. He and Tirel were quite alone. He turned his head, following the injured stag, trying to assess the prospect of a second shot. While his attention was still on this stage, another came within range. It was now, while the second deer passed before the king, whose eyes were turned away, that Walter Tirel drew his bow, aimed one of the arrows William had given him, and fired.

The king made no sound. As he fell forward on the arrow, he broke off the shaft, pushing the head deep into the wound in his neck, fatally cutting an artery. His last moment of awareness was of lying in a fever at Kingsholm. The faces of Flambard, Anselm, bishops, barons, courtiers and clerics passed behind his eyes in a flicker, then went out.

Running up, Walter Tirel found him unconscious. At that moment, there was no one else in sight, the forest was deathly quiet, no sound, not even from the horses, though they were tethered not far away. Tirel looked once more at the fallen body, lying motionless in a spreading pool of blood. Then he ran to find his horse, leapt on it and got quickly away. There was no pursuit.

****